Praise for th

'Intelligent and pacy thriller ... a tau.
revenge, perseverance and the struggle against inju..._
(Paula Hawkins)

'A stunning debut from an exciting new addition to the world of crime fiction.' (Stephen Booth)

Cold Dawn

'Stylish, authoritative crime writing from someone who knows ... vivid and gripping.' (Oliver Harris)

'A gripping and clever thriller in a magnificent setting ... I loved it.' (Sarah Ward)

Cold Summer

'Be prepared to find yourself caught up in this dark and gritty tale. Rick Castle is a character you'll back all the way. He doesn't always play by the rules, but that's what makes him so addictive. I absolutely loved this book. (Lisa Cutts, DC Nina Foster and East Rise series)

'The English summer may be cold, but the plot in this engrossing mystery is red hot ... this is a crime novel that oozes humanity, atmosphere, and storytelling at its very best.' (A.B. Patterson, the PI Harry Kenmare novels)

'Rick Castle is a compelling lead and Ellson delivers an exciting story that exudes a strong sense of place.' (Frank Zafiro, the River City series)

Also by James Ellson

The Trail
Cold Dawn

James Ellson was a police officer for 15 years, starting in London and finishing as a Detective Inspector at Moss Side in Manchester. When he left the police he started writing, and his debut novel *The Trail* was published in 2020. Both *The Trail* and the sequel *Cold Dawn* were longlisted for the Boardman Tasker Award.

James is a keen climber and mountaineer, and has visited Nepal many times. In 2004 he climbed 6,812-metre Ama Dablam, and in 2008 soloed the Matterhorn.

He lives in the Peak District with his wife, and manages their smallholding, which includes bees and an orchard.

Twitter @jamesellson3
facebook.com/james.ellson.98
www.jamesellson.com

COLD SUMMER

James Ellson

Cambium

First edition, 2023

Cambium Press

A CIP record for this book is available from the British Library

ISBN 978-1-7394421-4-9 (paperback)
ISBN 978-1-7394421-5-6 (ebook)

Printed in Great Britain by Clays Ltd, Elcograf S.p.A

1 3 5 7 9 8 6 4 2

For Lesley

Namaste!
Lexicon at the back

1

They followed the lorry all the way round Birmingham and onto the M6. As instructed, his driver maintained a distance of fifty to sixty metres. The fat man hugged the van's steering wheel, and occasionally wiped his hands with a filthy rag. A can rattled in the back, and bergs of grey cloud slid across the brown sky. England's dull weather matched its dull people.

The lorry was one of the largest artics, and had a dirty-white cab and a matching trailer. He stared at the two stickers on the rear bumper, SCHMITZ and GB. Schmitz he thought was German. GB was Great Britain – or Good Bye. *Namaste.*

Inside the trailer could have been almost anything. TVs, or toasters. Beds, or batteries. Fridges, or flowers.

There were some things it probably wasn't carrying. Dangerous or flammable liquids, chickens, or animals. No obvious air holes for one thing. It could have been carrying stolen goods, or it could even have been empty. There was none of the garish colouring or religious iconography of the trucks in Nepal. No advertisements or fixtures on the trailer that gave any clues. No stickers or name tags adorning the cab. Not even a line of spotlights or a cluster of aerials. There was no distinctive damage; only the usual marks and scrapes. Nothing to distinguish it from the thousands of similar lorries on England's motorways. Not even an obscene message in the grime.

There was only one thing of interest.

Two men in the cab. That was unusual in the days of sat nav and the relentless pressure on wage bills. He knew that, but Manoj had insisted.

A flock of large birds in arrowhead formation flew overhead. As if they were following the road, and perhaps they were.

His driver took a bag of toffee popcorn off the dashboard and holding the wheel between his knees, ripped off the corner and jugged out a mouthful. His name was Anoop, which was a fat man's name. His weight spilled sideways into the door pocket and onto the gearstick. Three people in the front would have been a squash. He already had a box of drinks and chocolate bars under his legs.

Next time, he would drive, and his nephew would navigate.

The artic indicated to pull off the motorway. Anoop closed the gap between the two vehicles, the drinks can clattering across the back. He glanced round. Rough wooden benches screwed to the floor lined each side. An empty can from last time.

Three hundred metres.

Two hundred.

One.

They followed the lorry onto the slip road signing Manchester. At the roundabout it turned left onto a dual carriageway. His driver followed.

He clapped his hands twice, and quickly. The noise sharp, slap-slap. Anoop accelerated and overtook. Then returned to the left-hand lane and slowed so that the van again matched the speed of the lorry. He checked the mirror. The artic now followed them, as per the plan.

At the next roundabout the convoy turned left. Then left again into an old industrial estate. A huge signboard covered in black sheeting and gaffa tape stood at the entrance. Plastic rubbish, tyre shreds and a hubcap littered the ground.

The convoy drove slowly through the deserted estate following the signs for supermarket deliveries. Past an empty car park, a defunct petrol station and along a service road until a trolley park – the ranks of trolleys still lined up – meant they could go no further. Anoop turned into the delivery yard, through the open gate and stopped next to the security guard's hut. Boarded-up like everything else. The artic lumbered past and nosed into an old unloading bay. The van's windscreen faced the rear of the lorry thirty metres away.

He nodded.

Anoop switched off the engine, and jugged out more popcorn.

The lorry driver climbed out first. Facing out, he reached a leg down, then jumped making a soft thud. He wore trucker's sandy boots and a thick lumberjack shirt. His shoulders were square as if he'd been sawn into creation. So different to Nepalese shoulders which sloped like river valleys. The passenger door swung open, and the passenger climbed down backwards, bottom sticking out and jacket riding up to reveal pasty-white skin. He walked around the back of the lorry, and met the driver on the offside. He had a red, jowly face. Two white British men in a lorry with a GB sticker. It made sense.

The door-like lorry driver opened a hatch which rose up and stayed. He pulled out tools. Short metal batons with handles taped for better grip. Like the racquets of professional tennis players. Larger wooden clubs. Coils of rope. Poles with a noose. Steel rods with jaws at one end and a handle and a lever at the other, known as graspers.

Like duellists, the two white men looked at the items for a few seconds. Thinking about what was coming, wanting to get it over.

It was what it was. It was what God wanted.

The artic driver moved first, stuffing a small baton in his belt. He slung a coil of rope around his shoulder and pulled on gauntlets. He picked up a grasper and a club. His hot-faced passenger put on gloves, and chose the same tools. He moved slowly, as if he wanted to delay things.

'Rather them than me,' said Anoop.

He buzzed down a window, and tapped a fingernail on the door. Hearing a slight ringing in his ears, he stared across the delivery yard at the huge lorry. He hoped his nephew was okay.

At last the two men had grabbed what they needed and walked to the back of the trailer. The passenger detoured to shut the yard gate.

Thunderous noise from a descending aeroplane filled the grey and brown sky. Banging, and screaming, and whining. The aeroplane's landing gear dropped down.

'Was it your idea to do it like this,' said Anoop, 'or Al Usra's?' Bits of popcorn flecked his spade-shaped beard.

Hant Khetan held up his hand.

'No talk.'

2

At the cemetery gates squirrels clicked in the canopy of the spreading oak. Starlings pecked amongst the gravestones, and bonfire smoke from the neighbouring allotments drifted over. A pebble-grey sky.

The coffin arrived. Its handles buffed to gleam, the mahogany box assembled with dovetailed joints. His old man would have approved, but his mother ambivalent. A moot point: decisions were now down to him.

Calix twisted his wrists in the handcuffs. One way, then the other. He flexed his fingers, and curled them back. And again. He rolled his shoulders as best he could, forward, then back. Back, then forward.

'Easy,' said the Strangeways guard. The stumpy Welshman stood a metre away, his laboured breath a constant reminder.

The four pallbearers let out the straps. They were tall silent men in black coats and black shoes. Calix should have been one of them, but it was against the rules. Everything was against the rules.

To the right of the new grave was the headstone of his old man, Brigadier David Coniston. Not a year old and lichen already clutching the granite. Calix let his eyes lead his head slowly around. Further back were four more guards, and outside the gates, wheels mounting the kerb, their van and escort vehicle. Five guards which he'd expected but no dibble which he'd been told were a possibility. Dibble were younger, fitter, but there were no dibble, and there was no dog. He'd been lucky.

One guard leant against the van, smoking. The other three stood ten metres behind Calix, spread out in a fan. One caught him staring, and he stared back.

It was a mistake.

The coffin landed, and stilled. Soil dribbled down. Two of the pallbearers pulled on the straps and rolled them up like firemen's hoses. The vicar, a thin nervous man, cleared his throat and began to speak. Calix listened as he glanced at the gathered faces. There was his mother's sister and husband and a dozen of her local friends.

He took a deep breath, and checked the edges of his peripheral vision.

'Now for the Lord's Prayer,' said the vicar. Eyes turned to the floor and some closed. 'Our father, which art in heaven.'

The last time Calix had heard the Lord's Prayer was in Nepal, beside another grave. He and Barney Williams were burying Barney's twin. Spencer – Spence.

'Hallowed be thy name.'

Calix braced.

'Thy Kingdom come. Thy will—'

Calix leapt over the grave. He staggered forward, but kept upright, and pushed through the people. They were catatonic, one tall woman stifling a shriek as he tore past. He took a few short paces, swerving around a gravestone, and avoiding a vase of wilted flowers. He jinked right onto the gravel path and accelerated. Feet crunching. Uphill, away from the gates and away from the guards.

The starlings rose and wheeled away, chattering to silence. Behind him, shouting, then more silence. His heart felt like it would explode. He'd been visualising it for weeks, playing it over and over like a pro athlete.

His foot slipped on the gravel. His stomach lurched.

'Coniston, don't be—' shouted one of the guards.

Don't be what? A fool? Stupid?

They were the fools. He wasn't simply bored with the Lord's Prayer. This was planned: cemetery, wall, field, copse. All he had to do was run faster than anyone else, and do it wearing handcuffs. He held his hands close to his chest and interlocked his fingers. His elbows rocked from side to side.

The gravel path ended, and taking the racing-driver line, he weaved his way through the headstones. He brushed a stone, only too aware a touch could send him flying.

'Coniston, we're gaining.'

Liar. Fucking liar. They were slow, and wore belts full of gear: batons and cuffs and notebooks and torches. They loved all that action man stuff, always comparing their latest three-cell Maglite. And he was more motivated. His sentence had been reduced by two years for talking to Castle, the disgraced dibble. Out on good behaviour after serving half. But three-and-a-half was still far too long. There were things he wanted to do.

One thing.

He jumped a culvert with a muddy trickle. Ran past a makeshift heap of grass cuttings, sweaty and yellow at the edges. He neared the far side of the cemetery. A man holding a spade stood in front of the wall. Next to him, the upper half of another man.

Gravediggers, both staring at him. Young men, too young to spend their time communing with the dead. Calix stared back. Have-a-gos? Maybe later in the pub, but not in the here and now. He ran past them, avoiding their scattered tools.

Their eyes didn't leave him for a second but they didn't move an inch.

'Okay?' stammered the man in the hole. His colleague held up a phone and tracked Calix as he ran past.

He reached the dry-stone wall, wider at the bottom than the top and leaning impossibly. Before the wall, a wire fence. Shoving a foot into the mesh he held onto a post and placed his other foot on the top. The fence wobbled and he half-slipped half-fell over. He hauled himself up. Reached over the top of the wall, flicked his leg up and rolled over. Ripping his trousers, grazing his hands. He felt bruised, tired, sick. Risked looking over his shoulder.

Behind the filming gravedigger, two guards were past the grass heap, the third close behind. The other two would be driving, radioing it in and trying to head him off. The dibble would send cars and a helicopter. A helicopter would be a disaster.

It would be what it would be.

His sister Megan would have been proud of him. Roles reversed, she'd have attempted something, maybe not fleeing from the funeral, but something. Overpowering her solicitor and walking out of prison in disguise. Sneaking out in the food lorry. He'd been living life for the two of them, ever since.

Only the field and the copse to go. The field was marked out as a football pitch, heavy under foot but flatter than the cemetery. He rounded a bench, the ground strewn with rips of orange peel. Ran across. At the centre circle he heard the click of a gate and glanced back.

There was a gate in the corner of the cemetery. A guard paused pitchside. He unclipped his belt and his gear hit the ground. A second guard behind him. Calix turned forward, stumbled, recovered. Kept running.

At the far side of the pitch he ran past a white-line machine and over a heap of corner flags. Charged into the copse, brambles pulling at his trousers. The wood cooler, darker. He slowed, kicking higher with his legs. His thoughts tumbled over each other. The car, the guards, the car, a cold beer, the car. Bird Bird, his mum, the car, his old man, Megan, his mum. Liver cancer had taken her, and quickly – four months from diagnosis to death. He felt dizzy, like he was falling.

Daylight streamed through the trees.

He veered onto a badger trail and charged on. Emerged at the road. He jumped a ditch onto the littered verge. An old trainer, a bleached plastic bottle, chip wrappers. He could hear a car. He looked right.

No car.

Only an old man in a cap walking his dog.

Calix could hear a guard thrashing through the wood. Then, the hoot of a car horn. He looked round.

The car. Blue, small, crap.

Fifty metres away. Reversing and hooting.

Calix ran towards it. They met in the middle, the car stopped, and he grabbed at a rear door handle.

Locked.

A guard emerged from the wood, and jumped the ditch. The man stumbled, fell, swore.

Calix hammered on the side of the car. The central door locking clicked. He opened the door and hurled himself across the back seat. The handcuffs bit into his wrists and drew blood. Blonde hair poked through the headrest.

'Coniston,' shouted the guard as he stood, and lurched forward.

The engine stalled.

The driver turned the key, the engine fired, the car jerked away, wheels spinning. The driver accelerated hard. Second gear. Third gear.

Calix lay on the back seat with his eyes closed, sucking in the air. His hands throbbed. His trousers were ripped, and his legs bloody and scratched. 'You didn't mention the wire fence.'

Hard braking slammed him against the front seats. A right turn. Then more violent acceleration, the engine protesting.

'Or the gate.'

He opened his eyes and glanced out of a window. The buildings and the trees were upside down – the whole world was upside down. He looked above – below – the buildings and trees. At the pebble-grey sky. He hoped his mum would understand. Megan would, and his old man would. The old soldier had always preferred fight to flight, unless flight led to fight.

'You going to say something?'

There was the sound of indicating and another right turn.

'You don't have to indicate.'

Calix glanced up between the seats at the rear-view mirror. The driver wore blue overalls and black gloves. They'd discussed forensics. They'd discussed the dibble, and Castle in particular. Despite the scandal, driven, decent, and seemingly omniscient.

Their eyes met in the mirror, and the driver started laughing. 'God, I'm going to get so fucking drunk tonight.'

Another burst of acceleration. More hard braking. Left turn, right turn. Back up through the gears. Finally, fourth gear.

'There's a phone in the bag on the back seat.'

Calix glanced in the bag, and relaxed.

A small butterfly with its wings outspread rested on the inside of the window. Red, orange, and gold, with black spots. Blue crescents along the borders. In prison, everything was grey, the colour of dishwater. The butterfly fluttered its wings. The blue on the wings was a light delicate shade, like eggshell.

He pulled himself up with his stomach muscles, and leant

forward slowly. Reached forward with his handcuffed hands. He clapped, flattening the Small Tortoiseshell between his palms and staining the skin red and gold.

The time had come, too, for the end of Hant Khetan.

3

Rick inspected his second toe. It was red and puffy, and throbbing as if he'd kicked a prisoner. Lots of people he'd like to have kicked, not only prisoners. The CPS clerk for losing his last file; Woods for oversleeping and missing the morning's search warrant; Robbo for cooperating with the internal investigation; everyone on the enquiry panel.

The wrong time of year for chilblains, he thought, rubbing in cream Maggie had bought him.

'You need to see this, Rick.'

Feeling a frisson down his spine, he looked up at the familiar voice. Maggie was an analyst in the Intelligence Unit, but also his girlfriend. It made finding a compromise between work and home even trickier.

'It's on the main screen.'

She wheeled off, her soft reflection caught in the glass door. Before joining the Job, Maggie had been a bomb disposal officer in Helmand. She'd been injured and subsequently discovered she couldn't use prosthetics because of stump disease. These two facts confirmed to Rick there was no God, and no hope for the human project. Now, her ghosts in addition to his flickered in the purple-black of the night.

He pulled on the sock, laced his shoe and followed her into the corridor. She was waiting, her crescent moon earrings still moving. They were a present from him.

'What is?'

'A YouTube video, trending.' Maggie turned and set off again.

Rick could hear a hubbub coming from the CID office, home to South Manchester's four teams of eight detectives. The noise sounded as if they were all there, together with their children. It felt like a prank although he knew it would be unlikely for Maggie to be involved. Playing it straight was one of the things he liked about her.

The corridor led into the open-plan room. A large TV sat high up on the wall in a corner, and staring up at the cracked screen stood twenty people. Detectives and trainees, and support staff attracted by the noise. Everyone was yabbering. As Maggie wheeled towards the screen, the crowd of people opened up, and Rick fell in behind her. The office reeked of stale milk, and had done ever since Downcliff dropped the carton. It always would.

'Coniston's escaped, boss. He'd been allowed out for his mother's funeral.' DC Bennett prodded his round-rimmed glasses. Next to him stood his partner DC Woods wearing a garden anorak.

Rick knew the name as well as his own. Calix Coniston was doing time at HMP Strangeways for a conspiracy with Hant Khetan, once the FBI's most wanted in South Asia and rumoured to be the next Osama Bin Laden. But that was history; Rick had arrested Khetan in Barnes the previous year after luring the Nepalese national to the UK. For his efforts, Rick had been suspended, investigated and demoted. But at least, Khetan was *inside*.

And until that morning, Coniston had been too. Rick had been sleeping easier, suffering less hot sweats, less daymares.

The solution: shove Coniston back inside – and fast.

Rick grabbed the remote and clicked forward, killing the advert for a national florist. Prison breakouts were unusual, and he could only remember a couple. He glanced round for Hunter. The two of them had an understanding. Things had taken place in the Khetan investigation which Rick admitted – to himself – shouldn't have.

Play.

For a few seconds the video was jerky and moved around fast. Gravestones, grass. Someone running towards the camera. The figure got closer. There was no doubt it was Coniston. Hands hugged to his chest due to the handcuffs, and running as if his life depended on it. 'Okay?' a voice spluttered. As the camera moved around, a gravedigger came into view, leaning on his spade. Coniston climbed over a fence and flopped over a wall.

'It's going viral,' said Bennett.

33,501 views. 5,607 likes. As Rick watched, the numbers ticked up.

The camera panned around, and back down the cemetery. Two prison officers were in pursuit, but already looked knackered. The camera returned to Coniston, running across a football field.

Rick watched the clip a second time, then switched the TV off and walked to the front. The room quietened. He felt like a military commander about to inspire his troops on the brink of battle. Coniston's late father, who'd been a brigadier in the Ghurkhas, and a man whom Rick had grown to respect, would have quoted Sun Tzu.

'Woods and Bennett, you get out to the scene. Kasim, Paulson, you two go with uniform to check Coniston's home address. The rest of you will receive taskings from DS Hunter. Gary, Maggie, in my office, please.'

Rick panned round the faces in the room. 'I want him back by lunchtime.'

In his office, he stood at his window and gave instructions via the radio to a new uniform inspector at Hedges Cemetery.

'Usual stuff, Mike. Don't let any of the prison guards go anywhere. Two detectives will be with you shortly.' Rick paused. 'Is Coniston tagged?'

'Yes, but the system's down. They'll let me know as soon as it's back up.'

'Helicopter?'

'Searching for a missing three-year-old in Bury. I've got all the available units criss-crossing the area.'

'Anything on the car reg?' Three storeys below Rick, a dog van rocked from side to side and the sound of vicious barking drifted up.

'No witnesses, yet. But we're hoping to find a CCTV camera nearby. Are you taking this?'

'Why wouldn't I be?' Rick turned from the window and threw the radio onto his desk. Files spilled and papers fluttered down.

Hunter walked in. 'Having a spot of Barney Rubble?'

Rick ignored him, his phone beeped with a message from Becky. *Don't forget to go and see Mum.*

'Where's Maggie?'

'She's upset about something.'

'What?'

Hunter shrugged, and undid a button on his shirt to scratch his chest.

Rick had left Maggie sleeping, wanting to make an early start on the night log, and he'd not yet spoken to her. Not properly.

'I need to go to the cemetery so we'll start without her. How the hell did Coniston escape? The prison guards should be sacked.'

'To be fair, he's given us the slip before.'

Rick picked up the scattered papers. Fair was one thing his sergeant wasn't. 'Do you think he planned it?'

Hunter tapped the screen on his phone. 'Possible he threatened a passing driver, but no one's called it in.'

'Still early.'

'Escaping from prison takes planning and contacts and know-how,' said Hunter, scrolling back and forth.

'He didn't plan his mother's funeral.'

'Weren't no surprise.'

'The Big Red then, or someone like him. Coniston used to deal for him. What about inside help?'

'Guards deliberately running slowly?'

'You saw the video.' Rick slipped the papers back into a file. 'No eager beavers like Paulson and Kasim.'

'Maybe,' said Hunter still reading his phone.

'So, help on the outside or help on the inside. Or both.' Rick paused. 'Are you expecting something?'

Hunter dropped the phone into his jacket pocket.

'Sort the taskings, then meet me at the scene. And ask the intel unit to find out if anyone's heard anything.'

Hunter walked to the door. He was wearing white trainers with a green flash which squeaked on the lino. The sergeant turned. 'You're taking this, then? After everything that happened in Aldershot and Barnes; and the enquiry, and your—'

'Yes!' Rick threw the file back onto the desk, the papers sliding out and toppling over the edge.

Hunter walked out. The squeaks receded, stopped, and restarted. The sergeant reappeared. 'I've got the stuff you wanted.'

Rick checked the canteen and the intel unit for Maggie. Scanning the car park, he spotted her car in the far corner. Maggie refused a disabled bay on principle. He checked the

16

photocopying room, and the PC's writing room. He put his head round the door of the prayer room. Empty. Which only left one room to try, and he pushed open the door.

'Maggie?'

Rick stepped inside, the door pulling shut slowly, then with a bang. 'Maggie?' His voice echoed. He took another couple of steps, his shoes clacking on the hard floor.

'You can't search in here.' Maggie's voice from the end cubicle.

Rick backed up to the basins. 'What's up?'

'How could you? Elaine's my friend.'

His stomach hollowed. The previous evening, Maggie had gone to the pub with Robbo's PA.

'She told me, Rick.' She paused. 'We got a bit drunk and she told me what happened last year.'

'Maggie, I can't now.'

'Always the Job first.'

The door opened, and Hunter stood on the threshold. 'Report just in of a burning car. More than likely, the bandit vehicle. Uniform on way.' He sniffed, as if he was taking the sea air. 'I'll wait in the yard.'

The door pulled shut.

'I'm sorry, Maggie. I wish I hadn't done it.'

'Rick, I'm not sure—'

'We'll talk about it tonight, Mags, I promise.' He paused. 'I love you.'

No reply came.

He stepped back out into the corridor, and letting the door slam, ran after Hunter. Maggie was right: already he was thinking how to maximise forensic opportunities from the getaway car.

4

The artic driver yanked across the locking bar on the trailer. The long vertical came free, and one of the rear doors swung open. The driver backed away, grasper and short club at the ready. The sickly-looking passenger retreated to the side.

Even sitting twenty metres away in the van, Hant could smell it. Fresh shit and stale urine. Barking followed. Loud angry barking. Beside him, Anoop seemed unaffected. The fat man finished the popcorn and stuffed the bag in the door pocket.

He glanced up at the monochrome sky, and held out his palm. Hazy cloud and rain in the distance. Always raining in England, even in summer.

The face of a large dog appeared in the trailer doorway. Then a second, and for a moment, the two dogs remained there, silhouetted in the darkness.

The dogs jumped out. They were over a metre tall with straight backs and lean bodies. Short brown fur with patches of black, and pointed ears. They stood shoulder to shoulder, turning round and snarling. Like macaques goading tourists at Chitwan.

The lorry driver advanced. The dogs parted and one bounded away. The driver lassoed the remaining dog and pulled the lever tight. He shouted at his second who ran forward to take the pole.

The dog strained away, gasping for breath. The driver clubbed the dog to the floor, and together, the two men dragged the dog to the edge of the compound. The passenger tied the dog by its collar to a post.

The second dog ran around snapping and rearing up.

Anoop picked his nose, bit his nails. He wiped his hands with the rag. He extracted the empty popcorn bag and straightened it and inspected it for crumbs, turned it upside down and tapped it. Unsuccessful, he stuffed it back in the pocket. Beside him, Hant sat still. He observed, he smelt, he listened. God was watching.

The fat man fiddled out another sweet bag from the pocket. Pink marshmallows. He ripped off the corner and ate a handful, one after the other.

'You no have *dharma*.'

'And what's darmer when it's at home?'

'Hindu rules, live right.'

'You mean like morals?'

Hant shook his head. 'No like. Is.'

There was action in the compound: one of the lorry men threw down a lump of bloody meat, staining the concrete.

The second dog approached. It was starving, desperate, mad, and not by mistake. The driver feinted with the club, and the dog backed away. The animal snarled, slobber oozing from its mouth and dribbling down. The driver circled the club in front of the dog's nose, one way, then the other, the dog mesmerised. He dropped the noose and cinched tight. The dog reared and issued a strangulated whelp. The driver stepped forward and struck the dog to the floor.

Hant opened the van door and climbed out. He brushed invisible dirt from his trousers and sleeves. He felt stiff after the drive, and would have liked to climb to a viewpoint and see a snow-capped mountain. He would like to have prayed and made an offering.

His obese driver scrabbled out of the van, and together they walked to the rear of the lorry. Anoop worked for him. Once, Manoj had worked for him, but now, temporarily at least, he worked for Manoj. They all answered to Al Usra. It was the way of the world.

The two of them walked up to the trailer, the stench intensifying. At the fenceline the two dogs wolfed chunks of meat. A large black bird appeared from nowhere and sat on the post. The lorry driver stashed the tools apart from the short metal batons, and his second filled a water bowl.

Hant slipped on the face mask of a ghostly fiend. The eye holes in the white plastic were covered by black mesh and ringed by large black sclera, and the dark cavernous mouth appeared to be screaming. Anoop and the men from the lorry took the cue to cover up. The masks spoke a thousand words for the situation, and reflected Hant's feelings if not the feelings of the three men working alongside him.

'Tape.'

Anoop used a roll of gaffa tape to cover the registration number. He bit the tape in his teeth and kept getting the tape caught on itself. After doing a bad job at the back he disappeared around the front. Anoop's last trip. However incompetent Hant's nephew turned out, he couldn't be as useless. And his nephew was family, almost *chhora*. A son.

The lorry driver opened the second trailer door. Light reached inside and fresh air battled with fetid. Dog shit dotted the floor like mounds of manure on a rice field. The trailer empty as a mountaintop.

The second white man propped a small ladder against the back, and climbed up with a power drill fitted with a screwdriver. He fixed a head torch over his head. He walked into the trailer, slaloming around the shit. His footsteps echoed.

Hant climbed halfway up the ladder and peered inside.

Humming in his ears. God would have looked after the boy, and if God hadn't, it was the boy's fault. He glanced back at Anoop.

'No watch here, watch road.'

His driver lolloped away, and he climbed up and followed the white man. Air holes had been drilled in the floor.

At the end of the trailer tarpaulins were strapped to the wall. The white man pulled one away, revealing a bank of inbuilt cupboards. All were screwed shut. The white man removed the forty-eight screws, pausing to breathe after each block of eight. He took off the panels and pulled out the soundproofing foam. It revealed a shiny door handle and new black bolts.

Hant put a finger to his lips, and listened.

He could hear movement.

5

At the dump site, a fire engine sat in the centre of the road with its doors open and lights flashing. Abandoned nearby were police cars, the dog unit, and a white forensic van. A small crowd was gathering.

Only a black shell remained of the getaway car. It blocked the gate to a field, and was no longer on fire but would never be driven again. Wisps of smoke persisted, the air heavy with the acrid smell. Two fire-fighters packed equipment, and police officers fixed crime scene tape and marshalled the onlookers. The crime scene investigator stood next to the burnt-out vehicle, peering inside. Further up the road, the dog handler ran his German Shepherd on a long leash.

Hunter parked next to the forensic van, and the two of them climbed out.

'How'd you get hold of it?' said Rick.

'What?'

'It.'

'Ah, that.' Hunter tapped his nose. 'Best you don't know.'

Rick walked over to the blackened car, Hunter lagging behind.

'Key's in the ignition,' said Tara. The CSI had long black hair and a nose ring, and cycled to work from Bolton. She was always raising money for good causes. 'Once it's cooled down, I'll get it lifted. Take a while for any forensics.' She paused. 'Tell Gary, he owes me five pounds sponsorship.'

Rick took out his wallet and handed Tara the money, then walked around the burnt-out car. Once, a dark blue VW Golf. The boot was open and empty, but the number plate was still present. The back seats had burnt away to reveal springs and the metal floor. The front seats remained intact, but the dashboard was a mess of melted plastic and glass fragments. Either the car had exploded or local kids had smashed all the windows.

Glass particles everywhere, as if there'd been a hailstorm. They crunched under his feet. They brought it all back.

His first week of nights as a DI. Seventeen bodies, and on the Saturday, seven. Two at the bus stop and five joy-riders, including Pearl and her brother. Only one survivor, Pearl's sister, Skye. Riddled with windscreen glass, and even five years later, only just alive.

Rick steadied himself against the shell of the car. It was still warm. He closed his eyes. His previous theory – arrest Khetan, and the flashbacks, visions and nightmares would stop – was in tatters. He did what Emma advised, took a deep breath, and counted to ten. Then he walked on, avoiding Tara's silent stare. She knew; at the nick, they all knew.

Slipping on gloves, he checked the door pockets. In the driver's door was a rolled-up magazine. He pulled out the charred remains, and unrolled it, pieces flaking off. The latest copy of *Rugby World*. The car owner's, or an unusual hobby for a TWOCer? Tara held open a forensic bag and he dropped it inside.

Hunter walked up, scratching his neck with the radio. 'Registered keeper is shown as Stephen Bowden in Fulham. Not reported stolen so he could be on holiday, or more likely, he's sold it and hasn't told the DVLA. I asked for a knock-on.'

'Anything from the dog?' said Rick.

'Might as well get a probationer to sniff round.' The sergeant tapped the screen of his phone half a dozen times.

'A bit odd the car's here,' said Tara. 'Two hundred and fifty miles north of where it was either stolen or sold. Why not just steal a local vehicle?'

'A lot of old cars make their way up north,' said Hunter. 'Nobody up here can afford new cars.'

'You should have stayed down there if you liked it so much.'

Rick left them to it. He'd heard rumours like everyone else. He walked up the road, trying to clear the smell in his nose and shift the images in his head.

Ditches, hedges, fields. Water seeped down the tarmac, and brambles waved their creepers. He wondered where Coniston and the driver had gone, and how. On foot, or in a vehicle. Taxi, bus, or a second car. He noted the bus stop outside Sycamore Close. A taxi was more likely, but top of the list was a second car, parked up beforehand by the getaway driver or a third person. A third person may have even been waiting.

If Rick had been Coniston? A second car, parked up beforehand, and only one accomplice. Following the investigation the previous year, he knew him better than most of his friends. Coniston was bright, unpredictable, and not afraid of physical discomfort. In Nepal, he'd walked or jogged for almost forty-eight hours to escape from Rick.

The last time he'd seen Coniston was interview room 3 at South Manchester. The prospect of seeing him again, and soon, wasn't the worst thing that could happen.

Maybe Coniston had walked – or run. And if he had, he wouldn't have gone with the driver. They'd have split, and Coniston would have disguised himself. House-to-house enquiries would hopefully yield witnesses and some answers.

The big question was why Coniston would risk adding years to his sentence. For pleasure or purpose? To get one over on Rick – in light of their history not a ridiculous theory – or for a reason Rick could only currently guess at.

Dave the dog man started waving.

About time.

Rick walked faster up the road, his swollen toe throbbing.

Dave pointed at a half-circle of stainless steel in the long glossy grass. His dog sat quietly behind him and watched Rick with charcoal eyes. Rick slipped on a pair of disposable gloves. He picked up part of a pair of handcuffs and dropped it into an exhibit bag. Nearby was the grey plastic strap from an electronic prison tag.

'He'd have needed bolt croppers for the handcuffs,' said Dave, 'But that thing! Only need scissors.'

Rick's phone rang.

As he pulled it out, another CID vehicle arrived with two more detectives. Paulson and Akram were young and showing promise. DC Kasim Akram climbed out of the car. He was slight and always immaculate. The only man in the office who ironed the back of his shirt.

'No sign of Coniston at his address.'

Nodding, Rick put his phone to his ear.

'Castle.'

'Got a witness,' said Mike, his voice squeaky with excitement.

6

Calix looked over his shoulder, but the road was deserted. A stone barn with a high window on one side and a meandering damson-blue river on the other. But there were no vehicles, and no people. He stood up on the pedals and yanked the bar ends. The bicycle weaved from side to side, but he kept going. Up yet another hill in the back lanes.

At the top he rested and leant against the dry-stone wall running alongside. He sucked up the clean air, listened. In the distance, he could hear a lorry and the honking of a horn. But no sirens, and no traffic that was close. He glanced behind him, then down across the fields to a pine wood and on the far side, another road. Sheep grazed in the field. They'd worn tracks, and the ground surrounding their drinker was bare.

An ordinary scene. But after the months in prison, ordinary felt extraordinary. He picked at the lichen on the wall. He sniffed his fingers. They stank of petrol, and would be a giveaway if anyone was suspicious and came too close.

He pushed off and coasted down. The rushing air made his eyes stream and his vision blur. Cycling felt ridiculous. Liberty felt wrong.

At the bottom of the hill he crossed a bridge and looked round again, but still there was no one.

He cycled on.

When Castle had once asked him what he believed in, Calix had told him two things. Never giving up, which he got from his sister Megan, and self-reliance which he got from his old man. Both were true, but there was also a third: getting things done. Part of his old man's job description as a brigadier in the army. Calix was never going to follow orders, but he understood about setting an aim and the steps and focus needed to achieve it.

Step one: escape from Strangeways.

Tick.

He punched the air, opened his mouth and drank a pint of freedom.

He reached a village and a signpost. Five miles to Staunton. Halfway to the town and the station. Standing next to the signpost, a phone box reminded him he needed to make a phone call. Not just for old time's sake, but to kick off the festivities.

On the far side of the houses, he stopped at a set of traffic lights. Nearby was a bus stop with people waiting. A young woman in a tight purple top stamped with the letter Z, reading a book. An older woman with two squabbling children wearing superhero costumes. A teenage boy wearing headphones and bright red trainers. Schoolgirls in yellow-braided blazers and short skirts playing on their phones and laughing. An old man holding two walking sticks.

The lights turned, and a car overtook him. In prison everyone looked and dressed the same. Young, male, pallid, wearing prison garb. And they were either manic or zonked.

'Excuse me.'

Calix started.

Crossing the road, a man in uniform. Pseudo-dibble. Community support or a special. In prison, they were known as badge collectors or snowmen.

Calix jammed his feet down on the pedals. His adrenalin

surged and he rocked the bike left to right as he accelerated away.

After thirty metres, he looked around.

Not a snowman, but a parking attendant with a shiny peaked hat and scrambled egg on his epaulettes. He stood in the middle of the road, staring after Calix and talking into his radio mic.

Calix cycled as fast as he could around the corner. Past a primary school, down a small hill, up a rise, all the time thinking through his options. The back lanes had seemed the safest route, but he could detour to the main road and continue to the station that way. Safety in numbers. The man might not have been interested in him, but he might have been. The mayor had recently spoken on TV about one big police family: dibble, pseudo-dibble, screws. Everyone and anyone in uniform.

Assistants at Aldi? Staff at Greggs? FFS, Mr Mayor!

He turned left and freewheeled steeply downhill, avoiding the potholes as the road curved around and flattened. At a notch in the hedge cut for a footpath, he dismounted and hauled his bike off the road. He pulled round the small rucksack left for him in the boot of the car with the bikes, and hung it on the handlebars. He slipped off the stars and stripes headover and stuffed it in the bag. In its place, he strapped on the cycle helmet. He looked like a prat, but prats didn't escape from custody. Distract & Blend was one of his former cellmate Darren's rules for evading the dibble. Next, Calix donned the fluorescent gilet. It was a paradox: in attracting attention, the gilet repelled it. Another of Darren's ideas, his top tip. 'With one of them you can get away with murder. Lit'ra – fucking – ally.'

Calix pulled on the rucksack, pushed the bike back onto the road and remounted. Glancing round, he cycled away.

At the main road, he signalled right and turned right. Look a prat, act a prat. Darren would be clapping. Five miles to the station which should take less than half an hour. Even on the car boot-sale bike.

A bus passed him, too close and belching smoke. Schoolboys in the back window flicked wanker signs. If only they knew.

He passed a sign. *Station, 2 miles.*

Cars passed in both directions. He overtook a dog walker and two joggers, no one paying him any attention. He wondered how his driver was doing. Now also on a bicycle, but heading to a different station on a different train line.

A siren ripped through the air.

Calix winced. He looked ahead, and behind, but couldn't see the vehicle. Not an ambulance and not a fire crew, but dibble. Castle, already? Minions of Castle? Castlettes, or a pair of Turrets or Towers.

Emergency vehicles had distinct two-tones, and in his cell he'd practised recognition by watching daytime TV. He listened and observed again. The vehicle was coming towards him, but still he couldn't see it. He could stop and hide, or ride on. He glanced at the semi-detached houses with scruffy front gardens. He could wheel up a drive and pretend he was visiting someone. Or he could sit it out.

The dibble car approached down the centre of the road, cars peeling away as if it was a snowplough. Blue flashing lights, screaming sirens. The car in front stopped at the kerb, and Calix swerved around it. The driver beeped his horn. Calix kept cycling, attracting attention but dispelling, or so he hoped, official scrutiny.

Three dibble officers sat in the car, eyes everywhere. Castle wasn't one of them, neither was his sidekick Hunter, nor the overgrown mountaineer playing at being dibble.

The car sped past, and the traffic resumed. Calix cycled onwards, the bar ends slippery with sweat. The sirens faded, and his pulse settled.

Castle was good, but not that good. It had to be coincidence. Had to be.

Maybe it wasn't.

He nodded at a postman unloading a box, and glanced into the shell of a former pub selling second-hand white goods. An old woman sat outside on a sofa stroking a cat. She wore a long purple coat covered in gold question-marks. He looked again. Not question-marks, but swirls. He was imagining things, Castle already getting to him.

The sirens grew louder again. Calix couldn't stop himself, but glanced behind, heart pounding like a blacksmith's hammer. The dibble car ploughed back down the centre of the road, cars streaming left and right – again. The dibble car turned right, and disappeared up a side road.

The sirens stopped. The main road returned to normal. Calix kept turning the pedals, but felt sick as a con during the last days of his sentence.

At the station, he pulled up at the cycle racks. For exactly two minutes he leant forward over the handlebars and closed his eyes, and as his drumming heart and trumpeting breath stabilised, he remembered.

One step at a time, like climbing Everest or winning a war.

7

Hunter drove past a primary school with children's artwork stuck in the windows, clusters of houses with mossy gutters, a village shop with peeling paintwork. Rick pondered the identity of the getaway driver.

One of TBR's soldiers, even TBR himself. Another con Coniston had met in prison. Darren Back, an Oldham psych job – although who was Rick to comment – had once shared a cell with Coniston and had visited after being released. He'd get Maggie to check with prison intel whether they had anything. An associate? There was Barney Williams, but Williams hated Coniston, blaming him for the death of his brother Spencer. He was unlikely to help him. On the other hand, Rick had a vague recollection that Williams played rugby. Leaving a magazine in the door pocket was a rookie mistake. Another action for Maggie. He sent her a couple of messages.

What else?

He'd left DS Sinclair in charge of the burnt-out car scene, and a list. House-to-house, 999 caller, CCTV, fingertip search, local bus and taxi companies.

Averaging one a day, prisoners escaping from custody weren't unusual. Most were absconders, walking out of an open prison, or failing to return after home leave. Escapes where an inmate broke out of a closed prison or from a prison van were rare: one or two a year. The last one nine months earlier when a prison van had been ambushed in Salford and two armed robbers escaped. Recaptured within weeks, and jailed with eleven others.

Very few escapees evaded recapture, and Coniston wasn't going to be one of them.

Rick's phone rang.

'Castle.'

He couldn't hear anything, not even deep breathing.

'No one,' said Rick.

'Never no one,' said Hunter. The sergeant had been in the Job twice as long as Rick, and had reached the stage of his career when his verbal inputs were twice as valuable as his actions. The only drawback, his actions were often negligible.

'Withheld number.'

'Course.'

'Surely not Coniston?'

'I'd bet on it.'

Making contact would be typical Coniston cockiness. A telecoms check was almost pointless, Coniston wasn't stupid. But routine enquiries solved cases, not moments of genius. You could be too cocky.

Rick phoned Paulson and delegated.

'Roger that.'

Paulson watched too many American crime dramas, but apart from that was solid in stature and capability.

They arrived at the cemetery at the same time as Robbo's black Range Rover. The superintendent parked alongside, and his tinted window buzzed down. A milkshake with a pink straw sat in the central console, and Holst's Mars blared. Robbo leant forward and turned down the volume. His cheeks were puffy, and the seat-belt pulled across his chest like a twist in a giant string of sausages.

'Gary.'

'Sir.'

It was the first time Rick had heard Hunter call anyone by their title, even if it was quiet and gabbled.

'Do you want a doughnut?' said Robbo, holding a paper bag out of the window. The small round doughnuts smelt sugary and sweet. They reminded Rick of Dad taking him to the local fair, and tasting them for the first time. They'd ridden on the dodgems, and one of Rick's front teeth had split his lip when bumped. Mum had been incandescent.

Hunter glanced at Rick, then shook his head for both of them.

Robbo retracted the bag. 'Holbrook's gone off with stress and won't be coming back. So, DI Castle, a fast result on Coniston would be good for the next DCI process.'

'When is it?' said Rick, leaning across Hunter.

'Chief super's just fixed it for mid-July.' Robbo plucked a doughnut from the bag. He took a bite. Sugary jam stained his lips and then was gone. 'No pressure.' He pushed the remainder of the doughnut into his mouth, and pulled away, the window buzzing up, Holst resuming, and Hunter itching his back against the seat as if he was a grizzly bear.

'Is Coniston Cat B?'

Rick nodded. The standard escape risk, but when they returned him, he'd be rebranded Cat A, and if Robbo could be trusted, Rick would get a nod for the DCI board.

They climbed out of the car.

A warm breeze whispered in the trees sheltering the entrance to the graveyard, and a noisy flock of birds pecked amongst the stones. The police incident caravan stood behind the prison van, and a row of cars stretched along the pavement. Police tape fluttered, constables dotted the scene. Another small crowd buzzed with expectancy.

A man wearing a red baseball hat plucked a Dictaphone from

a pocket and hurried towards them. Oliver, from Manchester News. His sense of smell for a story as attuned as a badger's for a hen-house.

'Coniston?' said Oliver, shoving the Dictaphone closer. He was mid-twenties, worked all hours, and on the way up.

Nodding, Rick signed the scene log. Like any professional relationship, his interaction with Oliver depended on reciprocity, and he never knew when Oliver could be useful.

'Quote?'

Rick thought for a moment. 'Two minutes in the sunshine is not worth two years on your sentence.'

'Would you say it's personal with Calix Coniston?'

Rick smiled and ducked under the tape. Hunter was waiting.

The uniform inspector stepped away from a group of people standing next to a corrugated shed. He was a thin man wearing a pristine short-sleeved shirt. He clutched a clipboard and the hairs stood on his arms.

'All boxed off, Mike?'

Hunter clicked his tongue, and stood aside to check his phone.

The inspector frowned at Hunter, nodded at Rick. 'Twenty-three people attended the funeral, including the vicar. We've taken a couple of first accounts and have details of everyone else. Nothing of note. The vicar's still here but everyone else has gone. Your DCs are speaking to the two gravediggers in the caravan. And the four guards are waiting in their van. They're refusing to give their names, only their numbers.'

'You said you had a witness?'

'Mr Jenkins. Albert. He's sitting on the bench.' Mike pointed to an old man nuzzling two small dogs under an oak tree.

'Gary, you speak to Jenkins, I'll get into the guards.'

Hunter bent down to scratch his calf.

'What?' said Rick.

He waited for a reply, but none came. 'Jesus! You get into the guards, and I'll speak to Jenkins.'

Rick walked over to the bench, feeling the lukewarm sun on his face. He hoped his bees were busy. He and Maggie should do an inspection at the weekend – even if she was still cross with him, maybe she'd control the smoker.

'Mr Jenkins, I'm DI Castle.' The old man shuffled up his dogs, and Rick sat down.

'I was telling your colleague, normally I've got three of them. One's with a nephew.'

'Yours or the dog's?'

Mr Jenkins frowned for a few seconds. 'Oh, I see. Funny. Ha-ha.'

Rick glanced at the ranks of gravestones, then back at Mr Jenkins. The old man took out a handkerchief and blew his nose. He wore multiple layers of shirts and coats, their collars a mess.

'You saw the car, Mr Jenkins?'

'Other side of the trees,' the old man said, pointing towards the top of the cemetery. 'I was walking the boys as I do every morning. To the corner, and back. Same every day since she passed.'

Rick nodded.

The old man petted his dogs. 'It was already there, near the bus stop, exhaust billowing out. Horrible stuff, I was worried about the boys. I didn't take any notice.'

'Anything might help.'

'Blue car, I think. As I got closer, I heard a noise and a man came out of the trees. Wearing handcuffs, like on TV. Me and the boys couldn't believe it.'

Rick murmured encouragement.

'He looked at me, not far away. Said something, I think. Not rude. Hello or Morning, something like that. Then he looked up the road and saw the car. It was waiting for him, obvious then.

Arranged, must have been. He jumped in, and the car shot off.'

Keeping eye contact, Rick said nothing. He was still hopeful.

The old man fed each dog a small biscuit. They licked his fingers, slobber staining his gloves. Rick cleared his throat.

'One thing was a bit odd.'

Rick's heart rate notched up. He wondered when the old man had last been hugged.

'When the lad tried to open a door, he couldn't because it was locked. He banged on the window. And then when he jumped in, the car stalled.'

'Anything else?'

The old man shook his head.

'Someone will come to your house to take a statement, Mr Jenkins, but you can go home now. Thank you. You've been very helpful.'

Rick walked over to the two Coniston headstones, paused for a moment next to the new one, then stepped across to the brigadier's. He read the inscription and bowed his head.

He remembered the old soldier's olive cravat, his rail thinness, and his belief in doing the right thing. He remembered David's love for his oddball son, for whom he had sacrificed his life. Rick still blamed himself for David's death. He remembered the two trips to Nepal and the constant battling with Calix.

Two minutes finished. Rick looked up, wondering if hostilities with Calix Coniston were about to resume. Part of him hoped recapturing Coniston wouldn't be quick.

He walked further up the cemetery through the rows of gravestones. Clasping his hands together, he broke into a trot. It was awkward and slow, and he slowed back to a walk. No doubt Coniston was determined. Had he escaped simply to defy being caged, to stick two fingers up at the law, or something else? A means to an end. Surely he realised he wouldn't stay out, and when he was caught, his sentence would be extended? The interesting detail from the old man was the getaway car's locked doors and jerky exit. Which suggested an amateur at the wheel. Again, he wondered about Barney Williams. Enough to arrest?

Behind him, a dog started howling, and he glanced round.

Mr Jenkins was waving.

Rick hurried back down the cemetery, his hopes rising.

The dog stopped yapping, and was rewarded by the old man with a treat.

'I remembered something else, Inspector. The driver was a woman. She had curly blonde hair which made me think of Marilyn Monroe. We both used to like her.'

'Is that right,' said Rick.

The noisier dog started chasing the quieter, more thoughtful-looking one. They trotted round and round in a small circle, faster, then about-turned and ran the opposite way. Suddenly, they stopped, the raucous dog rolled onto its back and played dead, and the quiet one turned a somersault.

8

Calix pretended to lock the bike. He strapped the helmet to the handlebars, and slipped off his rucksack. He took out a dark blue baseball cap and pulled it on. He took off the gilet and stuffed it in the bag. Then walked over to the clothes and shoes dumpster, and posted it through the slot. He imagined his driver in another station car park, dumping another rucksack. The gloves, the balaclava, the blonde wig.

The station did not seem to be staffed and he walked onto the platform through a side gate. He glanced up at the information board. Wrong platform, but a train to Piccadilly, central Manchester, was due in seven minutes.

Pulling his cap lower, he climbed the steps to the bridge and crossed. Below him, between the boards of the bridge, stretched the glistening rails. The churning water, the car-sized rocks. He tasted and smelt the wet air from the rushing river. Every bridge was the same, inside on the TV screen, or outside. His old man there one moment, and gone the next. Doing all this for him.

Calix grabbed the handrail and held it as he descended the steps to the far platform. He would have killed for a cigarette.

Half a dozen people were waiting. A man in a blue suit, two chattering women with shopping bags. A labourer with a tool bag. An old woman sat on the furthest bench; she was petting a small white dog, and smoking. Calix wondered about cadging a fag, but as quickly dismissed the idea, not wanting to draw attention.

A couple walked down the bridge steps and onto the platform. They were laughing. *They* were attracting attention. The principle of the fluorescent jacket. It seemed an odd time for the couple to be on the platform. They should be at work. Perhaps they were at work – and working for Castle.

The woman glanced in his direction.

Calix turned away, heart thrashing. Castle could have found the car already. Then again, the station was ten miles away and one of many options the dibble man could target.

He had no doubt it would be Castle who'd be in charge. Procedurally, the investigation would be assigned to South Manchester because the cemetery was on their patch. And only an idiot wouldn't assign Castle. No dibble knew more about him, or would be better able to predict his movements and actions. And no one would be more motivated than Castle, whom Calix had eluded twice before.

And to be fair, by whom he'd twice been caught. Castle was an obsessive detective, not afraid to break the occasional rule. The type of dibble who would chase you through red lights without slowing, then later beat himself up about it. Honours were about even, which made the current escape from Strangeways the decider.

Calix had spent many sleepless nights in prison thinking how he might retain his current advantage. Distraction was one tactic. Another was waiting for Castle's encyclopaedic knowledge of the Conistons and his unrelenting motivation to backfire. If Castle was likely to predict Calix would do x, Calix could do the opposite. Or he could double-bluff and do x. The main thing was to run Castle around, make him tired, point him at false leads and keep him guessing. Make him riled and prone to mistakes.

By which time, Calix's mission would be over, and he'd be in Australia on the trail of the van driver who'd run over Megan. Rod Stokes might have served prison time, but that wasn't enough.

He walked further down the platform, and read the timetable. Arrivals, departures, weekend schedules. He read them again.

He took out the phone his driver had brought for him. He pressed redial on the single number it had called.

'Castle.'

Easy as that. Calix could snap his fingers and the dibble man would answer. He could make him run, change direction, retrace his steps. If he wanted, have him dance the Harlem shuffle.

'Hello?'

Calix could feel the urgency in the voice, feel the man's passion. The desire seemed almost sexual.

Calix hummed, imitating a buzzing bee. A honeybee, he liked to think.

'Coniston?'

Calix hadn't expected that. He stabbed at the phone and ended the call. Castle was first-class dibble, and he shouldn't forget it. Should concentrate on the mission, not let *himself* get distracted.

The train pulled in, screeching to a halt. The automatic doors popped open, and announcements blared. He boarded and moved to an empty area of seats. Sat down, pulled his cap low and closed his eyes. Soon, he would be at the flat in Manchester and be able to relax. Have a beer, smoke a cigarette. A carton of beer, a pack of cigarettes.

Sensing movement, he opened his eyes. The old woman sat down in front of him, the dog at her feet. It stared at Calix with glassy eyes.

The train jolted to a start and Calix looked out of the window. Back gardens, a trampoline, a ball on a flat roof. The train whirred along.

They reached a station. Seven to Manchester.

Six.

He heard a siren but couldn't see it. Traffic queued in both directions over a bridge, but no dibble car.

Five.

In front of him, the dog started barking, its clean white fur bristling.

'Please have your tickets ready.'

Calix glanced behind him. He had no ticket, and no money. And he was unsure whether ticket inspectors were in the great dibble family and his mugshot sat on the inspectors' device.

The dog kept yapping. The old woman checked her pockets and tried to calm her pet, but the high-pitched barking continued.

'Quiet, Benny.' The old woman checked her pockets again. 'Benny, quiet, please.'

Calix leant forward, and put his hand on the dog's head. He pushed down, then stroked its ears, the glossy hollows. He liked animals, and they liked him. The dog calmed and lay down.

The ticket inspector stood over him. 'Ticket, please.'

'I haven't got one.'

'You'll need to pay a penalty fare.' The ticket inspector raised his console. 'You have twenty-one days to pay. Name?'

'Richard Tower.'

The inspector prodded the screen. 'Address?'

Calix used the road of Megan's best friend. Another tactic learnt in prison: when lying, stick very closely to the truth.

'Have you got any ID?'

'Left my wallet at home.'

'So how do I know you are who you say you are?' He glanced down at the screen. 'A Mr Tower.'

Calix shrugged.

'I know him,' said the old woman as she leaned over and tapped the collector on the arm. 'Ritchie.'

The ticket inspector stared at the old woman, then at Calix.

'Okay, then.' He completed the penalty fare form and printed it out. 'Twenty-one days to pay.'

The inspector bustled down the train. 'Tickets.'

Calix raised his eyebrows at the old woman.

She leant forward to whisper. 'I saw you putting clothes in the charity bin outside the station. One good turn and all that. Anyway, it's good to raise the heart rate once in a while.'

'Nice one,' said Calix.

He turned to the window. *Ritchie.* A second track curved towards them. Tens of thick cables ran overhead, and piles of construction material lay dumped alongside. Between them a gang of railway workers in high-vis jackets sat having a brew and a smoke.

At Piccadilly station, Calix helped the old woman off the train. He bent to tickle the dog's belly and watched the wave of hurrying passengers. At the end of the platform stood a posse of ticket inspectors, and above them hung CCTV cameras. He could run, or he could walk. He could hide, or he could preen. Paraphrasing Darren, but the gist was true.

Calix picked up the dog. 'Take my arm.'

The old woman slipped an arm through his, and together they shuffled forward.

'Do I smell?' said the woman.

Calix sniffed, then shook his head.

'Liar. I'm rotting in my shoes.'

They reached the queue at the inspectors. Calix clutched the penalty ticket in his hand holding the dog to his chest. He braced the old woman who was light as a stick of bamboo.

A female inspector with a red-rimmed hat pointed them to

the gate. It was large enough for pushchairs and concourse trolleys. She opened it with a pass, and the two of them pottered through. The gate clanged shut.

Together they walked into the station's grand entrance. Conifers stood in huge terracotta pots at each side like guards. The sunlight felt bright, and pigeons pecked about. A limousine pulled up and the birds scattered.

'Good luck,' said the old woman. She squeezed his hand.

Calix walked away, collecting a free newspaper from a vendor. Two hours since they'd torched the car, so too late to be featured. He hoped. The front-page picture showed migrants in a dinghy. *Abandoned refugee children to be housed in Manchester.* He checked the late news, but the box was empty.

The hall of residence was a twenty-minute walk. Calix kept in the shadow of the building line, avoiding eye contact and CCTV cameras. At the ring road he walked under the bridge. A rough sleeper without shoes thrust a polystyrene pot into his chest. He side-stepped and fell in behind a group of students. Two boys, two girls. The girls carrying books and smoking, the boys eating chips and talking.

He matched their progress, hoping they shielded him from the traffic. He was nearly there. Nothing for nearlies, his mum had used to say. Mum. The day had started with her. He hoped it wasn't wrong to appropriate her funeral. Maybe he'd talk to her later. Occasionally, he still talked to his old man.

Footsteps behind him. Clapping the pavement.

Calix whirled round. Two men were running towards him, and one more, holding handcuffs, was crossing the road. He turned back. Ahead, a man and a woman stood at the corner like sentries. They strode forwards. He looked for a ginnel but there was only the open doorway of a barber's shop and a flight of stairs.

One of the students dropped his packet of chips and sprinted diagonally across the road. The two girls screamed, the second boy shouted encouragement. Cars pulled up. The five officers converged on their man, the lead officer rugby-tackling him to the ground.

Calix walked past, and heart thudding but without looking back, turned left at the first corner. He walked a hundred metres, turned right.

Hartford Hall, Manchester University Hall of Residence

Underneath the sign was a map which he studied for a few seconds before finding the building he was looking for. He walked across a courtyard towards the accommodation block. A security guard stood outside the entrance. Calix about-turned and walked through an area of raised flowerbeds to the library. He read a couple of notices, then continued down the building line to the rear of the accommodation.

Students walked to and fro. Opposite, a new campus was being built. It was busy with workmen and beeping vehicles. A cement mixer whirled. Calix glanced back, but the guard wasn't following.

He walked across to the rear door of the accommodation block. *Loading and Unloading Only. Ask Porter for Key.*

It had been wedged open with a towel.

Calix slipped inside and walked through to the entrance. Room 57 was on the fifth floor. Outside, there was no sign of the security guard.

He took the stairs two at a time, his footsteps smacking the lino. Voices echoed down. He was so close. At the fifth floor, he exited the stairwell and padded down the corridor. It smelt of stale milk. He knocked on 57.

There was no answer.

He glanced up and down, knocked again.

'Who is it?' The voice sounded nervous.

'Who do you think?'

'It's unlocked.'

Calix went in. He slammed the door shut, locked it, and breathing hard with the effort up the stairs and the hours of relentless tension, sank to the floor.

He glanced up.

Standing over him was the six foot and three-quarter inch frame of Barney Williams.

'You took your time.'

9

A dozen detectives, analysts and data-handlers gathered in the incident room. They were surrounded by palimpsests of old investigations. Discarded briefing sheets, witness statements, and lists of phone numbers. Imperfectly wiped whiteboard timelines. House-to-house proformas, maps, and piles and piles of blank statement forms. The room needed a thorough sort-out, the filing of paperwork in the archives and a deep-clean. But the next investigation always appeared from nowhere, and like a damp spot on the ceiling, signalled a flood.

Rick stood at the front, wondering if it had been Coniston imitating the bee on the phone. The last conversation they'd had, in an interview room at South Manchester six months earlier, Coniston had mentioned an interest in keeping bees. The caller was definitely not a beekeeper. Honeybees hummed middle C, not low down the scale.

He waited for everyone to settle. Maggie sat by the door; Hunter at the back, doodling.

'Okay,' said Rick, pointing at the whiteboard. 'Map and time-line as we know them so far. At 11.22 this morning Calix Coniston escaped from custody. He was attending his mother's funeral at Hedges Cemetery when he ran off. Somehow, he eluded the guards and was picked up in a car. Ten minutes later the car was dumped and torched opposite a small housing estate called Sycamore Close.' Rick glanced at Hunter, but he was still drawing. 'For those of you who are new, Maggie's going to run through Coniston's record.'

Maggie turned to face the room.

'Two years ago Coniston conspired with Hant Khetan, a Nepalese national, to kidnap British trekkers during a trip to Nepal. Their agreed aim was to force FIFA to improve working practices in Qatar where Nepalese workers were building stadiums for the 2022 World Cup. The trekkers included the sons of Terry Williams, a FIFA vice-president. Spencer Williams died during the kidnap. Khetan's ulterior motive was revenge against Coniston's father, whom he held responsible for the death of his own father during the Falklands War. Calix Coniston was to some extent duped by Khetan, and his sentence was mitigated by the death of his father, Brigadier David Coniston.'

'It is complex,' said Rick, 'and reading the file is recommended.'

Hunter reached up and shoved open a window. He fumbled the stay, which clattered against the glass, and left it hanging.

'Last year,' said Maggie, 'DI Castle returned to Nepal with a small team to track down Khetan. He took Coniston with him. This operation was successful, but at some considerable cost. Khetan was lured to the UK and arrested, but in the process, he shot and injured Special Constable Russell Weatherbeater, and killed Terry Williams. Again, if you want to understand this case, read the file.'

No one moved or said a word. The room felt stuffy. The only sound, the flapping window stay. Rick secured the window, opened another one. He looked at the faces of his team, but they remained blank or looked away. The case had been a disaster and the needless deaths – Spencer and Terry Williams; Vicky Brant, an Australian trekker in the wrong place at the wrong time; David Coniston, the brigadier – still haunted him.

Calix Coniston, connected to all of them, still haunted him. And now he was adrift.

'That's the background,' said Rick. 'For now, concentrate on getting Coniston back into custody. A few questions to get you thinking. Who was driving the car? How did they leave the dump site, and where did they go? Why did Coniston escape? Who helped him? An inside or outside job, or both? Gary.'

Hunter walked to the front, scratching his neck.

'Registered keeper of the car is Stephen Bowden from London. Fulham. He told me the car was being used by his son Stuart Bowden, a student at Manchester Uni. The key was still in the ignition so it's possible that Stuart Bowden knows something.'

Paulson looked around, put down a foot-long baguette and raised a hand. He was always eating. He swam every morning before work, and arrived at the nick starving and smelling of chlorine.

Rick nodded.

'Sarge, how do you know you spoke to the actual Stephen Bowden?'

Hunter walked up to the junior detective and felt behind his ear. 'Damp.' He waited for the murmurs of laughter to die away. 'Passport seen by the Met officer who knocked at Bowden's door. Good enough for you?'

'What's up with you?' whispered Rick.

'Nothing's up with me,' said Hunter, loud enough for the room to hear.

Rick turned to Maggie. 'Anything from the prison?'

'They're sending someone over.' She looked down at her notes. 'Officer Yates.'

'I'd like you to sit in,' said Rick. She gave him a stony nod, and he moved on. 'We have three scenes: the cemetery, the pick-up point, and the dump site. Witnesses, CCTV, house-to-house for each one, starting with the pick-up. Kasim.'

'Yes, sir, thank you, sir.' If every DC was as polite and efficient, the inspectorate would be out of a job. And so would Hunter.

The young detective cleared his throat. 'I statemented Mr Jenkins, the dog walker.' He looked down and began to read. 'At about eleven o'clock—'

At the back of the room, the door opened and Superintendent Robinson stood on the threshold.

'Can I have a word, DI Castle?'

There was an awkward silence.

'I'm mid-briefing.'

'Now.'

Robbo walked away, his footsteps clip-clopping down the corridor.

Rick turned, proud of his team's silent reaction. 'DS Hunter will finish off, and I will see everyone back here at eight. Overtime code is six-two-two, show me as authorising.'

Robbo waited at the end of the corridor, pretending to read the fire extinguisher instructions. Rick walked up behind him. Rolls of fat bulged above the superintendent's collar.

'I've changed my mind,' said Robbo, turning round. 'You're not taking the job. You're still seeing a head doctor, and you've got too much history with Coniston. Somehow he always leads you to Khetan, and both of us into the shit.' He handed Rick a green file. 'I want you to sort this out. Needless to say, it doesn't reflect well on us.'

Domestic violence wasn't his remit, but Rick didn't argue. 'As you well know, Khetan's in Belmarsh. And it's bad practice to hand Coniston over now. You'd be criticised in a review.'

'The complainant's Velvet Carmichaels.'

Rick stilled. Velvet was Russell's teenage girlfriend, Russell his friend.

'This is a carbon dioxide extinguisher. Can you tell me why the hell we've got a carbon dioxide extinguisher in the CID corridor?'

'Listen, Robbo—'

'Sir.'

'Sir, I know—'

'No way.'

'I know the extensive case history as well as I know the caution.'

'Absolutely no way.'

'At least hear me out. Sir.'

'Thirty seconds.'

'Detective work is all about details, sir, not just finding them, but remembering them. You know that.' Robbo didn't know that. The superintendent had never been a detective, and possessed only a vague idea of the SIO detective method – taught on every Senior Investigating Officer course in the country. To Robbo, investigations were like sausage machines: either a sausage popped out, or it didn't.

'That's why we have computers.'

Rick added a second argument. 'I not only know all the background, I also know Coniston.'

'Time's up.'

'I know how he thinks,' said Rick, ignoring him, and tapping his head with a finger. 'I know what he's likely to do, who he's likely to talk to, where he's likely to hide. I'm the best person for the job and you know it.'

The superintendent inspected the fire extinguisher's maintenance chart. He knew Rick was right, but being right was only ever half the battle. Sometimes a lot less.

'You're keeping the DV file.'

'Fine.'

Robbo tapped the metal extinguisher.

'Okay, but there's plenty of small print. One, return Coniston to Strangeways, nothing more, nothing less. Two, no leaving GMP unless I authorise it. Three, regular updates so I don't look an arse in front of the chief super. Four, no more missed appointments with Doctor Emma. Got it?'

Rick nodded, but didn't move. 'Is this about last year?'

'What do you think.'

'My demotion's not enough, you had to wade into my personal life.'

'Your intractable pursuit of Khetan cost me any chance of future promotion or a nice quiet HQ job. I'm now stuck forever at South Manchester as deputy dog.' Not even an attempt at an American drawl.

'So you told Elaine?'

'Find Coniston, and make that file go away.' Robbo started down the stairs, the handrail bowing as he pulled on it for balance. 'And get the bloody fire extinguishers sorted.'

Rick drove to Magenta House to see Emma – room 331, imprinted on his brain like a watermark. He hadn't inspected his bees for a fortnight, but it was a risk he'd have to take. He couldn't ignore Robbo's instructions straight away.

A dull brown haze sat over the city, and all he could hear was traffic and sirens. He turned on the radio. Talk, classic, pop.

His car phone cut across the music, the ring tone reverberating around the interior as if a higher power was calling.

'Castle.' He waited for a few seconds. 'Hello?'

'Heard you've been demoted.'

Hairs rose on the back of Rick's neck.

'Coniston.' Rick's brain was scrambling. The silent calls *were* Coniston. From a phone box, or a pay as you go? Triangulation was a possibility. 'You're an idiot: your sentence will be extended.' In the absence of the brigadier, Rick couldn't help feeling avuncular towards his son.

'I couldn't wait.'

'To do what?'

'Start keeping bees.'

Rick hissed.

'Listen, Calix, tell me where you are, and I'll come and collect you. You can plead mistake.'

'Calix?'

Silence.

'Coniston!'

Pop music prevailed, loud and carefree.

Rick switched off the radio, and phoned Robbo. 'Coniston just phoned me.'

'What?'

'Coniston ju—'

'I can hear you, damn it. Why?'

'Who knows. I wondered about triangulation?'

A sharp intake of breath. A pause. Rick could almost hear the cogs whirring. 'Where's the immediate life or death justification?'

'It'll be the quickest way to get him back in Strangeways.'

'Rules are rules,' said Robbo, 'that's why you were demoted. You'll have to tap the keyboard and pound the streets like every other detective.'

Rick stabbed at the phone.

Alone again. He wondered what Coniston was up to. Flaunting his freedom or calling for a reason? Rick sensed it would be both: Coniston was a driven man, but couldn't resist a little grandstanding.

Ahead were yellow diversion signs. A crane appeared through the smog, then a boarded-up church, crows pecking in the weedy car park.

At Magenta House, Rick lingered in his parked car. Images were already filling his head. He sang *La La La*, he tidied a door pocket, polished the rear-view mirror. He ate an old Kit Kat he'd found lurking in the glovebox while he checked his phone. Work the great distracter. He asked himself the four questions from the SIO detective method. So simple yet so effective, like quadratics.

What did he know? Coniston had been picked up in a car. The driver had stalled. The driver had blonde hair and was probably wearing a wig; may have been reading a rugby magazine. The car had been driven to the dump site and torched.

What were his hypotheses? H1 – Coniston escaped as an end in itself. Because he could: for kicks, to show off. If that had been his aim, the YouTube engagement showed success. H2 – Coniston escaped as a means to an end. To see family, but he had no surviving close relatives. Meet a girlfriend? Find something out? Settle a score? Deliver something? H3 – Escape had been forced upon Coniston. Someone, inside or out, wanted him to do something. Something only Coniston could do. Someone with connections and money.

The Big Red, from the outside?

Hant Khetan, from his cell in Belmarsh? There was no way the Nepalese man could escape from the highest security prison in the country. Unless the unthinkable had happened, and there'd been two prison breakouts in a week. On the other hand, as unlikely as Khetan escaping from Belmarsh, as likely as the FBI's former most wanted in South Asia orchestrating a new plot using illicitly stashed phones from inside prison.

Rick stopped at a traffic light and watched a rough sleeper shuffle across, change his mind halfway, and shuffle back. Sacking tied with string for shoes in twenty-first century Britain.

Maggie made a monthly donation to a homeless charity. They'd spent most nights together for over a year, and he didn't want it to end.

The lights turned green, and Rick pulled away.

H1 seemed unlikely. Coniston would expect to be recaptured within a few weeks if not a few days. Would know he'd be placed on the prison's escape list, be forced to wear lurid clothing, and forgo all privileges. Would know his sentence would increase. H3 seemed very unlikely. Which left H2 – Coniston escaped in order to do something. But what?

Rick climbed out.

What did he need to know? and *How could he find the information he needed?* would have to wait.

The lift clacked higher. Clackety-clack like an old-fashioned train. It passed Emma's floor, and stopped at the fourth. Rick stepped out, but paused to look down through the gap between the lift and the hallway. Down into the chasm below, cold air rushing up; further down, all criss-crossing black struts and rivets.

He walked down the corridor and glanced into a few rooms. They were empty. He opened a door, and entered a room he judged to be directly above Emma's. Room 431.

At the window, he stared out into the coin-grey of Manchester. Weathered buildings, grimy vehicles, smoky sky. Two more rough sleepers were pushing a trolley down the street, taking it in turns to check the bins.

The door opened, and Emma walked in wearing a black trouser suit.

'Hello, Rick.'

'I couldn't—'

'It's okay.'

'Your spider plant. The box of tissues. I couldn't sit there.'

'It's fine, Rick. We can sit here.' She pulled a chair out from the table, and sat. She crossed her legs and opened a notebook. She wore chic pointed black shoes with two buckles. He noticed such things. He was a detective; he was paid to notice, not paid to sit and dwell. She was a psychotherapist, paid to sit and dwell on people like him.

'How is she?'

'Maggie?'

'No, Rick, not Maggie. Skye.'

He didn't trust himself to speak. Somehow, wedged between the driver's seat and the back seat, Skye had survived. The only nod to life in his first week of nights as a DI.

'Can you explain why she's so important to you?'

Rick shook his head. 'Not really.'

'Try.'

He glanced at the window, at the reflections of the gloom.

'Rick?'

'Did Maggie say something?'

'No.'

Rick didn't believe her. Skye had become a talisman, someone he made sporadic enquiries about, and had once or twice mentioned to Maggie. Skye had recuperated well for eighteen months, but then required further operations to remove more of the glass fragments. She was back in hospital for the seventh time. And there was no one to care about her. No trace of her parents, siblings both dead in the accident, foster home swamped.

'Rick, you have to say something, or I can't report back.' She wrote a note on her pad.

'You said—'

'I said, you have to say something.'

'Okay.' He looked at his watch. 'This time tomorrow, she'll be in theatre.'

'St Anne's?'

He nodded.

'Talk to me.'

'I suppose you could put it like this: she's my deal with the devil. If Skye's alright, then I'm alright.'

'What do you mean, alright?'

'I mean, I'm a decent human being, worthy of my place on the planet.'

Emma wrote another note. Her brown fountain pen scratched the page, as if her assessment was negative, and Skye was in danger.

His phone rang.

'Sorry,' said Rick, putting it to his ear.

'Yates is here from Strangeways,' said Maggie. 'Coniston's been having some interesting visitors.'

10

The second man from the lorry braced an arm against the false wall and hauled air through his mouth. Sweat marks ringed his neck and armpits. His breath smelt of teeth rot, the trailer of shit. Hant could have stayed outside, but he wanted to know as soon as possible. Always he wanted to know, but this time especially.

Hant nodded.

The white man slid the door away and stood back. Hant stepped forward and peered into the gloom, a faint tintinnabulation in his ears.

A metre wide, the secret compartment ran across the width of the lorry. Air holes in the floor, the same as the dog section. Stale air and the acrid smell from the bucket wafted out, but he couldn't see any people. Panic gripped his chest.

Slowly, his eyes adjusted to the murk, and faces began to form.

'Light!'

The white man passed the headtorch, and Hant slipped it over his mask. He looked again into the compartment, searching for the boy.

Movement. Shuffling and stretching on the hard wooden seat. The closest person, a young black man, glanced up with the wisp of a smile. Near the far corner, a woman Hant couldn't see was weeping. But that was to be expected. The headtorch picked out faces. Men and women, children. From all over: Iraq, Syria, Libya, Afghanistan, Nepal. Al Usra wasn't fussy: the dollar was king. They had been told to be silent, quieter than mice. Their lives might depend on it.

Hant still couldn't see the boy. He scanned more faces. A couple hugged and two children held hands. The young boy glanced up, then kissed the girl on the ear. An old man held a child on his lap. They stared at him with cold, drawn faces. In the far corner, next to the crying woman, sat his nephew.

Ram glanced at his uncle without recognition. But he was alive, moving, breathing. Hant's ears popped as if he was descending a mountain. They were all alive. He would make an offering soon. He always made an offering. Dogs were dogs, but whatever Manoj said, people were people and some were Nepalese.

'Now okay talk.' Hant cleared his throat, and beckoned them forward. 'Okay now leave.'

He weaved a path back to the ladder, and climbed down, glad of the clean air.

Migrants emerged. They stood in the trailer doorway, staring out. They carried small bags, very small bags. Bags were extra.

The migrants helped each other climb down. The lorry driver held the ladder, and his driver swung down the children. Hant was moved to see hard men soften. They said they did it for the money, but he didn't believe them. God was in them, even if they didn't know it.

His nephew was next. Ram was skinny, but tall for a Nepalese boy. Sixteen already. He jumped down with the ease and flexibility of a childhood spent in the foothills of Everest. Hant felt proud, but refrained from showing any emotion.

A migrant approached. He wore a black leather jacket and jeans and smart brown boots. He spoke.

Hant shook his head. Arabic, he thought.

'Thank you,' said the man. He sank to his knees, and leant forward and kissed the ground.

Behind him, the others dumped their bags and hurried to the edge of the compound. The women squatted together, and the men congregated by the security hut, urinating and hoiking. The black bird flew down and pecked around. The man with the brown boots stood up and ran stiffly at the bird, kicking at the air.

Hant collected the box of drinks and chocolate bars from the front of the van and set it down at the back. Migrants milled around and stretched. They drank the water and the milk, and the children ate the chocolate. Hant considered throwing Ram a chocolate bar, but he resisted. His nephew glanced at him, his face puckered. As if he'd eaten too many chillis.

The last two migrants reached the ladder. An Asian man passed down a bundle to a veiled woman. She held the bundle close to her chest, quietly sobbing. He jumped down, and together they walked over to Hant.

The woman unwound her veil. Her eyes were red-rimmed. Her lip was split and crusty blood covered her chin. The man's nose was bent, his face taut. The berry-red weal of a garrotte mark swelled on his neck. The woman pulled back a corner of cloth to reveal the half-turned head of a baby. Still, silent, its skin pallid with a grey sheen.

Hant placed his hands in the prayer position, bowed his head, and for a moment closed his eyes.

He'd seen it once before. The Al Usra network accepted babies, but many smugglers didn't. Babies cost double because they were trouble. They cried and screamed and couldn't be told to be silent. If a baby's caterwauling coincided with a border crossing or an inspection, the migrants risked discovery. Many had spent their life-savings, or represented their family's life-savings. So they took action. The compartment was a pressure cooker of hopes and fears, of dreams, and of panic-fuelled desperation and unchecked violence.

He opened his eyes and banged on the roof of the van.

'Five minutes,' his driver shouted.

Hant opened the doors of the van. The rattling drinks can fell to the ground and rolled under a wheel. He picked it up and squashed it and hurled it out of the compound. He tapped his ears, but it made no difference, he could still hear ringing.

11

In the sill of the balcony door nestled a battle-twig. It had a russet head with black bulbous eyes, and a long shiny body with short pale wing covers and a dark brown ribbed abdomen.

Before it had time to run, Calix scooped it up and balled his hands so it couldn't escape. Its legs and antennae tickled as it scuttled around its spherical cell. He walked to Barney's desk and dropped it into a mug. He scanned the desk for a better home. Books, files, laptop. He opened a drawer and took out a box of tissues. Listened for the sound of the shower, and satisfied, dumped the tissues in the drawer. He ripped away the top of the box and transferred the battle-twig. Then sat on the wheelie chair.

The battle-twig inspected the four corners of the box. Not unlike Calix when he'd first landed at Strangeways. The insect halted halfway along one side and waited. Calix shuffled back and forth on the wheelie chair. The curved pincers twitched.

He hated the common name of earwig, which was an old wives' tale. Calix prodded it with a finger. Battle-twigs weren't so different to humans. They had a brain. They ate, fought, mated, shat. Same as Beetle Beetle whom he'd found and incarcerated in a matchbox in Nepal.

Barney stepped out of the tiny bathroom wearing a towel, his hair wet, his stomach ripped.

'Meet Dennis,' said Calix, tipping up the box.

Barney nodded and slipped on a shirt. Calix went over to the galley and opened the fridge. He closed the door, and tore a hunk of bread from the loaf. He took a bite, and chewing, tore small pieces for Dennis. He dropped them into the box.

The intercom buzzed. Calix looked around for a hiding place. The balcony. The built-in cupboard. The bathroom.

'Pizza,' said Barney. He pressed the intercom and pulled on his jeans.

Calix carried the tissue box with Dennis out of the sightline of the flat door, and stood against the wall. He pressed Dennis down with his thumb so the insect couldn't move. They both stood still, Calix aware of each breath.

He heard Barney open the door. Footsteps padded down the hall. There was the rustle of bags.

'Thanks,' said Barney.

'We're doing free garlic bread.'

'Calix!' shouted Barney. 'Do you like garlic bread?'

Calix pressed down harder on Dennis.

'Calix?' A second shout.

Calix crushed the insect's exoskeleton into the bottom of the box.

Barney appeared from the cramped hallway, and in exaggerated slow-motion Calix put a finger to his lips. Barney turned and returned the way he'd come. The flat door slammed. Calix shook the tissue box, the corpse inverted and missing both antennae and a pincer. He took a tissue from the drawer and wrapped the body. He stepped out onto the balcony and placed the pyre in the ashtray on the table. He lit it. Flames engulfed the tissue and the corpse. There was a crackle from the burning body and a trail of smoke. And then it was over.

He went back inside.

'I'm sorry,' said Barney. 'I wasn't thinking.' On the low table sat the pizza boxes, and underneath a slab of beer. The smell of hot greasy food spread around the room.

Calix walked up to him. His friend was taller, lifted weights, played in the scrum in a rugby team. His friend had helped him escape from custody. His friend had been through a lot, much of it Calix's fault.

Calix slapped him.

Barney wasn't expecting it. He whipped his head away, and stepped back. 'Fuck, Calix, I said I'm sorry.'

Calix sat on a chair. 'I'm starving.' He opened two beers and pushed one across the table. He drank, the cold hoppy taste even better than he remembered. He drank again, gesturing Barney to sit. Barney kicked across the stool and flopped down. Inspected his beer as if it might be doctored.

They ate slices of pizza in silence, Barney avoiding Calix's gaze. Calix looked around. It wasn't really a flat. A bathroom and a large room with a galley section. The fridge whirred wherever you were. He pushed home a floppy slice of insipid pizza. They made it better inside: crisper and spicier.

'Took nerve to pick me up. Thanks.' Calix held out his bottle.

Barney nodded, licking his fingers and trying not to smile. He picked up his beer and clinked. 'Craziest thing I've ever done.'

Calix drank to him, and with him. Carrot and stick – basics. Calix's old man had sometimes talked about how to make his men follow and obey when they were being shot at. Calix had pretended not to listen, but wished now he could put that right. Maybe in a way he was.

Barney plucked out a mushroom. 'Ram's not going to come.'

'Why not?'

'Because he's only sixteen and lives in a village in Nepal. He probably hasn't even got a passport.'

'You read his letter, his uncle's sorting it out.'

'You really think so? Special K himself?'

'He regards the boy as his own son. Anyway, all that matters is Khetan's in the UK. If Ram can lead us to him, great, if not, then we'll find him another way.'

'You don't even know Khetan's here. If he's not in Belmarsh, he's probably back in Nepal.' Barney picked out more mushrooms. 'You said it was a rumour.'

'He's definitely not in Belmarsh, hasn't been for months. The Americans had him for a bit. Then the Chinese got involved and he was released. He's now returned to the UK to raise some money for his next campaign.'

'That's just prison gossip.'

'Someone saw him.'

'*Who?*'

Calix shrugged. 'A friend of a friend.'

'You had friends in there?' said, Barney, scooping up more pizza.

'A few.'

'Where did they see him?'

'In Manchester.'

Barney grunted and stuffed in the rest of the slice.

'You don't know Armstrong walked on the moon,' said Calix, 'but you believe he did.'

'There are photos and footage of the space walks. What have you got?'

'He's here, I know it.' Calix could feel it, although he didn't want to say so. Barney already thought he was half man, half biscuit.

While Barney finished the rest of his pizza like a contractor, Calix considered his remaining slices. He peeled off the chunks of pepperoni and ate them. He ate the olives. He scuffed up the cheese and ate that. Barney stared at the wastage like a hungry dog. Calix pushed it over and finished his beer while he watched Barney eat every crust and every soggy crumb.

He opened another beer to celebrate, but could only manage the occasional sip. Unsure whether he'd overeaten, or like a child, was overexcited. Still one more phone call to make.

Calix stood alone on the balcony. He leant on the rail, smoking and staring out across the bright lights of the big city. A plane rumbled overhead, and cars zipped across the motorway flyover, their lights flaring and fading like a time-lapse film of flowers. Buses trailed up and down the Oxford Road, the passengers blurred through their steamed-up windows. Below him a night club rocked. Minicabs pulled up and disgorged beautiful young people wearing bizarre and colourful clothes. Girls in short skirts and skimpy tops queued outside while their tattooed boyfriends argued with over-muscled bouncers.

He tapped the cigarette and watched the ash falling, falling and falling.

The air throbbed with the heavy bass of the club. Voices rose and fell. Cars screeched away from traffic lights. Car horns poked at the city.

Calix flicked the cigarette into the air. It spun, and fell from view. He sank to his knees, clutching the rail for support. He retched. He leant forward and vomited pizza and beer until there was nothing left. Today he'd given his all and now he was empty.

12

Rick was halfway up the back stairs when his phone rang. Yates was waiting in his office. The display showed withheld number. He took the call.

There was a pause, Rick sensing the deliberation, the stage-management.

'Coniston?'

'Very good.'

Rick ignored the sarcasm. 'What do you want?'

'To help you.'

'Let's help each other – hand yourself in.' Still, Rick could feel the brigadier's hand on his shoulder.

'If I give you information, will I get a reward?'

'Information about what?'

'Khetan.'

Rick stilled, his arms turning goosebumpy. Khetan was his second bête noire, but now safely ensconced in Belmarsh. What had Coniston heard? An escape attempt, a bomb plot organised from within prison?

'Did you hear me?'

'What do you mean, he's in Belmarsh.'

'He's not. He's running around in the fresh air too.'

'What?'

The line dropped.

Rick ripped off his jacket and loosened his tie. Coniston was either enjoying a sixty-second chain pull, or—

He phoned Belmarsh, and as he waited for someone to answer, climbed the stairs and took refuge in the photocopying room. Kicked the door shut, took off his jacket.

A prison official answered and put him through to custody.

A PC opened the door, Rick shook his head, and the PC went out.

Finally, and without looking them up, Rick gave Khetan's date of birth and prisoner number. Only one other person for whom he could do the same.

'Hant Khetan is no longer a prisoner.'

Rick removed his tie, half-strangling himself in the process. 'You're sure?' Two breakouts in a week would not only be a record, but also would have dominated the headlines.

'He was released six weeks ago.'

'*Released!* Released where?'

'Release code 27C.'

'In English?'

'Classified.'

'Released to another prison?'

'I don't know, I'm sorry, sir.'

Rick rang off. He phoned the Prisons Index. Again he relayed the details of Khetan, and waited. *Released.*

'Sir?'

'Yes?'

'Hant Khetan is not currently being held in a British prison. I'm—'

Rick threw the phone down. Picked it up, collected his jacket and his tie and opened the door. He felt hot and cold all over. One man would know the reason why, even if he said he didn't. Yates could wait.

Robbo was sitting at his desk eating a slice of birthday cake with a fork. The slice was big enough to hold a candle and half of the word Mary, one of the typists.

'Hant Khetan's no longer being held in a British prison.'

Robbo looked at Rick, then down at the cake. He placed his fork on the plate and pushed it away. He wiped his lips with a red and gold serviette.

'Well, where is he?'

'Don't act as if you didn't know.'

Robbo snorted, stood up like a man twice his age, and turned to the window. He looked out into the yard. 'I'm thinking of buying a minicab when I retire.'

'You owe me an explanation.'

'I owe you nothing, DI Castle. You owe me for still having a job.'

'I worked for two years and put my life on the line to put Khetan behind bars. Saving dozens, if not hundreds of lives. Yes, I cut a few corners, but there's been an enquiry and I was demoted. You can't keep punishing me.'

Robbo glanced down at the slice of birthday cake. 'Okay, okay.' He dabbed a finger in the icing and licked it. 'Okay. I knew Khetan had been released, but I don't know why, or where he is now. The file's got a Top Secret rating.' He looked up and raised his eyebrows.

Rick wanted to throw something, kick something, punch something. Felt only hot. Angry as a firestarter. He walked to the door. 'Rumour in the PCs' writing room is that the typist who doesn't like Mary laced the cake with laxatives.'

He went out, leaving the door wide open.

13

When Rick walked into his office, Yates was reading a free newspaper and dunking a biscuit into a mug of tea.

'Make yourself at home, why don't you.'

The uniformed prison officer mumbled an apology. He was a large bald man with cauliflower ears.

Rick sat down. In front of him Yates folded the newspaper and brushed crumbs from his shirt. His epaulettes showed three bars meaning he was a custodial manager, the approximate equivalent of a police inspector.

'I've just had what personnel call *a difficult meeting*.' He hoped he wasn't going to have another one.

Yates removed paperwork from a file and set it down. 'The governor is professionally embarrassed. The supervising officer has been suspended, and there's going to be an enquiry. The officers shouldn't have been in a huddle. There should have been a dog.'

Rick moved his chair back. Yates' breath smelt like a squatters' kitchen.

'You want to know about Coniston. We've locked down his cell, and tomorrow we'll search it and interview his cellmate, Jacob Vogel.'

'Tomorrow's no good – the search and interview need to happen now.'

'I can try to speak to the governor,' said Yates. He looked as persuasive as a PCSO at closing time on a Friday night.

'The prison service is already at fault for losing Coniston. You don't want to make things worse by hampering our attempts to recapture him, do you? Put the public at risk?'

'As I said, I can speak to—'

'You need to *tell* him. Or do you want me to write you a note?' Yates nodded mechanically. 'I'll tell him.'

'Mention I'm friendly with Oliver at Manchester News.'

'You've made your point.'

'Also, I need the names of the prison officers who were escorting him at the funeral.'

'I can't release those, governor's instructions. I can however give you the details of Coniston's visitors and authorised phone numbers.' He handed Rick a sheet, then snatched it back. 'Wrong one, sorry.' He handed Rick a different sheet.

It showed a list of five people. Coniston's grandfather Joe who'd visited every month before his death, and his mother who'd visited once a fortnight. The Big Red, a mid-layer drugs dealer who Coniston had once worked for, had been five times, the last time, three months previously. Barney Williams, Spencer's surviving twin, had visited the previous May, and three times in the previous two months. Darren Back, a former cellmate, had visited twice, once in September and once in the week before Christmas.

'And these are his two authorised phone numbers.' Yates handed Rick another sheet. 'His mother and grandfather.'

'You don't mind if I take photocopies,' said Rick, standing up. He leant forward to take a biscuit, and as he did so knocked over Yates' mug. Tea spilt across the desk and onto the prison officer's lap.

'Fuck!' Yates pushed his chair back and stood up.

'Very sorry,' said Rick. 'Paper towels in the gents, end of the corridor.'

Yates brushed tea from his papers, shuffled them up and put them in his file. He stared at Rick with small porcine eyes, then exited without saying a word.

The heavy footsteps receded.

Rick opened Yates' file, removed the list of the guards and slipped it onto his printer. Pressed photocopy. No paper. He took paper from a cupboard and refilled the tray. Hearing footsteps, he glanced at the door. The heavy guy in accounts lumbered past. He photocopied the first sheet, swapped sheets. Heard someone at the door.

Looked up.

Only Hunter. 'They're waiting in the incident room.'

'I'm coming, just finishing up with Yates.'

'What's up?' said Hunter.

'Coniston phoned me. Spoke this time.'

'Told you. What did he say?'

'Not much. Just flaunting his liberty,' said Rick, photocopying the last sheet. He decided not to mention Khetan. His colleagues including Hunter already thought he was obsessed as a fruitbat. 'On the off chance, I asked Paulson to trace the calls.'

'Almost forgot,' said Hunter, placing a small evidence bag on the table. A sweet smell leeched out.

Rick returned the papers to Yates' file and locked the cannabis in a drawer. 'Thanks.'

Yates walked in.

'Want me to show him out, boss?' said Hunter with a wry smile.

Rick thanked Yates for coming in and apologised for his grumpiness. The two men walked out, the heavy steps of Yates, and alongside, or so he imagined, the gambolling steps of Hunter.

Rick turned to the window, and stared out across the concrete blocks of Manchester. The cold sky. His priority was Coniston, but at the same time he could make discreet enquiries about Khetan. The Nepalese man could lead him to Coniston, and vice versa. Maggie had an old sapper colleague who now worked at Six. If she was still talking to him. Get Coniston behind bars, and hopefully by then, he'd at least have an explanation for Khetan's release. Maybe someone at Six or their counterparts across the Atlantic would feel the same way as he did. Another fruitbat.

Rick heaved the casement home. The day had seen a double blow for justice, and it wasn't over yet.

He stood there, hands still gripping the wood, an idea forming.

Had Coniston escaped in order to track down Khetan? It made sense. The two prison exits weren't a coincidence – they rarely occurred in police work – but linked. Coniston had escaped to hunt down Khetan, and take whatever form of revenge he considered appropriate. Which was unlikely to be a formal warning.

If he was right, the other fruitbat was Coniston.

They were *both* pursuing Khetan.

Rick heaved the casement back up and bathed in the cool summer air.

At the back of the incident room Rick poured coffee from the dented thermos and grabbed the last, bedraggled pastry. He felt starving. Maggie often brought him something to eat when they were working late. But not today.

The room felt stuffy and smelt of fish and chips. Hunter sat on a desk at the side with his eyes closed. Paulson proffered a box of ketchup-laden chips.

Rick shook his head. 'Okay, everyone.' The room quietened. 'Coniston's already playing silly buggers and has phoned me a couple of times. Paulson is tracing the calls, but I don't expect an easy result. So we crack on as usual. Strangeways have provided details of the four guards and Coniston's recent visitors. Maggie's checking out the guards as we speak, and this is a list of his visitors and phone numbers.' He handed the nearest person a wedge of paper. 'Gary, can you tell us about Stuart Bowden.'

Rick swallowed a piece of pastry, and assumed he'd eaten the rest.

Hunter opened his eyes and wiggled forward on the desk. 'Two days ago, Bowden was twenty-one and decided to drink a beer in twenty-one bars.' He scratched behind his ear. 'Bowden's car keys were in his jacket pocket and at some point, probably in or after the Three Feathers, he took off his jacket. Yesterday, when he woke up, he realised his keys were missing. Wasn't bothered as he owned a spare set. Until that is, he went to use his car and it wasn't where he'd left it.'

'Go on,' said Rick.

'Same day, dinner time, at the back of his halls of residence. On a meter. He assumed it had been lifted, but when he phoned the meter company they said they hadn't taken it. Says he tried to report it, but the number was engaged.'

'Do you believe him?'

'Maybe.' Hunter's phone beeped and he looked down at the screen. 'Maybe not.'

'Previous?'

Hunter shook his head.

'Alibi?'

'No, in bed asleep.'

'So he could have been the driver?'

'Yes. Or the thief might know Bowden and where he parks his car. If he doesn't know him, then he might have seen him park it and followed him around for the afternoon, or he might have stolen the keys and got lucky pressing the key fob. Both scenarios are unlikely, but possible. More likely, the thief knows Bowden.'

'The getaway driver,' said Kasim, 'could be Bowden, the key thief, the car thief, or even a fourth person.' In front of him lay a pristine detective's attaché case.

Hunter pretended to clap.

'The remains of a rugby magazine were found in the torched car,' said Rick. 'Barney Williams is an associate of Coniston and a Manchester student, and I think he plays rugby – two years ago, I remember seeing sports photos in his family home. Confirm whether he does, Kasim, and find out if he knows Bowden.'

'Yes, sir.'

'Exciting isn't it?' said Hunter.

The door opened, and Maggie entered.

'Hunter's playing up,' whispered Rick after she'd joined him at the front. He hoped the aside would produce an affectionate glance, but she turned to face the room without acknowledgement. Her face was pale. He wanted to give her a hug.

'Four guards,' said Maggie. 'Sakit N Patel, Rashim Swales, William Twite, and Harry Agar. Agar's close to retirement and heavily in debt. Twite was cautioned for shoplifting when he was fourteen. Swales is a dual national with Spain, and has a conviction there for drug smuggling. Seems the prison service didn't know about that. And Patel lives in the next road to Coniston's family home.'

Hunter slid off the desk, and again pretended to clap. Maggie bowed her head.

'There are four guards,' said Rick, 'so one each, Woods, Bennett, Kasim, Paulson.' After receiving four nods, he moved on to the other actions. There'd been nothing so far from the CCTV and house-to-house enquiries. But that was the nature of police work: a beach of stones to turn over and only a handful with anything interesting under them. A sandy beach and one big rock would be like winning a race with only one entrant.

He glanced at his watch. 'Thanks everyone. Back here for seven tomorrow.' Hunter gave a mocking salute and walked out.

'Mags, have you got a minute?'

The wash-up of detectives and staff stilled, and conversation stopped. Rick felt sorry for Maggie. Felt sorry for the situation. The room emptied quickly, leaving the two of them in painful silence.

'Do you want another brew?'

'No, thanks,' said Maggie.

He felt like a stranger, at best a colleague. Not like her lover, and, or so he thought, her best friend. He touched her arm, but she stiffened, and he retracted his hand.

'I've got another enquiry for you, bit more sensitive.' She'd worked with him long enough, knew him well enough, to understand what he meant.

'You really think now's a good time?'

'Sorry.' He again went to touch her arm. Again, she retracted.

'Is this about Skye?'

'No.'

'You spoke to Emma.'

'I worry about you.'

Rick's stomach heaved, and he waited for it to settle. He was grateful he'd eaten only a pastry. 'So, it's about Elaine?'

'It's about you. You blackmailed Robbo last year. He was a friend of yours, yet you used him. I'm not sure I really know you, Rick. Or what you're prepared to do for the Job.'

'Khetan is responsible for tens, maybe hundreds of deaths. Including Spencer and Terry Williams. David Coniston—'

'The Job will always be there.' She paused. 'I think it's best you sleep at your flat tonight. I'll see you tomorrow.' She wheeled out.

Rick poured out the dregs of the coffee. There was one thing more important than the Job. He sipped at the mug, then hurled it at the wall.

14

Rick parked outside his parents' house in Chesterfield. As he climbed out he cranked his neck sideways in case his mum was looking out of the window. Their family joke over the sole fact strangers knew about the town. Dad no longer laughing had been one of the first clues he wasn't well.

Opposite the house, a patchwork of green and russet fields gave way to the darker brown moorland. Stretching in undulating hummocks as far as you could see. A footpath opposite led all the way to the highest point on Kinder Plateau at 633 metres. Rick had walked there a few times with his parents, Mum packing a lunch and a flask of coffee, Dad a can of beer. His dad had always liked a can of beer at lunchtime.

Rick heard rapping on a windowpane. The outside light came on, and his mum waved at a window.

He sat in the kitchen while she made coffee. She wore his old grey checked shirt, and an apron with a print of Durdle Door. The room smelt sweet. A jam pan sat drying on the draining board, and alongside stood a tray of jars of jam. Books on wildflowers and a puzzle magazine covered half the table, and a stack of library books sat on a stool by the door. His mum took a milk bottle from the fridge. Photos on the front: Becky and

Julian on a gondola; Rick and Maggie in a canoe; Dad on a garden bench at Three Views.

The lid of a jam jar popped making his mum start.

'Will you take a jar back with you?' She put the milk back, the harsh light of the fridge emphasising the lines on her face. She looked tired. 'Rhubarb and ginger.'

Rick nodded. 'Maggie's favourite.'

His mum pushed two mugs of coffee onto the table and sat down. 'Thanks for driving all this way.'

Rick clasped her hand on the table. It felt thin and cold. 'You need a bit of heating in the evenings.'

'It's June.'

Rick sipped his coffee. Mum drank hers in great gulps as if she had a steel-lined mouth.

'How's Dad?'

Another lid popped.

'That's a good sign,' they said together.

His mum smiled. 'Thanks for coming, darling.' She wrapped her hand around his hand holding his mug. 'It gets a bit lonely here without him.' She sighed. 'He's getting worse, but that's to be expected. Forgetting how to put on his trousers, tie his shoes. He's like a different person, now, so perhaps that's easier.'

'Is it?'

'No.' She stood and rinsed her mug under the tap and inverted it on the drainer. 'I have to force myself to remember. How he used to walk at the front of the rambling group, even on a twelve-miler.' She dried the jam pan and set it on the side. 'Will you put it away before you go?'

'Of course I will. Sit down, Mum, please.'

'What is it?' She sat and looked at him expectantly. She unhooked the top of her apron and tucked it away. 'I knew something wasn't right. Is it you and Maggie?'

Rick looked down into the depths of his mug. The coffee

almost black. 'No, Mum, we're fine. I want to talk about Dad.'

'What about him?'

'Well, I don't want to get your hopes up, but I've been reading up on the beneficial effects of cannabis for Alzheimer's sufferers.'

'Cannabis – isn't that illegal? No, Rick, no, no, no. I don't want you to risk your job.'

He took her hand again. Still freezing. 'Can I get you another jumper?'

'No, darling, I'm fine. Roger, well, it's one of those things. It is what it is, isn't that what they say?'

'Mum, that's nonsense.'

'But you're a police officer. A detective chief inspector.'

'A DI!'

'Still.'

'Family before the Job. Brigadier David Coniston taught me that, told me before he jumped off the suspension bridge in Nepal.' Rick glanced down at the floor, a runner bean slice protruding from under the fridge. Maggie knew he thought that. Didn't she?

'Rick, darling,' said his mother, touching his arm. 'You might get into trouble at work.'

'I'll be okay.'

'Go on then, tell me.'

'I don't want to raise your hopes too much, but there's been a study in Norway looking at the beneficial effects of cannabis for Alzheimer's patients. Three hundred and fifty people in the study, six-month trial. One in three people showed a marked improvement.'

'What kind of improvement?'

'Recognising loved ones.'

'Oh, Rick.' She clasped his wrist with both of her hands. They were rough and scratched from her gardening. They always had been, always would be.

*

Rick drove back across the dark and blustery Peak District. The damp road wound through small steep-sided villages, then curved across the undulating moorland. He felt bombarded. Dad, Skye's op the following day. Coniston. Did Barney Williams know Bowden? Did Coniston know Patel from his childhood? Or was Darren Back returning a favour from their time inside. Or TBR freeing an asset?

And then there was Khetan, who was free as a bird. Free as Coniston. Both of them were flying around, and Rick was back to square one.

All the previous year had been for nothing. And now Maggie had found out about him pressurising Robbo. More than upset, she was disappointed in him as a person. As a partner. As a future—

The car phone rang, loud as a tannoy.

'I thought I told you to go home, Kasim.'

'Sakit Patel had five k deposited into his current account last month.'

The young detective's excitement reminded Rick of himself when he'd been new into the CID. He still got the fluttery feeling. He had it now. 'What's the source?'

'My cousin – he's a financial investigator.'

'In the Job?'

'Birmingham. He wants me to do the course, says it's the way to really hurt career criminals. I was wondering about a warrant for Patel.'

'Looking for what?'

'I'm not sure. Surveillance, then?'

'Not yet. Find out if there's a UC working in the prison, and if there is, task him with finding a link between Coniston and Patel.'

'Yes, sir.'

'See you tomorrow.' Rick paused. 'Kasim?'

'Yes, sir?'

'Well done.'

The phone call changed his priorities, or maybe it didn't. The prison officer could have been bribed to let Coniston escape. By Coniston, or TBR on behalf of Coniston, or by someone else. And why? It was an interesting lead but until they had more, it didn't change his hypotheses or his plan for the morning.

Coniston the priority. Khetan on hold.

He opened the window and blasted himself with cold air. It reminded him of a train journey with Dad when he'd stuck his head out of the window in a tunnel to show off. A cinder had lodged in his eye, and he'd cried. Dad had chided him, then taken him to A&E. Had welled up when Rick was given the all-clear, and slapped his legs in the hospital car park.

Rick closed the window, his eyes streaming. One day it would all be over for Dad. One day it would all be over.

15

Rick drove to work, his cold hands gripping a cold steering wheel. Spots of rain on the windscreen. A sepulchral sky. Four lines of enquiry: TBR, Darren Back, Barney Williams, Sakit Patel. Which one to brace first?

He sat, held at traffic lights. Steam rose from a boiler vent on the nearest house. Curtains still drawn.

The car phone rang.

'Hello.'

'Morning, sir. Jane, the station officer.'

Slight disappointment. 'Yes, Jane?'

'There's an old woman here to see you.'

'It's five-thirty.' His excuse, a cold bed. And accused of a cold heart.

'Said she's an early riser. She saw the witness appeal on the local news and she's seen Coniston.'

'Don't let her out of your sight.'

A car crossed the junction, then a line of bicycles with flashing LEDs on their helmets and wheels. In the middle was a racing wheelchair, the rider wearing a bright yellow helmet. Maggie. She sped past, and twisting his head, he watched her go. Four days a week she rose at five and cycled; two days she trained in the gym. He'd sponsored her for the big day, now only three weeks away.

Green light.

Rick turned down a back road. Gunned the car down to a bridge and back up the other side. Over a level crossing and into the car park of an abandoned pub. He climbed out and waited on the corner like a flasher.

The line of flashing bicycles approached. Determined lean men and women wearing Lycra, and hewn like stone. Maggie in the middle, pounding her rims with bespoke gloves. Maggie concentrating, in the moment, oblivious.

Gone.

But it left him with an idea to get back in her good books – he needed a favour tracing Khetan. He got back in the car and drove to work. He'd helped her make the racing gloves a few weeks back.

Their Sunday project after a lazy morning in bed with the papers and coffee. 'It says here,' Maggie told him, 'men in demanding, stressful jobs make the best lovers.' After testing the theory, they spent the afternoon boiling crystals, then moulding the hot glutinous plastic balls into the shape of her gripped hands. To withstand the repeated pressure on the rims they had to be rock hard, but to be effective they had to fit the unique shape of a person's hand. Once they were dry, he and Maggie super-glued rubber to the surface. More than half the crystals were left over, and for a laugh they made Rick a pair, too.

Before he could punch the code into the keypad, the back door swung open. Jane wore a short-sleeved blue and white checked shirt which exposed her puffy red arms, and always reminded him of a dinner lady at school who could carry six plates, stacked hand to armpit.

'Her name's Mrs Grieve. Says she saw him on a train.'

They walked down the corridor.

'Tea?'

'You?'

'Her.'

'Yes, sir, three cups.' She pushed up her glasses and rubbed her eyes. 'And a prisoner's breakfast.'

'You're an angel.'

'If only my other half thought that.'

They reached the station office. A TV sat on a desk, the screen showing pictures but the sound muted. A dark-skinned man was carrying a buggy-type pushchair with a young girl through a muddy bog. Rick stopped. It was raining hard, the man's hair dripping and his clothes saturated. A dustbin liner was tucked around the girl and a clear plastic bag covered her head. They were followed by a grim-faced woman holding the hands of two older children. They were all soaked, their feet and calves caked in thick mud. Behind them were more people, and when the camera scanned back, a large crowd was revealed. Surging forward and back as they were constrained by riot police armed with batons and long shields. Tickertape scrolled across. *Thousands of migrants battle with riot police in Macedonian quagmire on border with Greece.*

'Shocking, isn't it?' said Jane over his shoulder. 'She's in room 3.'

Rick walked on. He felt sorry for the Macedonian family and the crowd behind them, but also for the police officers caught up in their fury. He'd been in a riot near the Arndale, a drunken Friday night which had spilled into looting and vandalism. His team had been pelted with bottles and cans of piss, and three taken to hospital. He blamed the politicians, their inability to broker and agree. Their inability to organise a car-boot sale.

Outside the door Rick hesitated, knowing he could, should, still delegate.

He knocked, and opened the door.

A warm fug spilled out. Condensation fogged the windows and the room smelt of old potatoes. An old woman wearing a thick coat and a crocheted crimson hat sat at the table, a small white dog at her feet. Non-matching shoes, one with a built-up heel. On the table sat empty microwave wrappers. She cupped her tea with yellow fingerless gloves. He stepped inside and shut the door.

'Mrs Grieve, I'm DI Castle.'

The dog yapped, then yawned and lay down.

'Quiet, Benny.' She looked up. 'Are you good with dogs?'

He was better with bees, and hoped he was better with people. But on current evidence, he wasn't sure. He could lie or gibber, but experience had taught him a moment of candour could yield the same in return.

'Not really.' He pulled out the second chair and sat down.

'Your boy got on the train at Old Town. I'd been to see my sister. She's eighty-seven. Between you and me she's gone a bit—' She made circles with a finger around her ear. 'The boy helped me with Benny at Piccadilly. *He's* good with dogs.'

Benny jumped up at Rick and sniffed his balls. He squatted and stroked the dog. It licked his fingers. He forced himself to keep his hand there. One-upmanship against Coniston was ridiculous. If it was him. The fugitive liked animals, but so did most of the population.

'Can you describe him?'

'At my age they all look the same.'

'Colour?'

'White.'

'Height?'

'Tall.'

'Hair?'

'No idea.'

'Anything else?'

She shook her head.

'Thank you, Mrs Grieve. I'll get Jane to bring you another cup of tea. We'll show you some photos.' Rick stood and pushed the chair back under the table.

'Oh, he got a ticket.'

'A ticket?'

'A penalty fare. From the ticket collector.'

'Did he give a name?'

'Richard Tower. Remembered it by thinking of Richard the Lionheart and my tower-block. You'll do that with names when you're my age.'

Richard, a long form of Rick. Tower was a synonym for Castle. Had to be Coniston. Too clever by half.

Rick bent towards the old woman. People-watchers, dog-walkers, curtain-twitchers, busy-bodies, he loved them all. He kissed the top of her head, her stiff grey curls like frosted grass.

Fifteen minutes later Rick left the police station. Paulson drove his car, and Woods and Bennett sat in the back bickering like children. Four followed in the crime squad van. They were heading for the Hartford Halls of Residence, the rationale recorded in his policy book. One, Williams had visited Coniston three times in the last six weeks. Two, Williams might know fellow-student Bowden, and Bowden might have lent him his car. Three, thanks to Mrs Grieve, they knew Coniston had caught a train back to Manchester Piccadilly which was not so far from Williams' term address.

En route, Hunter phoned. 'Where are you?'

'Where are you?'

'At the nick.'

'I don't care about the rest, Gary, but you have to turn up. Meet us at Hartford Halls. I've sent Kasim to the magistrate's court for the warrant.'

Rick clicked off the phone, the car quiet as a crypt. He switched on the heater and opened the vents. It was meant to be summer.

16

Calix slipped on jeans and opened the balcony door. Cool air from a glaucous sky poured into the stuffy room. Breathing deeply, he surveyed his freedom. Opposite, the new student block shrouded in scaffolding and orange plastic pulsed with activity. Labourers streamed through the turnstiles, a crane moved overhead, drills whined. On the corner, in the first-floor studio of a fitness centre, runners pounded the treadmills. Neither appealed: work, nor leisure.

Behind him, Barney's phone trilled on the desk. It turned half-circles, drumming and drumming. Then it stopped. Calix picked it up. Withheld number. He checked for messages. No messages.

It could have been Castle. Calix saw him everywhere, sensed him constantly.

He shuffled onto the balcony, toes feeling the bite of the door sill. He glanced down but no kin of the battle-twig sheltered. A spray of vomit stained the glass door, but rain had washed the balcony clean. Lighting a cigarette, he inched forward, glancing left and right along the line of identical balconies. Above him, more identical balconies, like a bank of mushrooms.

He leant on the rail. Below him, cars queued for an

underground car park and people walked purposefully. Two dark blue cars and a small white van joined the queue. The second car pulled alongside the first car, windows lowered, and a conversation took place. The second car U-turned and drove away at speed. Calix smoked the cigarette. Concentrated on the inhale, the fuzz of the burning nicotine, the pucker of his lips.

A key turned in the main door. He tensed, forgetting for a moment where he was, and where he wasn't. Locks and keys and the smell of shit. And shouting and shouting and damaged, dangerous people.

Barney entered the room, carrying a wok. 'Got this from Firash on the next floor, and flour from Elly next door.' He paused. 'You okay?'

'You had a missed call.'

'Who?'

Calix shrugged, hauling on the cigarette.

'I'm starving.'

Calix flicked the butt away and walked back into the room, feet now feeling the carpet. Thin, but still carpet. In a mug he mixed water with some of the flour and a sachet of salt from a takeaway. He set the wok on the hob.

Barney switched on the kettle, and waited, twiddling with his phone. 'You're on the news.'

Calix tipped out the dough and pulled away a lump. He flattened the dough in his palm. 'Rolling pin?'

'Funny,' said Barney, not looking up. 'You're famous. TV, Twitter, everywhere.'

Calix glanced around. Then picked up the mug and smashed off the handle. He sprinkled flour on the side and rolled out the dough until it was flat. Sprinkled more flour. Rolled. Threw the chapatti in the smoking wok.

Barney picked up the pieces of handle. 'Fuck, Calix.'

Thirty seconds later brown spots appeared on the chapatti.

Calix peeled it up and flipped it over. He'd wanted to make chapattis for months, wanted to cook something, anything, but chapattis were simple and reminded him of Nepal. Another thirty seconds, and he removed it. The chapatti felt warm, and for water and flour, smelt fantastic. He ripped it in half and handed a piece to Barney.

They stood together, chewing like connoisseurs. In the corridor footsteps marched up and down.

'Hey, Calix?'

'What?'

Barney shook his head. 'Nothing.' He gathered books and papers and shoved them in a satchel. 'You going to be all right here?'

Calix glanced around the room. His new cage. He made more chapattis. They settled his stomach. They reminded him of the cave and the snow-capped mountains, the sparkling snow. Of his old man.

Barney stood in the bathroom doorway cleaning his teeth, looking at Calix and not looking at Calix.

Heavy banging rattled the door.

Barney stilled his toothbrush. Calix grabbed his arm and put a finger to his lips.

'Police, open the door!' Castle's voice, duller, harsher than on the phone.

Barney set the toothbrush down and spat in the sink. Looked at Calix for instruction. Same old.

Calix felt angry. He'd told no one about his driver so how did Castle know? Had Barney told someone, or left something in the car? His friend stood in front of him, white spew on his lips. Blame wouldn't be helpful. Possible, too, he'd been recognised at Piccadilly and followed. He thought through his options. Castle might not have a warrant. He could hide – if he'd been a battle-twig. Fight or flight were his old man's options, but fighting the

Greater Manchester dibble was a non-starter.

'Williams, are you in there? Open up!' The doorframe shook with hammering. 'One minute or it goes in.' A different voice, duller still.

'You got a screwdriver?' whispered Calix.

Barney shook his head.

'Get me three minutes.' Calix gripped Barney's muscled shoulders. If it came down to bench pressing, or jumping, or throwing, then Barney was the man. 'Remember why you're doing this: for Spencer, for your dad.'

Barney nodded, pulled himself away and walked to the door. 'Who is it? Firash, is that you? I told you I'll clean your wok.' He glanced over his shoulder.

Calix raised a thumb and headed to the balcony. Barney felt like a younger brother, annoying and ordinary, but when it came down to it, supportive.

There was more banging on the door. 'Police, stand back!'

'Firash?'

'It's not fucking Firash.'

'Have you got a warrant?'

'Course we got a bloody warrant!'

'Push it under the door, then.'

Calix pocketed Barney's phone, stepped onto the balcony and closed the door.

Drills still screamed in the building site, joggers still beat the running machines. Clouds scudded, the sky funereal. His mum wouldn't understand, or maybe she would. Visiting him at Strangeways, never once missing a fortnight, she'd never moralised, never criticised, never judged. Only loved.

17

They drove into Bradford through drizzle and rush-hour traffic. People waited at bus stops, and umbrellas dotted the busy pavements. Hant fingered the road atlas, and Anoop ate the last of his greasy chips. Their penultimate drop, and then he could acknowledge the boy.

Following the signs for Middle Horton, they turned into a tangle of backstreets. A police car sat outside one house. The officer looked up as they drove past. Hant turned a page of the map book, turned back. He looked through the spy hole into the back of the van. The remaining migrants and Ram were quiet. They were tired, hungry, scared. It had been a long night. A puncture and an enforced wait in a layby while they waited for morning to buy a new tyre.

'Stop,' said Hant.

Anoop pulled over and parked, the tyres squelching along the kerb. His driver couldn't even steer. They sat in a wide empty road behind a block of flats. Trees lined the pavements, and rain dripped onto the roof. Through the branches, the pale sky was brightening.

A road crew with a mini-digger worked at the end of the road. Pop music boomed from one of the flats. An Asian woman walked past, pushing a pram through the puddles. She bumped the pram down .onto the road and crossed. The child started bawling. She manoeuvred the pram back up onto the pavement. One of the road crew wolf-whistled.

Hant put on dark glasses, flipped up his hood and climbed out. Britain was awash with people, and a few more would make no difference.

He walked round to the rear doors, and checked up and down the pavement. Glanced up at the flats. A bicycle chained to railings, pot plants. He fixed the sheet so it hung off the bumper and covered the number plate. He unlocked the door, and opened it a crack.

'Wassef.'

The new name for the Syrian family. A couple with a ten-year-old boy climbed out with their bags. They moved awkwardly, eyes shrouded with sleep. The woman wore a blue hajib, and her husband a black leather jacket. The boy only had one ear and smelt of urine. In the distance, sirens split the air. The man and woman looked at Hant. He waited. The sirens faded. Always, there were sirens, and he'd like to have said that, reassured the couple, reassured the boy, reassured himself.

'Follow.'

He walked along the street, away from the road crew. At the corner he waited for the Wassefs. A bus trundled past, people pottered along the far pavement. Boxes of fruit and veg sat outside an open-fronted shop.

The Syrian family turned the corner, and shuffled closer.

Two things happened at once. A van stopped outside the shop, three men climbing out, and a stocky white man crossed the road diagonally across the junction. Hant walked further, his pace quickening, and the Wassefs following. The stocky white man stopped to tie up his shoe. The group of men opened the sliding door of the van, and began to unload. A woman walked towards him, talking on a mobile phone. She wore jeans and trainers.

Hant stood at the entrance to the block of flats. He could run up the road, or disappear through the flats. He could hide, and phone Manoj. The Wassefs would be detained, held in an immigration centre, and deported. The stocky man tied a second shoelace, the woman neared.

He could hear the booming of a waterfall, like the one near Saklis. After the monsoon rain, it was a torrent. He walked into the entrance of the flats, and broke into a run. At the wheelie bin enclosure, he stopped and waited. He looked through the wooden slats. Flies buzzed. The bins stank of fish.

The Wassefs looked up and down, and sat on the low wall. The woman on the phone walked past. The stocky man didn't appear.

Hant waited five minutes.

Wassef helped his son stand on the wall and pee into the bushes. His wife opened a carton of the milk, and they passed it around.

Hant waited another five minutes. Five minutes was a long time. Anoop would be wondering. He sent him a text. *Wait.*

He tossed a coin, heads it was okay to return to the Wassefs. He lived by *dharma*, so God would look after him. God would look after all of them.

Heads.

After picking up the coin, he strolled back. He felt better, felt a weight had been lifted and God was alongside him. He removed the piece of paper from his pocket. Time to go to work. His job was to ensure the Wassefs were placed, and wouldn't inform on Al Usra.

Mrs Wassef offered him the milk. Shaking his head, he handed her the paper with a name and phone number. He'd obtained the details from *Syrians in Britain*, a support group he'd found on the internet. The volunteer would help the family settle, and prevent them coming to notice of the authorities and pressured to give up the network in return for the right to stay.

'No police. Understand?'

Wassef nodded.

Hant drew a line across his neck.

Mrs Wassef shielded her son's face. She understood, they both understood. Hant handed Wassef a mobile phone and a hundred pounds.

The Wassefs looked at the money and the phone. Hant's money. He knelt by the boy, the youngster's dirty knees reminding him of his childhood. He took a Rubik's Cube from his jacket pocket, one of several he'd bought. The six sides were complete. He clicked it back and forth a few times so the puzzle remained set. The boy reached out, and took the Cube. He clicked it around. He concentrated like a child, stared like an adult.

Hant stood.

'God is watching.'

He walked away, but at the corner glanced back. Wassef was on the phone, his son clicking the puzzle. The wife stroked her child's hair.

Hant turned and hurried back towards the van. One more drop, and then he could embrace Ram.

The toy, the phone, even the money was nothing. The twenty migrants had each paid ten thousand pounds. His cut was ten per cent, Manoj thirty. The money was crazy, and had just increased. Following the sex attacks in Germany, attitudes across Europe had hardened and borders strengthened. Al Usra doubled its prices. Ten lorries would mean they made two million pounds a week. Every week.

He climbed back into the van.

'Drive.'

The fat man U-turned, drove to the junction and pulled out into the traffic. Hant tilted his head so an ear was parallel to the ground and banged his skull. He tried the other way and banged again. He could still hear the waterfall near Saklis.

18

The cramped corridor was as narrow and as brightly lit as a passageway in a brothel. Stained with black marks and blue-penned graffiti, the walls wore the scars and scrapes of student life. Waiting at the stairwell, Woods, Bennett, and red-eyed Paulson eating a sandwich. No sign of Kasim and the warrant.

Rick stood to the side while Hunter jabbed on Williams' door with the end of his extended baton.

There was no response.

'Give me that,' said Rick, grabbing Hunter's baton.

He crashed it against the door half a dozen times, then stood back. The cheap pine now marked with a cluster of overlapping circular dents halfway up.

'Alright!' Williams' voice.

'It's DI Castle,' shouted Rick. 'I thought you'd at least give me the time of day.'

'And why's that?' said Williams, now the other side of the door.

'Because after flying halfway round the world and back, I finally got Khetan. And banged him up at Her Majesty's Pleasure.'

Williams remained silent.

'I came to see you last year, Barney, at the car rentals at Heathrow. Easy Cars wasn't it?'

Still nothing.

'Do you remember what you said to me when I told you I was going after him? You told me to *Get that bastard*. Well, I did. And he's now in Belmarsh, and will be for years to come. Hopefully, you and your mum have got some closure now.' Until six weeks ago, it was the truth.

The door opened on a chain, revealing a vertical slice of Barney Williams. Behind him, a cupboard door lay open preventing a view into the flat. An unseen TV blared with a daytime chat show.

Two years since Rick had first met him, walking back across the suspension bridge in Nepal after he'd negotiated the boy's release from Khetan. Williams had been thin, his face pale, his eyes bloodshot. As if he was returning from a war zone. Later he'd been diagnosed with post-traumatic stress disorder. The student in front of him was very different, even stockier than in the foyer of Easy Cars the year before. Ruddy-faced, too. From beer or agitation?

'But not my dad.'

'No, and I'm sorry for your loss. You know that, you saw me at the funeral. You also know, because you attended the inquest, that my actions outside your parents' house in Barnes couldn't have saved him.'

Williams toe-poked the door.

'You're lying about Khetan. I heard he's out.'

'Who told you that?'

Williams shook his head.

Rick felt the warmth of incredulity. It was a bad gaffe. Williams was a student, and didn't mix with criminals. The only person he was likely to have heard it from was Coniston, and although it was possible Coniston had told him during a prison visit, it still suggested Williams had aided and abetted Coniston's escape.

Rick sighed with the pretence of making a big concession. 'I'll tell you what I know, Barney, *if* you let us come in.'

'What do you want?'

'We're looking for Calix Coniston. Is he here?'

'Here?' Repetition was the instinctive response of a liar.

'Yes,' said Rick. Beside him, Hunter yanked up a sleeve and scratched his arm. White tracks like aeroplane trails.

'No.'

'Can you turn down the TV?'

'In a minute.'

'You know he's escaped?'

'Of course. It's everywhere: TV, YouTube, Twitter.'

'Has he contacted you?'

'No.'

'So can we have a quick look?'

'I'd prefer to wait for the warrant.'

'You've been watching too much TV,' said Hunter.

'I know my rights. I'm reading law.'

'Oh, help me, God.' Hunter shoved his foot into the crack of the door.

'Last chance, Barney,' said Rick. 'If Coniston's not here, what's the problem? Two minutes and we'll be gone.'

'The principle of it.' The student smiled thinly, lied badly.

Raising an eyebrow, Hunter braced the door.

Rick shook his head.

Hunter scowled and removed his foot.

The door pushed shut.

Rick thumped the retractable baton down on the floor leaving a dent in the lino. Then tossed it back to Hunter, who racked it back in his belt, but only after pretending to blow smoke from the end as if he was acting in an Am-Dram production of *Billy the Kid*.

'We'll wait,' said Rick.

Upstairs for thinking, downstairs for dancing. Even if Coniston was hiding inside, an illegal entry would not only invoke another disciplinary, but scupper his chances at the next DCI board. An alternative was to arrest Williams on suspicion of being the getaway driver, but without proper grounds, there was a risk the court would throw the case out. They could borrow a key from the caretaker, but a court might not like that either. He had no choice, but to wait for Kasim and the warrant.

Williams' body language revealed his discomfort, more, Rick thought, than antipathy towards the police. He was either harbouring Coniston, or he was embarrassed about something or someone else. Drugs, stolen property, a girl. A boy?

Williams hated Coniston like Caesar hated Brutus yet had visited him several times in Strangeways. The warrant would be worth waiting for. They were on the fifth floor – even Coniston wasn't that nutty.

'Wait here, Gary. As soon as Kasim brings the warrant, we'll go in.'

'Where are you going?'

'Phone calls.'

At the end of the corridor Paulson blocked the door like a bouncer. He was round-shouldered and had pecs like breeze blocks. Woods put away his Sudoku magazine and Bennett passed around a packet of gum.

Rick phoned the crime squad sergeant DS Davies, and explained the impasse. 'Sam, you roll on to TBR's address. Call me straight away if you get a hit.'

'On it.'

'Always a vacancy in CID if you're interested.' Rick pocketed the phone, hoping Sam would one day come across. Always thinking two or three moves ahead, he was the perfect person to lead young officers in their first plain clothes posting. They were keen as puppies, and liable to piss in the dog bowl.

He turned to Woods. 'I want you and Bennett and Paulson to visit Darren Back. Call the office for transport and two more to help. Same as Sam, get a hit, call me straight away.'

Two nods and a 'Roger that.' They turned and clumped down the stairwell.

Rick turned to Hunter. 'What's up?'

'Nothing.'

'If there is something, Gary, let's hear it. And if there isn't, I need more from you for a little while.'

'You'll get him.'

'Not just him.' Rick lowered his voice. 'Khetan's out, too.'

'You're taking the Mickey Bliss?'

Rick shook his head. 'Someone let him out of Belmarsh.'

'Who?'

'Above my pay grade apparently. Someone from Six, I imagine.'

'I hope they got a bargain.'

'I'm going to find out. One of Maggie's old sapper colleagues now works at Legoland.' Rick waited while a student came out of their room, locked their door, and went down the stairs.

'Robbo tell you that?'

Rick shook his head. 'Coniston. Robbo confirmed it.'

'I need a lie down.'

'Goes no further for the time being.'

Hunter nodded, scratched the back of his neck.

Rick followed the others down the stairwell, his tinny footsteps echoing on the metal-edged lino. He'd pay fifty pounds to swap the two sergeants. Five hundred to find Coniston. A lot more to smooth things with Maggie.

But that would be easy. Life was about the journey, the process, the ups and downs. At least, that's what people said.

*

Rick sat in his car in the underground car park. Shafts of light through thick bars pierced the deep shadow. An iridescent puddle of fuel lay across the next bay and in the next but one, an abandoned car battery sat in a shopping trolley.

He checked his phone for messages, but there was nothing from Maggie, the hospital, or Kasim. Only from Oliver. *Was Barney Williams the driver who picked up Coniston?* The voice message was possibly an inspired guess, or more likely, he'd followed one of the CID cars. The journalist had previous for it.

He phoned Kasim.

'I'm next up to see the magistrate, sir. Seems like every other house in Manchester's going to get busted. Should be with you in twenty.'

Which was enough time to make two more calls. He started with Maggie, but she didn't pick up. He left a message. 'Saw you this morning, Mags. Looking good! And, Mags, I've got a favour to ask, Job-related. Can you call me?'

Next he phoned the hospital. As he waited to be put through, he saw the churning river. The mobile crane creaking on its stanchions as it raised the stolen car, draining like a colander. The crane operator talking about a game show and Rick telling him to shut the fuck up. Then they heard a voice, a cry. Rick slithered down the wooded bank, and amongst chest-high scrub lay Skye. She was bloody and bleeding, and dying.

'St Anne's. Which department?'

'Ward 17.' He waited again, looked at his watch. Ten minutes to the warrant appearing. Fifty-fifty, Coniston was in Williams' room.

'17.'

The number – always – like an electric shock.

'DI Castle.'

'Rick Castle. Nepal?' Her voice held derision.

'Yes,' said Rick. He was well known in Manchester, people split in their viewpoints. 'Is Skye Peters-Green out of theatre yet?'

'Unfortunately—' said the nurse. Rick felt stabs in his stomach. 'Skye's operation was delayed, now postponed a week.'

'Thanks for your help,' said Rick, managing to keep his voice neutral. The NHS was under similar pressures to the police, and in inner city Manchester they were comrades on the front line. Even if she wasn't a fan.

He tried Maggie again.

The driver's door heaved open.

A large-framed police officer wearing full uniform gripped Rick's arm and hauled him out. Grabbed him up in a bear-hug and squeezed.

Rick pocketed his phone, forced a smile.

'Hello, Russell.'

'Why are you sitting here? Gloomy as a morgue.'

'You come to assist?'

'Sergeant Davies called me.' Russell's military-style boots were shinier than Rick had ever seen on a police officer. Sharp creases down the short sleeves of his shirt. The owner of Nepal Adventures took off his helmet and placed it on the roof.

'Still like being a special?'

'I love it, can't get enough. Arrested a burglar at the weekend. Had half a dozen silver necklaces under his collar, and a screwdriver down his sleeve. Had a go, too.'

'You okay?'

'I was lucky. Rather than running, he threatened me with the screwdriver. Using approved arrest and restraint methods, I detained him and radioed for the van.' He leant forward. 'I beat the crap out of him, then called the van. I don't think he'll do it again, not round here anyway.'

103

'Did he make a complaint?'

'Course not. He wanted my autograph – arrested by Russell Weatherbeater, five-time Everest summiteer!'

Rick's phone beeped with a message. *5 minutes, Kasim*

'Are you still seeing Velvet?' Robbo's file lurking in the back of his mind.

'Nah.'

'What happened?'

'She doesn't want to spend her time with an old hop-along like me.'

Russell's radio crackled and he walked away, towards a barred window. Rick stared. The mountaineer was limping. Russell spoke into his mic, and walked back, his left leg over-compensating for his right. Heat suddenly coursing through him, Rick loosened his tie and undid his top button.

'How's Maggie?'

'Okay.'

'Not okay?' Russell knew him, in the same way he knew Russell. Hearing the words, but listening to the body language.

'She's fine.'

Russell nodded. He didn't blunder or bluster. He was a mountaineer, a giant, a legend, but his day job was moulding teams of strangers as he led them up and down mountains. *If* he still could climb mountains. Yet, whenever they caught up, he never moaned, never mentioned Barnes.

'Did Sam brief you?'

'Barney Williams' flat—'

'And we're looking for Coniston,' said Rick, interested to see Russell's reaction.

'Sam said. Got to say I'm not surprised Coniston skipped class – he's loop-the-loop. Although on a day-to-day level, I found him okay. There are worse people to get stuck on a mountain with.'

104

Rick's phone beeped. *1 minute, Kasim*

'We're on, Russ.'

The special cum mountaineer pulled on his helmet and secured the chinstrap. He took out his baton and gripped it as if he was about to stab an icefall and start climbing. A second baton hung from his belt.

Before Rick could comment, Kasim drove into the underground car park like a rally-driver competing in the Paris-Dakar. The young PC jumped out, and ran over, clutching the warrant. His reflection blurry in the purple-edged puddle, and behind him, the engine of the CID pool car steaming and whirring.

19

Calix looked down from the balcony at the ground, five floors below. Maybe, if there'd been a bouncy castle or a swimming pool, or a limousine cabriolet, like in films. But there was only cold, hard concrete. He heard the thud, felt the thud, saw a blinding flash of white light. Then nothing. He pictured the pool of blood spreading slowly outwards, dripping down to the gutter in the road, channelling along to the drain.

He straightened. Not down, so up.

Above him were three more storeys and the roof. Eaves half a metre wide projected out. If he climbed up, he could lunge and grab. And fall. It didn't matter. The lines of mortar between the burnt-red brickwork were thin, and although they would allow his fingers to purchase, he'd struggle to remain stationary, yet alone ascend. Alain Robert, he was not.

Not up.

Along, then. He glanced left and right – identical. In a roundabout way, he knew Elly, so right. He walked to the side of the balcony, feeling sick. He wasn't really going to do it, just see if it was possible.

Elly's balcony perched five metres away. Between the balconies a drainpipe dropped from the roof to the floor. Smooth as glass but at regular intervals it was attached to the brickwork. Even better was a thin ledge which connected the base of the balconies. It was only the width of a matchbox, but meant traversing wasn't impossible.

A pigeon flapped past, close enough for him to feel its heavy wingbeats. He'd rescued a pigeon once, mended its leg. Toose never had told him whether the bird survived. Big Scottish Toose. Alreet, man?

Behind him, the TV blared in Barney's room. His view inside obstructed by the blind.

He looked out at the building site opposite. A cacophony of banging and drilling and shouting. He should have been a hod-carrier or a brickie. Good honest work for a good honest wage. Knackered in the evening, beer and chips in the pub for tea.

'Calix!'

Only a whisper, but he whirled round, steadying himself with the handrail.

'Castle's gone, and most of the dibble,' whispered Barney through the partly open window. 'But they've left someone outside the door. I think they've gone to get a warrant.'

Through the gap in the blind were acres of level floor, a television, half a slab of beer. His mouth felt dry. Too much bread for breakfast.

'I think they'll check the balcony.'

'Really.'

Calix climbed up and over the balcony rail, fitted the toes of his shoes through the slats, and stood. He hugged the rail, and glanced down at the wide pavement. At all the concrete. The killer concrete.

Barney pushed the window wider. 'You sure?'

Calix nodded. 'Shut the window and watch the door.'

Barney nodded. The worry etched on his face was surprising, and touching. The window closed.

And Calix was alone.

He glanced down at a rough sleeper shuffling along, at a cyclist with chunky headphones, at three giggling schoolchildren. He looked up, looked along. Wiped his greasy hands on his trousers. He took a deep breath. He'd escaped from base camp at Mosom Kharka and run for fifty hours, day and night, up and down what felt like mountains, to evade Castle in Nepal. He could do this.

He could. He took another deep breath. The sooner he started, the sooner he'd finish. Finish. The end. Good night, that's all folks!

Facing the wall he slid his fingers along a thin line of mortar and gripped downwards. He edged one of his feet along the narrow ledge, gripped tighter with his fingers, and moved his other foot away from the safety of the balcony and onto the rail. He stayed there, an X shape on the side of the building, balanced but only just. His body pulsing like a leopard about to spring.

He made a rule, only one hand or foot at a time. He slid his far hand further along, adjusted the fingers, locked down with the fingertips. There was space for only the first knuckles. He moved his other hand, then edged his feet along.

Halfway to the drainpipe.

Melancholic flute music drifted up from below. Wiping a hand on his trousers, he couldn't stop himself looking down. Vehicles were turning in for the car park. The rough sleeper sat on the pavement, legs straight out in front of him. He was playing a recorder, charming the snake above him.

Ten per cent of the time, maybe.

Calix moved his leading hand, adjusted his fingers, locked down. Moved his trailing hand, his feet. Caught snatches of conversation buffeted by the building site.

He reached the drainpipe and halfway.

The smooth pipe offered no respite, the screwed attachments

flush with the brick. A mistake, and a bad mistake, too, not to check Elly was inside her room. He should have knocked on the wall.

The snake-charmer played on.

Calix moved a hand, moved a foot, and slid over the drainpipe, like a snake. 'Sss!' So close, his balls squashed against the pipe.

He moved again. Halfway from halfway. Three-quarter way to full way. Third base, in sight of the home plate. Home run, home edge, home teeter. His brain befuddled, crazy with adrenalin.

Below him, a screech of tyres and a bang. A car hooted. The rough sleeper stopped playing. Calix froze. More cars hooted. A man started shouting. Calix looked down, expecting people to be looking up. But no one was looking up. A dog lay on the road, and people and vehicles were gathering. He could help: he had a soft spot for dogs.

The world, he thought, wasn't looking at him, he was looking at the world.

He slid a hand, locked his fingers, moved his feet, and reached Elly's balcony. He grasped the fat iron bars and shoved his feet between the slats.

The rough sleeper's tuneless recorder-playing resumed. It brought back Megan playing at home, she'd been six, Calix four or five. He'd used it once or twice to fire frozen peas at birds from his bedroom window.

He climbed up and over, and dropped down onto the balcony. He strolled around the vast flat expanse, playing air guitar, pretending to beat the drums, smoke a fat cigar.

Below him, the rough sleeper and the cars had gone, and the black dog lay at the curb.

Calix turned and knocked on the glass balcony door. He heard a siren, the muzak of Manchester.

He knocked louder. The siren came closer, then went quiet. He hammered on the door, like Castle.

The blind was drawn back, and a girl stood there in her nightwear. She was small, Asian, and wore baggy pink pyjamas with large pockets. Her eyes flared. She took a step back, and the blind dropped.

He knocked again, softer.

The girl pushed open a window.

'Elly?'

She stared at him with large green eyes.

'I'm a friend of Barney. Cal–vin.'

The window closed and the blind was drawn back. The girl turned a key in the lock, and the balcony door opened. Calix stepped inside, and shut the door behind him.

'You are Elly?'

She nodded, but kept her hands in her pockets as if she was holding a rape alarm or a pepper spray.

The layout of the room was different, the bed close to the window. Calix sat down on the end. Sunlight streamed through the window, making an oblong of light on the black and white duvet. It made a rainbow on his thigh. He picked out the colours, red to violet. He lay back and closed his eyes. He could sleep a thousand years.

He sat up.

Elly was sitting in a chair, her feet curled up underneath her. She was playing on her phone, her nails making soft plinking noises. The duvet was damp from his sweat-soaked clothes.

'Sorry.'

She looked up, and shook her head.

'Have you got a cigarette?'

'I don't smoke.'

'A dog was run over. You may have heard the bang, and the shouting. They've left it there in the gutter. Bastards.'

'I was asleep.' She said it neutrally, and he waited for a smile, but it didn't come.

In the corridor there were heavy footsteps and muffled voices. A dibble radio splurged – and went silent.

Calix put a finger to his lips, and held it there for the count of five. He swivelled round, pulled over a pillow, and turned back. One of Elly's hands was again in her pocket. He set the pillow across his knees and looked straight into her green eyes. He hoped the threat would be enough, and if it wasn't, what then?

20

The corridor was overflowing with the four of them. Kasim, Russell, Hunter, and Rick. He toe-punted the cheap door, took Russell's second baton from his belt and hammered on the circular marks from before.

'We've now got a warrant, Barney. I'll count to three. One.'

A student with a string-bag of books stood at the end of the corridor.

'Two!'

Rick readied. The door somewhere between the straw house and the stick house.

'Three.'

The door opened, and Williams backed away into the room. Kasim and Russell rushed in, the special leading with his left leg. Rick followed, and Hunter shut the door.

Russell grabbed Williams and shoved him face-first into a wall. 'Show me your hands.'

'Alright, alright.'

'Clear,' yelled Kasim from the bathroom.

Williams faced the wall, his legs apart, his hands to the sides. The model prisoner. Russell stowed his baton, and grabbing one hand at a time, handcuffed him in the rear stack position. He tightened up the cuffs, but didn't double-lock them. Any movement from Williams would tighten them further. Russell patted the student down, Williams moaning as he moved his hands and unintentionally tightening the handcuffs. Russell turned him around. Williams' nose was bleeding.

Rick turned off the TV.

'Christ, Russell.'

He turned to Hunter. 'You take over from Russell, and Russell, you swap with Kasim. Start searching the bathroom.'

The flat smelt like the lounge on a cross-Channel ferry. Body odour, stale alcohol, cigarette smoke. Williams didn't smoke, but Coniston did.

Rick yanked open the blinds and opened the window. Cold air and a thick band of sunlight sliced into the room. It made Rick think of the Sycamore Road apiary and his bees. Out gathering nectar and pollen, even now. In his peripheral vision he caught Williams blinking. Hungover or an involuntary reveal of deceit? Or both? If he was hung over, had he been celebrating?

'Gary, search Williams again.'

'Calix is not in my pockets.' Williams' voice was cut with sniffs as he tried to stem the bleeding. Blood blotted his shirt and the carpet. The carpet cheaper to replace than the shirt.

'It's the principle of it,' said Rick.

Hunter patted their prisoner down one limb at a time, turned out his pockets, felt around his collar, checked his shoes, and his belt. Pushed his fingers through his hair. Nodded at Rick.

'Front-stack him, and for God's sake give him a tissue.'

Hunter repositioned the cuffs, and Kasim handed Williams some toilet paper. Hunter pressed him down onto a chair. Kasim began to bag the shoes.

Rick glanced around. There were two rooms, a living room with a bed, a desk and a galley area, and a tiny ensuite bathroom. Pizza boxes and beer bottles sat piled against the pedal-bin. Too many for one person. But, no sleeping bag, no blankets, no cushions on the floor.

He set a copy of the warrant down. 'Do you want a cigarette?'

Williams looked up, a wad of bloody tissue hanging from each nostril. 'I don't smoke.'

'I can smell smoke.'

'You should be a detective.'

Russell stood in the doorway of the bathroom. 'Sounds like he needs teaching some manners?'

'We're okay, Russell, you crack on with the bathroom.'

Rick pulled up a chair and sat down in front of Williams. Eye-level. An early lesson from his advanced interviewing course: in order to access the truth, concentrate on what made Williams human, not what made him criminal – or *assist* a criminal.

'How's your nose?'

Williams eyed Rick suspiciously. An obvious tactic, but humans couldn't help themselves. 'Okay.'

'How's the rugby?'

Williams adjusted a nostril plug. 'Won our last game.'

Rick's recollection had proved correct. 'And your course?'

'Useful.' A glimmer appeared in Williams' eyes.

Rick matched it. Reset. First name. 'It was difficult, Barney, to talk properly in the corridor.'

Williams said nothing. He didn't disagree.

'I did my best for your family, Barney, and for the other families who lost loved ones.' Williams looked confused, as if he was thinking about something else. Had Coniston told him about Khetan? If he had, it made it even more likely Williams was the getaway driver at the funeral. Two and two, Rick was making seven. Getting ahead of himself. Evidence required.

'I cut corners, I was demoted.'

Williams scowled. 'If you'd arrested Khetan as he entered the UK, my dad would still be alive.'

'The enquiry found the border force to be culpable.'

'The whole system's to blame. Border force, police, prison service, home office.'

Again, Rick wondered what Williams knew, and who had told him. He could smell Coniston, his cigarette smoke, his stories and his manipulation. Slowly, he surveyed the room, looked back at Williams. 'Looks like you had a good night, Barney. Did you have a few people round?'

'No comment.'

'He's studying law, boss,' said Hunter.

Rick ignored him. 'Was Coniston one of them, Barney?'

'No comment.'

'Where were you yesterday?

'No comment.'

Russell loomed in the internal doorway. Slapped the door.

Sore, sulking prisoners, either from physical or verbal abuse, were ten times harder to persuade to talk, a hundred times harder to ease into an admission.

'Need to have a word, Russell. In the corridor.'

Rick glanced at Hunter, who nodded. They also knew each other well. Continue with the search, Kasim to guard Williams.

Rick followed the special into the corridor, and closed the door behind him. Russell limped to the stairwell, and looked over the banister. Waited, not meeting Rick's eye.

'Does your leg hurt?' said Rick, lowering his voice. Same tactics as for Williams.

'No.' Russell paused. 'It's a bit stiff in the mornings. Eases up. Worse in cold weather.'

Rick winced inside. Russell was a cold weather specialist, and climbed predominantly overseas at altitude. The Alps, Pakistan, Nepal. 'What about leading expeditions?'

'I've got a new ops manager, Kathy. She's doing them. Means I can deal a bit more with admin, with clients, and this stuff. The four-hour shifts for specials really suit me.'

'Are you still climbing?'

'Some,' said Russell. 'Inside, at Stanage, occasional trip to the Lakes.'

'I'm sorry.'

'Don't be.' The mountaineer, ex-mountaineer, stared at the ground floor, ten metres below. 'I've climbed a lot, Rick. It's time to do some other stuff.'

Rick glanced down the corridor, then back at Russell. His friend. 'You can't carry two batons, Russell.'

His phone rang. Woods.

'No answer at Darren Back's address, boss. Neighbour across the hall says he's been kicked out. How're you getting on?'

'A lorryload of intangibles. See you back at the nick.'

Rick walked back to Williams' room, Russell following.

'I found something, Rick.'

'What?'

'In a cupboard under the sink. A box of gloves, same as we use.'

'Nice one.' Rick opened the dented door. 'Guard the door.' He went inside, pushing it back behind him.

Rick sat at the desk.

An angle lamp, books, a line of ring binders. Laptop. A pedestal with three drawers. He started at the bottom. Looking for anything to connect Williams to either Coniston or Bowden.

Magazines. *Men's Fitness*, and underneath, a wad of soft porn. He pushed the drawer back. Stationery and a few coins in the middle drawer. From the top drawer he removed financial statements, a phone bill, receipts, and two handwritten letters. It would all have to be taken back to the nick, copied, and checked. Above the desk hung a cork notice board crammed with photos. Most showed drunk students horsing around. A couple of family shots. None of Coniston.

'Take a look at these, Gary. See if you can spot Bowden.'

Hunter walked over, and Rick watched Barney watching the sergeant scrutinising the photos. The student's face flickered, but he knew he was being watched.

The two detectives swapped back. Rick opened the laptop. He tried Hotmail. *Inbox. Sent. Deleted.* Nothing grabbed his attention – they might have used pseudonyms – and he checked through the open tabs. Williams had been watching the gravedigger's video on YouTube, but so had thousands of other people. Browsing history might reveal something, and he folded it up and put it in an evidence bag.

'Bathroom's finished,' said Kasim.

'Kitchen stuff, the bin,' said Rick. He leant back against the chair. There was something missing.

'Barney, where's your mobile?'

'I don't know.' Williams cleared his throat. 'I had it last night.'

Another intangible.

He watched Kasim take a sheet of plastic from the kitbag, and lay it flat by the front door. He tipped out the refuse bin and shook it up and down. Began to pick through the rubbish.

Hunter turned on the TV and flicked through the channels. He settled for a numbers quiz show.

Rick glanced again at the photos above the desk. Some taken at a football game, but most showed partying and high jinks, beer bottles and glasses thrust at the camera. One photo showed Williams and his friends wearing stupid ties. Another showed them dressed in sheets, pretending to be Romans. In the next photo, there were half a dozen people partying in a garden. Williams was wearing a dress and a wig.

A blonde wig.

Rick felt a hit of dopamine. At last, he had a tangible. He glanced at Kasim, ripping off pieces of tape with his teeth and bagging items seized from the bin. At Hunter, scratching an elbow through his crumpled shirtsleeve. At Russell, peering through the crack in the door. At Williams, staring at the blood-stained carpet.

At Coniston, laughing at all of them.

Two could laugh.

At the entrance to the car park, a marked police van ferrying Williams pulled away from the kerb. A flicker of blue lights, a peal of whistles.

Rick phoned the crime squad sergeant.

'On our way in, boss. We searched TBR's place, but there was no trace of Coniston, and Redman said nothing. One thing, though. I got my boys to speak to a few of the neighbours, and last night the woman opposite saw a man in half-blues at TBR's door.'

'Police?'

'Maybe. She's retired civvy staff so noticed the epaulettes and serge trousers. God knows why she's living there.'

'Description?'

'White, large, late thirties. Bald.'

Rick pocketed the phone and jogged to his car. The custody suite was filling up, and the day was getting interesting.

21

Sheffield, the final drop. Undulating countryside and a series of rounded grassy summits backdropped the city. They were hills not mountains, and climbing them required daytrips not expeditions.

Hant checked up and down the side-street. Not bothering with glasses or a hood, he unlocked the van doors. A Nepalese couple from his neighbouring village sat on one bench, and, opposite them, was Ram. The boy was lean, maybe too lean.

'*Namaste!*' Two voices in unison, the boy remaining silent.

Blinking in the light, Ambika climbed out followed by Samir dragging their cheap plastic holdall. They turned to face the sun and closed their eyes for a few seconds like porters at home. She was a small, thin woman with a bent back from subsistence farming, but Samir, a carpenter, was muscled, and fissured as bark.

Hant began to close the doors, and nodded at his nephew. Ram half-smiled. It wasn't much, but it was something. Soon, they could talk.

He locked up, and started for the high street, glancing back halfway. The couple followed, Ambika with the help of a walking pole. At the corner Hant waited, and then set off again until he reached the Annapurna restaurant.

The closed sign hung down, but the owner was expecting the

three of them. He went inside, holding the door for his people. The two of them shuffled inside, and he shut the door. Turned the nestled key.

Spices wafted, and prayer-flags draped from the ceiling. The tables were laid, and behind them, large tableaux of snow-capped mountains and colourful villages dominated the walls. At the back of the restaurant were doors to the kitchen and to the bar. Two women sat on stools folding napkins and polishing cutlery. A small man prodding a calculator looked up.

'Yash?'

Hant nodded. 'You are Padam?'

'And these are—'

'Work very hard,' said Samir, stepping forward. 'Kitchen, table.' He shrugged.

'Work good,' said his wife. She sounded wheezy.

'Sick?' said Padam.

'Work okay,' said Ambika.

The restaurant owner clapped a finger to his lips, then turned to Hant and pointed.

Hant took a roll of banknotes from his pocket, and counted out five hundred pounds. He laid them on the bar next to the calculator. 'Ambika need some week in hospital but work good.'

Padam counted the money. 'Okay, okay! Sit, we're all going to eat something, then we start work.'

Loud knocking reverberated the door to the street. Padam glanced at the front windows, swore. Hant stood and ushered his people through the door into the kitchen.

Pop music played on a radio, and the smell of chopped onions hung thickly. The knocking sounded again. Shouting, too. He peeked out of the kitchen door at Padam, wondering if it was what he thought it was. The restaurant owner screeched instructions to his staff in the kitchen.

Hant closed the door and braced it with a mop. Two chefs in

120

spattered white aprons stopped chopping and stared. Knocking sounded at a door at the far end of the kitchen. Hant eyed the magnets of cleavers and knives traversing the wall. The racks of glasses. The stack of bottles, floor to ceiling. Large pans simmered across a huge grid of hobs. He couldn't have wished for a better arsenal.

'Immigration, open up.'

Hant translated, and Ambika clutched Samir for support. One chef turned the volume up on the stereo. The other wiped his hands and took up position at one end of a large chest freezer.

In the dining room, Padam shouted through the front door. A dog started barking at the back of the kitchen.

The chefs shifted the freezer. Beneath it was a jagged hole, and a set of rough steps disappearing into darkness.

Hant stepped down into the gloom. He waited for Ambika and held out his hand. Samir followed and the three of them descended. It felt cold and damp. He could see boxes and a wooden chair at the bottom. He felt his feet down the steps, he felt for his head. At the bottom he stepped into a cave-like room. The walls rough and unfinished, the ceiling held with scaffolds and extending joists. A bucket in the corner. There was a second chair, a small table and a metal cabinet lying on its back. Inside were an archer's bow and a set of arrows.

'Ssh,' whispered a chef, peering down into the hideaway. He tossed down a cigarette lighter. Then, together with his colleague, hefted the freezer back into place.

Dark.

Pop music filtered down.

Hant patted around for the lighter, the floor clammy and rough. He felt the lighter, manipulated it straight, and flicked it. He directed Ambika to a chair, insisted Samir take the second chair. He sat on the steps, and relaxed his thumb on the lighter. No connection on his phone.

He inspected their cell. Unless they dug, there was no way out. He sat back on the steps, and let darkness prevail. God would prevail. If he had lived his life through *dharma*, God would prevail. If Padam and Samir and Ambika had lived their life with *dharma*, God would prevail for all of them.

The pop music stopped. Voices and footsteps. Doors banged, an argument. The voices receded. A dog barked, and lumbered around. Hant used the lighter to step forward and find the bow and arrow. He handed the lighter to Samir. The bow was a metre and a half long, black and yellow, and taut as cable. The arrows metal-tipped. He fitted one in the bow, and swivelled to point up the steps. Samir nodded with encouragement. Hant pulled the bow back, and took aim.

He set the bow down next to the steps, and Samir let the light extinguish. Darkness.

Twenty minutes passed. Hant reached out and squeezed Ambika's hand. He reached for Samir's hand. He held both.

'*Dhanyabad.*' Thank you. Samir squeezed harder. '*Dhanyabad.*'

'Okay.'

'She need operation, kidney. Di-ally-sis. Learn English words.'

Hant nodded in the dark.

'Want good school, children.'

'Ssh.'

Another twenty minutes passed. Two or three more months, and even with his people travelling for free, he'd have paid back Manoj for funding both years of Hant's FIFA campaign. *And* he'd have built up a war chest. He'd be able to return to Nepal and decide what was next. Not for Manoj, not for Al Usra, but for Hant Khetan and the Nepalese people, wherever they were in the world. Qatar, USA, UK, wherever. That was right, that was *dharma*.

One hour. Ambika squatted over the bucket. Hant

remembered Ram and Anoop, sitting in the van in the side-street. His driver rifling the cab looking for a sugary snack, and Ram searching for an eye-hole, or pondering his immediate future. Next week, Hant would be driving and Ram would be learning the business.

Footsteps resumed above. The freezer was lifted away, and light poured into the hole.

'Okay,' shouted Padam.

The three of them hugged, and climbed out. They hugged the two grubby chefs. Pop music resumed. Samir and Ambika danced a strange little dance. In the dining area, Padam poured shots of raksi. Hant sent a text message to Anoop. He drank, checking the eyes of the five people in front of him. Padam poured a second round, for the taken waitresses. Hant drank again. He prodded his ears, the ringing returned.

22

Calix remained in Elly's room all morning. She made him a strong cup of tea and a jam sandwich with chunks of butter. They listened to Castle and the dibble moving around next door. They listened to Radio 1. Barney's neighbour sat in a chair and played games on her phone, tapping away with two fingers. To begin with, he watched her like a raptor, but gradually he relaxed, and let her move around the room. After an hour, he let her get dressed in the tiny bathroom.

The dibble stayed hours, and when they finally clomped down the corridor, they took Barney with them. Elly said it was lunchtime, and she'd missed her morning lectures. She bustled with a toasted sandwich maker. He said she could put butter in the microwave to make it spreadable. She paused to stare at him with the buttery knife in mid-air, and for a moment he thought she might stab him. Her eyes were like polished emeralds.

Calix went to stand in the balcony doorway. Opposite, the building site banged and flapped as if it was a normal day. He looked along the building line towards Barney's room, and down to the pavement. His stomach churned as he imagined what could have been. He pulled on an imaginary cigarette, threw it down and ground it out.

Elly handed him a plate and a glass of milk.

'All boys like milk.'

Calix sat. He ate a mouthful of toasted cheese sandwich. Dipped it in the ketchup, and still chewing, drank some of the milk. It was cold and creamy. He looked up.

'We need to talk.'

'It's okay, I know who you are. Your name's not Calvin.'

Calix nodded. He chomped another mouthful of sandwich. He ate badly, hot cheese spurting out onto the plate. All wanted men ate badly. He fingered up the spilt cheese, tidied up his plate.

'Do you know about hedgehogs?' He straightened his second triangle next to the remaining pool of ketchup.

'They like milk.' Elly put down her nibbled sandwich. 'Tell me about hedgehogs.'

'Mainly they eat invertebrates – slugs, worms, frogs. But also mice and voles. Eggs, sometimes, even birds. They can climb, and swim.'

Elly fetched a glass of water and drank it. She looked at him through the bottom of the glass. She put it down. Calix finished the food and the milk.

'I have to go to a lecture.'

'I guessed.'

'You didn't want to talk to me about hedgehogs, did you?'

'I did, and I didn't.'

'You want to know if you can trust me.'

Calix put down his plate.

'When my elder brother Simon was sixteen, he was arrested for being drunk and disorderly. He was thrown in the back of a police van, taken to a patch of waste ground and beaten. They left him there to make his own way home. His nose was broken, and he needed sixteen stitches in hospital. He wasn't a troublemaker, and it was a case of being in the wrong place at

125

the wrong time. He never really recovered. Dropped out of school without A levels despite a string of As at GCSE. Now removes the last few feathers from plucked chickens in a factory.'

There was a loud rapping at the door.

'It's the police. I know you're in, the key's in the lock.' Castle's voice, enunciated and intelligent. A cut above.

Calix shook his head at Elly, held a finger to his lips. He glanced at the balcony, heard the judder of the drills on the building site. He'd done it once, he could do it again. Climb all the way round the campus building if he had to.

'We'll come back later.' Castle knocked on the door opposite Elly's. 'Anyone home, it's the police.'

Calix sensed a trick.

Elly sat motionless.

The two of them heard the student who lived opposite speak to Castle.

Calix crept to Elly's door, and listened. So close, he could have touched him. The dibble were knocking on every door and appealing for information. He crept back, and whispered instructions to Elly. He'd told her about hedgehogs, she'd told him about her brother.

'I know people,' whispered Calix. 'I know The Big Red.'

'We all know people,' said Elly, pointing to the end of a line of floor to ceiling cupboards.

Calix opened the door, and pulled the coats and dresses apart. He wriggled into the back, and stood in the corner. Pulled the clothing across. Elly slipped on a pair of orange shoes and closed the door. The wardrobe smelt of perfume and women. Girls. He closed his eyes, and inhaled. It wasn't the worst place to hide, and a hundred times better than a second balcony climb.

He heard Elly remove the chain on the front door.

Silence.

The darkness paled like the break of sunrise. He made out the shoulders of coats and tops. He reached out and felt a brushed cotton coat, a silk dress. He inhaled the closet's musky fragrance.

Still, there was silence.

He wondered if she'd left, walked out into the arms of Castle and told all. He grabbed a fistful of dress. He breathed, he breathed again. The wonderful smell of a girl's bedroom concentrated in a cupboard. It reminded him of Tania who'd lived on his corridor when he'd been a student. She never wore a bra. They'd had a thing, a bit of a thing. She wasn't sure, she was confused.

Elly's voice.

And Castle's.

Coming into the main room. She was leading Castle to him. Elly! He clutched a coat hanger, he could strangle the inspector dibble.

'I saw it on the news,' said Elly. 'And I heard you crashing around next door.'

'Sorry if we woke you up, ma'am.'

Ma'am!

'That's okay, officer.'

Officer!

'How well do you know your neighbour, Barney Williams?'

'We nod in the corridor.'

'If you do see anything, or remember anything, please give me a call.'

Footsteps moved to the door. The door clunked shut, and the chain rattled across. Calix sunk to the floor of the wardrobe, coats and blouses falling on top of him. He wondered if he could have done it. Castle was like family.

The cupboard door opened.

127

'Okay if I go to a lecture, now?'

Calix uncurled his fingers to reveal a selection of buttons, then tossed them high into the room like confetti. Somehow, he'd stumbled across a moll.

23

Strangeways loomed above dull Manchester suburbia. High blank walls topped with rolls of barbed wire and security cameras. Observation posts, warning notices. Muffled shouts and screaming, and the feeling of worse evils being concocted.

Rick sat in his car in the car park, facing the guardhouse.

Cars pulled in alongside. Big men, grim-faced and carrying nothing, climbed out and approached the prison. They formed an orderly queue, heads down, and slowly filed inside.

Big men began to emerge. Keychains dangled, one held a newspaper. Two or three stopped to light cigarettes. Car doors slammed, and the prison officers began to drive home.

A bald man in his late thirties emerged from the guardhouse. He held a thin file. Looked up at the blue sky, at a distant aeroplane disappearing in cirrus. He walked into the car park.

Rick leant across and pushed open the passenger door.

'Yates!'

The prison officer walked over.

'Get in.'

'What if I say, No?'

'We can do it officially.'

Yates looked over his shoulder, then climbed in.

Rick started the engine and pulled out of the car park. Traffic was heavy and bad-tempered. Everyone was in a rush.

'How was your shift?'

Yates clicked his tongue. 'Where are we going?'

'You'll see.'

Rick headed to South Manchester and further south, out into the country. They passed a field with horses, a small copse of trees. He turned down a lane and stopped at the apiary.

Yates muttered to himself, but climbed out holding the file.

They sat on the bench facing the horseshoe of hives. The air hummed with thousands of bees, flitting away from the hives, and zipping back again. Each bee knew which of the fifteen hives in the horseshoe was home, landed unerringly at the entrance and crawled inside with their cargo – nectar, pollen, water or propolis. Then emerged, a short while later, to embark on another mission. All day, they worked nonstop. Even trainee detectives would pale.

'Why have you brought me here?'

'Because it reminds me there's a context to what we do, what we witness, and what we're trying to achieve.'

Yates sighed. His neck was red and blotchy.

'I was on my way to see you, anyway.' He nodded at the file.

'What have you got for me, Paul?'

Yates looked across at Rick, his brow furrowed.

'Paul?'

'Not much, I'm afraid. Odds and ends from the cell-search. And nothing from the interview with Vogel. I've brought the interview transcript, for what it's worth.'

'Mmm.'

Rick stood up. 'There are three types of bee in each hive, Paul. The sole queen, and the only fertilised female. The workers, who make up ninety-nine per cent of the bees.

They're unfertilised females. And a couple of hundred drones, the male bees. Drones have only one role which is to mate with the queen. They don't forage or clean or guard or nurse the brood, and as befits their low utility, they don't survive the winter. In October drones are kicked out of the front of the hive, and die in the scrub.'

'Is that right?'

'Last night,' said Rick, 'why did you go and see TBR?'

Yates shook his head.

Rick surveyed the hives, turned to face Yates. 'I need some utility from you, Paul.'

Yates ran a hand along the arm of the bench. 'It's funny, I wanted to be a police officer, but I couldn't get in. Applied three times, then joined prisons. Every time I see my dad, he says, Don't you feel like you've been banged up with them? Still, after fifteen years. And he's right, I bloody do.'

Rick sat down and stared across.

'I'd like a guar—'

'Tell me.'

'I was going to, just not today.'

'Tell me right now, from the beginning.'

Yates glanced around. The apiary was quiet, no one in sight and Rick's car the only vehicle. Traffic droned on a distant road.

'Before I came to see you yesterday I was stopped outside the prison by TBR. It seems weeks ago, now. He told me to slow your investigation down, and gave me two hundred quid. He promised more. At the time I didn't think I had any choice, he's well connected inside. But, it didn't sit right, and I couldn't face my dad ever finding out. So last night, I went to see him and returned the money. He said there'd be consequences.'

'Which explains your reluctance to hand over the guards' details?'

Yates nodded. 'I was going to give you everything in a week or two.' He took a piece of paper out of his file and passed it over. The sheet Rick had photocopied.

'I'm sorry.'

'What about the interview with Vogel?'

'Nothing, as per the transcript.'

'What about the cell search? You said, you found odds and ends.'

'That's the truth, but odds and ends are what you want, right?' The prison officer removed a clear sealed bag from his file.

Rick held it up. It contained an envelope addressed to Coniston. His home address had been crossed through and Strangeways Prison written in bold type. The two stamps were foreign, one showing a mountain, the other a temple. Rick recognised Bodhnath Stupa, one of the most famous landmarks in Nepal. He peered at the postmark.

Kathmandu, Nepal.

His pulse quickened. The only person Coniston knew in Nepal was Hant Khetan. A connection which more than justified the shenanigans with Yates.

His phone rang. Hunter.

'Where are you?'

'Talking to an informant.'

'Just had a nod from Williams' brief – they're ready to go.'

'Tell him ten minutes.' Not a hope, but the message would keep both solicitor and client expectant, and agitated.

Rick pocketed his phone. 'Anything else, Paul?'

Yates handed him another clear sealed bag. 'This.'

The bag contained a photo of Coniston and an Asian boy standing in a river next to a chest-high dam. During Rick's enquiry to Nepal the year before, Russell had carried an instant camera and must have taken it.

In the background of the photo Rick recognised the camp at Mosom Kharka in the foothills of Everest. Multicoloured prayer-flags looped between the tents, and behind them snow-capped mountains sparkled under a perfect azure sky. The boy was Ram, Khetan's nephew. Coniston had built the dam with Ram, part of his effort to win the boy's trust. Which in turn, had been part of Rick's strategy to persuade Ram to provide information on the whereabouts of his uncle. The photo made him rethink the first exhibit.

'Was the photo in the envelope?'

'No. It was stuck on Coniston's cell wall.'

Khetan could have sent the envelope, but the photo would have been from Ram, and therefore, the envelope more likely, too. 'Anything else?'

Yates handed Rick a sheet of paper with a list from the cell search. Photos of Coniston's family; three letters from his mother. Books; magazines; a newspaper. Clothing; toiletries. A television.

Rick returned to the photo. He turned it over.

Camdai nai tyaham herna.

'Do you know what it means?'

Yates shook his head. 'Didn't see it.'

Rick stared at the Nepali handwriting. *Herna*, hernia. *Camdai* like *camion*, lorry in French. A GCSE in Nepali would have been so much more useful.

He glanced at his watch: ten minutes was up.

'Yesterday, Paul, you told me Coniston's only allowed to make phone calls to two specific numbers. What about making unauthorised calls?'

'He will be, almost definitely. Most prisoners do, and our search teams regularly find SIM cards and handsets.'

'What about letters going out – do you read them?'

Yates nodded. 'We say we do.'

'So, thinking aloud, if Coniston wanted to send an unsanctioned letter, he could bribe a guard, or slip it to a friend during a visit?'

Yates nodded, playing with his wedding ring. 'Look, Rick, Mr Castle, sir, I'm really sorry about all of this.'

'I'm sure you are. Last question: does Sakit Patel work on Coniston's wing?'

'Not on the same wing. But Sak runs the prison garden and Coniston is – was – one of only a dozen or so prisoners who signed up.'

'Okay,' said Rick, 'that's it.'

'That's it?' Yates sighed deeply. 'What are you going to do?'

'For now,' said Rick, 'nothing.'

The prison officer passed Rick the file and stood up. He took a couple of steps, surveying the horseshoe of hives. The back of his neck looked sore.

Rick walked back to the car, Yates following behind. The prison officer waited while Rick reversed out of the verge and onto the road. The central locking clicked. Rick wound down the window.

'Walk back will do you good, Paul. Consider it the penalty for veering over the line.'

Yates looked like he'd swallowed a bee.

The car edged forward. 'One more thing,' said Rick.

The prison officer turned.

'Buy some mints.'

Rick drove away. There was no point in visiting the apiary, no point in being a beekeeper, if he didn't leave in better humour than when he'd arrived.

Rick waited until he hit the main road back to Manchester, then stuck the blue light on the roof. He turned on the siren and blatted back to the nick. Blues and twos was his rock 'n' roll.

The bribing of Yates suggested TBR helped spring Coniston from prison and supported hypothesis H3, Coniston was forced to escape. Slowing the investigation would give more time for Coniston to achieve whatever it was Redman wanted him for. But what? TBR employed heavies to pressure people, and although Coniston had once moved a bit of weed, he was hardly significant in his dealing operation. It suggested something more personal, something requiring Coniston's particular skill-set. Intelligence, an affinity for animals, and determination.

Approaching the nick, Rick switched off the noise and the lights. Feeling untouchable, he parked in his old DCI bay in the backyard. He took out his phone and looked up the translation of the Nepali on the back of the photo.

See you soon.

Khetan's nephew Ram had sent Coniston a photo with a message that he would see him soon. Coniston was heading back to Nepal. To track down Khetan?

His phone buzzed in his hand. Hunter.

'I'm here. Two minutes.'

'There's a problem. Williams says he doesn't feel well. Doctor's seen him, and the interview's been delayed until tomorrow. Brief has gone home.'

'Who is it?'

'Fullilove.'

Rick grinned. The two of them had history. In respect of Williams, a round each. Tomorrow, he'd knock them out, both Williams and his brief.

He explained about the photo.

'So you think Coniston's going to do a flit to Nepal?'

'Tell me you've done a port alert.'

'Sea and airports, major rail stations. Also, all licensed premises plus pet and corner shops. I have been in the Job almost thirty years.'

Rick hardly noticed the sarcasm. He was already performing the investigative backflip to connect the photo to Khetan. Already planning a third visit to Nepal in as many years. Russell as guide and interpreter. Paulson and Kasim as bagmen, willing to run and run, and not complain. Or scratch.

He threw the phone on the dash and took out the photo of Coniston and Ram next to the dam. They'd had a falling out in Nepal, but maybe they'd patched it up. Maybe, they'd been in regular contact on WhatsApp or Facebook. Maybe that's what the message referred to, see you again *virtually*.

Possible, too, Ram didn't even know Coniston was going to escape. If the photo had arrived in the envelope, then it appeared he didn't even know Coniston was in prison. But then why should he – the boy lived in a village in the foothills of Everest.

Rick was coming down from the earlier high. He felt like an apple scrumper, gorged on low-hanging fruit and slightly drunk. The prize apples still out of reach.

His phone buzzed again.

'Castle.'

'Sir, it's Kasim, I heard you were back.'

Rick updated the young DC on the Sakit information.

'So can I arrest him?'

'Did you find out about a UC?'

'There is one, and he's been tasked, but I'm still waiting to hear back.'

'Wait another day, it might give you something for interview.'

'Yes, sir. Thank you, sir.'

The back door of the nick slammed. Rick pocketed the phone and glanced across the yard. Maggie was heading towards her car. He climbed out and ran over. Past the squad cars, and the carrier, through the pools of yellow light.

'Maggie.'

Ignoring him, she pulled open the driver's door of her car. She wore a salmon-pink blouse and her chunky beads.

'You've not been answering my calls.'

She lined up her wheelchair at an angle to the car.

'Thanks for hanging on for the Williams interview. The custody sergeant is McAllister and he's a devil for procedural detail. If a prisoner says he doesn't feel well, and the doctor agrees, then there's no arguing. Even if it's a scam pulled by the brief.'

'That's okay.'

'Mags, can we talk?'

She turned to face him.

'I'm sorry about Elaine. I am. But the damage was done last year. Khetan was responsible for so much and I would have done anything to get him.'

'The Job's changed you, Rick – *is* changing you.'

'I haven't.' He paused. Maybe he had – no one stayed the same for ever, but his moral beliefs were solid as a wood of ancient oaks. 'It's not.'

She looked into his eyes for the first time in a couple of days. 'I know you're not really like that. Not really.'

Rick wrinkled his nose. He hoped the ridiculous gesture would break their impasse. He'd used it once or twice in interview, not that he was going to tell Maggie.

Her stare softened and she tried not to laugh. 'I'm sorry for being grumpy.'

'No, Mags, I'm sorry!' Rick knelt down and gave her a hug. 'Is it Siobhan again?' He pulled away.

'No, it's not her.'

'What, then?'

'No one. It's me, I'm getting old. I've got wrinkles, look.'

'No, you haven't!' Rick looked more closely. 'There's

nothing there.' He kissed her cheek. 'Friends again?'

'Friends,' said Maggie, pecking him on the forehead.

'More than friends,' said Rick, kissing her on the lips.

'Not here,' whispered Maggie, giggling, and manoeuvring her chair back alongside the car.

She pushed a fist into the car seat and using it as a pivot, swung her body from the chair into the car. She spun the chair around and flipped up the rear handle so the seat concertinaed. She removed the wheels one a time, and slotted them into the passenger footwell. She spread a towel on the seat, and with a steadying hand on the roof, lifted the chair up and across herself.

Rick knew better than to help, or even to offer to help. Maggie was as stubborn as a power-cut.

She put her key in the ignition, and Rick stepped back. She shut the door and the window buzzed down.

'What was the favour you wanted?'

'Khetan's out of Belmarsh.'

'What?'

The yard suddenly seemed dark. Cold. Blurred figures moved in an upstairs room in the police station.

'After all of that work.' She paused. 'Why was he released?'

'That's what I'd like to find out. I wondered whether you could contact your old sapper colleague. Duncan, isn't that his name? The one who became a spook when he left the army.'

'Duncan,' said Maggie, nodding. 'Leave it with me.'

'Thanks.'

The window began to rise.

'Mags?'

The window stopped.

'Yes?'

'I could come round.'

'You could.'

Rick sensed a problem and his heart thumped. Like anyone else, at night he wanted to be warm and loved, and told everything would be okay. 'But?'

'You'll have to make the bed – you're so much better at it than me.'

'I can do that,' he said, smiling.

Maggie raised her window, and drove away. Rick placed an imaginary golf ball on the ground, lined up his feet, took a practice swing, then wellied the ball over the backyard fence and into the shadowed streets of South Manchester.

24

Rick glanced at the clock radio – 02:50. He hoped Coniston was also awake, and worrying about a police team crashing through the front door.

The phone rang.

He rolled over, snatched it up.

Not his phone.

'Hello,' said Maggie, holding her mobile to her ear. 'What?' she said a few seconds later. Rick waited, presuming it was bad news. One of her parents or her brother.

Finally, she slid the phone back onto her bedside table. She looked wan, and sipped from a glass of water.

'Is everything okay?'

'That was Duncan,' said Maggie. 'And you won't believe what he told me.'

Rick sat up, turned on a light.

'What?'

'He's working the night shift.' Maggie took another sip of water and put down the glass. 'This can never come back to him, you've got to promise. He only told me because we were good friends in the sappers, and—'

'And?' said Rick wondering how good.

'I covered for him once.'

Again, Rick wondered. So much of Maggie's history he didn't know. 'Of course not, I promise.' Glad that his promises were still currency with Maggie.

'Khetan was extradited to the Americans.'

'For fuck's sake.' Rick climbed out of the bed and went to the window. He drew the curtains back and stared out into the darkness.

'Do you want to hear the rest of it or not?'

'Yes.'

'Apparently, the Americans pulled rank, citing murders of US nationals and involvement in bombing international facilities.'

'So what the hell have they done with Khetan?'

'Wait for it. There's more, quite a lot more.'

Outside, parked cars sat outside quiet houses. Nothing was moving, everything in shades of brown and black.

'Then,' said Maggie. 'You won't believe this, Rick.' She sounded disbelieving herself. 'The US implemented a secret prisoner exchange with China, an agreement based on a complex three-way deal involving Nepal. In return for five American diplomats accused of spying, China took custody of Hant Khetan. I use the term *custody* only very lightly.'

'They let him go?'

'Within a fortnight. The intelligence hypothesis is that the Chinese wanted him to again cause havoc for the west.'

'For fuck's sake.'

'You already said that.'

'What did Nepal get?'

'In return for staying silent about one of its citizens, a national *kayaka* – a hero – in respect of his pressure on FIFA to change their policy on worker's rights in Qatar, Nepal are getting two multi-million pound hydro-electric dams. China is funding them and supplying the know-how.'

'It's a disgrace. And if it got out, an international scandal.'

'I know. The UK's official position is denial. But in private, the intelligence service is hopping mad.'

'Do they know where he is?'

'Nope.'

'Two years I've thought about little else. Of putting my career on the line, and a lot else besides. Russell was shot.'

'I know, I know.'

They shared the silence, the semi-darkness, the intensity of being awake in the middle of the night. Both of them alive with incredulity, frustration, anger.

A car drove past.

'Maggie.'

'What?'

'Thanks for finding out.'

'What are you going to do?'

'Nothing. Nothing I can do. Find Coniston and move on.'

He padded out to the bathroom and took a piss. Maggie was right, he couldn't believe it. No one would believe it, not Hunter, not Russell, not Robbo. Not the brigadier, or Barney Williams. Not Coniston. And not the general public. States, including the British state, ruled the word like titans. Like automatons.

Rick went into the kitchen, and stared at the remains of the pasta and the empty bottles of beer. He ate a congealing tube of rigatoni, then picked up the bowl, and posted it through the swing-top of the bin. It landed at the bottom with a sharp *crack*. He grabbed a bottle and hurled it at the wall, fragments of glass spraying all round.

'Rick?' shouted Maggie, sounding half-asleep.

He showered, shaved, and dressed. There was no way he would sleep now, so he might as well go to work.

In the bedroom, Maggie was already unconscious. He blew

her a kiss, cleaned up in the kitchen, then left, wondering if she would also head in early.

A bright moon watched him, high in the night sky. He opened the car window and let the cold air blow in. He turned at a set of traffic lights, the moon swinging overhead. As if the planets were aligning and the moon was pinpointing the police station.

Another Maggie came to mind. Mrs T, wearing a jumper of EU flags, wearing a Cossack hat, wearing a headscarf and riding on a tank, taking on the Argentines. She'd been a *kayaka* of the brigadier, and renowned for surviving on very little sleep. If Mrs T could run a country on four hours lying down, then he could recapture Coniston.

And Khetan.

25

The police station ticked with night shift officers. Lights shone in every room, and custody and the PCs' writing room were busy as daytime.

Rick pinched bread from the top of the CID fridge and dropped it in the toaster in his office. He made a cup of strong coffee, and spread the toast with last year's honey. He licked the spoon. Some beekeepers could tell which flowers the bees had visited, but they didn't have an escaped prisoner to find. And a second, who'd been *let go*.

He sat at his desk, reviewing the reports on his desk and compiling a list of enquiries. The wheat and the chaff, and Rick, the combine harvester.

Chaff. CCTV enquiries at the cemetery, the pick-up point, and the dump site. Anniversary visits and house-to-house, likewise. CCTV trawl along the route of Bowden's pub crawl. Statement from the ticket inspector. Statement from Salisbury, Coniston's next-door neighbour. The other neighbours – the Finchams – were on holiday in Australia. The name was familiar: two years ago, Coniston had stuffed their dead cat.

Wheat. CCTV from Old Town station showed Coniston arriving on a bicycle, dumping a fluorescent jacket. CCTV from Piccadilly station showed him getting off the train with Mrs

Grieve and walking out into Manchester. The phone calls from Coniston – Paulson had traced the phone number to a pay as you go SIM card showing no messages and no other phone calls. Paulson's theory, which Rick agreed with, was that fearing triangulation, Coniston had chucked the phone. Williams' phone was missing. Had he leant it to Coniston as a replacement?

The photo of Ram and the Nepalese correspondence found in Coniston's cell. Had Coniston escaped in order to return to Nepal to hunt down Khetan?

It was possible Williams would know all the answers.

A cleaner popped her head in the door, and emptied his bin. Asked him if he wanted his desk polished, or his computer screen. Scalps were extra. He wasn't there, yet.

Outstanding. Interview Williams. Room-to-room enquiries at Hartford Hall. Find, then brace Darren Back. Arrest TBR and interview him about bribing Yates. Arrest Sakit Patel, house search and interview. Financial enquiries.

He made more coffee and started an interview plan for Williams.

Nine a.m. In Rick's office, Hunter and Maggie, all three on the phone, all waiting for answers. The atmosphere tense, expectant, and better than any drug. Withdrawal just the same.

Maggie was made up and wearing her white blouse with black triangles. Her eyes were bloodshot. *Does he know about Khetan?* she mouthed, pointing at Hunter.

Rick nodded. He ended his call and tried Robbo's mobile, left a terse message. The superintendent started late, finished early, as if he was living a hundred years earlier.

'Thanks for your help,' said Maggie on the phone. She placed it in her lap and looked across at Rick. They shared a moment – leaving the pasta in a hurry, the fresh sheets. 'Finally got through to admin at the university. The day Coniston escaped, Williams missed his ten-thirty lecture.'

Another nail in Williams' coffin.

Hunter pocketed his phone. He stretched out an arm, pulled the shirtsleeve back, and scratched all the way along. Like an unhurried road sweeper.

'Williams is fit. Brief's here.'

'Let's do it,' said Rick.

He waited outside the interview room while Hunter went to sign out Williams. Gary had left him his tabloid newspaper, and he glanced at the front page. *British Jobs for British Workers.* Underneath, a photo at an airport showed UK Border Controls and a large crowd of people pushing and shoving. The article blamed migrants for exacerbating most of the country's problems. Increased levels of crime, longer waits at hospitals and doctors' surgeries, larger class sizes in schools, more litter on the streets. A councillor from Basingford was quoted. '*Enough is enough. We're being squeezed both ways: less money from the government but more people to spend it on.*' To the right of the article was a box titled, *This is what YOU say.* The opinions were racist, xenophobic, nimbyist. One man blamed migrants for his local football team losing as he was unemployed and couldn't afford to go and watch them.

Hunter returned alone.

'Five minutes. Fullilove's making a phone call.'

Rick handed back the newspaper to Hunter. She'd started already. 'Do you agree with this, Gary?'

'I know you won't.'

Rick's views on migrants, like his views on the legalisation of cannabis, were neither the official line nor popular in the canteen. 'Do you?'

'Some,' said Hunter. 'There's a team of Rumanians ripping the Arndale.'

'A tiny proportion of migrants are criminal, same as Brits.'

'Last night on the news they said a quarter of rough sleepers in Manchester are migrants. We haven't the space or the services or the jobs for all these people.'

'Most of them are doing the jobs we don't want to do or have insufficient people qualified. Chefs, carers, nurses. Doctors.'

'If they have skills then we should let them in but only temporarily. In Australia, they have a points system.'

They stopped talking as the door to the custody hall opened. Williams appeared, wearing a red t-shirt with a thick silver stripe. He was escorted by Frank the civilian jailer, who was bald and invariably grumpy. Bringing up the rear was Williams' solicitor Sandra Fullilove, wearing an orange jumpsuit. The custody door pulled shut, guillotining gawps from police and prisoners alike.

The five of them trooped into the stuffy interview room. Scowling, Frank cleared the table of sandwich and crisp wrappers and an empty Coke can.

He exited, shutting the door.

Rick gestured, and Williams and Fullilove sat down. Hunter fiddled with the recording equipment. The solicitor from Butts & Pickering passed over a business card. Long pale fingers, painted fingernails.

'How are you, Rick?'

Hunter stopped fiddling. Eyes popping.

Williams stilled.

'I'm okay.'

Rick sat opposite Williams. He arched his fingers and studied the inverted heart-shape, trying not to remember. Hunter sat next to the equipment. He flicked a switch, a beep sounded, a red light shone. The sergeant sighed, and like a schoolboy reciting a sonnet in assembly, gave the caution.

Rick took a breath.

'Can you describe, Barney, your friendship with Calix Coniston?'

Fullilove tutted, and crossed her legs.

'He's not a friend.'

'How would you describe him?'

'If I saw him in the street, I would avoid him.'

'Why?'

'You know why.'

'For the tape.'

'Two years ago I went on a trekking expedition to Nepal. Calix was seemingly just another trekker, but it turned out he'd conspired with Hant Khetan. My brother Spencer and I were kidnapped, and my brother died. Calix was duped, yes, but I still hold him responsible for Spencer's death.'

'You know he escaped yesterday from prison?'

'I don't live on the Isle of Wight.' Williams squeezed his hands and clicked the thumbs. Because he'd been held hostage by Khetan in a cave for weeks, or because he was nervous.

'Do you know anything about it?'

'Inspector Castle, my client just said he did.'

'I'll rephrase. Barney, did you help Coniston escape?'

'No.'

'Have you helped him since he escaped?'

'No.'

'Have you seen him since he escaped?'

'No.'

'This is your chance, Barney, to tell us if you do know anything. Anything at all.'

'My client couldn't be clearer, Detective Inspector. If you haven't got any more questions, then—'

Rick glanced at Hunter. He was sketching on a pad. He turned back to Williams. The student looked confident. 'You're studying law, Barney?'

'Is that relevant?' said Fullilove.

Rick counted silently to five. 'Miss Fullilove, please, we're never going to get started yet alone finish.'

'Ms.'

'Ms.' He turned to Barney. 'Are you studying law at Manchester University?'

'I am.'

'Presumably you want a job afterwards?'

'I do.'

'As a solicitor?'

Williams nodded.

'For the tape.'

'Yes.'

'Like Ms Fullilove here?'

Williams smiled. 'I suppose.'

'So you understand that a conviction for assisting or harbouring Coniston, or for perverting the course of justice, will bar you from entering the legal profession?'

'I do.'

'What might seem now like a good idea will look very different in a few years' time – when the only job you can get is stacking shelves or driving a minicab.'

'I don't know anything.'

'I might be able to do something.'

'Honestly, I don't know anything.'

The word hung between the four of them like a flashing neon light. A naïve legal student's error, or a deliberate red rag. Hunter kept doodling.

'Okay, then. The day before yesterday, what did you do in the morning?'

'Lectures.'

'All morning?'

'Some of it.'

'Were you in a lecture at eleven twenty-five?'

'Eleven twenty-five exactly?'

'That's the time Coniston was picked up in a car. You know

that. It was on the disclosure sheet as well as on the news.'

'I was at the cinema. The Ruzzo does cheap tickets for students in the morning.'

'Could you give us a few details?'

'I went to a nine o'clock lecture on probate, but bunked my ten-thirty. Can't stand constitutional law. Nothing else 'til the afternoon so I went to see a film, *Drowning By Numbers*. It was the ten-thirty programme and finished about twelve-thirty.'

'What's the story?'

'You don't know it?'

'Humour me.'

'I could have looked it up.'

'Did you?'

'No.' He paused. 'Three women who have the same name of Cissie Colpitts each murder their husbands by drowning. The numbers one to a hundred are placed randomly through the film. Number one was on a tree, number two was on a bath, and so on.'

'Where was number one hundred?'

Williams stared at Rick without expression for a few seconds and then glanced at Hunter. The sergeant stopped drawing, and looked up. Fullilove wrote on her pad.

'On a rowing boat,' said Williams. 'I was back in my seat by then.' He winked.

Rick stared, wondering whether he'd imagined the facial tic. He glanced at Hunter. The sergeant raised an eyebrow, confirming what Rick thought he'd seen. But then, Hunter was Hunter. Had Williams made a slip, or was he taking the piss? If so, he'd under-estimated his suspect. But not his solicitor – maybe it was Sandra's idea. He rewound the interview in his head. Had she drawn a boat on her notepad? The interview was running away from him like a coked-up shoplifter.

'Did you see the film with anyone else?'

'No.'

'Okay,' said Rick. 'You went to a lecture, then to see a film. What about in the afternoon?'

'I studied in my room.'

'Who with?'

'No one.'

Rick made a mark on his pad. 'Monday evening?'

'I don't remember.'

'Lot of pizza boxes and beer bottles for one person.'

Williams glanced at his solicitor, then back at Rick.

'Do you know Stuart Bowden?'

'No. Who's he?'

Rick drew another line on his pad. A second mistake? 'You initially said No, as if you recognised the name. Do you?'

'Inspector, my client has said that he doesn't know him. Please move on.'

Rick ignored her. 'He's another Manchester student.'

'So are ten thousand other people,' said Williams.

'Where were you on Saturday evening, two days before Coniston escaped?'

'I went out, I think.'

'Who with?'

'I'm not sure.'

'Where did you go?'

'I don't know. Most nights I go out. Everyone does. They all meld into one. We go out, get pissed or whatever and we go home. Boring, really.'

'Stuart Bowden's car was used to scoop Coniston from the cemetery. And on Saturday night his car key was stolen from his pocket in a bar or pub in the city centre. Do you know anything about that theft?'

'No.'

'Or taking Bowden's car the next day, Sunday?'

'No.'

'Are you sure?'

'Yes.'

'*Inspector.*'

'Okay, Barney, let's talk about visiting Coniston in Strangeways. In the last six weeks you visited him three times. A man you would avoid in the street. Why?'

'I'm specialising in criminal law.'

Williams said it without hesitation, and almost as if he'd been primed. Rick glanced again at Fullilove's business card. Butts & Pickering. Coincidence?

'One of the lecturers advised that if we were going to spend our careers sending people to, or saving people from, prison, then it was a good idea to go and see one. Visiting Coniston was an ideal opportunity. About time he did something for me.'

'What was the name of the lecturer?'

'Edgerton. Dr Edgerton.'

'We will check.'

'Fine.'

Rick glanced over at Hunter who was shading his doodle. 'Gary?' The sergeant looked up. 'Anything?'

Hunter passed his sheet of paper, the top and bottom quarters neatly folded back to leave a proud canvas. Which held the sketch of a Punch and Judy tent on a beach. Shaded stripes on the tent, and behind, a calm sea and circular sun. Punch and Judy were playing cards while sausages cooked on a barbeque. The bobby was polishing his boots. Rick refolded the paper in half and scored it flat. He folded it in half again and scored it flat again, driving his fingernail back and forth. No doubt he was the hapless bobby; Fullilove, Judy; and Williams, Punch. Maybe he'd been distracted, but the message was loud and clear.

Rick slotted the sheet in the back of his file, and closed the cover. 'I want to go back to the film. What did you do afterwards?'

Williams paused. 'I come out, buy a sandwich, walk back to my room eating it.'

'Tell me about the sandwich.'

'Is that a joke?'

'Where did you buy it?'

'I can't remember.'

'What sort of sandwich?'

'Cheese, I think.'

'What else?'

'I buy crisps and a drink.'

'What flavour?'

Williams looked away. 'Cheese and onion.'

'The drink?'

'Coke.'

'Diet?'

'Yes. No. I don't remember.'

'Who did you sit behind when you were watching the film?'

'What?' He frowned. 'An old guy.'

'Describe him.'

Williams puckered his mouth. 'I don't know. Bald.'

'Which way did you walk home?'

Williams sighed. 'I'm not sure. There're different ways.'

'I'm sure there are, but which one did you take?'

'Really, Inspector,' said Fullilove. 'I don't see these questions as relevant.'

Rick disagreed with her on three counts. Not only were his questions relevant, and Williams' answers damning, but Fullilove knew it. He picked up her card and turned it over in his fingers. He put it down. 'Barney, something has been bothering me since your solicitor handed me her card. Why are you using Butts & Pickering? Why not the duty brief? Or a local firm?'

Williams opened his mouth, but didn't speak.

'Communications between a lawyer and a client are

legally privileged, Inspector, you can't ask that.'

'Your solicitor, Barney, is confusing her privilege with client privilege. Whether you answer or not, is up to you. Perhaps you haven't reached that stage of your course?' Rick glanced at Fullilove. 'And perhaps your solicitor has forgotten.'

Williams turned towards her.

'My advice is not to answer.'

'In any case my question concerns your decision *before* you even spoke to a solicitor. My question is why you chose Butts & Pickering?'

Williams said nothing.

'Butts & Pickering is the same firm used by Coniston.' Rick opened his file and made a third mark on the pad. 'Chance? I don't think so.'

Fullilove uncrossed her legs, and held her notepad to her chest like a shield. 'My advice is still not to answer.'

'You don't know what to say, Barney, do you? Because the truth is that Coniston told you to use them, didn't he? Otherwise, why would you be using them? There must be twenty firms that are closer to South Manchester.'

Fullilove stood up. 'Inspector, I'd like to speak to my client in private.'

'Barney? You don't have to if you don't want to.'

'Inspector, I'm warning you, I'm going to make a complaint.'

'I want to talk to her.'

Rick nodded at Hunter.

'Interview suspended.' He stopped the recording, and sealed the discs.

Rick opened the door, and Sandra walked out followed by Williams. Fun while it lasted, he thought. Frank escorted the two of them into the next room, and the door pulled shut.

'Couldn't you just scribble a note like a normal person?' whispered Rick.

'Drawing takes my mind off the itching. Doctor's orders.'

Rick removed the scored paper from the file, and unfolded it. The sketch was good, very good. Playing card detail, glowing charcoal, and a likeness in the bobby's face.

26

Calix slid Elly's balcony door open a couple of inches. Cool air streamed inside. It was still early and the building site opposite was quiet. A pair of pigeons cackled and roughhoused in a flower bed, sending petals and green leaves airborne.

He pulled over a chair, sat. He lit a cigarette and blew the smoke through the gap as instructed by his moll. She didn't smoke, her room was a non-smoking room, and yet she'd bought him – remembered to buy him – a pack of cigarettes. He sat, he smoked, he listened for sounds next door, for footsteps in the corridor. Only the sleepy purr of Elly, turned away from him, towards the wall, legs curled up. He sat, he listened, he smoked. He dozed.

'Ow!'

Elly stopped twisting his ear.

'I was awake most of the night,' said Calix. 'Barney didn't come home.'

'They've still got him.' She yawned, and stretched, revealing a fold of brown stomach and a pierced belly-button.

'Or he's staying away.'

Elly slid the balcony door wider, and passed him another mug of strong tea. She pulled up the other chair, and sat next to him. Held her mug in both hands.

A motorbike accelerated beneath them, then slowed, and turned, and accelerated back. The rider glanced upwards. Calix didn't think the rider could see him, but he wasn't sure. Too late. He surveyed back up the road. No other vehicles, or pedestrians. He observed the windows on other buildings: all opaque oblongs of greyed glass with slots and flashes of light. But no faces, no people, no spotters, no Castle with binoculars or telescope.

'So,' said Calix, 'what are you studying?' He lowered his gaze to the mess of petals and leaves surrounding the flower bed where the pigeons had play-fought.

'What am I studying?'

'You know, what subject?'

Elly sipped her tea. 'The varied uses of hedgehogs and other small animals by the Roman Army.'

Calix clicked his tongue in amusement.

Elly put her mug under her chair, and picked up her phone. He watched, out of the corners of his eyes. She started playing a game, arranging irregular shapes so they were regular. So many questions she wasn't asking him. He either trusted her or he didn't.

She kept playing, her fingers tip-tapping, and the phone issuing tinny beeps of encouragement. Her face rapt. Molls by definition were unknowable, incomprehensible, indecipherable. He glanced outside, at the rusting balcony rail. Expendable.

Calix closed the door of Elly's tiny bathroom. He pushed Barney's mobile onto a shelf with cotton wool and ear buds. He splashed cold water on his face, and cleaned his teeth with Elly's toothbrush. In the mirror he looked tired, and rough: sunken eyes and two-day stubble. He spied Elly's razor, but thought better of it. She'd bought him smokes.

He peeled off his socks and removed his trousers and shorts. Leaving the taps alone, he stepped into the shower tray.

He squatted, and inserted two fingers into his anus. He prodded carefully until he felt the corner of a plastic bag, and gripping as well as possible, pulled.

The small plastic bag fell into the tray. It was soiled, and the acrid smell instant. He washed the bag under a tap, and cleaned the tray. At least his old man would have approved of that. He took off his shirt, and showered.

Darren had taught him stuffing soon after he'd first been sent to prison. Stuffing, and packing, and the advantages of both. Packing was better for the longer term, and the method favoured by drug mules to transport class A into the country. Stuffing was better overnight, and useful for moving contraband into prison. Darren hadn't mentioned it could be used to smuggle things out of prison, but it had proved equally effective. Despite it being his mother's funeral, he'd been strip-searched three times. Once in the holding area, waiting for the van; again, when the van crew took over custody; and the third time when he was unloaded at the cemetery. There were other things he'd liked to have brought out, but only one thing which was essential.

He towelled off, and patted the bag dry. He inspected Elly's lipsticks, her talcs and lotions, her range of tweezers. He sniffed her perfumes and sprayed her deodorant, the tiny room transmogrifying from toilet to tart's boudoir. He dressed.

'You almost done?' whispered Elly at the door. 'I need to go to a lecture.'

'Two minutes.'

She hadn't asked what he was doing – molls accepted things, and didn't ask difficult questions.

Calix sat on the lid of the bog and removed the inner bag. It was dry and unsoiled which was a relief. He removed the SIM card and set it on the side. He flushed both bags away. He took down Barney's phone and removed the SIM. Swapped it for the stuffed SIM, then powered up the phone.

A photo of Spencer astride a mountain bike appeared. Calix entered the PIN number – the date of Spencer's death, and divulged by Barney during a prison visit when he was trying to make Calix feel guilty. Messages began to pop up. There were unlikely to be many as few people knew his number.

Two messages from before his breakout:

TBR. *Jonny Fireplace got an 18 rap see you make JF welcome*

Darren B. *New doll goes like a Christmas cracker!! Hang in there, C*

Neither was the message he was hoping for. Calix stared at the screen. A third message appeared. It was from the right person, but the right message?

He tapped open the text from Ram, sent the day before he escaped:

Hello callixx arrive Dover

He closed his eyes and opened them again. The message remained, but still there was no mention of Khetan. He stared at it until the screen faded and went dark.

27

'First interview I've downstreamed for ages,' said Robbo.

Rick followed his boss out of the custody suite and into a dusty stairwell. Posters of dull divisional objectives lined the walls. Robbo turned towards him. His cheeks had lost their definition, his face a flabby round. Two pustules marked the end of his nose.

'Frankly, Rick, I'm a bit disappointed. All this hoopla associated with you 'tecs, you especially.' He paused. 'You know the DCI job remit includes leading on interview training.'

'As I'm sure you've realised, sir, I'm only halfway through this one. Before I can rebut Williams' story, I need to know what it is. Yes, he has an elaborate alibi but it falls apart at the edges. You will have picked up on the tell-tales when I asked him about what he did afterwards and his route home. Great detail on his story, but very little on anything else. Uncertainty, hesitation, use of the present tense, subliminal suggestion.'

'Sorry?'

'Williams' lunch was very similar to the rubbish Frank cleared away from the table in the interview room. In the cinema, the man in the row in front of Williams was bald – like Frank.'

The door to the custody suite buzzed open, and Maggie

pushed out. She waited by the door, but Robbo turned, and lumbered up the stairs.

Maggie moved forward. Her hair had dried. She rested her calloused hands. She had a grip as strong as a bricklayer's.

'Can you get someone out to the Arts Cinema?'

'Will do.'

'Then can you interrogate Williams' phone number. Incoming and outgoing calls, messages. And check Williams' claim with Dr Edgerton.'

Maggie nodded, and Rick winked his thanks.

The custody door buzzed open a second time.

'They're ready,' said Hunter.

Rick couldn't stop thinking about the bobby polishing his shoes, the sausages on the barbeque, Punch's poker hand. Unlike Robbo, there was no excuse for Hunter – he knew what Rick was doing.

Knew Rick was about to nail Williams down.

Hunter switched the recording equipment back on. The machine beeped and the red light showed they were live. Hunter bent down and scratched his puffy ankle. Rick felt like his dad was watching. Dad in triplicate: Hunter in his new avuncular role, Robbo behind the screen, and Dad who always lurked behind everything Rick did and said.

He offered round the jug of water he'd brought in. Sandra declined, and Hunter appeared not to notice. Williams nodded, and Rick poured out two glasses. He pushed one across the table, and drank half a glass. He'd run the cold tap specially.

'Okay, now?'

Williams nodded. He drained the glass of water, pursing his lips as if it was whisky.

Rick offered him a refill.

'No.' Williams shook his head. 'Thanks.'

Fullilove scowled, and crossed her legs. She knew Rick was grooming her client.

'Remember the suspension bridge, Barney? You were so thin after the weeks in the cave. Your hair matted and grown wild. Your quite decent beard.' Rick smiled, and added a soft chuckle.

'Is this relevant, Inspector?'

'I think so.' Rick focussed on Barney, not giving the solicitor the distraction she wanted. 'You found even climbing the ladder onto the bridge, Barney, a bit of a struggle. You rested at the top. Behind you, Mount Mera loomed in the distance. Pristine snow slopes, a shimmering blue sky. Swimming-pool blue. You looked – you were – shellshocked. Somehow, you staggered past me, and across the bridge. And there on the far side, waited Russell Weatherbeater, and my colleague Kate. Russell carried you down the ladder and force-fed you Mars bars. Kate held your hand, and hugged you. Cried with you.' Rick leant forward and locked on Barney's eyes. 'We – Russell, Kate, me, Greater Manchester Police – tracked you down, negotiated your release, and escorted you home.'

Williams nodded, and squeezed his fingers.

'We carried you on and off for three days on a stretcher. Hired extra porters but we all took turns, including Kate. On the steeper sections, Russell carried you on his back. We ate double *dal baht* in the evenings.' Rick paused, but there was not a flicker of a smile. 'Barney, you can get yourself out of this. But you have to help us. You have to help yourself.'

Williams sighed, and looked away.

'No comment.'

Rick laughed, this time for real. In his peripheral vision, he saw Hunter folding a piece of paper to make another canvas.

'Is there any reason you can think of why Coniston might want to return to Nepal?'

'Don't even think about answering that,' said Fullilove. 'He's not one of your trainees, Inspector.' Williams glanced at his solicitor, then at Rick.

'No comment.'

Rick pulled closer the box of exhibits which sat on the floor. He toyed again with the running order, and began.

'Exhibit KA/17, your running trainers. There's windscreen glass in the soles which matches the getaway vehicle.' He placed the exhibit bag on the table. 'Any comment?'

'Half the shoes in the country contain windscreen glass,' said Fullilove.

'So half don't.' He shook the bag. 'Barney?'

'No comment.'

Rick replaced the exhibit bag with another. 'Exhibit RW/4, box of nitrile gloves found in the bathroom cupboard. Blue, medium-sized.'

'They were there when I moved in. I may have moved them to a different shelf.'

'Which would explain your fingerprints on the box?'

Williams nodded.

'For the tape.'

'Yes.'

'The gloves match three pairs found in the boot of the getaway vehicle. Any comment?'

'They're also very common,' said Fullilove, brushing invisible dust from her knees.

'Not so,' said Rick. 'They're all right-handed. The manufacturers told us a batch of fifty boxes was affected. Nine pairs are missing from RW/4, three of which are very likely to be the ones recovered from the boot of the getaway vehicle. Barney?'

'No comment.'

'Okay, then. One of these pieces of evidence means little, but together they point the finger.' Rick swapped exhibit bags. 'Exhibit KA/7, a photo of you wearing a dress and a curly blonde wig found on your pinboard.'

'It was taken at a fancy-dress party a couple of weeks ago. I borrowed the wig from Elly next door; ask her if you don't believe me.'

'Where is it now?'

'I don't know, I lost it that night.'

'Don't forget, Barney, a jury may one day listen to the recording of this interview. Of course you're training to be a solicitor so you know that. If I was on the jury, I'd be wondering why you haven't asked me why I'm asking a question about a curly blonde wig, and also why you told me who you borrowed the wig from, but not the dress.'

Barney reddened.

'It's a shame this interview is not being video-recorded, but for the benefit of the tape, Mr Barney Williams has turned red as a post box.'

'I disagree,' said Fullilove. 'Totally. He looks the same as he did when we came in. And if he does look any pinker, then it's because it's too hot in here. I may also be a little flushed.'

Hunter whistled a flat one-two.

'For the sake of clarity, Barney, I'm asking you because a witness described the driver of the getaway vehicle as having curly blonde hair.'

'Could have been a woman,' said Ms Fullilove.

Rick expected another whistle from Hunter, but second-guessing him took the throw of a dice. Second-guessing Coniston the throw of six dice. He returned the photo to the exhibits' box, and placed another bag on the table.

'Exhibit KA/19, a mobile phone bill in your name. However, we didn't find your phone, Barney. Where is it?'

'I don't know. That's the truth.'

'And the rest isn't?'

'Ignore that,' said Fullilove. She looked at Rick. 'Cheap.'

Unlike the restaurant she'd chosen.

He ignored the glint in her eye.

'When did you last use your phone, Barney?'

'Yesterday morning, I thought. I used it to check my Facebook page. Maybe I didn't.'

Rick didn't linger on the point. It was possible Williams was telling the truth about the phone, but in stating so had all but confirmed his complicity. Rick would bet his pension Coniston had taken it.

'Onto the statements. Alex Tidy, a pizza delivery driver has described how he delivered two pizzas to your door on Monday evening. A man fitting your description answered the door. When he offered free garlic bread, you, or a man looking like you and paying with a credit card in your name, shouted over his shoulder a word the driver didn't recognise. A nickname, he thought, something like *Gallics*. Which to my mind, sounds very like *Calix!*'

'That was me. I agree. But the driver misheard.'

Rick started counting. At seventeen, Barney spoke:

'I shouted, Garlics.'

Hunter guffawed.

Fullilove and Williams turned towards him, and in his head, Rick high-fived his colleague. The pair turned back.

'Garlics, not Calix.' Rick made a note on his pad. 'So, windscreen glass, right-handed gloves, curly blonde wig, and a word sounding like Calix. You have to ask yourself, Barney, if twelve good and true hear all that, whether they'll deliberate for long.'

'Beyond all reasonable doubt is the test, Inspector. And there is reasonable doubt. Plenty.'

'The risk you, Barney, and not your solicitor will have to take.' Rick topped up his glass, and offered the jug to Williams. The suspect ignored him. 'You say you want to be a lawyer,

Barney, but as I said earlier, you can't be a lawyer with a conviction for assisting or harbouring.'

Williams grabbed his glass, water splashing out.

Rick tensed, ready to jump his chair back. Even Hunter sat up and felt for his telescopic baton.

Williams stared at Rick with cold hard eyes. He jogged the glass up and down, spilling more water. 'I'm grateful to you and the police for securing my release two years ago, I am. But it's you who doesn't understand.'

He crushed the glass in his hand.

'I told you back at Hartford, Khetan killed my brother and my dad.'

Blood began seeping through his fingers.

'You bloody idiot,' said Hunter, standing to hit the alarm button. A klaxon sounded and his sketching floated down onto the desk. It showed the shoe-shining bobby laying a poker hand down between Punch and Judy. Four aces. Underneath, a red-stained pool spread across the table.

In the monitoring room Rick stood alongside Maggie and watched through the one-way glass as the force medical examiner bandaged Williams. Two uniformed constables stood guard.

'Good and bad news,' said Maggie.

She sounded like the old Maggie, his girlfriend Maggie. Who he made excuses to meet during the day. Who sent him amusing text messages, and left cakes and buns on his desk.

'Fullilove's not making a complaint. But mainly it's bad news. Can't get hold of Dr Edgerton. And Williams' alibi checks out. CCTV at the Ruzzo cinema shows Williams buying a ticket at 10.18 and exiting at 12.37. Also, his phone. Normal pattern of use until twenty minutes before you executed the warrant. Then nothing, no incoming, no outgoing, no messages. Currently switched off. CPS say it's not enough.'

Rick *knew* Williams was the driver, but it didn't matter. He inspected the lines running across his palms. He would find love and father three children; he would be unlucky in love, and discover he was sterile; a disaster waited around the corner. He'd fail his DCI board. Skye wouldn't make it. Dad would never recover his memory however much cannabis he consumed.

McTavish, the dour instructor on his SIO course had advice for every scenario. *Keep your eyes on the wee goal, and if the left back is from the Dalglish clan, go up the left friggin' wing.*

Rick looked at Maggie, wanting to pick up her calloused hand and point out the lines on it. To tell her, tell himself, that it was going to be alright. That it was all going to be alright: his dad would recover, he would make it with Maggie, he would find Coniston *and* Khetan.

'Redo the Ruzzo cinema CCTV. Go back the previous week, hammer it.'

Maggie nodded.

He phoned Hunter.

'When you bail Williams, stick a surveillance team on him.'

28

The *Okay* hand car wash was an old petrol station. The islands for the pumps and the overhead gantry remained, the plastic turned grey and brown. Moss grew in the cracks, and pine needles filled the gutters. The old shop served as an office and breakout room, the old garage as a storage area. On the first floor was a two-bedroom flat, scruffy, but the utilities worked. Cheap if you paid cash, and Hant always paid cash.

At six the car wash closed and the migrant workers went home. Polish men and boys from a previous wave of migration. The UK needed them to do the jobs they were unwilling or too lazy to do. Like washing cars, looking after the elderly, picking fruit and vegetables. At home in Nepal the extended family did these jobs. The UK, Hant thought, was a strange country: their people had no values, no *dharma*. A god they didn't believe in. Migrants were poor, and often saddled with young children and sick relatives, but they wanted jobs and better lives and they were prepared to work hard for them. Bringing them into the country was good for the lazy and dysfunctional British. New genes would draw the indigenous population back to the real world, and if they didn't, would replace them while they were tapping on their phones.

He drove the van from the parking at the back to the forecourt where Ram waited with a bucket and a sponge. His nephew was kicking a wall. He looked out of place, like an animal in a zoo. Hant turned on the high-pressure hose and pointed it at the windscreen. He gave instructions. Together, they worked around the van: windows, roof, bodywork, wheels. He drenched the teenager – accident, *mapha garnuhos!* – and turned off the hose.

Working on opposite sides, they wiped off the excess water. Hant unlocked the metal box near the rear wheel arch; he checked the contents, and locked it. It was his insurance, and not cheap.

'Okay. Here is first lesson. Clean van, no stop police. All lights work, no stop police. Understand?'

Ram nodded, and replied in Nepali.

Hant slapped him. 'English.'

Ram felt his reddening cheek. 'Good car—' He paused. 'Good car, no police.' Hant nodded and dummied another slap. The boy jumped back.

The van steamed in the evening sun, the sky light blue and cloudless. It was one of the few days in England Hant could remember when it wasn't raining or looked like it was about to start. He coiled the hose and watched Ram work. His nephew sponged off the van, buffed both sides of the windows. He vacuumed the cab, then the back. He sprayed cleaner on the dash and the seats.

Hant sat in the driver's seat. The van smelt of oranges, the steering wheel felt sticky. Ram put the equipment away, set the padlock. Hant pressed the horn and banged on the roof of the cab. Ram climbed in. He wore jeans and a yellow sweatshirt, trainers. His hair was damp. He looked like a British national.

'Seatbelt,' said Hant, yanking his own belt.

Ram clipped his seatbelt.

'*Ramro*,' said Hant. Good.

His nephew scowled at the double standards.

Laughing, Hant drove out of the car wash and into the light traffic of Westbury. He headed for the ring road, Ram staring out of the window as if he was on the moon. A queue outside a fish and chip shop: two fat women with a pushchair, a tattooed man naked to the waist, a jogger stretching against the wall. Then a pub, people milling outside, getting drunk and pretending to be happy. A supermarket, the car park rammed. Dog walkers. In Nepal, no one walked a dog except the servant of a state governor.

The ring road was busy but moving, and Hant matched the speed of other vehicles. Ram stared out, still mesmerised. Dark sleek cars like Bengal monitors, and bright four-wheel drive jeeps darting in and out of the traffic like danphes. A low loader with four shiny red and black tractors. Another carrying a house.

'*Kahaan?*'

Hant leant over with an outstretched hand, but the boy edged away.

'Where?'

Hant nodded. 'Wait and see.' It would be lesson two for the boy.

Hant turned off the ring road, and at a traffic light, consulted his phone. Shelley Street, left, third on the right. He glanced down beside him. A wheel brace stuck out from under the seat, and an old t-shirt filled the door pocket. He leant down, and felt around in the rag. His fingers gripped the handle of a pair of kitchen scissors, sharp but cheap. He'd bought five pairs for £9.99. A future lesson for the boy: knives worried police, everyday items didn't. He pushed them up his sleeve, the boy oblivious.

He didn't park the van in Shelley Street, but the next one. He ensured it faced the way they'd come, and there was half a car's distance in front. So much for the boy to learn; later, he'd talk him through the day. Not now. If he told him now, the boy would ask why.

They walked to Shelley Street. Cars parked bumper to bumper, kids playing football in the road. Hant looked up and down. The boy glanced into the cars, and stared at the houses, bristling with satellite dishes and boiler vents. Number 25B.

Hant rang the bell, and stood back. Tubs of brilliant multicoloured flowers sat on the window ledges either side of the door. The boy waited by the gate, but that was okay.

He rang the bell again. A curtain twitched two houses along.

The door opened to reveal an old woman. She was smoking, and wore purple slippers with matching pom-poms. It looked like a child had made them.

'Mrs Rao?'

The woman coughed like a vacuum cleaner and held the door for support. She nodded, her eyes watery from her hacking cough.

'Anoop's mother?'

'He not live here.'

Whether his driver lived there or not was beside the point. Hant fingered out the scissors, and glanced back at the gate. The boy's attention was now on his uncle. Good. Lesson two about to begin.

Hant snipped the air, and let the familiar metallic twang fade away. He snipped again. He stepped to the right and cut the bright flowers from the tub, leaving stalks like scythed rice. The old woman's mouth dropped open. Ash fell from her cigarette. He stepped left, and butchered the second tub.

'Say Anoop, no talk.'

The old woman pushed the door, but Hant wedged a foot. 'What you say him?'

'No talk.' She nodded like a toy.

171

Hant withdrew his foot and the door shut with a click.

The two of them walked back to the van in silence. Ram no longer looked around, but stared at the crumbling pavement. Hant dropped the scissors down a drain. A bribe sometimes worked, as did violence, but to guarantee someone did, or didn't do something, threatening their family was infallible. *Dharma* began at home.

They drove away, the indicator echoing in Hant's ears. Beating time like a village drummer.

29

Opposite Elly's room, the building site vibrated and groaned. Workmen shouted and wolf-whistled. They'd hooked up a column of overlapping tubes from the top of the scaffolding to a skip at the bottom. Building detritus thundered down.

Calix sat at the balcony door, smoking and staring out. Occasionally, he walked over to the partition with Barney's room and held a glass to the wall. His friend still wasn't back from the police station.

Could he trust him? He lit another cigarette and worked through the logic. Yes, otherwise he would have been arrested and returned to Strangeways. Then again, as the pressure on Barney mounted – your whole life before you shit – he wasn't sure his friend wouldn't crack. He tapped ash from the cigarette. Barney not returning didn't clarify matters: he could have been charged, or moved to a safe-house.

His old man always had a Plan B. He pulled out Barney's mobile and phoned TBR.

'Heard you're a free dog.'

'You hear everything, Red.' Calix swapped hands with the phone. 'Do you know where Khetan is putting his head down? And how he got out of Belmarsh?' He swapped the phone back. 'I kept quiet in there.'

'I already come good on that. Paid to slow down the squealers.'

Calix didn't know what TBR was talking about, but asking too many questions, even any questions, wasn't sensible. He waited, nodding his head to the drum 'n' bass he could hear in the background.

'I'm a businessman.'

'How much?'

'The house, dog.'

Calix toe-tapped the sill of the balcony door. 'That's a high price.'

'The market's illiquid.'

'Works both ways.'

'You always were a smart dog.'

Calix pocketed the phone. If sending the machine guns to high ground to give covering fire didn't work, then the mortars would have to be used. Gleaning the whereabouts of Khetan from Ram was Plan A, TBR the mortars. His old man the field marshal.

The day ticked by. The workmen broke for lunch, and sat in small groups with flasks and snap boxes. They smoked and gassed, and threw scraps for the pigeons.

Calix felt his eyelids closing. Pinching his cheeks, he was reminded of his old man's stories of doing sentry duty as a recruit. His constant battle with sleep, and his tactics: chewing gum, yanking out hairs, pinching his face. He pictured the family dinners when his old man wasn't on manoeuvres. Calix and Megan fighting over the pork crackling, their mother keeping order. Later, the two siblings smoking behind the shed, and later still, smoking weed in the wood. He was doing all this for his old man, for Megan, for the three of them.

A key turned in the lock.

Calix leapt up, and backed out of sight. He slid open the wardrobe, a not unpleasant prospect.

'It's me.' Elly's voice.

She walked into the main room. She wore a red leather jacket and a pink cotton hat, and looked relaxed as a deckchair. A fisherman's fly was hooked into her hat. He pictured her wearing a real mink and holding up a sawn off.

The cushions and blankets still lay on the floor from where Calix had tried to sleep. He could have tidied up, should have tidied up. It was her room.

'Did you see anyone?'

Elly shook her head. 'There's a notice on the main door. And everyone's talking about it. About you. About two years ago, and last year.' She plonked a carrier bag on the side. 'I got a takeout – Vietnamese.'

Calix folded blankets, and Elly made her strong tea. They sat cross-legged in the middle of the floor, and ate with the cheap wooden chopsticks. Mixed chicken rice, super hot, and greasy crackers. He was good with his hands and adept with the chopsticks. He ate quickly, surprised at his hunger. The rice, eating on the floor, the intensity of his project, reminded him of Nepal. Despite things, he'd been okay in Nepal. Not very okay, but okay.

Elly leant over and nabbed one of his prawns. He clutched at it mid-air, and for a second they wrestled, but he loosened his pinch. He drank half his tea, not sure why he'd let her win. Elly picked up her drink, still chewing the pilfered prawn. She peered at him over the rim of her mug.

'Hedgehog lecture, was it?'

She nodded. 'The Romans bred them for longer spines, larger animals. They took them in cages when they went to war. Sort of mascots.'

'Is that so?'

Elly put down her half-eaten tray, and nodded it was his to finish. She wiped her lips with a serviette and scrunched it away into the paper bag.

'What now?'

They heard the noise at the same time. A key in next door's lock, the door opening and slammed shut. Whoever had entered was not trying to be quiet. Music boomed out, then stopped. The television likewise. Whoever had occupied Barney's room was not only not being quiet, but intent on making a noise.

'You want me to?' said Elly, her eyes flicking at Barney's room.

Calix nodded.

She finished her tea and went out, shutting the door with a click.

Calix waited at the threshold of the balcony. He lit a cigarette, and blew out tramlines of smoke. A dustcart rumbled along the road, and two men loaded great bins of stinking refuse. Outside, the afternoon dawdled like a tired child.

Elly came back.

'Sit,' said Calix, stubbing out the cigarette.

She sat.

'It is Barney, but he was a bit odd. Unfriendly, rude even. Didn't mention you. I asked how he was, what had happened.'

'What did he say – exactly?'

'He said he stunk, he needed a shower. I should stay away. He then tried to make a joke of it, I should move out!' Elly took off her hat and mussed her hair.

'Anything else?'

'He said, he was late with Professor Edgerton's assignment.'

'Who's he?'

Elly grabbed her phone and tapped the screen. 'Teaches criminal law… last assignment he set was advising a client who's been arrested following a surveillance operation.'

Barney's door slammed. 'See ya, Elly!' Footsteps thumped away down the corridor.

Ninety minutes later, Calix put on his trainers. He tucked the cigarette packet in his back pocket. He pulled open Elly's cupboard drawers and rifled through the contents. She observed him as if she was watching a demonstration and later might be asked questions. He found her hats and scarves and rummaged back and forth. After selecting a dark headover, he took a pillow from the bed and removed the case. He ripped down the seam, opened it out and folded it along the diagonal. Tied the corners in a knot. Then arranged his left arm in a makeshift sling. It wasn't perfect, but it would do.

'Your purse.'

'It's okay,' said Elly, standing up. 'I'm coming with you.'

30

Rick waited for his mum in the car park at Three Views. A gardener shuffled along the border of the lawn with edging shears. A stream trickled into a pool, and together with the regular *clip-clip* of the shears, the plash of the falling water soothed his Coniston headache. He didn't have time, but he forced himself to make time. Always hoping for a glimpse of the old Dad. The real Dad. Normal Dad.

He phoned Hunter.

'Any movement?'

'Williams opened his blinds, but that's it so far.'

'You all plotted up?'

'Ready as ferrets in a poacher's knapsack.'

Rick redialled.

'Anything yet from the UC, Kasim?'

'Was about to phone you, sir. It's rumoured that Coniston was *tight* with Patel, and had unlocked his handcuffs so he could escape at the cemetery. Of course, we know that's not true, Coniston's handcuffs were chopped. What now?'

'Arrest and interview, house search.'

'Yes, sir, thank you, sir.'

Rick's phone lit up with a call from Robbo. He blew his

cheeks out. It was the way the police hierarchy was meant to work: check up on staff below, pull a face when a supervisor called. There was no sign of his mum, so he answered.

'If it's not too much to ask, I'd like an update.'

'I've got surveillance running on Williams which might lead us to Coniston. Having interviewed him I'm sure he was the driver. Even better would be triangulating his phone. My hunch is he's lent it to Coniston. I wondered if you'd changed your mind on authorising.'

'And what do I write in the box asking for the imminent risk to life?'

'His conspiracy with Khetan led to three deaths.'

'That was two years ago.'

Rick took a deep breath. 'I think Coniston is going after Khetan.'

'It's you with the conspiracy theory. How many more times, No.' Rick puffed his cheeks out again. 'How long have you had this now?'

'Three days.'

'You've got a week.'

'Another week?'

'Four more days.'

An old Volvo pulled onto the gravel and parked next to Rick's car. His mum climbed out wearing a dress and make-up and carrying a cake tin.

'Got to go, Hunter's calling.' A lie, used both up and down the chain.

Dad's ensuite smelt like a school locker-room. Rick opened a window, and his mum set out the cake and crockery on the small table.

'I feel guilty when I'm here, and guilty when I'm not here.' She glanced over her shoulder at the open door. Still no sign or sound of Dad. She picked up his cardigan from the armchair and hung it in a cupboard.

'You're here,' said Rick. 'That's all that counts, for both of you.'

He bent down towards the cake. It smelt the same as usual.

'You did add?'

She nodded.

Rick's phone buzzed with a text from Hunter. *No change, no change*

Through the window, the gardener reached a corner of the lawn, lifted and swivelled the shears and snipped back into the corner. Rick closed his eyes, and massaged his neck. *Clip-clip. Clip-clip.*

'I don't want to!' Dad's voice from the corridor. 'Am I in borstal?'

Michael walked into the room, propelling Dad by the arm and shoulder. He mouthed hello at Rick.

'They've come specially to see you, Roger, brought you a cake.'

'A cake!'

Dad wore a yellow t-shirt with a palm tree motif, and jeans without a belt. Slip on shoes. It was all wrong, and Rick felt sorry for his mum. She cringed, then set her face, nodding as if she was talking to herself.

'Roger, darling!' She pecked his cheek. Behind them, Michael slipped out and shut the door.

'Hello, Dad.'

His dad looked at him, and tilted his head. 'Do I know you?' He walked over to the window, and pulled it shut.

'I was doing a puzzle of the Queen's Silver Jubilee. 1977. I bet you didn't know the Royal Mint produced 37 million crowns to celebrate.' He shuffled over to a chest of drawers. 'I've got one somewhere.'

Rick caught his mum's eye. He smiled and shrugged and tried to convey love and reassurance and understanding and going with the flow.

'Roger, come and sit down, and have some cake.'

Mum boiled the kettle, and made tea. She sat down, cut the cake. Dad rummaged in the drawer, finally yanking it out and emptying it on the bed. Handkerchiefs and socks were cast aside. He emptied a box of medals, a tin of pens and pencils. He opened another drawer and removed a shoebox. Emptied it on the bed and worked his way through.

'He used to be so neat and tidy.' She poured three cups of tea, and ate a Garibaldi.

Rick's phone buzzed a second time. 'Sorry, Mum, I'd better take this.'

'It's fine, darling.'

Rick stood and went over to the window. The gardener was cleaning his shears with a rag. 'Gary?'

'Williams is on the move. Leaving Hartford now.'

'Okay, keep me updated.'

'Found it!' said Dad. 'Look!'

Rick examined the coin in its pink protective casing. The queen, so young-looking, the coin buffed, immaculate. He steered Dad to a chair and eased him down.

'Mum's made you a cake.'

'Is it fruit?'

'It is.'

They watched him eat an enormous slice. Start to finish, no conversation, no drinking tea. Like someone sawed a log, or pumped a tyre. Dad tried the tea. He pulled a face. No sugar, Rick knew. It killed Mum to add sugar; a new habit, and so downmarket.

Rick's phone buzzed. *Sorry*, he mouthed at Mum.

She shook her head.

'Gary?'

'Williams is doing anti-surveillance. Walked round and round a tower block, doubled back through an alley and eyes all over. We could be on here.'

'Leaving now.' Rick shoved his chair under the table. Dad was eating another huge slice of cake.

'He's always had hollow legs.'

Rick necked the remainder of his tea. Don't expect a miracle, he'd told his mum. But maybe something, if Dad ate the whole cake, and a few more like it. Even a small change, a hint of recognition.

'Can I go now?' said Dad, standing up. He opened the door and walked out. Rick squeezed his mum's hand. She let it lie for a few seconds, then crying silently, began to cut up the cake and pile the slabs into the tin.

Rick jogged out to the car, ready to shoot Coniston if they found him.

On the way to the city centre, he fitted his earpiece and Hunter assigned him callsign Delta 7. Grey clouds lumbered overhead and spits of rain spotted the dusty windscreen.

The team were plotted up around a McDonald's, and waiting for the next instruction. Delta 3 stood in the queue inside the restaurant, Delta 4 sat at a bus stop opposite, and everyone else waited in cars a block or more away. Rick wedged his car into a metered bay outside a barber's.

Hunter phoned. 'Williams came straight here from Hartford. Long queue so only just been served; has sat down to eat. What did the super say—'

'He's on the move, Delta 3.'

'Talk later,' said Rick. In the barber's, a youth with a green Mohican swept the floor.

'Got him, Delta 4. He's out, out, out. Turned right. Now

caught at a traffic light.' Rick edged the car out of the space. 'Green man, he's crossing. Straight on. Now into a newsagent, I'll stop to look at the notices.'

'Delta 6,' said Hunter, 'replace Delta 4 when target exits.'

'Buying cigarettes, Delta 4.'

Coniston smoked, but Williams didn't. Rick chewed a nail, and puttered in first gear to the end of the street. He waited. A car beeped behind him, and he pulled over the junction.

'Target's out, out, Delta 6. Right, as before. Crossing the road by the university. The library I think. Into the park. Through the park.'

Rick reversed back into the junction, U-turned and drove back. Cars hooted. He needed a driver, he was the DCI. He was the DI.

'He's exited the park, Delta 6. Down a side-street, and onto Lower North. There's a bus. He's running for it. Definite no, no for me. Sarge?'

'Delta 2-2,' said Hunter.

'All mine, Delta 2-2.'

Rick scanned the A-Z, and holding it in his left hand, drove to the end of the street. He gunned the car across, and to the T-junction. Stopped for a woman pushing a buggy. Left was one-way, the wrong way, so he went forward another block. Left was again one-way. He turned left, hugging the parked cars. A driver in a transit shook his wrist.

'Bus heading for Stockport, 56A. Can't see target, Delta 2-2.'

Rick spotted the bus, and a small cheap scooter tootling behind it. He was too close, and showing out. He turned into the entrance of a tiny garage unit, and leaving the engine running, flopped down onto the passenger seat.

'Held at roundabout, Delta 2-2. Now on, over roundabout, still heading for Stockport.'

A woman in oily overalls knocked on the window with a

spanner. Rick straightened, mouthed an apology, and reversed the correct way into the one-way street. He drove towards Stockport, and imagined the other surveillance cars doing the same, tracking the bus like wasps to an ice-cream.

'Held at a bus stop, Delta 2-2. No sign of the target.'

Rick drove over a roundabout, past a man selling roses. An array of bouquets, and a roughly written sign: £3-50 each. Maggie loved roses, loved all flowers. His heart-rate purred. Police work, real police work made him feel good.

'Target is getting off the bus. Off, off, off, Delta 2-2.'

'Delta 8, please,' said Hunter.

'I'm down, have eyes, Delta 8.'

Rick slowed, bumped up the kerb, and waited. An old mattress and a cooker sat in a tiny front garden. On the dirty front door a broom handle poked out of the letterbox.

'He's turned down Thomas Street. Stopped at a tatty bike shop. Gone inside. I can't stop or go in.'

'Delta 2-3,' said Hunter.

Rick searched the internet for bike shops on Thomas Street. *ABC cycles, cheap and cheerful repairs.* He cross-searched the police database. Two cycle mechanics had couriered drugs for TBR. The drug-dealer's involvement would also explain Williams' anti-surveillance tactics. He picked off the chewed nail and it started bleeding. The front door opened and a young boy wearing shorts stood on the threshold. A woman appeared, slapped the boy on the leg and slammed the door. The broom handle was yanked inside. Rick wrote down the address and called it in. He sucked his finger.

Hunter phoned. 'What did the super say about triangulating his mobile?'

'He said No, so we'd better not lose Williams.'

'We won't, but if we do, I know someone.'

Rick picked another nail. He wiped the blood off his phone.

A plate was pushed out through the letterbox and smashed on the ground. Inside the house there was shouting. He made a second call to the control room.

He phoned Hunter. 'Is there a back entrance?'

'It's not on the street map.'

'Window?'

'I'll burn Delta 8.' Hunter switched to the surveillance radio. 'Enter the shop, Delta 8.'

Rick slammed the steering wheel. If they lost Williams, then what? Get Hunter's mate to triangulate Williams' phone? It would prove Maggie right, show he was changing and slipping down the slippery slope. Blackmailing Robbo last year, obtaining the cannabis for Dad, now circumventing procedure. For each one, the ends justified the means. Dad's health, or the Job. No profit or personal advantage.

'Target's not there, Delta 8. Am I okay to put the brake-pads on expenses?'

'No!' shouted Rick. 'Take them back.'

A marked police car bumped up the pavement in front of his car. The two officers, one tall, one tiny, nodded in his direction. Rick climbed out, thought better about it, and climbed back in.

He phoned Hunter, and shouted again: 'Do Williams' phone, and whatever you have to, to get hold of Darren Back.'

31

The CCTV room at Hartford doubled as the porters' office. It smelt of egg sandwiches. Battered lockers lined the back wall and a column of traffic cones stood in a corner. Radios and cudgel-length torches sat recharging.

Rick, Hunter, and Paulson crowded behind Max, the head porter and general fixit man, and stared at the bank of screens. Paulson smelt of the swimming pool. Students entered and left the building all day and all night. Rick jabbed his teeth with a finger. No sign of Darren Back, and triangulation not the miracle clue he'd hoped for. Williams' phone had been switched off while he was in custody which took them no further forward. It could have run out of battery, or manually powered down. The location at the time was the vicinity of Williams' room, conceivably half of the building.

Hunter beckoned Rick to the back of the room.

'Max is ex-Job, he's quite happy to let us into a few rooms.' Hunter poked at his nose, squashing it flat one way, then the other. 'So?'

Rick took a deep breath. He'd slipped down the slope, but he hadn't fallen to the bottom. They couldn't search 350 rooms looking for Coniston, and anything less was dartboard policing.

'You stay here with Paulson, recheck the CCTV. I'll kill Woods if he hasn't done it properly.'

Leaving them to it, he went outside.

Three skateboarders rattled past, one sliding down a banister on a set of steps. He decided to walk round the building before driving away, and he followed the three boarders. They wore baggy black t-shirts with low-slung jeans, and talked in code. Shrubs and a flowerbed covered in woodchip ran down the side of the campus. The case flip-flopped around his head; he was starting to think Williams' visit to the bike shop was a distraction. He reached the corner and turned. Opposite, a similar sized campus was being built, and workmen in yellow helmets dotted the site.

Halfway along the rear of the building there was a door. *Loading and Unloading Only. Ask Porter for Key.*

Woods!

He surveyed the building line across the road, then finished the circuit and returned to the CCTV room. Hunter and Kasim hadn't moved, Max was at the kettle.

'There's a back door, Gary, no external camera, but there's a couple across the street that might reach. Try the council, and Paulson, you knock the shops.'

After two minutes back in his office, there was a queue of five people. Kasim, Bennett, Tara, Maggie, and Robbo. He could have written a paper on prioritisation: rank, importance to the case, and personal preference. Maggie said her update was urgent, but said she'd come back, and the other three followed her away. Robbo closed the door.

The superintendent was jacketless, and his crisp white shirt bulged over the front of his trousers. Rick made him an instant coffee in a mug. Robbo doubled the milk and spooned in a heap of sugar.

'Have you looked at the Carmichaels file?'

'No.'

'I want him out – whether he's your friend or not.'

'He's done a lot for the Job.'

'Out, and soon.'

Rick stared blankly at the superintendent.

'Coniston?'

'We're getting closer. I'll tell you.' Rick drank some of his coffee. Black, despite preferring it with milk. Being in the presence of Robbo made him eschew every calorie.

'Got something else for you.'

Rick made a face.

'Do you want to get back to DCI?'

Rick scratched an old bee sting on the back of his hand, and felt like Hunter. He glanced at his phone, but there were no messages.

'I assume that's a Yes.' Robbo tried his coffee, then added more sugar. 'This is a bit sensitive. Consider it a personal favour. Yesterday, I found dog shit on the bonnet of my car, and today the windscreen wipers have been bent. CCTV's not working; software issue, waiting for technical.' He sipped his coffee. 'You got any biscuits?'

Rick shook his head. 'Who've you pissed off?'

'Funny.'

'Apart from me.'

'My wife, and Elaine. But this isn't them, and they've already acted. Janice took my golf clubs to the dump, and Elaine's stopped talking to me – and making me cakes.'

'Why are you asking me?'

'Because Gary Hunter works for you, and between the two of you, you cover the best and worst of detective policing.' Robbo drained his coffee, pushed the mug onto Rick's desk and padded out. In the bottom of the mug lay a light-brown sludge.

'Next,' yelled Rick.

Maggie wheeled in. She wore an orange blouse and black half-length trousers with a silver trim.

'Williams' alibi is false. I watched the Ruzzo CCTV 'til I was seeing double.' She turned on the monitor at the back of the room.

Television news appeared, and a breaking story about the migration crisis. A young boy in a red t-shirt and blue shorts lay face down on a beach, his head in the water. He was dead, the result of an inflatable boat packed with migrants having sunk.

The two of them stared at the boy, washed up on the sand like an old shoe or piece of driftwood.

'Difficult to imagine what he went through,' said Maggie. There were tears in her eyes. Small waves rolled up the beach, and broke over the body.

'The boy,' said a commentator, 'is one of a dozen Syrian refugees feared drowned as they tried to cross the Mediterranean heading for the Greek island of Kos.' The narration paused as an official walked into the water and scooped up the body. The boy hung limply, water dripping down.

'This is happening in Europe. *Europe.*' She switched channels to the DVD player. 'Migration's a good thing.'

'I agree.'

'Our fertility rate is falling and if we're not careful we'll end up with ghost towns like in China. Migration helps, but we need to have children, too.'

Rick raised his eyebrows. Maggie meant the country, not the two of them. Didn't she? They weren't married, and they'd never even talked about it.

'Don't you think?'

'I think there are too many people in the world,' said Rick.

Maggie waited for him to continue.

'Not only in terms of food capacity but also for social

cohesion. People need to get out to the countryside, the coast, even the local park, and if they don't, they get frustrated, pent-up and bored. Which leads to disorder and crime. Overpopulation is at the centre of all the world's current problems – but no one ever mentions it.'

'So, you don't want children?' Maggie clattered the DVD into the machine.

'The DVD's not working,' said Rick. Of course he did.

'Now you tell me.' She swiped a sideways glance at him, and ejected the disc.

'Sorry.'

She set down the remote. 'I'll summarise it. Williams arrived at the cinema at 10.18 and left at 12.33, that much fits his story. But I collected the previous fortnight's CCTV and started watching. When *Drowning* starts showing, it plays every weekday morning at 10.30. Four days before Coniston's escape, I hit the jackpot. Williams arrived at the cinema at 10.23 and left at 12.32. The next day, he saw the film again.'

'And on the day itself?'

'He didn't leave or re-enter through the front, I double-checked, but he could easily have ducked out through a fire-exit.'

'Giving him enough time – just – to drive the getaway car and make it back for the credits. Clever. Not definitive, but enough to get Williams back in for another interview. Thanks.'

Maggie handed him the DVD, and turned to go. Behind her, Kasim appeared in the doorway. Rick held up two fingers, and the young detective withdrew. 'Maggie.' She looked round, her face pre-set. 'You know you'd have made a first-class detective.'

'Against the rules,' she said, thumping down on the arms of the chair with her fists. It creaked underneath her. 'No legs, you may have noticed.'

'I meant *before*: before Helmand, before the army, before any of that. If you'd joined the Job instead.'

'The Job might be your answer to everything, but it's not mine.'

'Mags, do you never think—'

'No, I don't.' She paused. 'That's the thing about life, there's no rewind button.'

He'd meant it as a compliment, that he was on her side, and wanted her to know. 'I treat you like a detective – in my mind you *are* a detective.'

She stared at Rick for a few seconds, then finally nodded. 'I know you do.' Her words barely a whisper, her face uneasy. She grabbed his hand and pulled him closer. Kissed him gently on the lips.

'Kasim!' she called over his shoulder.

As Maggie went out, Kasim walked in. Looking smart as a mannequin in a men's outfitters.

'Got an update, sir, on Sakit Patel. As discussed, arrested and interviewed him this morning. He folded almost immediately. Said the five k was a payment to turn a blind eye while a drugs package was delivered at visiting. He'll be sacked eventually, but there's a possibility he might continue as an informant. The NCS are coming over.'

'What did he say about Coniston?'

'Knows him to recognise, and knows where his mother lived. Saw him a couple of times in the prison garden, but no idea about the break. Seemed genuine. Sorry, sir.'

'That's the Job for you, Kasim. One step forward, one step back, until the step forward reveals a hidden world. It was a good idea – although next time, use one of our financial investigators.'

'Yes, sir.'

'Word of advice, too, Kasim. Don't become an FI – they're accountants who occasionally wear body armour. If you want to be an accountant, leave and earn ten times the salary.'

'I couldn't leave, sir,' said Kasim, 'I love it.'

Rick felt a stab of brotherhood pride. Most police lost their enthusiasm for the Job, but his motivation had never waned. If anything, he was more determined. 'Cheer up, I'm not reassigning you to the property store, and seeing as you like the financial stuff, can you chase up the FI's report on Coniston and Williams?'

'Yes, sir. Thank you, sir. Straight away, sir.' He turned, and almost bumped into Bennett who'd slid into the room and was polishing his glasses.

'Two minutes, Simon.'

Bennett nodded, kept polishing.

Rick phoned Hunter. 'Anything?'

'Yeah, I'm at the council control room. Mother of miracles, their camera covers that door and is working. Just started watching – from the time Coniston got off at Piccadilly.'

'Alleluiah!'

Rick put the phone down. 'Now, Mr Bennett?' His light-hearted mood evaporated as fast as it had arrived. Bennett had once been as keen as Kasim and Paulson, but working with Woods had killed his enthusiasm. It would have killed anyone's.

Bennett hooked his glasses around his ears, and placed a file on Rick's desk. 'Report from technical on Williams' laptop. In brief, no emails or other messaging to Coniston, or Hant Khetan. But, browsing history shows plenty of interest in both of their antecedents, and their criminal cases. It also reveals Williams' recent fascination for anti-surveillance tactics.'

Rick made a note. 'Woods made a hash of the Hartford CCTV trawl.'

'He's better with people.'

'You don't mind partnering him?'

Bennett shook his head. 'He's seen most things, and lets me lead the play.'

There was a light *tap-tap* on the door, and both men looked over at the waiting SOCO. She was sucking a lolly. Rick beckoned Tara forward. 'Thanks, Simon.' Rick pulled over the file, and Bennett walked out.

'Tara?'

'Nothing really on the car. A few fibres, that's it. The rugby magazine was too burnt to be of any use. Better luck with the photo of Williams and the Nepalese boy. Part of the address on the envelope is impressed into the photo, so very likely the photo arrived in the envelope. And the photo's real, not photoshopped. Fingerprints and DNA don't match anyone on the database. As you requested, I specifically checked Khetan.'

'Okay, thanks.' Rick took the proffered paperwork. 'Do you know what's up with Gary?'

Tara downed her spent lollystick in the bin, and unwrapped another sweet. 'Have you heard about his mum?' Her tongue was orange.

Rick shook his head.

'You'd better ask him.'

The SOCO exited, and finally he was alone. He stacked the new reports, and finished his notes while they were fresh. Williams was still not only the best lead, but becoming the only lead. Find Williams, find Coniston; find Coniston, and that's where it would end. No way Robbo would authorise another trip to Nepal to get Khetan.

He made coffee and unearthed the Carmichaels file. He read quietly, the clock ticking and his stomach rumbling. The complaint against Russell Weatherbeater had been made by the next-door neighbour of Velvet Carmichaels on behalf of the girl. Pattern of behaviour supported by two further complaints, both prisoners Russell had arrested. To which Rick could add what he'd seen in Williams' room at Hartford. He examined photos of Velvet's injuries; a black eye, and bruising to her arms. He listened to a 999 call, and read statements of attending officers.

He watched a clip of a custody video, one prisoner shying from Russell like a beaten dog. He read the doctor's report from the second prisoner. The conclusion was unambiguous: Russell had become a violent man. Rick had his theory as to why, and being responsible, it was only fair he solved it. For Velvet, for Russell, for the Job. One to ponder, amongst everything else.

He phoned Russell to request an interview, listened to a Nepal Adventures sales pitch, and left a message.

Draining the coffee, he turned to Robbo's second fly in his soup. Damage to his car. Had the uniform superintendent forgotten everything? Ten minutes, no more would Rick spend. He worked through his four questions starting with, *What do you know?* One phone call later, he knew there'd been no other reported damage. Which presented two hypotheses: a member of the public with a grudge, or someone who worked at the station.

After ten minutes, he phoned Hunter.

'Anything?'

'Nope.'

Paulson appeared in the doorway. 'Sandwich?'

Rick nodded.

'Chicken, or tuna?'

Rick ate, browsing the internet. He needed to do something to make it up to Maggie, something to show he was serious about her, something unexpected. He typed *used racing wheelchairs for sale* into Amazon. Nothing. He tried *second-hand racing wheelchairs*. Again, nothing. He tried eBay. Still nothing. He typed racing wheelchairs into a search engine, and at last, there were plenty of hits. The first for a company called PushPower, the next for Sitting Comfortably. He clicked through. PushPower sold five models. At random he selected the Elite XP racer. The effusive description made it sound as if the machine would win races by itself. Interested in a price, Rick clicked *Buy*. Up popped a maze of questions – seat angle, camber, kneel width – but, nothing about the number of gears. He figured he'd need twenty-one, same as a bicycle. He reversed back a page. The Elite XP had one gear. He checked other models, and cross-checked Sitting Comfortably. Every model was the same: one gear.

His phone rang.

Hunter's number.

Rick snatched it up.

'Got him.' Hunter's voice was flat, but that was Hunter. He only got excited if he didn't want to do something, or a prisoner didn't want to do something.

'You've nicked him?'

'What? No. On the CCTV. Entered Hartford via the unloading door about twenty minutes after he left Piccadilly station.'

'Get back there, and lock it down. No one in or out.'

Rick stuffed in the remaining half sandwich, no idea whether it was chicken or tuna, and ran down the corridor.

32

In the nearest park to Hartford a dozen teenagers played football between goals made from discarded clothing. They shouted and swore, and chased the ball like dogs. Two girls flew a red and green kite while their parents played cards across a picnic table. On the far side of the pond a group of mothers with prams and young children fed the swans and their cygnets. A baby was crying. The park was a green oasis in the desert of monotone Manchester.

Calix and Elly slipped out of the groundsman's hut and walked around the kiosk to the area of benches. There'd been no rush, and with his insistence on taking it in turns to keep watch through the night, the late start had been a chance to doze. His mouth tasted burnt, and he felt like he'd slept on a plane, but Elly looked as if she was straight out of a box.

They sat on a bench. He put the rolled-up sling between them. The air smelt of sweet popcorn and coffee. She sat with her legs crossed, jigging her feet up and down. She wore her red leather jacket and pink hat with the fish-hooks. The jacket had intricate hexagonal stitching across the padded shoulders, and large metallic fasteners on the lapels. Calix lit a cigarette, and checked the three access gates. He identified an emergency exit, a tree which grew over the railings. A decision to make: leave her, or take her?

He smoked down the cigarette.

Then pulled across Elly's bag. A cheap white cotton bag with a bookshop logo. Elly didn't murmur. He took out her purse and counted the cash. Six pounds and seven pence – enough for coffee and pastries at the kiosk. He removed her bank card, and glanced at the photo on her student ID. So young, and striking a pose even there. He rummaged through the rest of the bag. A black cardigan, and three pairs of knickers. Moisturiser, toothbrush, toothpaste. A box of face-paints. Her phone. He removed the battery, and hurled the phone into the pond. The splash attracted the swans, and the card-players glanced across.

'Why're you here?' said Calix. Elly pointed her foot, and her shoe fell off. 'That shit about your brother.'

'I'm an orphan.'

'I don't believe you.'

'My father beat me.'

'No, he didn't.'

Elly picked up her shoe. 'We're all insects. Groping towards something terrible or divine.'

'Is that a quote?'

'Philip K. Dick.' She pulled on her shoe. 'I don't do drugs, don't know any rock-climbers.'

Calix repeated Dick's line in his head. It was as if she'd looked it up especially for him, but he still wasn't sure. He looked at his watch, considered another cigarette. If the park was an oasis, he and Elly were nomads.

'Put it another way, why should I risk taking you with me?'

Elly watched a customer at the popcorn cabinet in front of the kiosk. The old Korean woman came out the front, wiping her hands on a cloth. 'Two reasons. I bring a second set of eyes and ears, and a second brain. And I brought my face-paints.'

Calix rechecked the exits. Elly had thought about it. She'd forgotten Barney, but she'd thought about it. She'd also forgotten her most useful contribution – as a hostage.

They watched the swans circling around the cygnets.

'Orange bills mean they're mutes. Trumpeters have black bills and come in two flavours. Whistlers have a small yellow spot near the eye. Whoopers have a yellow base, and are noisy devils. Bewick's are similar, but smaller and quieter.'

Elly turned her glass-green eyes on him.

'I like animals. I stuff them, but I like them. You ought to know that.'

'Okay.'

'You don't know why I'm doing what I'm doing.'

'I know enough.'

'You don't know what's next.'

'Do you?'

Calix lit another cigarette, and watched the kite riding the thermals, rising and rising, then thundering downwards, its red tail stretched taut. He pulled out his phone – Barney's handset, Calix's SIM card – and from memory dialled a number.

'Hello.' The voice sounded both aggressive and suspicious.

'You still with Wendy?'

'Nah, she's potatoes! Long time, Capeman, I heard you're out in the sunshine. What can I do yer for?'

Calix read out the details on Elly's bank card, and requested her account be used as far from Manchester as possible. He said he might need a second favour, too, and said he would phone again with details. Darren assured him the armourer would be put on notice.

He pocketed the phone, and pulled on the cigarette. Elly looked at him stoically. 'My account's overdrawn all the way.'

Calix nodded, not believing anything she said. It wouldn't have surprised him if her old man was a billionaire, and Elly a trust fund baby.

'You need some money, right?' said Elly. 'Let's rob the kiosk. I've often sat around this pond and wondered about it. She's a small woman. You ask for a punnet of popcorn, and I'll slip in the kiosk and raid the till.'

However desperate, he wasn't going to terrify an old woman. It would also alert the Welsh dibble yet alone the local ones, but perhaps she knew that. He could set another test, but there wasn't time. He stubbed out the cigarette.

'Enough.'

He stood up, flipped over his hood and walked a few metres away. Turned back. 'You coming?'

In Failston, they walked past Sakit's. The guard's house was quiet, the windows shut and the pale green blinds drawn. But, the three cars on the drive suggested Sakit was at home.

The two of them walked on. They held hands like girlfriend and boyfriend. She wore her pink hat with fish-hooks, Calix his hoodie. They turned right, and right again into his parents' road. His mother, his old man, and Megan. His road now. It was steep, always impassable in snow. They slowed, Elly's hand warmed. They passed the fallen oak tree, ever more rotten, the garden with the covered sailing boat, the tall beech hedges. White painted stones marked the grass verges.

'They're new,' said Calix, pointing at the stones.

Elly squeezed his hand as if their relationship was real. He liked the feeling, couldn't help it.

33

In the sallow haze of rush-hour a group of students gathered outside Hartford Hall. Cars and buses streamed along the surrounding streets, occupants glancing at the line of police vehicles and patrolling officers. Robbo stood nearby, kowtowing with a senior university administrator. He wore full uniform, his cap brushed, his white gloves like a puppet's.

Rick sat in his car, waiting for a call from Hunter in the council CCTV room. He'd assigned three detectives to help him watch the footage. He watched a skateboarder turn a trick. Behind him, tower blocks of silvery glass stretched into the sky. If Coniston hadn't exited, he was still inside Hartford. Which would return Rick to the dilemma of whether or not to search 350 rooms. He couldn't not. He'd ask the administrator for written permission but go ahead regardless. If a judge got to scrutinise his decision, it would be on their head to release Coniston. Rick would have done his job. The Job would have prevailed.

Rick's phone buzzed.

'Gary?'

'Going to take all day.'

'Okay.'

Robbo wouldn't stay – he never stayed. Like a child, the superintendent needed feeding every couple of hours.

Rick heard Russell on the police radio. He phoned the special constable who was on foot patrol in South Manchester and asked him to attend Hartford.

One skateboarder rode the banister down the steps. Two young officers intervened, and there was a scuffle. The van arrived, and the boy was handcuffed and taken away. The drone of traffic resumed.

Weatherbeater opened the passenger door, and climbed in nursing his helmet. 'Do you think he's in there?'

'Difficult to predict Coniston,' said Rick, glancing at the crowd of students, and the accommodation block rising above them. He respected their fugitive for it. 'But yes, right under our nose.'

The mountaineer adjusted the seat and stretched out his legs. 'Is this about Velvet?'

'It's about you.'

His friend stared through the windscreen. Robbo was speaking to a reporter, and the group of students growing.

'I think, Russell, you've got a problem.'

The mountaineer opened the car door and pushed it wide.

'If you get out, you're on your own. Stay, and I'll help you.'

Russell looked sideways. He stretched his head up and down, and sighed. He made a fist and cupped it, inspected the tight pale skin across his knuckles. He released his fingers. 'What do you mean, help?'

'Make the internal enquiry go away.'

Russell considered for a moment, then reached out and closed the door.

'There are two conditions. First, the violence stops, now, here – in my car. Second, you get professional help.'

Russell stroked the dark blue baize of his helmet. 'I like her, I really like her. I mean, I think I love her. It's just, she's young and—' He huffed on the silver-coloured badge and polished it on his trousers.

Rick cycled through some of his memories with the mountaineer and part-time police officer. The first time he'd met him at the Nepal Adventures office, inspecting the climbing wall entrance to a rear window. The plane ride to Lukla where the sycophantic Sandhurst recruits had lauded him like a war hero. His unflappable man-mountain presence in the Nepalese foothills. And perhaps he was heroic, the five-times Everest summiteer and arrest-table-topping special constable. Maggie had once told Rick that if she needed help, the sort of help the emergency services couldn't or wouldn't provide, she would ask Russell. Rick hadn't been sure what to think.

'Remain a special?'

'Remain a special,' said Rick.

'Alright.' Russell climbed out of the car. He fitted his helmet, and strode off towards Hartford. His stride asymmetric, and tragic as a Shakespeare play.

Hunter arrived, slewing his car to a halt in front of Rick's. The former flying squad officer climbed out, and leaving the door open slouched over.

Rick began to hope, he couldn't stop himself. Hunter had driven. Had left his door open. Hadn't dawdled. Rick buzzed down the window.

The sergeant ran a puffy hand across his throat. And a second time.

Rick hit the steering wheel.

'Fuck!'

'Coniston came out the unloading door yesterday afternoon. Had his arm in a sling. With a girl.'

'I thought because—' said Rick, pointing at Hunter's car door.

Hunter glanced back. 'Sorry.' He sniffed, and itched his nose. 'Want me to chew Woods?'

Rick climbed out of the car. 'Show me.'

Hunter took his phone from his breast pocket and flicked the screen. 'There.' The screen showed the rear of the campus building, the unloading door open and Coniston walking out behind a small Asian girl.

'Hostage?' said Rick.

'Possibly.'

Oliver appeared from nowhere, Dictaphone at the ready. 'What's happening?'

'Not a good time,' said Rick. 'I'll be in touch.'

The journalist shrugged. He wrote crime fiction in his spare time and tended to get creative if he wasn't kept updated.

The two detectives walked over to the group of students. 'Excuse me,' said Rick, holding up Hunter's phone, 'Anyone know who this girl is?' He showed a boy with headphones, a Japanese girl, two students in gym kit, a girl with long blonde hair.

'Elly Simmonds,' said the blonde girl. 'She lives on my corridor.'

'Have you got five minutes?'

She nodded.

Rick passed the phone back to Hunter, and whispered instructions. 'Let Robbo know the score, and stand everybody down. Take Russell and secure Simmonds' room. Search it for forced entry, signs of a struggle. Task Kasim to do Simmonds' background, and get Tara up there to confirm it's Coniston. I'll speak to this informant in my car.' Mentioning the SOCO reminded him he needed to speak to Hunter about his mum. Now wasn't the time.

Rick ushered the blonde student back to his car, and they climbed in. Robbo looked over in their direction but didn't approach. Police cars began driving away.

'So—'

'Mary. Mary Phelps. Is Elly okay?'

Rick twisted his body back against the door, and looked across at the young student. She was freckly, and had a splodge of green paint on her cheek. 'I don't know. Can you tell me everything you know about her.'

'I'm not like her friend or anything. She's way too cool for me. I don't really know who her friends are. She never has anyone round to her room.' Mary undid her hair and rethreaded it through a red elastic. 'Sorry, I don't know what you want.'

'Anything, everything.'

'She's doing philosophy, plays snake on her phone in the lift, lives on takeaways. The first time I met her, we were moving in, she told me her father was Sri Lankan, her mother French, and they live in an apartment in Paris. I thought you know, Wow! She's on my corridor as I said. Two doors down; me, Ison, her, Barney.'

'Barney Williams?'

'That's right. The hunk of the corridor. The building, really. He plays rugby for the university.'

'Are they friends, Barney and Elly?'

'I don't know. I don't think so. Not friend friends.'

'Anything else?'

Mary shook her head.

Rick thanked her, gave her a card, and watched her walk away. She looked round once as if she couldn't believe it was happening. No one could ever believe it was happening.

Maggie was waiting in his office. The plant she'd given him sat on the edge of the desk. He'd forgotten its name and forgotten to water it, and it was dying. It suddenly seemed important, and he reversed out and went to the kitchenette for some water. A mug didn't seem enough so he filled a small saucepan and returned. He poured the water into the pot, the cracked earth drinking the water without trace. Maggie watched him watching the water pour out into the saucer.

'I give it fifty-fifty.' She opened a folder. 'Kasim's been in touch, and I've dug up everything I can find on Elly Simmonds.'

Rick opened the window. Evens was better than he'd expected. Robbo's car stood in its reserved spot, the yard deserted. In the distance, the jingle of an ice cream van.

'From Hartford's admin office: second-year student, studying English Lit. Bright, but indifferent. Potential for a first. Little involvement in student life. Home address in East Anglia, lives with her mother – a fortune-teller, apparently. No siblings. Admin have a home phone number and a mobile for Elly. She has no convictions, but does have a caution for stabbing a classmate with a compass when she was fourteen. Social services also have a file. Two months after the caution, her father drowned when he fell off a cross-Channel ferry. An accident according to Dover police and the coroner.'

'Her mobile?'

'Switched off.'

Behind Maggie the door opened, and Robbo stood on the threshold. He held his hat in one hand and his white gloves in the other.

'Has he kidnapped her?'

'It's a possibility.'

'And there I was, thinking you had it all wrapped up. Two more days and I'm going to ask DCI Gibbs to take over.' The superintendent shook his head, and wandered away leaving the door open.

Maggie went across, shut the door, and came back.

'Does he always barge in like that?'

Rick see-sawed his head.

Maggie clicked her tongue. 'Rick, is it Skye's op this week?'

'It was meant to be. Postponed.' He could hear the crane operator chuntering. Heard himself swearing, and between their words, a keening. The hairs had stood on the back of his neck, and they stood now. Somehow, she wasn't dead. He knelt in the scrub and started giving mouth to mouth, and chest compressions. She was so small and thin, he was scared he might blow too hard or break her ribcage. The paramedics when they'd finally arrived not hopeful or even interested. *Another one off that scummy estate.*

Rick looked back into the room. At Maggie. He needed her, but he couldn't tell her that. It was the last thing she wanted to hear. 'How many gears are there on your wheelchair racer?'

'One, they all have one. Why?'

'Just wondered.'

Maggie wheeled to the door. She turned. 'If you want, next time you visit your dad at Three Views, I'll come with you.'

Rick nodded. He waited until he heard her moving down the corridor, then crumpled a sheet of paper, dropped it on the floor, dribbled it around his desk and whacked it through the open doorway. The crowd roared. At last something had gone right.

34

Under leaden skies, a nondescript lorry stood on the hard shoulder of the motorway. Further along, a white crime-scene tent. The six lanes of road were empty of traffic, the only vehicles belonging to the emergency services and the undertakers. Fire engines, ambulances, police cars, and a line of hearses parked one behind the other, the gaps between them equal. As if it mattered, and perhaps it did. Uniformed men and women moved around with purpose. Behind them, the nearest hill was flecked with sheep.

The lorry's rear doors were open, and its tail-lift halfway down. Two people in light blue forensic suits stood waiting.

Two more appeared from within the lorry carrying a bodybag. They passed it to the pair on the lift who passed it down to two more standing on the hard shoulder. The bodybag was ferried to the tent.

Water dripped from the lorry's undercarriage and formed a pool underneath. The sheep wandered around the hillside.

The video ended and DS Jim Hazelhurst turned to face South Manchester's detectives. He was in Liverpool for a month-long court case, and had promised Rick he'd come over and do a training session. The timing wasn't ideal, but life had to go on.

Eating, sleeping, a semblance of other enquiries. The Coniston case wasn't everything. Maggie's position, not his. Not Hunter's, not Kasim's.

'I know you're in the middle of a job so I won't blah on,' said Hazelhurst. He was a tall man with wide shoulders, and still in good shape. 'A quick briefing on the National Crime Agency, and an input on people-smuggling is what DI Castle requested. I'll do my best. The NCA leads the UK's fight against serious and organised crime. We have international reach and the mandate and powers to work with law enforcement organisations around the world.' He flicked onto his next slide. 'Five main strands of business: child exploitation, border policing, cybercrime, organised crime, and linking them all up, economic crime.'

Sitting at the back, Rick drifted off into considering the Coniston case. *What did he know?* Coniston had escaped from prison, Williams had driven the getaway car and continued to help him. TBR and Darren Back had visited Coniston in prison recently. Khetan's nephew Ram had sent Coniston a photo with the caption, See you soon. Khetan was a free man, released by MI6 on orders from across the Atlantic.

In front of him DS Hazelhurst progressed through the slides. 'Organised crime presents a number of specific threats. Shout them out.'

'Drugs,' said Bennett.

'Firearms,' said Woods. 'Kidnap, identity theft, money laundering.'

There was a pause.

'People-smuggling,' said Kasim.

'And people-trafficking,' said Hazelhurst. 'One more obvious one?'

'Theft?' said Woods.

'What sort?'

'Big ones,' said Hunter.

There was a ripple of laughter.

'You're not from up here,' said Hazelhurst.

'I used to be Met,' said Hunter. 'Croydon.'

'I thought I recognised you. You went to the flying squad – Gary Hunter. Gary Hunter and Mr Castle in one CID office. One room!'

A few of the junior detectives glanced in Rick's direction. He was used to it, had heard a lot worse although usually when people didn't know he could hear. Hunter scratched his wrist. His sergeant liked an argument, occasionally liked more than an argument.

Rick readied. However, Hunter seemed subdued, and for a day or two, now he thought about it.

The next slide – a dozen men wearing robes, sleeping in a garage – appeared on the screen, and Hazelhurst continued. The moment was over, and Rick returned to mulling the Coniston case.

He mined further back into the history. Hant Khetan, the FBI's most wanted man in South Asia was responsible for the deaths of the fathers of both Coniston and Williams. He wondered if that was the connection with Elly Simmonds: Khetan was somehow involved in pushing her father off a ferry? Was she involved with Coniston and Williams, or was she their hostage? Her mother a fortune-teller revealed everything and nothing about the student.

So much he didn't know. *Hypotheses?* H1, Coniston escaped as an end in itself, could be discounted. H2, Coniston escaped as a means to an end. What end? Revenge against Khetan seemed the most likely option. But how, now Khetan was hiding somewhere in Asia. Then, H3, escape forced on Coniston by an organised crime group. TBR had bribed Yates to slow the investigation, his motive unclear. Darren Back not in that league.

What did he need to know? More on Elly Simmonds. An

account from Darren Back. The whereabouts of Coniston – if Rick had that, he had everything.

'Good effort,' said Hazelhurst. 'We'll move on to people-smuggling.' He flicked forward another slide. It showed a crowd of Asian women and children, sparsely clothed and scared-looking. One young girl in a faded yellow dress stared at the camera. Hooped earrings, bracelet, a fat lip. 'What's the difference between smuggling and trafficking?'

Kasim cleared his throat. 'Smuggling is getting people from A to B. Transport. Trafficking is using them when they get there. Exploitation.'

'Spot on,' said Jim. 'You want to watch him, Mr Castle. He'll be after your job.' He forwarded another slide – six young white girls climbing out of a horsebox in a motorway service station. 'People-smuggling is similar to importing drugs, but more of a political hot potato. Plenty of opportunities for cross-selling so a people-smuggler might also be a trafficker, might also be exploiting children. Almost certainly, they'll be laundering money. Money is at the root of everything, and there's a lot of money to be made.'

Rick wandered off again. The whereabouts of Coniston. Heading to the coast and a small boat. A light aircraft? Europe, then Nepal? He'd need money and help. Rewind to TBR. Surveillance? Rewind further. Coniston exits from Hartford with Simmonds. What would they want first? Food. Cigarettes. Coniston smoked. Worth a speculative trawl of all the local newsagents. But, then what? A sighting was almost worthless. Would he hire a car? So far, Coniston had used a bicycle and taken the train. Second guessing him was hard. Respect to him – again.

'What can you do for us?' said Hazelhurst. 'We need information, intelligence, and informants; the three Is. What can we do for you? Deal with your intel. We can run proactive operations as well as turn up and deal with your prisoners.

'Questions?'

Maybe, Rick was crediting his opponent too much. With or without Williams and Elly Simmonds, Coniston couldn't leave the country. He or they would come to notice. The ports, the major railway stations, even the private airfields were on high alert. He would just have to wait. He stared at the final slide – a reprise of the lorry from the video. The slide was black and white and looked like a print in a museum. The light-coloured lorry, tent, empty road and hooded forensic officers against the backdrop of the dark sky.

The lorry.

And there it was, staring him in the face.

'Do they smuggle anybody in the opposite direction?'

Hazelhurst nodded. 'It does happen. Last year, a nominal from an OCG tried to leave the UK by hiding in the back of a lorry. He was wanted for supplying drugs and attempted murder. Border police at Folkestone found, and arrested him. There's not much demand, and prices are lower.'

Rick nodded. So it was possible that the two of them, or the three of them, were going to be smuggled out of the country. *Or had been.* Which meant the end. The end of the Coniston investigation, the end of his vague hope to nail Khetan on the back of it. The end of his effort to get his old job back. Along with his self-esteem. His stomach lurched like the final throw of a washing-machine.

But it wasn't the end, not until he *knew* Coniston had left the UK.

'Couple more questions, Jim.' Rick had fifty. What did the NCA know about people-smugglers in Manchester, their collection and drop-off points, the fixers, the drivers, the nominals behind it? Names and places. The hard intel.

*

Rick ate lunch in the back of the surveillance van in the yard. The superintendent's black Range Rover stood in its marked bay. Wing mirrors folded inwards, bodywork gleaming. Behind Robbo's car pigeons perched on the razor wire of the perimeter wall. The yard was deserted save for two PCs smoking at the back door of the station.

He was multi-tasking. Maggie would laugh.

The sky cerulean blue, and looking up he could have been in Nepal. Even if it was only 14C, at least it looked like the summer.

The PCs shared a joke, stubbed out their cigarettes, and buzzed back into the building.

Rick finished the vending machine bap and balled the excess of cling film. He bit into an apple.

He wanted to be alone and figure his next move with Coniston. Hazelhurst had refused any smuggling intel until he'd spoken to his boss. None would be forthcoming. The squads were all the same: they sucked up divisional intel but disseminated next to nothing. And what they did, was out of date.

The station door opened, and Robbo stepped out. He waddled across the yard to his car, and clicked it open. He leant inside and took something from the dashboard. Rick lifted his binoculars. Robbo wiggled out a sweet from a packet of wine-gums. Rick lowered the glasses. Robbo walked round to the back of the car. He lifted the rear windscreen wiper, then looked around the yard. The yard was empty. Rick realised he had neither corroboration of the broken front wipers, nor a witness to the shit on the bonnet. He lifted his camera.

Robbo flexed the rear wiper back and forth.

Rick rested a finger on the camera's shutter release; if Robbo damaged his own car, Rick would be DCI before the end of the day.

The superintendent folded the windscreen wiper down. He

checked both sides of the car, and walked round the front. He glanced across the yard, locked the car, and walked back to the building.

The pigeons returned to the razor wire. Rick finished the apple, the whole thing. Chomped through the core, and chewed up the pips.

Finally, he spat out the stalk. He'd decided; he had to do something. Another tip from his SIO course: *If you're stuck reactively, go proactive.* He phoned Hunter.

'I want you to start surveillance on TBR.'

'Not Back?'

'Out of interest, if I'd said Back, would you have said, "Not TBR?"?'

'No.'

'Meaning?'

'You got me,' said Hunter.

Rick ended the call, then phoned Gary again. 'Are you okay?'

'Why wouldn't I be?'

'Is your mum okay?'

Hunter said nothing.

'Gary?'

'Old girl passed a couple of days ago.'

'Gary, I'm sorry.' Rick retracted his pen in and out. 'Forget the surveillance and go home, you shouldn't be here.'

'After we've got Coniston back, maybe.' Hunter paused. 'You don't think it'll affect you, and then, well, then it does.'

'Yes,' said Rick. He put the phone quietly down beside him. It explained Hunter's erratic behaviour, but wished it hadn't.

A police car with a flat tyre drove into the back yard and parked alongside the marked bays. The barrier clanged down. Behind it, Jenny, one of Maggie's basketball teammates, crossed the entranceway.

Rick climbed out of the surveillance van, and ran after her. He ducked under the barrier and called out. She turned around and wheeled back up. Her mass of black frizzy hair sported flashes of silver.

'Hello Rick.' She beamed. The smiliest person he knew. 'How's Maggie?'

'We had a bit of a falling out, and I wanted to ask a couple of questions about racing wheelchairs – if you've got a minute.'

'For you, Rick, anything.' She winked.

'I had a look on the internet, thought it would be like buying a bicycle.'

Jenny cackled. 'About as similar to a bicycle as a lawnmower. How long you got? Don't answer that, Maggie's told me about you. Bicycles work by turning a crank to makes the wheels turn. A relatively indirect transfer of power. Technically, racers don't have a drive wheel which continues spinning when your hands stop pushing.'

'Which explains why racers don't have gears.'

'Attaboy. And also explains why racing is more like running than cycling as in order to maintain speed going downhill, you have to keep pushing. But unlike running, a racer's hands only push the rims between two o'clock and seven o'clock so you lose a lot of momentum.'

'Going uphill is hard work – and not helped by not having gears.'

'She said you were a smart cookie.'

'I'm thinking of buying one.'

Jenny hooted. 'You! You can't sit still.' She paused. 'Sorry, I can see you're serious. Bit more you should know, then. Moving a racer is like swimming – you have to learn a stroke, and it's pretty uncomfortable. To maximise power generation, the racer must fit you exactly.'

'Explains why I couldn't find any second-hand.'

'Be like wearing their pants – you'd always feel awkward.'
She laughed. 'To buy one you need to go for a fitting – and,
Rick, beware: it takes ages.'

Rick kissed her. 'Thanks.'

'People will talk,' she said, laughing as she wheeled off. 'Got
the hots for you, boy, she has!'

Rick ducked back under the barrier and walked across the
yard. Jenny's bonhomie was infectious and he felt more
optimistic about a future with Maggie.

But not about catching Coniston.

Or Khetan.

He picked up a pebble and hurled it at the taunting pigeons.

35

Rope, tape, buckets. Two hammers.

Hant slammed the van doors and climbed into the front with Ram. The DIY store hadn't been busy and there were few vehicles, but still their van sat in the correct bay, not one for cars or vehicles with trailers. Hant followed the rules, told Ram to obey God and follow the rules. Unless the rules didn't suit.

Staring through the windscreen, Ram unwrapped another toffee, and chewed in moody silence. A painter in spattered overalls loaded tins of paint into a trailer. Two women bickered at the boot of their car. A store assistant smoked by the sliding doors of the entrance. Jumbo sacks of gravel lined up.

'You want to come England,' said Hant. It was true, but it had suited him, too. The packet of sweets was his blatant attempt at amity.

The painters drove away. One of the women climbed in her car and locked the doors. The other woman banged on the window.

'I want—'

'What?'

Ram shook his head. He was a teenager. He was in a strange country. He was scared. The woman drove away, the second woman running after her, yelling. The boy smiled – finally. Ram was family, technically his nephew, but after Hant's brother had been seized by Maoists – and never returned – more like a son.

'Work me six months, maybe twelve. Make lot money, then go home Nepal. Build guest lodge, live *dharma*. You many children. *Thik chha?*' Okay?

'*Thik chha.*'

Hant started the engine, and slapped Ram's leg. The boy's body language told a different story. He drove out of the car park, past an artic being unloaded of wheelbarrows and timber. He could smell the dogs, hear the whispering, see the fright of the hidden migrants. Only a few days before the next delivery.

Grey clouds trundled across a hazy sky. Rain a possibility at any moment in Manchester. Hant missed Nepal, the harsh sunlight and the sparkling mountains, the predictability of the weather. They queued at a traffic light. In the car next to them two children in the back watched films on headrest consoles. Multicoloured lights flicked across their faces. Ram watched them watching, all three mesmerised. The lights turned green, the vehicles shunted forward, and Hant headed back to the *Okay* car wash.

They drove past a swimming pool, a caravan hire centre, a veterinary clinic, and reached a roundabout. A police car turned in behind them. The van was clean, the lights worked. Hant was driving under the speed limit. The van was insured and taxed. The boy oblivious of the police, of the danger. Hant braked, and stopped unnecessarily at a pedestrian crossing for a man pushing a disabled child. Not only was the van legal, but he was a considerate driver. He drove through another roundabout, the police car still following.

Police sirens blared. Blue flicker in the mirrors.

Hant slowed, pulled over, expecting the police car to pass. Hoped it would pass. The boy leant forward to watch in his wing mirror.

'*Bandar ko chaak!*'

Hant stopped the van. '*Chaina Nepali, Ram. Chaina English. Chaina.*' No Nepali, no English, nothing.

Two police climbed out of the car. Laughing, they approached along the pavement. Hant lowered the passenger window and one police peered in. Without moving and in silence, Hant prayed to God, and itemised the supplies in the back. Tape was tape, and hammers were hammers. You could torture with a car battery, kill with a beer bottle.

'No seat belt.' The police scowled.

Hant gripped the arms of his seat, heard a faint ringing in his ears. The boy had one thing to remember. One thing.

'Cannabis, Pete?' said the first police to the second police. He sniffed the air like a cartoon character. It was a barefaced lie. He kept his eyes on Ram and Hant. He wore white shirt sleeves, his tie tucked under an epaulette. A gold-coloured chain hung around his neck. He opened the passenger door. 'Out, both of you.'

The second police waited by Hant's door. Hant climbed out, and the second police followed him to the pavement.

Ram glanced at Hant. He was scared, sorry, awaiting guidance. Hant shook his head.

'Where're you from?'

'Manchester,' said Hant.

'Where were you born?'

'Westbury.'

'And my Aunt Fanny's a coalminer.'

The first police sniggered. 'What's in there?' He squatted and pointed to a metal box near the rear wheel arch. Secured with a number code.

'Spare key.'

Hant muttered a few words to God as the police lined him and Ram up against the van. Face the van, hands on the van, feet apart. Like criminals. The second police patted him down. He smelt of women's perfume. He felt up the inside of Hant's legs, squeezed his balls. Found nothing except the two hundred pounds cash in Hant's pocket. He sealed it in a plastic bag. 'Evidence.'

Then it was Ram's turn. The first police patted him down. Turned out the toffee papers from his pocket. They whirled to the ground, and blew away. The first police kept patting.

'Aye, aye, what have we here?' The first police backed off and took out his baton. The second police handcuffed Hant.

Hant twisted around in the cuffs. The ringing in his ears strengthened.

'*Dekhanunu*,' said Hant.

The second police yanked Hant's cuffs. 'English.'

'Show him.'

Ram unzipped his trouser flies, and delved inside.

'Slowly,' shouted the first police.

Ram produced a mobile phone.

The first police laughed, and the second police laughed with him. They laughed like idiots. Ram looked like a half-drowned dog.

'Open it,' said the first police, pointing with his baton at the metal box. Hant had hoped they'd forgotten, had hoped God was listening. He offered a silent prayer.

The handcuffs made the number dials tricky to turn. The first police prodded him with his baton. Hant kept fiddling. God, where are you?

Another prod from the baton.

'I trying. Swear father's life.' His father was dead, killed by a British soldier in the Falklands War. By David Coniston. The Ghurkhas and the British were meant to have been on the same side.

A police radio crackled.

'Got a shout.' The second police ran back to the car.

The first police unlocked Hant's cuffs, and whispered in his ear. 'Best you fuck off to where you've come from.' Behind him, the police siren briefly buzzed, like an angry wasp.

The two police drove away, lights flashing and sirens wailing, and taking Hant's two hundred pounds. Ram sat on the kerb and cradled his phone like a new mother. He started crying. Hant snatched the phone and slapped him. He pulled the boy to his feet, opened the van door and pushed him inside. He walked round the front, climbed in and locked the doors.

'God was listening,' said Hant. He said another prayer.

Ram stopped bawling and started sniffling. Hant inspected the phone. The last call, a week ago. He checked the messages.

Two days ago, a text from an unknown number. *Okay*

It was a reply to Ram's text sent earlier the same day. *Hello callixx arrive Dover*

Callixx?

'Calix Coniston?'

Ram nodded, but kept his head down.

'*Bandar ko chaak!*'

Hant tossed the phone into the back of the van. It bounced off a seat, landed heavily and slid along the floor until it hit the rear doors and fell silent. Ram glanced into the back, and across at him. Without warning, Hant jabbed the boy in the face. Then turned on the radio and pulled out into the traffic.

36

Rick worked the case. Sitting at his desk, he pounded the streets and knocked on doors. Modern policing. Interrogated databases, made phone calls, typed reports, issued taskings.

He circulated briefings for every patrol in Manchester. Descriptions and the latest intel on Coniston and Elly Simmonds, and Darren Back. He sent a fresh CHiS tasking. The hundred or so Manchester informants would be tasked with similar information, and paid for results. He called Oliver. Favour for a favour on credit, Rick promised. The phone crashed down. He reviewed the files and drank three cups of coffee.

He phoned Hunter.

'Any movement from TBR?' said Rick.

'I said I'd call you.' Hunter might or he might not, that was the problem.

'Well?'

'Two of his goons have turned up, Starfish and Thompson. They brought a litre bottle of whisky, so maybe they're having a quiet night in.'

Or maybe they were fuelling up.

Rick stared out of the window into the backyard, his hands feeling for the radiator. Cold as the case. Come on! He felt like a football manager who kept losing. Only so much he could do –

aside from running onto the pitch and kicking the ball himself.

Maybe he would. He put on his coat, grabbed his baton and cuffs. He'd spend an hour trawling the streets.

Maggie caught him at the door.

A tease of perfume.

'Do you want to go and see your dad for half an hour?'

'Not really.'

'Together?'

At Three Views Rick moved Dad's table into the window of his room. He began to sort the Pelmanism cards, only vaguely aware of Maggie chatting to Dad. Half his team were sat up on TBR, the other half gone home for an evening with their families. No one worked 24/7 anymore. Not even him.

He could be trawling the streets for Darren Back.

'Rick?' said Maggie.

'Sorry.'

Thirteen sets of four like playing cards. He removed half so there were thirteen sets of two. Bright yellow suns, footballs, dogs— He shuffled them, and spread them face down over the table. He felt a little nervous. It was a test of sorts. At Michael's suggestion, they'd played a month back, the three of them. Dad made one pair, and even that Rick suspected had been luck. Now, after Dad had consumed more than half of Mum's cake, he hoped it might be different. Two pairs, even one pair if it was won using his memory would be something.

Maggie was inspecting Dad's hands, and the two of them were laughing.

The room smelt of sleep and stale urine. Rick didn't want to compute. When the Coniston case had finished, he and Maggie should take Dad to the apiary and get him into a bee-suit.

Maggie led Dad over. Rick had not told her about the test, not told her anything at all.

'Pelmanism, Dad.'

'At Christmas we used to play Newmarket for matchsticks. I don't think I've got any. Oh dear, I'm sorry.'

'We, Dad?'

His dad didn't answer.

They sat, Dad at the head of the table. Rick went over the rules, and Maggie suggested a jigsaw puzzle if Dad would prefer. Sometimes, she could be so interfering.

Dad went first. Slowly, he turned over a card, and Rick wondered if his dexterity was also deteriorating. Life became ever more complex, then stopped and uncoiled. The card was a dark blue reservoir which became purple near a dam. Maggie prompted Dad to turn a second card. He turned the one next to it. Statistically, as good as any, but Rick already felt disappointed. A red building crane towering above a cityscape.

'Blue reservoir, and red crane,' said Maggie. 'You want to remember them, Roger.' She prompted him to turn them back over. They were going to be there until Rick had retired from the Job. Coniston still on the run, Khetan a Nepalese deity.

Maggie's turn. She turned over a house.

'All that training you're doing!'

She smiled, the sunlight catching her very faint freckles. She sat just outside touching distance, Dad in-between. He laughed with them, but they both knew he didn't understand the joke. Maggie turned over a black and white chequered football, and prompted Dad before turning the cards back.

Rick revealed a shaggy Old English Sheepdog. Then a football, a second football.

'Another football,' said Maggie.

Rick felt his stomach tighten. 'Dad?'

Dad turned over the same two cards as his first go – the nearest two.

'Try a different card next time, Roger.' Maggie squeezed

Dad's arm. She turned over the footballs, then a second Sheepdog. She turned over the first dog. 'Two pairs for me.' Rick pulled a face, but Maggie ignored him. She turned over a rainbow, then a galloping black horse.

His go, but his phone rang. 'Sorry.' He withdrew to the room's entrance. The acrid smell intensified. 'Gary?'

'They're on the move, all three of them.'

'I'm coming.'

'No point 'til we see where they're headed. Probably just the pub.'

Hunter would head to the pub, but not TBR. He preferred basement clubs or parties in empty warehouses. *If* he was at leisure. But he might not be.

Rick put the phone down. Maggie shot him a look. So far, so bad.

'It's my go,' she said, turning over the second horse, then the first. She turned over a second rainbow, then the first. She revealed a card they hadn't seen before. A silver crescent moon in a black sky. She turned over a bright yellow sun with yellow rays as if a child had drawn it. 'Two more pairs for me.'

Rick sighed. Reducing the field would make it easier for Dad. Perhaps Maggie was doing the right thing, but he couldn't let her win. He revealed the second house, then the first house. He revealed the second moon, then the first moon. He revealed another new card, a crenulated black castle. Like Bodiam or Tattershall. 'Hey, Dad. A castle, like us!'

Maggie tutted. 'Is that why we're playing this?!' Her face relaxed into a grin. 'Honestly!'

Rick grinned back, but Dad's face remained passive. Rick revealed a camouflaged Land Rover, then flipped the cards over. 'Your go, Dad.'

His dad took his time, again staring at the cards. Rick glanced at Maggie who shook her head. 'What am I meant to be doing again?' said Dad.

'Pairs, Dad. You turn over a card, and if say it's a reservoir, you try to remember where the other reservoir is.'

Dad fingered his first card, the reservoir. Rick nodded. Dad turned it over. He fingered a second card, the red crane. Rick shook his head, and Dad withdrew his hand.

'Come on, Dad. Where's the other reservoir?'

Dad ventured out a hand and moved it spider-like over the cards. Five pairs down, sixteen cards left. Rick shook his head, kept shaking. Dad touched three-quarters of the cards before Rick nodded. Dad turned it over.

'Hooray!'

Maggie clapped. 'Well done, Roger.'

Rick's phone buzzed. He put it to his ear. 'Gary?'

'They're heading Failston way.'

Rick balled his fist. Coniston's family home – now his – was in Failston.

'I'm coming.'

He stood up. 'I'm sorry, Maggie.'

Without even looking at him, she swiped the suns, then the castles. He hoped it was a good omen. It left the score as Rick two and Maggie five. Dad had scored one.

The screen of his phone flashed before he heard it. He smothered the buzz. 'Gary?'

'They've driven past Coniston's. All eyes into the house.'

'And now?'

'They're parked up at the back of a primary school. Waiting or deciding, I'm not sure.'

'On way.'

'Sorry, Dad,' said Rick. He whispered to Maggie: 'TBR and his crew have just driven past Coniston's address. I'll pick you up later.' She held up a thumb. He kissed the top of her head. Dad's head, too.

'Get off,' said Dad, flapping his hand as if he was scaring a bird.

Rick drove out of the car park as if he had nine lives. From behind, hooting and flashing of lights. Accelerating away, he phoned Hunter on the car phone.

'Update?'

'All three have decamped into the road two over from Coniston. Single file, balaclavas. They're on a mission. TBR's holding a staple gun, Thompson a baseball bat.'

'What channel you on?'

'Seventy-three. A footie is behind them – Foxtrot 1.'

Rick adjusted the police radio to listen directly to the surveillance team.

'They've gone down an alley and into Copthorne Road, Foxtrot 1.' One road over from Coniston, the name familiar.

'They're going to Sakit's address. The Strangeways guard.'

'Etiquette, please, sir.' Hunter's voice, enjoying himself.

'Permission,' said Rick. He was, too. He slammed the car into second and executed a double overtake. More hooting and flashing of lights. He was about two minutes away.

'Yes, sir?' Mocking.

'Sakit lives at number nineteen.'

'They're keeping to the shadows.' The low mutter of Foxtrot 1.

Rick kept it in third, the car whining. One minute out.

'They're at the front door, looking around.'

Rick braked hard, double-declutched into second. A distant memory of his driving course surfaced and dived. Turned left, right, left and he was there, could see an unmarked pool car parked by the kerb with its lights on. Hunter.

'They're forcing the door. They're in, in, in.' The footie now screeching.

Rick skidded to a stop behind the pool car, and jumped out. In front of him, the passenger door opened.

'Uniform are on way,' said Hunter. 'I called the footie back, didn't think we should show out.'

Rick opened the boot of the pool car and hauled out a round shield. 'We can't just sit here, come on!'

He started running, and at the same time shouted instructions on the surveillance channel. 'Tango 2 and 3 round the back, Tango 4 and footie units meet me at the front. Round shields if you have them.' He ran into Copthorne Road. Sirens muttered in the distance.

He sprinted halfway down the road. Two people were waiting in the shadows outside Sakit's. Paulson and the footie who Rick knew by face, but not name.

'Batons and cuffs?'

Paulson nodded, the footie shook his head.

Hunter ran up from behind holding a round shield. 'Who wants it?' He winked.

Shouting and screaming emanated from inside the house. Semi-detached, cars on the drive, the front door half-open. Neighbours emerging.

'Hunter, behind me, then Paulson.'

Rick hurried down the path. Slowly, he pushed open the splintered front door. Calm before the storm. He took a deep breath. So much for desk policing.

He charged in, screaming 'Pol–ice!'

Chaos in the back room. Patel sat in the centre. He was taped to the back of a chair, his hands tied and his face bleeding. The three wannabe mobsters stood around him, TBR waving the staple gun. Hysterical screaming from upstairs.

Rick entered, baton in one hand, shield in the other. TBR whirled round, wielding the staple gun. Rick smashed the top of the shield into TBR's nose. There was a crack and a spurt of blood and TBR staggered back. Fell down. Rick sensed a presence to his right. He lashed out rightwards with the shield, felt a connection, and heard another man groan and go down. Starfish. Shouting from behind him. Hunter and

Paulson. Sirens so loud it seemed they were inside the house.

One more mobster. To his left, Thompson, armed with a baseball bat.

Rick struck out with the baton, connecting with a shoulder. Thompson yelled out. Rick hit him again and again.

Thompson went down.

Paulson loomed over the moaning Thompson, Hunter over the groaning Starfish. TBR was out for the count.

Then there were uniformed police officers everywhere. Three for each gang member, more in the back garden. Voices of authority upstairs.

Rick loosened his grip on the round shield, and backed up to the door. In the Brixton Riots they'd used dustbin lids. The march of progress.

Hunter glanced over.

'Blimey, boss.'

The two of them leant against the bonnet of a chunky police van belonging to a tactical support unit armed with eight PCs and a sergeant. The bonnet was warm, but not as warm as Rick. He was boiling, even his fingers.

A black Range Rover pulled up and the driver's window buzzed down. Robbo's podgy face looked out. Rick imagined the superintendent's electronic gates on his drive, his automatic garage door, coffee maker, breadmaker, his row of TV remotes.

'Coniston?'

Rick shook his head. 'Patel has been taken to hospital with a suspected broken arm and staple gun injuries to his face. Wife and kids are with relatives and family liaison. They're shocked, but okay. TBR, Starfish, and Thompson are in custody for aggravated burglary. I'll get into them in the morning, but I'm not that hopeful for a lead on Coniston. We've searched up and down for him, the loft, shed, garage. No trace.'

'Too many coincidences.'

Rick nodded.

The window rose and the Range Rover drove away. Hunter clapped silently and slowly.

The sergeant scratched his leg. 'Why'd they target Sakit?'

'Either they think he's grassed, or as a warning so he doesn't. Or there's something connecting TBR, Sakit, and Coniston we don't know about.'

A white repair van reversed up and parked. A heavily tattooed man climbed out, pulled on a toolbelt, grabbed a rechargeable drill and walked up the path to Sakit's front door.

'Coniston's close,' said Hunter. 'I can smell him.'

In his head, Rick slow-clapped Hunter. What he needed was actionable intelligence or a verifiable sighting from a member of the public. Not hunches from his sergeant. Nor humphreys, hieroglyphics or half-baked ideas overheard in the CID office, or whatever else went on in Robbo's head between meals.

He stood up, reluctant to leave the warmth of the bonnet. 'Get Sam and his crew to search Coniston's h a again. Stand the surveillance team down, and I'll see you back at the nick for a debrief.'

He drove back to Three Views, but Maggie had left. Michael told him she'd caught a taxi. He sat in his car in the car park and looked along the line of shadowed windows to Dad's room. Dad inside, sitting, standing, being, becoming someone else.

His phone buzzed.

A text from the Crime Squad sergeant Sam Davies. *Negative at Coniston's h a*

He switched on the phone's ring tone, and it sounded within seconds. Without looking he took the call.

'Sam?'

'Not Sam, no. Is that DCI Castle, South Manchester?'

'Yes.'

'DS Morris, sir, Bradford CID. PNC says you're the OIC for a conspiracy involving a Nepalese national. Hant Khetan, also known as Special K.'

'I am.' Rick sat up as if he'd been jabbed with a Taser. All his senses on high alert.

'Good news, I think. He's just come back to me on prints.'

'In Bradford?'

'Maybe. They were on a Rubik's Cube.'

Rick thumped the roof of the car. He played air drums on the steering wheel, flapped the sun visor as if it was a high hat. He started the car and drove out of the car park, hooting the horn, and turning on the radio. Any station, as long as it was loud.

37

The Finchams' master bedroom was huge, and chintzy. Tassels hung down from the white waffle bedspread, embossed red and gold wallpaper covered the walls. There was an old-fashioned dressing table with three mirrors and a red stool which fitted underneath. The view from the bay window was of the rear garden which ran steeply up to a thick wood. Rotting silver birch trees towered above the fence on the left, and a hedge gave way to a bamboo thicket on the right. It was possible to squeeze between the privet and the bamboo from one garden to another. Calix had done it enough times.

Between the bed and the dressing table there was enough room to park a car. Calix carried up two kitchen chairs, and a folding card table from the lounge, and plonked them down. Staying upstairs would avoid them being seen by callers at the door, or passers-by. Or nosy neighbours, especially Salisbury who ran the Neighbourhood Watch.

Elly sat on a chair, and pulled out a box of chocolates from under the bed.

Calix went into a front bedroom, and peered out. Down the empty road, past the new white stones, the beech hedges, the sailing boat with its fluttering blue and white pennant. To the corner. He looked the other way, into his own front garden. The front door was boarded up, and the garden unkempt. The bronze statue of Athena needed buffing.

He saw his old man mowing the lawn around her, and cleaning the mower afterwards. Using a wire brush, adjusting the spark plug. Careful, particular, and good with his hands. The one trait Calix had inherited.

He checked his phone for messages, then went downstairs. In the kitchen a wall calendar showed a three-week holiday in Australia, one week spent. Every year regular as Christmas, the Finchams went on holiday to see their daughter in Sydney. For a few years, he'd looked after their cat. The flap in the back door was now boarded, and Riley stood in a cabinet in the dining room. It wasn't perfect, but not his worst job. The Finchams had been delighted.

Calix unhooked the key for their runaround car, and pulse jumping, went into the integral garage. The small yellow car sat ready. He unlocked the door, and sat in the driver's seat. He'd liked to have tried the engine, to be certain, but Salisbury had the hearing of a dog. He returned inside, opened the freezer and the fridge. He looked in the kitchen cupboards. Bread and cheese; jams; biscuits; pizzas, ready meals. They'd be fine for a week, at worst two. He collected the chess set and some magazines from the lounge, a couple of beers, and went back upstairs. The Finchams really should have changed the codes for the key safe and the burglar alarm.

Elly was filing her nails.

'*Grr.*' She raked the air.

Chocolate foils littered the bed.

Calix set up the chess board, the pieces hand-carved ivory. Everything a memory: Spencer and Barney playing every day at the cave, and the search by Khetan's goons. They'd stamped on the chessmen, broken the chessmen. Stamped on the three of them, but not broken them.

Elly unwrapped another chocolate, and Calix lit a cigarette. She moved the white pawn in front of her king with the ease of someone who played a lot, or never.

A dibble siren ripped the air.

Calix shot to the front bedroom, and peered out. Two dibble cars in convoy sped past, braked hard at the corner and disappeared. Their sirens receded, then strengthened, then stopped. The next road over, Sakit's road. Halfway down, Sakit's house.

He returned to the master bedroom and looked out from the bay. There was no sign of dibble, no sign of Castle. When he sat back down, Elly asked the question with her jade-coloured eyes. He unravelled a chocolate wrapper and reformed it into a miniature cup, and tapped the cigarette free of ash by way of an answer.

They played on. Calix moved a pawn to confront the white pawn, and Elly moved her king's bishop to c4. Already, he felt like he was losing.

He lost.

He lit another cigarette, and Elly opened a beer. She leant back on her chair, and laughed, and swigged the beer.

Calix made another chocolate foil cup, and tapped more ash. He checked his phone for a message from Ram. He stood, checked the street view from the front bedroom, and the garden view from the back. Still no sign of anyone, still no message. He swatted a fly on the glass, and padded back.

'Big bed,' said Elly.

Calix sat on the end, and dissected the fly with his long thumbnail. Elly flicked through a magazine.

'I told you it would be boring.'

'I'm not bored. And you didn't.'

'*Grr.*'

One of the dibble cars returned, along with an unmarked car

and four plain clothes. Detectives or baby detectives, but not Castle. They parked nose to tail around the statue, and making wisecracks, surrounded his house. One unlocked the padlock, and in they went. Elly came to stand alongside him in the front bedroom. She smelt sweet and beery. Their clothing touched as if she conducted electricity.

The dibble were quick. After ten minutes, they exited, clipped the padlock, and zoomed away.

Calix and Elly sat back at the card table, and stared across. Elly ripped a page out of a magazine.

'A recipe.'

Calix started laughing. He laughed long enough and hard enough to be able to listen to the waves of sound. He couldn't remember the last time he'd laughed so it hurt. It felt good, and bad. It made him wonder about the next time.

He heard a soft *tink-tink* on a window. He held his hand out flat to get Elly's attention, then pointed to his ear. The *tink-tink* came again. He moved to the bay window and looked down. At last. He trotted downstairs, and unlocked the back door.

Barney stepped inside. His stubble made him look older. He dumped a small rucksack onto the freezer, and looked out of the window. Calix locked the door.

'You okay?'

Barney nodded, his face registering surprise at being asked. They padded up the stairs, and into the vast bedroom. Barney stopped in the doorway. He held his bag by a twist of canvas out to the side like a circus strongman.

'Why's she here?'

'I don't know really.'

'College is so dull,' said Elly. It sounded weak, and not for the first time, Calix felt unsure.

'Has he told you what we're about?'

Elly shook her head.

Barney dropped his bag by the door, and stepped forward. He picked up a chess piece, the black king, and turned it over in his fingers. Calix knew what his friend was thinking, knew Elly couldn't know. He was sorry she was there and didn't know, and not sorry. Barney set the king down on the board. He found the black queen and set it alongside, then the bishops and the knights. He set the entire board. A new game.

Calix carried up a third kitchen chair, and the three of them sat in a circle. Calix lit a cigarette.

'We've got wheels, and food. Just need the weapon.'

'And the target,' said Barney.

Calix nodded, breathing out plumes of smoke. He checked the phone. The message he'd been waiting for was there.

Hello Callixx arrive Manchester with hant speak you soon friend ram

38

There was just time before Rick drove to Bradford to interview one of the aggravated burglars. He'd hardly slept, couldn't stop thinking about Khetan. Could it be possible, one of the FBI's most wanted was back in the UK? Possible too he'd never even left. And if so, was that the reason his flashbacks hadn't ended – he'd begun to think Coniston was responsible, but maybe his subconscious somehow knew about Khetan. A discussion to have with Emma.

Rick waited outside interview room 1 until the corridor was empty. He removed a chair from the next room and stood on it outside the door. He stretched down to open it, pushed it open, and stood up. He leant inside with a piece of gaffa tape, reached above the door and into the top corner and stuck it onto the lens of the CCTV camera. He withdrew his hand, stepped down and returned the chair.

Then sat in the first room, waiting for Hunter.

All three burglars were looking at lengthy sentences, irrespective of whether they were carrying a weapon. The gavel of joint enterprise. Starfish was the youngest, just having turned eighteen, and had a quarter of the previous of the other two. He might talk, might be lured into a deal.

Hunter signed him out of custody, and persuaded him into the interview room without a brief in return for a McDonald's breakfast. Rick's idea, and his money.

'You like gherkins, Mr Hunter?'

'Not so much.' Hunter pulled one out of his burger with a tea stirrer and flipped it across the table.

'Ta very much.'

The two of them ate with noisy enjoyment. They played a couple of games of noughts and crosses, Hunter losing each time. When they'd finished eating, they balled their rubbish and competed at lobbing it into the bin. Rick drained his tea, squashed the cup, and threw it on top of the overflowing packaging. Hunter had his uses.

'Tony,' said Rick.

'Yes, Mr Castle?' Starfish wore a new black tracksuit and orange trainers. Normally, rings and a large necklace. He was lanky and gormless-looking. Rick wondered if it was going to be that easy.

'Do you know where Calix Coniston is?'

'No, Mr Castle. Mr Castle?'

'Yes, Tony?'

'No tapes, Mr Castle?'

'No, Tony. No tapes. We're not interviewing you about last night. This is an intelligence interview, and not recorded.' He glanced up at the covered CCTV camera. Not tape-recorded or filmed.

'Tony.'

'Yes, Mr Castle?'

'Have you heard the expression, there's no such thing as a free lunch?' Rick set down a small notebook and a pen on the table.

'No.'

Rick paused. There was no such thing as easy. 'Would you like another McDonald's, Tony?'

'Well, I wouldn't say, No.' Surely, no one could be that guileless, that simple. Rick wondered if it was all a show. In fact, Starfish had a high IQ and could recite passages of Keats and Shakespeare.

'I'm going to need something in return.'

'You mean some money?'

'No. I mean some information.' Rick picked up the pen and pressed the top half a dozen times, extending and retracting the tip. *Click, click, click.*

'About what? I don't know much.'

'That,' said Hunter, scratching his leg, 'might be the understatement of the year.'

'About Calix Coniston,' said Rick. He put the pen down, picked it up again.

'I don't know anything about him, God's truth, so strike me down.'

'How about TBR?'

'Eh-eh,' said Starfish, shaking his head. 'I made that clear to Mr Hunter. I say no comment on last night and about my co-constricters, Tommo and Mr Red.'

'One more chance, Tony. Otherwise it's the end of Maccy-Dees for a very long time.'

Hunter sighed and scratched his leg. 'Come on Tony, you can do this. Remember what I was saying to you.'

'What about Darren Back, Tony? He's done one, and we'd like to know where he is. It'll never come back to you, we promise.' He glanced at Hunter and back to the overgrown boy in front of him.

'God's truth,' said Hunter. 'So strike me down. Strike us both down.'

'I'm sorry,' said Starfish. 'I cannot say. Mr Red would not be happy.' He pulled a pained face.

Rick picked up the pen, extended and retracted a few times. He glanced up at the camera. He could feel Hunter watching him.

Click, click, click.

The Coniston case was stuck. Yes, he had a promising line of enquiry on Khetan, but not on Coniston. The Strangeways fugitive was eluding him, beating him. Coniston was winning.

'Last chance, Tony.'

Rick clicked out the pen tip.

'Sorry, Mr Castle.'

Rick raised the pen and jabbed it down onto the back of Tony's hand. At the same time, roared: 'Where's Darren, Tony? I know you know. You went to the same crappy school together, you were inseparable until you were fourteen.'

Tony yelled and whipped his hand away, the pen extending like a flag from between his metacarpals.

Rick plucked it out.

Another yell.

The pen bloody, and dripping.

'Alright! Darren's at a flophouse in the northern quarter.'

Rick waited, clicking the pen in and out.

'Fuck! At the end of Semion Street. There's a McDonald's near there, that's where I seen him.'

Rick stood up. He took out his wallet and dropped a couple of ten-pound notes on the table. 'Get him another breakfast, Gary. And get him cleaned up.'

He went out, leaving the door to pull shut behind him.

Carrot and stick, basics.

Straight to Semion Street. A convoy of three cars, Rick driven by Hunter, and following, Woods and Bennett, and Kasim and Paulson. Hunter was silent, driving fast, jinking in and out of the lane, hands working hard on the steering wheel. Rick was still buzzing, but doing his best to appear calm. Like the sky, marbled purple and grey. The sun was even trying to break through.

'Did you clean him up?'

Hunter nodded. He glanced in the rearview to check the others were following. Scratched behind his ear.

'Do you think he'll say anything?'

'Nope. It's his only chance TBR will believe he didn't talk. Blab about one thing, blab about *every*thing. And I told him so.'

Silence resumed. Halfway to Semion. If they found Darren Back, then maybe they'd get Coniston. At least get something on him. Hunter braked heavily, changed down, accelerated. The car dipped and rose, like a speedboat hitting the waves. The car was used to it. They were all used to it.

'We need to speak, boss.'

Rick's phone rang. 'Later.'

He held the phone to his ear. 'Castle.'

'It's DS Morris, sir, I got the message you were delayed. Wondered how long you're going to be?'

'Midday?'

'Fine, I'll see if I can get my informant to come with me. Costa Coffee in the town centre.'

Hunter turned into Semion Street. Rick looked over his shoulder. The two CID cars were still behind them.

They dumped the cars where they could and gathered on the pavement. Rick nodded at his team. Apprehension in their faces. The task, or him?

The flophouse was obvious. The end terrace was in a state of disrepair, paint peeling, the ground floor window cracked, and the front door boarded up. Rick whispered to Woods to watch the front and to guard the cars. He led the others around the back. Paulson held the battering ram. Radios were turned down low, pulses were notching higher. Rick felt a tingling sensation – having had no sleep and a mug of tea for breakfast, he was running on empty.

A panel in the side fence was missing. Beer cans and rubbish strewn in the backyard. Three metres by four, a basketball hoop stood rusting, the netting missing. Graffiti on the back door: *Fuck Off.*

Rick nodded at Paulson. The detective shouldered the ram, steadied, swung back and smashed the door open first time.

In they went, Rick leading.

Shouts from upstairs, the air fetid. Rotting food, sewage, cannabis. They worked together, one searching, one safeguarding the searcher. Rick and Hunter climbed the stairs, stepped over junk mail and fast-food wrappers. The carpet missing.

The landing was dark, and the light switches didn't work. Rick turned on his pen torch. The first room was empty except for discarded clothing, the window hung with a dusty sheet. A shout of Boss! from downstairs.

Rick reversed into the landing.

'Five in the front room,' shouted Bennett. 'But not Darren. They're okay. We're okay.'

Rick slammed the banister.

A woman was sleeping in the next room. Hunter ripped the sheet from the window and opened it. Fresh air cascaded in. 'Police,' said Hunter. The woman groaned, hid her head under a pillow. 'We're after Darren Back,' said Rick. A muffled shout of abuse.

Rick checked under the bed and in the cupboard. Half a dozen shoes, a used condom, a post office jacket.

Next room. The bay window at the front, large, built in cupboards. A double bed with the shapes of people sleeping. Rick ripped down the sheet on the windows, and glanced outside at Woods looking up. 'Wakey, wakey, rise and shine,' shouted Hunter. He yanked the duvet from the bed.

Three women and one man lay in their underwear. The women, still really girls, were thin, and delicate-looking. Needed a decent meal.

'Ah, ain't that cute,' said Hunter. 'All Charlie and the Chocolate Factory.'

'Not sure which version you read,' said Rick. He offered silent thanks to whoever was in charge – God, Darwin, his morning tea leaves. 'Darren, get up. You're coming with us.'

Back reached down for the duvet but gave up, lay back and closed his eyes. 'For what?'

'Assisting an offender.'

'Who?'

'Calix Coniston.'

Back scowled.

'Really?' said the girl on the nearside of him. 'Calix Coniston?' 'He's lovely,' said the topless girl on the far side. She reached down to touch herself. 'Loves animals, apparently,' said the first girl. 'Well, I'll be his tiger any day of the week,' said the third.

Rick grabbed Darren's foot and yanked him off the bed.

'Get dressed. And you three, shut about Coniston. He's unpredictable, and not who you think he is.'

Rick jammed the handcuffed Back into the rear of the CID car, alongside Paulson. Woods climbed in and Rick slammed the door, banged on the roof.

'You go with them, Gary. Back to South Manchester and book him in.' Above them, the sun was about to show.

Hunter tossed Rick a set of car keys. 'Where are you going?'

'Bradford, with Maggie. I'll tell you later.'

Hunter nodded. No moaning, no jokes. No time for Rick to ask after his health.

'Are you okay, boss?'

'Me?'

'Twice in less than twenty-four hours, you've lost it.'

'For the record, I didn't lose it, either time. And look where we are, now: we've finally got hold of Darren Back and have an angle on Coniston.'

'*If* he knows anything, and *if* he talks.'

'You're beginning to sound like Robbo.'

'And you're beginning to act like Robocop.'

Two of the CID cars drove away with Back, and Rick turned to their remaining vehicle. A sudden shaft of sunlight hit the bonnet and revealed the reflection of a person. Their upper body, and a face – Coniston. Criminal, loser, escaper.

Rick whirled round.

No one.

He turned back, looked again at the bonnet of the CID car. The image was Rick Castle. Him. Detective, winner, seeker.

Maybe, Coniston and him were both seekers. Maybe, they could work together.

39

The cafe in Bradford was busy. The smell of coffee hung thickly and a melancholic jazz eased out of hidden speakers. Modern art lined the walls and cacti sat on tables.

Rick sat with DS Dave Morris and Maggie at a table in the back corner. He glanced at the clock, nervous the informant wouldn't show. She was already twenty minutes late. A baby at the next table started crying. Maggie glanced over, her eyes lingering.

Rick swivelled the handle of his cup, one way then the other. 'You're sure the prints are Khetan's?'

Morris had sandy hair and a boyish face. He didn't look police which made him ideal for running informants. He nodded. 'Full match.'

By itself it meant nothing. Khetan could have touched the toy in Nepal, or anywhere in South Asia. It could have been months ago. But it could mean— The nature of policework to raise hopes, and dash them.

Rick checked the clock. Thirty minutes. His coffee was cold. Pushed the handle one way, then the other. He knocked over the cup, coffee spilling into the saucer and across the table. Maggie looked at him as if he was deranged. He mopped up.

Forty minutes. He'd give it an hour. Probably two.

'One thing's puzzling me, Dave,' said Maggie. 'Why are Rima and her son's fingerprints not smothering anyone else's?'

'Rima – that's not her real name – is quite cute about these things.' Morris smiled. 'In Syria, would you believe, she once dated a cop.'

'The boy's father?'

'No, before that. Meeting Rima has made me realise migrants aren't just figures on a TV screen, but real people with complex histories and hopes and dreams like the rest of us. Before the fighting started, she was a pharmacist. Her husband was a journalist and her son went to school. He had a pet rabbit called Bitir for fuck's sake.'

'Peter?' said Maggie.

Morris nodded. 'The boy's all she's got left now. Her husband's dead, her house ruined. She's got nothing, just the clothes she arrived in. She has to start over, and giving up a smuggler was something she knew she'd get paid for. And having dated a cop, she knew what to do.'

Rick checked the clock, then his phone. A missed call and a text from Robbo. *Tell me you're not in Bradford*

Hunter?

'Here she is,' said Morris, standing up.

A woman in a pale orange hajib stood just inside the entrance, glancing around. She held the hand of a ten-year-old boy wearing a dark hoodie. Morris escorted them over and made the introductions, then walked to the counter. Maggie shuffled up, and they sat down. Rima was in her late twenties and wearing pale lipstick and eyeshadow.

'I've got something for you, Amin,' said Maggie. From her bag she withdrew a football programme. 'Manchester United last Saturday.'

The boy's eyes widened, and he glanced at his mother. She nodded and whispered to him in Arabic.

'Thank you,' said Amin, pulling back his hood and revealing he was missing an ear. His mother tried to smile at Maggie. Morris sat down with another coffee and a plate of flapjacks. The boy like a horse in a starting gate.

Rick knew how the boy felt. He leant forward. 'Rima, I'm interested in the fingerprints on the Rubik's Cube. Would you recognise the man who gave it to you?'

'I don't know. His head clothe, and he wear glasses.' Beside her, Amin attacked the flapjack. Rick tapped on his phone and brought up a photo of Khetan. He pushed it across the table, his stomach tightening.

She studied the screen. Her son used both hands to eat the flapjack, up, down, up, down to the plate. Syrup-coated crumbs everywhere.

'I think so, but I'm not sure.'

Witnesses! Never sure, always stuck in no man's land. Rick pulled the cactus closer, leaving a wake of spilt coffee. He jabbed a spike with a finger. The boy whispered in his mother's ear.

'Of course he can,' said Rick. 'And he can take the others home.' Rima put another flapjack on the boy's plate. Rick poked his phone. 'Take another look.'

She shook her head, the tassels on her hajib stroking her shoulders. 'I no sure.'

Rick pulled his phone back. 'Have you any way of contacting him again?' Rima shook her head. Rick tapped the cactus spike with his thumb. 'Do you know where he collected you?'

'I sorry, I don't know. I try help. I want help.' Her voice was soft, hesitant.

'Can you describe the journey?'

She shook her head. 'No windows in van.' Beside her, and with Maggie's tutelage, Amin was working out how many points United could get by the end of the season.

'How long was it?'

'One hour and half, two hour maybe.'

'Round and round Bradford?' Rick drew circles in the air. 'Or did you start somewhere else?'

'Some round and round.' She copied Rick's circles and her son did some more. 'But most on fast road. *Vroom.*'

'*Vroom,*' imitated her son. '*Vroom, vroom.*'

Rick smiled at the boy, nodded at Rima. 'Can you describe the place where you emerged from the lorry, and swapped to the van?'

'It was next to a big building. Like a factory. Big place with roads and round-roads.' More circles in the air.

'Roundabouts?'

'Yes, I think. Old petrol station, I remember also.'

'What else?'

'Go lorry to van fast. Men not want us to see.'

Rick needed more, something unique to identify the location. Rima probably knew something, and she wanted to help, so it was a case of uncorking the answer. He watched Maggie flick through the matchday programme with the boy. At the counter a waitress frothed milk into a jug. The smell of fresh coffee stung the air. 'Rima, what could you smell?'

'Only us. We smell after sit in lorry for days.'

'What could you hear?'

She shook her head.

'Think!'

Maggie and the boy looked up, Maggie shooting daggers. People at other tables looked across. The door of the café opened, and a bell jangled. New customers entered.

'Aeroplanes. There were lots of aeroplanes. Amin likes aeroplanes, he saw them first. We counted them. Five big aeroplanes, in a big circle in sky.'

Rick turned to Morris. 'Has Bradford got an airport?'

'A small one. Doesn't sound like it. Sounds like a big one with planes in a holding pattern.'

Rick turned back to Rima. 'Okay, good, we're getting somewhere. Petrol station, large building, a factory maybe. Were there any big pipes or silos?' He tapped his phone to find a picture to help. He found an oil refinery and held it up.

'No. Only one big building. Place for lorries load and unload. But old. Closed. Rubbish in car park.'

'A car park?'

'I see through fence. White line for cars. And also lot of— I don't know the word. For shopping with wheels?'

'Shopping trolleys?'

'I think, yes.'

Rick found a photo. 'These?'

'Yes.'

Rick kept asking questions, but no other hints emerged. What she'd told him might be enough, but might not be.

Rima stroked Amin's head. 'Something I want tell you, now. Baby die in lorry.'

'Your baby?' Rick stilled his breathing.

Rima shook her head. 'Baby die because crying. Crying and crying. We told, Quiet or you found by police.' She wagged her finger. 'Sent back to Syria. But baby crying and crying. Father of baby get blanket and— I still feel sick. And guilty Amin is okay.' She wept quietly into her hands.

DS Morris and Maggie were silent. Rick was silent. He listened to the soft rustle of Amin turning the pages of the football programme. When the boy reached the end, he turned it over and started again.

It rained heavily on the drive back to South Manchester. The wipers screeched back and forth, and the tyres sloshed through the surface water. The summer was broken, but Rick didn't care. He was feeling cock-a-hoop with the lead on Khetan. Who'd have thought?

248

'You were nice with the boy,' said Maggie.

'So were you.'

'I want to have a baby.'

'What?' Rick looked across at her.

'Look out!'

Another driver hooted and veered to the edge of the overtaking lane. Rick steered back into the centre, and slowed. Rima's terrible story. And the baby in the café, mewling and bawling. Sucking a bottle, the new mother pandering, her friend cooing. Rick's stomach filled with butterflies. He wanted a son to kick a football with, to teach beekeeping. Rick a dad, Dad a granddad. It would cement his relationship with Maggie forever. He'd have to marry her. Ask her. He'd been thinking very, very tentatively about how. But he was getting ahead, and wondered if Maggie was pregnant.

'One day.'

Rick's stomach settled. She wasn't pregnant. A girl would be fine, too. Better than fine. She'd have her mother's smile and easy laugh. Her principled but sensible outlook. Two children, one if not both to follow him into the Job, shore up the thin blue line. He overtook a motorhome, then eased back into the centre lane. He'd made one crucial assumption.

'With me?'

'I don't know.'

The phone rang.

'Castle.' His voice no longer ebullient, but flat.

'It's Gary, phoning from custody. As we thought, in respect of Sakit, and Coniston's escape and whereabouts, TBR and Thompson were tight as witches. And—' Hunter took a deep breath.

'What?'

'Sakit's refusing to make a statement. And CPS won't charge without, so I had to bail them.' Rick thumped the wheel, and silently, swore black and blue. 'Custody skipper wants a word. Here he is—'

'Sergeant Paine, sir. Duty inspector's reviewed Back and wants to know when you're going to be interviewing.'

'Just finished taking a statement. Be with you in an hour.'

A sleek white car with a rear spoiler overtook at a stupid speed.

Maggie tutted.

At the speeding car or his lie, Rick wasn't sure. 'Did you tell Robbo we were coming to Bradford, Maggie?'

'Of course not! He's got snitches all over the nick – rewards them with extra rest days.'

'Being confined to Manchester is Robbo throwing his weight around.'

'I don't disagree.'

Rick changed the subject. 'I'm sorry I left you at Three Views with Dad.'

'That's okay. Going out with you has never been straightforward.' She glanced across at him. 'I quite like Pelmanism – and I'm better than you!'

'I finish strongly.'

'Is that right?'

They both laughed. And for a while it felt like their relationship at the start.

Lights flared on the car in front.

Rick braked violently, the car bonnet dipping and his seatbelt cutting across him. He stared at the wipers, marching back and forth. Remembered he was meant to be investigating the criminal damage to Robbo's Range Rover. He had an idea for the suspect, but as yet no evidence.

'Rick'

'Yes?'

'Are you going to tell the CTU about Khetan?'

'Probably not.'

'Robbo?'

'Look what happened last time. Khetan didn't spend five minutes in custody. If that got out, it would be a scandal.'

'And what do you propose this time?'

'I'm going to leak it to Oliver, and let him tell the world.'

He was forced to slow as they passed two identical coaches from Blackpool, pictures on the back and sides of smiling families playing on sandy beaches. On holiday he always found himself counting the days.

'No one can verify Khetan's in the UK, so I need to firm it up. If I do, *then* I'll inform CTU *and* the NCA.' Despite playing it down to Maggie, in his head Rick was playing it up. Khetan *could* be in the UK. And would explain Coniston's breakout from Strangeways.

Maggie shook her head. 'I'm worried for you, Rick. One of the findings of the internal enquiry into the shooting of Russell and the murder of Terry Williams last year was your failure to notify CTU.'

'I know.'

They fell silent, and Rick looked straight ahead and drove like an automaton.

His defence had been that he'd assumed Robbo would have done it. The enquiry disagreed, finding that the buck stopped with Rick as SIO. Which was probably fair, but still reflected an oversight from the more senior officers. He'd accepted responsibility, blaming a lost action by a junior detective. The truth, however, was he'd considered it, but had never issued the action and skirted the issue of CTU whenever it had arisen. He'd wanted Khetan to stand trial and for victims – those still alive – and their families to get their day in court. For justice to be done. And not for Khetan to become a pawn in geopolitical chess, far removed from the people the international politicians were meant to represent.

The three-way US / China / Nepal deal a month later showed that he might as well not have bothered.

Last time, and despite the terrible consequences, he'd been right not to inform CTU. Operationally, it would have been no different. And he had no intention of informing them this time.

The car phone sounded again. Robbo's name flashed up on the screen, and both their hands reached out. Rick was a fraction faster, and cancelled the call. Maggie's hand covered his, and for a moment longer than necessary, her pale, warm hand remained there.

'That dead baby, Rick.'

He nodded.

The rain eased, and the pale-yellow sky shimmered with brightness. Rick turned off the motorway and switched off the wipers. If he'd been playing poker, he was all in.

40

Darren Back was eating and unavailable for interview. Detained suspects, more rights than an endangered species.

Rick bought food from the nearest takeaway, and met with Hunter and Maggie in his office. Holding chopsticks in one hand and a square box of egg fried noodles in the other, he stared at a wall map of northwest England. Maggie sat at Rick's computer, and Hunter, worse than a child for staying still, walked around while he ate.

The case had turned upside down. If Khetan was in the UK, Coniston wouldn't be going to Nepal to look for him, but staying put. In addition, it was possible Khetan's nephew Ram was travelling to the UK to see one or both of Coniston and Khetan. The pieces fitted in a smashed plate way; they went together, but left cracks and inconsistencies.

The problem was the pieces: they didn't exist.

Rick ate a prawn. Hypothesis 2b – Coniston escaped from Strangeways to take revenge on Khetan for the death of his father. Assisted by Williams, similarly motivated. Three questions remained. The role of Ram. More crucially, whether Khetan was in the UK, and if so, where.

If Rick was right, the way forward suggested itself. Find

Coniston, find Khetan. Or find Khetan, find Coniston. Success would make Robbo order an entire Chinese menu, and stand Rick in good stead for the DCI promotion. So, brace Darren Back for information on Coniston, and if nothing was forthcoming, concentrate on Khetan. It made sense in his head. He put the noodle box down and turned.

'Why's Ram coming to the UK?'

'Apart from Coniston and his Uncle Khetan, he only knows one person,' said Maggie. 'His grandfather Harri Subba the ex-Ghurkha. Ram's not shown on a port or airport list so he's either not here yet, or has entered illegally. If he's here illegally, and Khetan's running migrants, that seems a good possibility for his passage. Maybe to assist his uncle when he arrives.'

Rick ate a greasy prawn cracker, looking over Maggie's shoulder at her computer where she'd pulled up Ram's family tree. Part of his investigation the previous year.

'After the interview with Back, Gary, I want you to drive down to Aldershot, and talk to Harri Subba. Get a warrant and search his flat. Take Woods and Bennett, and Russell Weather-beater. He wants to go back to see where he was shot, see if he can draw a line under it.' The mountaineer hadn't said so explicitly, but revisiting scenes had sometimes helped Rick. He suddenly remembered Skye, lying in the hospital bed. Going back to the river had helped him know all the facts, but the feelings had remained. Sadness, guilt, longing – for what, he wasn't sure. To turn back the clock and make things happen differently?

'Aye, aye, cap'ain.' Hunter spooned up the last of his rice and dumped the container in the bin. He opened a can of ginger beer, took a long pull.

'We don't actually know Khetan's in the UK,' said Maggie. 'Rima was unsure when you showed her his photo, and he could have touched the Rubik's Cube thousands of miles away.'

'Fair point,' said Rick. He ate another cracker and stared at the map. 'But, apart from Back, it's the best we've got.'

'I still can't believe,' said Maggie, 'our government released Khetan from custody. They *let him go*.'

'Just plain wrong,' said Hunter.

'We're agreed then?' said Rick. 'We go after them both. And we don't tell Robbo.'

'Soldiers,' said Hunter, 'aren't we Maggie?'

She mock-saluted.

'Okay,' said Rick. 'Khetan appears to be involved in a people-smuggling operation. Criminals like everyone else are lazy, so they may well use the same location for the transfer of migrants from lorry to van. If we can identify the transfer site, we'll get Khetan.' He paused as Kasim ran into the office.

'Financial Investigator got a ping, sir.' The young detective's face was flushed, his tie askew, his words gabbled. 'Not Coniston or Williams, but Elly Simmonds, the girl missing from Hartford. Hope it was okay to add her, sir?' Rick nodded. 'She – rather, her cash card – withdrew ten pounds in Scunthorpe yesterday lunchtime. And twenty pounds in Leeds last night, but the system was down.'

'CCTV?'

Kasim shook his head, and cleared his throat. 'Wanted to tell you straight away.'

'Get the CCTV, and come back.'

The young detective nodded.

'And Kasim, I've changed my mind. Do the FI course, you'll be the most revered man in the station.'

'That's you, sir. Locker-room at least.' He about-turned and rushed out of the room.

Hunter picked a scab on his nose. 'I've seen and heard it all now.'

Leeds, Scunthorpe? Rick wasn't sure. The amounts seemed

low, the places hours apart. How were they travelling from one to the other? By public transport or by stealing a car? Or had they teamed up with someone else? Darren Back was in custody. TBR?

'Back to you, Maggie. What do we know about the transfer site?'

'We have three descriptive details. One, it takes a van ninety to 120 minutes to drive there from Bradford; two, there's a largish airport nearby; three, there are ranks of shopping trolleys.' She tapped on the keyboard, and the printer whirred. Her map showed two circles around Bradford. Between them lay Manchester, Sheffield, Blackburn, and York. Not much further were Blackpool, Liverpool, and Hull. Three ports where the lorry could have entered the country, but Rima hadn't mentioned the sea, salty air, gulls.

Rick's mobile rang.

'It's Lou. You left a message about the domestic violence case – Violet Carmichaels. Is now a good time?'

'As it's you.' Rick walked to the door, Maggie throwing him a glance. 'Won't be a moment.'

Next door, the licensing officer was at his desk, but two doors along, the photocopying room was empty. A notice on the photocopier explained why. He shut the door. He'd have stopped working if he'd been similarly abused.

'There's no victim statement,' said Rick, 'so it's a third-party prosecution. They never get home at court. No statements from neighbours or any other witnesses. Just the transcript of the 999 call and the doctor's report. No similar fact – the accused is of good character.'

'Look, Rick, you know as well as anyone that DV is a CPS priority. Also a GMP and government priority.'

'The accused has acknowledged he's got a problem and is undergoing counselling. He's a special constable and done a lot for the Job.'

'He's a well-known climber, a minor celebrity, and should be treated like everyone else.'

'Exactly,' said Rick. 'Not receive a triple punishment. A prison sentence, lose his position in the specials, and be castigated in the community. He's giving back to society, and he's getting help.'

'I'm not sure.'

'He was shot on duty as a police officer. The first volunteer officer to be shot on duty for years.'

'Is this personal, Rick?'

'Of course, it's personal. It's Russell Weatherbeater. I was in charge when he got shot.' The door opened, and a man wearing white dungarees holding a toolbox stood on the threshold. 'Sorry, Lou, I've got a case to nail.'

'Mmm. Arguing with you is always fun. This is a meal at the Taverna in Lightfields without Maggie kind of favour. I'll see what I can do.'

'All yours,' said Rick to the engineer, and pocketed the phone. He returned to his office, Maggie glancing up as he entered. It was a Catch-22 situation: explaining and not explaining both made him look as if he had something to hide. He didn't, but felt like he did.

'CPS, internal matter.'

Nodding, Maggie read from her computer screen. 'For passengers, Manchester is the third largest UK airport; Liverpool the twelfth; Leeds Bradford the fourteenth; Humberside the thirty-fourth. The others outside the top fifty. Manchester has twenty-three million passengers a year, Liverpool four, Leeds three. In terms of flights, Manchester has 163,000 a year.' She opened a drawer, took out Rick's calculator. 'Not many at night, so one every couple of minutes.' She tapped again. 'Liverpool, every ten minutes or so.'

'I'm no egghead,' said Hunter, 'but if he's anywhere, Khetan's in Manchester.'

'Supermarkets, Maggie?' It seemed incredible, but they could have bumped into Khetan filling up with petrol. Coniston's jailbreak made increasing sense. Ram the wild card.

'Not phoned them yet, but I know at least one disused site. Prestwich, near the public order centre.'

Robbo walked into the room. Light-coloured crumbs soiled the front of his dark blue jumper.

'Sir, just the person,' said Rick. 'Got an update on Coniston, and on the more delicate matter. I'll walk with you.'

Rick followed his boss along the corridor, past the kitchenette which reeked of baked beans, past the parade room, noisy as a playground, past the clanking photocopying room. The last door was the prayer room. They entered, Rick shutting both the external door, and the door to the narrow atrium.

The room was cool and quiet, and empty. He'd only been inside once before, a couple of days earlier, when he'd been searching for Maggie. At the front was a small altar, and on each side two rows of chairs. Cushions and mats were grouped at the back. There were drapes along the walls, and fresh flowers on a table. Red- and blue-tinged light entered through a stained-glass window.

'I'm not sure this place is appropriate, sir. I'm an atheist.' Rick could smell the flowers; they reminded him of the apiary.

'You've got an answer for everything, only not the ones I want. Try me on Bradford.'

'What the bookies would call even money. Khetan's finger-prints were found on a Rubik's Cube seized by Bradford CID. Still making enquiries, but looks promising.'

'That wouldn't get my wallet out of my pocket.'

'We'll kick a few doors, I'm confident. Likewise with your car. I've got a suspect.'

Robbo looked at his watch, the expensive face catching the coloured light from the stained glass.

'Who?'

'When I'm sure, I'll let you know.'

'The Carmichaels file?'

'All but sorted.'

Robbo went out, late for a meeting. Rick sat on a chair and looked at the altar, at the shelf of prayer books, at the stained glass. Inhaled the delicate aroma. He bowed his head and prayed to a God he didn't believe in.

RAM'S FAMILY TREE

DCI Rick Castle

June 2015

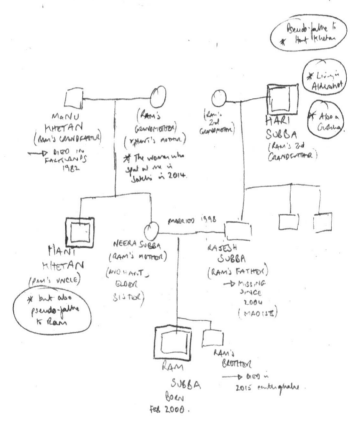

41

Interview room 3 and the smell of wet trainers. Home from home.

The door shoved open. The Welsh custody sergeant stood, glowered, signed Back over. The prisoner wore jeans and a t-shirt and entered with a swagger. He was chewing gum, and looked lively as a wild cat.

Hunter unwrapped the tapes.

'What's the secret with all the women?'

Back eased out his chair. 'Either you got it, or you ain't.'

Hunter slapped the tape doors shut. 'Oh, I got it all right.' Scratching his groin, he dumped the cellophane in the bin. He pressed record. The tapes beeped and fell silent. Hunter sat down, winked at Back.

B movie over, it was time for the main feature.

Back chewed faster, glancing at Hunter, then back at Rick. He smiled. 'Ha!'

'Calix Coniston has escaped from prison,' said Rick.

'No comment.'

'You shared a cell in Strangeways with Coniston for ninety-seven days.'

'No comment.' Back chewed, and tilted his head one way, then the other. His albino eyes darting all over.

'Since your release, you've visited Coniston twice. Once in September, and just before Christmas.'

'No comment.' Back chewed and chewed. He would get bored, only the brain-dead and political detainees didn't get bored.

'Have you seen Coniston since he escaped?'

'No comment.'

'Have you spoken to him?'

'No comment.'

'Have you assisted Coniston in any way since he broke out? For example: offered him a place to rest his head, given him cash or clothing.'

'No comment.'

'Yesterday, did you happen to visit Scunthorpe – or Leeds?'

Back juddered his chair back and stood. Hunter leapt up, took a step, and put a hand on Back's shoulder and pressed down. Back resisted, and Hunter jabbed him in the side. Their prisoner didn't speak, but sat slowly. He looked at Rick. 'No comment. No fucking comment.'

'Cuffs?' said Hunter.

'Darren?' said Rick.

'No comment.'

'Look, I know you'll say no comment 'til the end of time, but we all want something. Tell me what I want to know, and I'll tell you something in return.'

'No comment.'

'What do you want, Darren?'

'No comment.'

'You, Darren, are what we call a professional.' Rick caught Hunter's eye and ran a finger across his throat. Hunter clicked off the tapes. The real interview still to start. Hunter escorted Back into the custody suite and Rick followed behind. He whispered instructions to the jailer.

The reception area smelt even worse than the interview room. The Scottish fell-running custody sergeant stood up and bawled at a prisoner. The arresting officer, a stout female probationer, looked embarrassed.

Rick hung back.

The door to the rest of the station buzzed open, and Kasim walked in. In his hand, a brown wallet file. 'Sir, I've got the financial investigator's report. Thought it might be relevant to your interview.'

Rick nodded and followed the young 'tec back out. The custody door felt heavier than usual, the result of his early morning ride. Push-Power had set up a racing wheelchair, but he'd only managed three miles. He felt like he'd swum the Channel. Maggie regularly rode ten miles, occasionally twenty.

At the bottom of the nearest stairwell Kasim handed Rick the report. He opened the cover and flicked through.

1. *The Strangeways prison guards at Hedges Cemetery*
2. *TBR and Darren Back*
3. *Coniston's bank account*
4. *Coniston's 10k transfer to Anthony Back, September 2015*
5. *Coniston's 5k transfer to Barney Williams, February 2016*

He already knew the information on Sakit Patel, and there was nothing untoward about the other three guards, Swales, Twite, and Agar. He turned to the second section. Neither TBR, nor Back had a bank account or credit cards. Their National Insurance numbers showed they didn't claim benefits. They used cash, or, and more likely in TBR's case, used false details.

Coniston's bank account was more interesting. His current account held over ninety thousand pounds – several times Rick's, annoyingly. It was the result of losing both parents and being the only surviving child. And Coniston was going to become wealthier as his mother's estate had not been finalised. There'd been no transactions since his escape.

The fourth section blew his mind. The day Terry Williams had been murdered in Barnes, Coniston had transferred ten k to Anthony Back, Darren's younger brother. From memory, Rick thought Anthony didn't even have a criminal record. The payment, then, likely to be destined for Darren. But why? It implicated Coniston in Terry Williams' murder. Darren Back, too.

'Have you read this?'

'Yes, sir.' Kasim paused. 'How well do you know Anthony Back, sir?'

'Go on.'

'He's clean, works as a cashier in a petrol station. I statemented him a few times when I was in the shoplifting squad. He's alright, really. For one of them.'

Rick's head was spinning. He'd been handed a detonator for the interview with Back, but at the same time information that ripped into his hypotheses.

He skimmed the final section of the report. A month before Coniston had escaped, he'd transferred five k to Barney Williams. Williams had withdrawn it in four amounts the following week. That information seemed more straightforward, all but confirming Williams had assisted Coniston to break out.

But his hypotheses were in disarray. H2, Coniston escaped as a means to an end, he had thought meant Coniston going after Khetan, H2a. But, if the previous year Coniston had conspired with Khetan in the murder of Terry Williams, it made no sense. And doubly so, in light of the recent payment to Barney Williams.

Rick slapped the wall, the noise echoing up the stairwell. Rectangles of light covered the stairs. 'Questions, Kasim. You might not know the answers, but then again you might. Why is

Coniston's bank account not frozen while he's in prison? And how can he access it there?'

Kasim looked sheepish. 'I did have a quick chat with my cousin.' He cleared his throat. 'It's possible for prisoners to access their bank accounts, but it has to be authorised by the prison governor, and can be done only by way of a letter. The ten k and five k transfers were made online. Probably from an illegal phone.'

'Not sure you need to go on the FI course.'

Rick folded his hand around the banister. It felt cool, solid. He needed to adapt his hypotheses to the new information. H1, end in itself, out. H3, forced to escape, out; Coniston was paying people, calling the shots. Which left H2, means to an end. But what end? H2a, Coniston and Williams, and possibly Darren Back, were hunting Khetan. H2b, Coniston was again conspiring with Khetan, and Williams, too. But why? Another FIFA target?

The door to custody buzzed open. Frank the jailer stood there wheezing. 'Ready for you, sir.'

Maggie appeared at the end of the corridor. She waved a piece of paper at Rick, and he waited until she drew up. 'I've compiled a list of seven disused supermarket sites and three DIY stores in Manchester.' She handed him the paper. She wore pale pink lipstick. She wanted a baby.

'Phone DC Morris, and see if he can arrange for Rima to go on tour with us.' Maggie nodded. 'How was training this morning?' He resisted the urge to tell her about his own ride.

Kasim took a step backwards. The custody door started beeping because it had been open too long. 'Sir,' said Frank.

'Okay, I'm on track for under three hours.'

'Kasim,' said Rick, 'you'll sponsor Maggie, won't you?'

'Course I will. I'll get the whole office to sign up.'

Rick jogged down the corridor to custody. He'd make it up to them in overtime. 'Thanks,' he shouted over his shoulder.

'Both of you.' He slowed to a walk. Good detectives never ran anywhere – they used the time to think. Kasim probably already knew that.

He entered the bedlam, the custody door clunking heavily behind him.

'They're in the cage, sir,' said Frank, shuffling as if he was wearing two left shoes.

The cage was the outside area designated for prisoners' smoking, and accessible only from the custody suite. Darren Back stood at one end, his arms poking through the wire and smoking. Hunter stood next to him. The two men were talking, and as Rick approached, Hunter nodded.

Frank unlocked the door and Rick stepped inside the cage. The floor strewn with fag butts and chewing gum splodges. Through the wire, half the backyard sat in sunlight, half in shadow.

The jailer shuffled away.

Hunter scratched his ear.

Rick stared at the prisoner. Back's neck between his hairline and his collar was thick and red, like a raw steak.

'Your younger brother works in the petrol station on Booth Street. Anthony's a good lad, not got a record. Not even a caution.' Rick paused. 'Last year, however, ten thousand pounds was paid into his bank account by Calix Coniston. At the exact time of Terry Williams' murder.'

Back pulled on the cigarette, the end flaring softly.

'If you've got something, fucking charge me.'

'That can wait, but recapturing Coniston can't.'

Back remained looking out across the dark and the light of the yard. He stood still as a statue.

'Anthony really is a good lad. Not even a possession charge. Your mum must be proud. But maybe it's because he hasn't been stopped enough. Maybe, if we started stopping him, we'd find something. If we looked hard enough, wanted to find it enough. And believe me, we want to find it, and we will find it.'

Back flicked away the cigarette and turned to face Rick. He wasn't handcuffed. Rick stiffened and Hunter took a half-pace. Their reaction instinctive and together.

'Ha! You pair of cunts.'

Rick stared into Back's ghostly eyes. He was glad neither his mum nor Maggie had heard his speech.

'You'll leave my brother alone?'

'You have my word.'

'So?'

'Tell Coniston I want to meet him.'

'You'll have to bail me.'

Rick nodded.

'That's it?'

'That's it.'

Rick turned and called for the jailer. Already, time was moving too slowly. In his head, he bellowed like a rhino separated from its young.

42

Calix squeezed through the gap in the hedge with next door. Bamboo whipped his face and stones pressed into his knees. The gap was smaller than he remembered. Staying on his knees, he surveyed his back garden. The tractor tyre sandpit where he'd first encountered beetles, the plum tree where he'd snared birds and squirrels, the wood where he'd smoked with Megan. His old man's beloved lawn. It needed mowing and the garden cutting back. Not today.

He crawled forward to a silver birch, and looked down on the house. Taking his time, he inspected every window for signs of movement or anything unusual. Nothing he could see. It was possible but unlikely Castle was watching, and a risk he had to take. He glanced behind him at the Finchams' roof protruding above the hedge. He wondered what Barney and Elly were talking about.

A goldfinch landed on the flags and pecked at the seedhead of a dandelion. He watched it awhile, never having had the taxidermy pleasure. Red and gold and black, the cloak of an emperor.

The bird flew off, and Calix crawled up to the house. The lounge looked as it always had done: brown leather suite, dark brown furniture. Staying low, he made his way to the back porch and stood up. Under a shelf stood a raggedy line of Wellington boots. He felt around in the largest pair and pulled out a pair of socks. Inside them was a set of keys. He grabbed a pair of gardening gloves, unlocked the back door and went inside.

The kitchen annex smelt of washing powder. In a cupboard, the boiler chugged quietly. Home. He'd lived there for over a decade. He saw his mother emptying his schoolbag, putting his gym kit into the washer, finding the packet of cigarettes. Someone playing a prank, he'd protested. She knew, of course she knew.

He heard the scrunching of gravel. A man with a bright orange delivery bag was limping up the drive.

Calix ducked down. Fluorescent garb always made him think twice. A clutch of leaflets skidded along the hall floor, the letterbox pinged. As the man limped away, Calix thought he recognised him. Someone from his childhood, or from Strangeways? Dibble – a stooge of Castle?

He observed the man walk away, looking for a hop with the wrong leg. But the leafleteer hobbled consistently, and was either genuine, or a master of dibblecraft.

Feeling the burn of risk intensify, Calix climbed the stairs, past the photos of his old man in military uniforms – khaki, ceremonial, number twos? He felt the keen stare of his old man watching him. Two flights led to the attic, his room. His tools; his workbench; and his animals, all looking at him with cold glassy eyes.

He went to the window where he'd once left food for Bird Bird. The feeder was still attached to the frame. He pushed it open and looked out, straining to hear a squawk and searching for a flash of red or blue that would give the parrot away. But he heard and saw no sign. He wondered if she was still alive, whether she'd raised young. Whether he would ever feed a fledgling. He banged the window shut.

And paused a moment.

He turned. On the bed was a book, *No Future Without Forgiveness* by Desmond Tutu, and a note from his mother.

Calix
Time to get on with the rest of your life, and make something
of yourself. Make a dead woman happy.
Mum

He picked it up and sat down. Took a moment.

The chinking of gravel made him move to a window. He couldn't see anyone. He looked out the back of the house. No one.

He read the note again. The blunt phrasing was unlike his mum, but maybe she'd wanted him to remember it. He stared at the paper. She'd always had high hopes for him, ensuring he did his homework, insisting on three sciences at GCSE. He wondered if she'd been fulfilled, trailing around the world for his old man's army postings, and later keeping house. The odd bit of charity work, but no career. Two children, but Megan accidentally killed, and Calix jailed – and not like other children. He'd never invited friends around for tea, not once taken home a girlfriend. Maybe she'd have liked Elly. Maybe she wouldn't have.

He ran his fingers across the duvet.

She knew everything about Khetan – the kidnap and Spencer's death, the sequence of events on the suspension bridge leading to his old man's death, the murder of Barney's old man. Surely, she didn't forgive Khetan for ripping their family – and Barney's family – apart? Surely, she was not asking for him to do the same?

From a desk drawer, he pocketed a knife and a headtorch.

He went down one flight of stairs, and along the corridor to the hatch in the ceiling. Three quarters of the attic was his room, but the rest had been used by his old man to store suitcases, bits of carpet, and miscellanea. He popped the hatch, pulled down the ladder, and climbed up.

Warm stale air wafted down. He switched on the light.

There wasn't much to see. A cluster of cases, half a dozen rolls of carpet. Wooden joists poked up through the insulation. He put on the gardening gloves and rolled up a strip. He rolled it back, rolled up its neighbour. Halfway across he found the red handtowel. He unfolded it.

And there, as if it was hibernating, lay the handgun.

His old man had brought it back from the Falklands. On the last day of the campaign, almost the last action, he'd used it to kill an Argie as he and his platoon had stormed Mount William. His old man was a hero – whatever anyone said about the accident with the grenade.

Calix picked it up, and fingered the crosshatched grip, the smooth barrel. The gun felt all its nine hundred grams. With his right index finger, he pressed the release button and the magazine dropped from the grip. It was empty. He pulled back the slide and checked the chamber. Empty. He released the slide. Then, raising the gun to shoulder height, he stretched out his arm, closed his left eye and looked through the sights at Hant Khetan.

He squeezed the trigger.

The hammer fell and the gun clicked. His heart pounded as if it was for real. He pushed up the safety catch.

He could hear his old man. It's a Browning Hi-Power, semi-automatic, nine millimetre. It takes a magazine of thirteen rounds in a double stack. Always hoping Calix would follow in his footsteps, join the army, better still the Ghurkhas. Calix always a disappointment, Megan the prodigal child.

Calix unrolled the rest of the towel. There was a small cleaning kit and a spare magazine. But nothing else. He picked up the cleaning kit and turned the towel over. He put the gardening gloves back on and checked the area around the towel. Nothing. He rolled the gun back in the towel and put it next to the hatch. He searched the loft. It took him an hour: he rolled up every strip of insulation, checked the water tank, the carpet. Even the suitcases.

He climbed down the ladder with his find, and started on the house. His parents' bedroom. It made sense not to keep the two things together, but if you were keeping a gun, why not keep a box of ammunition.

In the back of his old man's wardrobe he discovered a safe. After another hour he found the key, hidden in an old aerosol lid in a bathroom cabinet. Jackpot.

Or so it seemed briefly. But there was only jewellery, old copies of his parents' wills, and five Krugerands.

Two hours later he gave up. He collected his razor and toothbrush from the bathroom, ibuprofen for Barney, dental floss for Elly, and went downstairs. After locking the door, he replaced the key in the boot, stuffed his old man's khaki smock into a rucksack, and returned next door.

Barney and Elly were upstairs in the main bedroom. Barney was playing solo chess, turning the board every move. Always winning, always losing. Elly dozed on the bed, her legs folded down at the end, and her pink hat pushed back. She looked pale, vulnerable.

'Success?' said Barney.

Calix put his bag of things on the bed, and sat down. 'Yes, and no.' He lit a cigarette, his hands shaking.

Elly sat up. She adjusted her hat, tucking her hair underneath.

'I dreamt I was in a tent in the desert. An oasis with date trees. I was trying to escape on a camel, but it wouldn't stand up.' She opened Calix's rucksack. She took out the gun and held it in one hand. She pointed it at Calix, at Barney. 'It's heavy.' She held it under her chin, the barrel pointing upwards. 'Bang!'

'You don't have to be here,' said Calix. 'In fact, I think you should go.'

Barney picked up his black knight. 'Tell her, she deserves to know.'

'Yes, tell me,' said Elly. 'Whatever it is.'

'And if I don't?' said Calix.

'I'll sing the Birdie song.'

'Okay, okay.' Calix raised his hands in mockery. He pulled on the cigarette. 'Okay.' He took a deep breath. 'My old man was a soldier in the Ghurkhas. An officer. In the Falklands War he was a young lieutenant and led a platoon of thirty men, mostly young Nepalese. During the fighting, a grenade landed near my old man. He hurled it away, but it landed amongst his own men, killing Manu Khetan, Hant Khetan's father. Two years ago, Hant Khetan kidnapped me and Barney in Nepal. My old man died trying to rescue us. A year later, Hant murdered Barney's old man. For a time he was the FBI's most wanted in South Asia.'

'What happened?'

'To cut a long story short, Khetan was lured to the UK and arrested by a Manchester detective called Castle. A dibble who knew what was right, and was prepared to act accordingly. However, Khetan was quickly released.'

'Why?'

'I don't know. All I know is that he's here in England, and I – we – have a chance to resolve the situation. For good.' He nodded at the gun.

Elly replaced it in the rucksack. She lay back and stared at the ceiling. Barney took a white pawn with the black knight, and swivelled the board. Calix smoked down the cigarette.

His phone buzzed.

'Just the person.' Not that he would charge Darren with having a great mind. 'I need that second favour – you mentioned the armourer.'

'It's a nickname.'

'For what?'

'What do you think.'

Calix described the gun and made the requisition. Some days, five minutes talking to Darren was four and a half minutes too long.

'What did you want?'

'Eh?'

'You rang me.'

'I been arrested. Just bailed by that dibble you're friendly with.'

Being thought of as friendly with the dibble was not a good look. But sensing there was more, Calix said nothing.

'He wants to meet with you.'

'Why?'

'He didn't say.'

Calix hung up, but kept hold of the phone. It had to be a trap, and an obvious one. Even so, he was tempted.

Barney moved his white bishop. Turned the chessboard. Moved his black castle. Turned the board. Elly rolled onto her side and wedged her hands under her head. She stared out of the large window, at the tops of the trees and the rushing clouds. Calix picked his nails and lit another cigarette.

His phone buzzed again. The number a landline he didn't recognise. He let it ring out, puffing like an old man on the cigarette. It rang again, the same number.

'Hello?'

'Hello, sir, will you take a reverse charge call from Ram Subba?'

'I will.' Calix stubbed out the cigarette on the edge of the chair while he was connected. There was a click, a handover from the telephonist. 'Ram?'

'I want live you, Calix.'

'Okay. *Ramro.*' Fine. He paused. 'Are you with Hant?'

'*Ho.*' Yes.

'*Kahaan?*' Where?

'*Thaahaa chhaina.*' I don't know.

Calix heard a slap and a yelp. Then the line went dead. He phoned the number back, but it rang, and rang. He tried a second time. He phoned the operator. She told him it was a telephone box in Manchester, but she couldn't give him any further details. He threw the phone onto the bed, and went to stand by the window. Black-bellied clouds marshalled in the distance, the air felt heavy and humid. A thunderstorm was imminent.

He made another phone call, Barney and Elly watching him like sycophantic generals.

'The house is yours.'

'Okay, dog.'

Drum 'n' bass thumped down the phone.

43

A giant oak tree guarded the arched entrance to the Hedges Cemetery. The pavement was buckled with the roots and reminded Rick of walking through a rhododendron forest in Nepal. He'd been chasing Coniston, then.

He looked around, but there was no sign of him. The car park deserted. The fugitive was unlikely to show, and if the roles had been reversed, he wouldn't. He risked adjusting the handcuffs tucked into the waistband at the back of his trousers.

Notices signalled a community working party, directions to the nearest florist, a vacancy for a gravedigger.

He walked through the metal arch and looked up the graveyard, replaying Coniston's escape and flight. Well planned and executed, and in other circumstances, the brigadier would have been proud. Rick detoured left and stopped in front of the two Coniston gravestones. He bowed his head, reflected a moment. Couldn't choose your son, couldn't choose your father. The human condition.

A breaking twig made him turn.

Coniston, alone, unburdened. His blue eyes sparkled and his sclerae were clear as those on a Nepalese *chorten*. As if he'd slept.

'I didn't think you'd show.'

'Knew *you* would.' Coniston stopped just out of grabbing distance. 'Those close to me said it would be a trap.'

'But?' said Rick, wondering who Coniston meant. TBR, Back, or Williams. All of them? Or none of them. Coniston, slippery as an eel. Rick knew that, and revelled in it.

'It's why I wanted to meet here. You respected my old man, and I didn't think you'd act dishonourably in front of him.'

Rick stepped away. 'Take a moment.'

Coniston moved closer to the headstones. He bent down in front of his mother's and laid a sprig of heather. He reached forward and touched the stone. He stood up, stepped sideways, and squatted down again. Laid another sprig, leant forward to touch the stone, following the inscription with his fingers. *Brigadier David Coniston, 1959-2014. Loved his men and his family.*

Rick felt the back of his neck prickle.

Coniston stood up, dressed back. Rick moved closer, within grabbing distance. Coniston didn't flinch.

'I've been looking into your accounts.' Like an international athlete, Rick visualised a grab. 'They're far healthier than mine.'

'Only so many chocolate bars and phone cards you can consume in Strangeways.'

'You sent five k to Barney Williams.'

'Maybe.'

'And on the day Terry Williams was murdered by Khetan, you sent ten k to Anthony Back. What I don't understand, and here's my question, is why you conspired with Khetan to kill Terry Williams?'

'I didn't.'

A grab would be simple, quick. Deep breath. Then, step forward, yank Coniston off-balance, and handcuff. One second, two seconds, three seconds.

'Are you taping this?'

'No.'

'Let's just say the third party involved needed something for his trouble.'

Rick thought back, but only for a moment. 'You paid the gunman at Barnes. Not to kill Terry Williams, but to kill Khetan. Of course.'

A car drove past the graveyard. Coniston glanced around, turned back, but didn't speak.

'Where is Khetan now?'

'Why is he even out?' Coniston's voice held anger. It was an emotion they shared, something Rick could use.

'Nepal is getting two massive hydro-electric dams. They'll provide cheap electricity and raise living standards for over a million people.'

'And the US?'

Rick shrugged, impressed by Coniston's geopolitical appraisal. 'Releasing Khetan was a decision I can assure you I had nothing to do with, and which has infuriated me.'

'I know he's in the UK – in England, somewhere up north.'

In the next row, birds flittered amongst the lichen-covered headstones. Two chasing each other, flashes of yellow.

'Calix?'

'You'll have me on the dibble payroll next.'

'We want the same thing.'

'You said that in Nepal.'

'Are you familiar with the prisoner's dilemma?'

'Intimately. Whether to take a shower, eat the canteen food, whether to close my eyes at night.'

'It's a thought experiment. Two members of a criminal gang are locked up. Each prisoner is held in solitary confinement and cannot speak to or pass a message to the other. The police don't have enough evidence to convict them on the main charge. Their fallback is to sentence both men to a year in prison on a lesser charge. But before they do, they offer each prisoner a deal. There are four possible outcomes:

'If prisoner A and prisoner B betray each other, they will serve two years in prison. If A betrays B but B stays silent, A will be released and B will serve three years. And vice versa. Finally, if they both remain silent, both will serve one year.'

One of the chasing birds rested on Mrs Coniston's headstone. Seemed to eye the two of them quizzically before flying off.

'The two prisoners A and B,' said Rick, 'should work together for the best outcome, but might not.'

'You and me?'

'If we work *together*, we can locate Khetan and lock him up for the rest of his life. If we don't, he might serve nothing.'

'It didn't happen last time,' said Coniston. He looked over his shoulder at the entrance to the graveyard and the road. Turned back.

'No, it didn't. But this time, it'll be different. If we're successful in recapturing Khetan, I'll leak it to the press along with the circumstances of his previous release. There'll be national outrage, and questions in the Commons, followed by a public enquiry.'

'I'll think about it.'

Rick stepped forward and brushed a cobweb from the brigadier's headstone. He stepped back. 'He'd be unimpressed.'

Coniston raised an eyebrow.

'Your father was a senior army commander and made a lot of decisions. To make them, he gathered information, and when he could, reflected on the pros and cons. But if time was short, or the situation dictated, he was decisive.'

'I'm not my old man.'

'You're not.' No one was, thought Rick. Everyone thought they were an improved version, but the truth was often different. 'He was his own man.'

The two of them stared at the headstone. Reread the inscription.

'Okay,' said Coniston. 'If you're pushing me.'

'I am.'

'The answer's, No.'

A minicab pulled up at the entrance to the cemetery. *Pete's Cabs*. The driver executed a three-point-turn, but didn't drive away. The engine left running.

'Neither of us will get what we want,' said Rick.

'That's what you think.'

The minicab driver hooted.

Like the brigadier, Rick could also be decisive. It hadn't been his intention, despite his visualisation, but if Coniston refused to work cooperatively, then arresting him would be the better outcome. And leave Coniston with the worst. He could mull the prisoner's dilemma for weeks at a time back in his cell.

Turning to face his fugitive, Rick pulled the handcuffs from the back of his trousers. He grabbed Coniston's hand, yanked him around and off-balance, and snapped one half of the cuffs on his wrist. Three seconds, as he'd pictured.

'I gave you a chance to cooperate.'

Coniston reached down to his ankle, and drew out a short length of scaffolding bar from the back of a trouser leg. Rick stepped back, but was stopped by the brigadier's headstone. Helping his son, even now. Without warning or backswing, Coniston lashed out. Rick swayed back but not fast enough, the bar striking a glancing blow to his head. He toppled over the back of the headstone.

Coniston peered down, resting his still-handcuffed hand on top of the stone. 'I knew I shouldn't have trusted you.'

Rick sprawled on the ground, woozy as a recruit on passing out day. Somehow, he opened his eyes, stared up.

'You should have done. If you'd agreed to work with me, I wouldn't have produced my handcuffs.'

His eyes flickered shut.

Footsteps, running.

Eyes, open.

Coniston, gone.

Rick hauled himself up the gravestone, and watched the minicab drive away. A bird with a flash of yellow settled on a neighbouring headstone. Quizzical, still.

44

Ram's eye was bloodshot and swollen, the eyelid black, blue, and purple. His cheek was puffy and crusty red. His nose was bent and cut. His face pale. He smelt of antiseptic and cigarettes. The boy sat in the flat's saggy armchair. It was a huge chair with a fold-out leg rest and shaped sides to keep your head from lolling to the side. Covered with a yellow braided material, faded but functional. His nephew sat like a village elder, not talking, not smiling while Hant ran around like a third wife.

The brilliant colours reminded Hant of a *chorten*. The boy's eyes were equally cold and condemning, and followed Hant as he hurried in and out of the room with swabs and drinks, and even bits to eat.

He'd hit the boy too hard in the phone box. But now there were problems: if they were stopped by the police, they might be questioned; and the boy was sullen, silent, and would be difficult to motivate. Tomorrow, another delivery of migrants and work to do.

Hant went into the kitchen to refill the boy's glass with water. He stood at the chipped enamel sink and looked out of the window at the migrants washing cars. Hosing, sponging, scrubbing, dressed in their matching yellow t-shirts. He could hear high-pitched ringing. He pinched his nose and blew out his ears, but the noise persisted. A scooter pulled up with two people. The rider took off his helmet – black with orange flames – and spoke to the nearest washer. Hant thought he'd seen him on the forecourt before. Probably enquiring about a job.

He returned to the main room and set the glass down by the armchair. He sat on the floor cross-legged, ready to make his peace with the boy. But first with God.

He looked up at his nephew.

God told him to get off the floor, Hant was not a dog, the boy not the Dalai Lama.

Hant pulled over a crate and sat level with the boy. It helped him find the words to speak to him. God knew what he was doing.

He told the boy he was sorry. He spoke Nepali as a concession. Other concessions, too. A visit to the cinema, tonight if he wanted, and all the popcorn he could eat. And a trip to see the boy's grandfather Harri, in the Belle Vue nursing home in Aldershot. Next week, or the week after.

The boy sipped the water, trying not to grin.

'Okay.'

The boy had only to work for him for six months. After six months Hant would have paid back Manoj, would have given free passage to many of their people, and have created a war chest. He would be able go home to Nepal and plot afresh. *Dharma.* The boy could stay in England, Hant would procure a British passport for him, or the boy could return to Nepal. It would be up to Ram to choose. In Australia… You know, Australia?

'*Chaina.*' No. The boy's reply dripped with sarcasm. He was better, getting better, Hant was getting through.

So, in Australia, the native people go on walkabout when they're about your age. They head into the desert alone, and fend for themselves for six months. They find food and water, and shelter. And after six months, they return to the villages. They return as men. You work six months for me, you return as a man. Your work six months for me, I give you money and control of your future.

There was a knock on the door.

Hant wasn't expecting anyone. No one knew their address. He half-ran into the kitchen and took a knife from the drawer. Holding it by his leg, he peered out of the back bedroom window. At the door were the two lads from the scooter, one holding a phone. Their bike leant on its stand at the foot of the steep flight of stone steps behind them. They were pasty and stringy-looking.

One of them knocked again. The second pointed to an open window in the bathroom.

Hant opened the door a crack and looked out. The knife by his leg, the knife ready.

'Yes?'

'Do you want any eggs?' said the boy who'd knocked.

'Smile,' said the second boy, holding up his phone and pointing it at Hant.

He looked the boys over, glanced down at their bike. He looked around the rear yard of the car wash, but there was no one. And only two vehicles, the boys' scooter and his van. He wondered if he'd misunderstood.

'What is eggs?'

'Eggs?' The first boy sniggered. 'Eggs is eggs.' He clucked and flapped his arms like a chicken.

The boy with the phone retreated down a step. 'Come on, Starfish.'

Hant considered. Either way, he and Ram would have to move out of the car wash and find somewhere else. The two boys backed down the steps, laughing but still looking up as if

Hant was Ravana. As if they *knew* he was Ravana. The boys reached halfway down the steps. They did know.

Hant opened the door wider and rushed out.

The boys turned and flew down. Threading an arm through his flame-covered helmet, the first boy straddled the bike and started the ignition. Hant wasn't wearing shoes and the rough stone of the steps bit into his feet. The scooter puttered forward, the second helmet crashing to the ground and rolling away. The second boy didn't delay for his helmet but ran alongside the scooter. At the foot of the steps, Hant dropped the knife and grabbed a broom. He sprinted after the bike. The second boy tried to mount the scooter, but couldn't. Hant held the broom like a spear. The scooter sped along the side of the building, and rounding the corner, barged through the melée of half-washed cars and yellow-shirted washers. The second boy still not astride.

'Thief,' shouted Hant.

No one seemed to understand. The washers stood and laughed as if it was all some big joke.

The scooter bumped down onto the road and the second boy mounted. Hant threw the broom at the rear wheel, but it fell short and tumbled into the gutter.

The scooter accelerated, its engine screeching in protest. Hant chased up the road, the boys weaving in and out of the traffic, and the pillion passenger glancing behind. They turned up a side street and disappeared from view. Hant slowed, and finally stopped by a lamppost with a loose panel.

'*Bandar ko chaak.*'

He slapped the panel back and forth until it clattered to the ground, then picked grit and spots of tar from the soles of his feet. A gringo's pads, now.

45

'Next left,' said Rick, glancing at his phone, then back at the road.

Number five on Maggie's list was an old Value supermarket in Chadwick, a suburb which sat astride the ring road in north-east Manchester.

Hunter turned off the main road into an industrial estate, and Rick checked behind that the others were following. Maggie sat alongside Kasim, and in the back were Rima and Amin. The two vehicles passed a large sign covered in black plastic and tape. Crows circled overhead and the air smelt of chemicals.

They turned right at a roundabout and into the supermarket site. On the left was a boarded-up petrol station. Chains and padlocks hung from the pumps and a closed sign hung on the door. *Forever* graffitied underneath. They came to another roundabout. Deliveries were to the left, parking and store straight ahead.

'Straight,' said Rick.

Fifty metres in front of them sat the Value store. Two storeys high, stretching left and right. As they drove past, Rick peered at the lines of tall shelving and long row of empty checkouts. Not a single person. It was eerie, like an apocalyptic film. They turned away from the store and down the far side of the complex. On the left was a small wood and behind it the main road which he could hear but not see. To their right was a huge parking area which, according to the sign, had space for 405 cars. A couple of cans rattled about the deserted lot and plastic rubbish had collected in wind eddies. Dandelions dotted the concrete. He half expected to see a posse of Triffids.

Hunter continued to where they'd started, but this time turned left to deliveries. On the left was another wood. The trees screened the site from casual observers. At number four on the list a railway track had run alongside and every time a train passed, hundreds of potential witnesses would have stared out of the windows.

'Harri Subba?' said Rick.

'As I said on the phone, Harri's not a well man. He's in a care home, and his flat's been taken back by the council. Not had any visitors but the home received a strange phone call enquiring about Harri. The manager will phone me if there's any more contact. I've put the local cop shop on notice. What happened to your face?'

'Later.'

Rick had been close to convincing Coniston to work together. Even closer to nabbing him. And now? Back to slower, more speculative policework.

Hunter buzzed down the window, scratched his arm across the edge of the glass.

They reached the end of the road and the cage marshalling area. Behind the sign were hundreds of supermarket trolleys. Hunter turned through the open gate into the deliveries compound. The security hut next to the gate was boarded up. A steel palisade fence surrounded the compound. Hunter parked in the middle.

Rick climbed out. To the left of the gate were three unloading bays, their huge roller doors padlocked to the ground. Opposite the bays two skips overflowed with rubbish, and nearby, a stack of cardboard tied in bundles, and a cage of orange gas cylinders. Behind the security hut stood a container from the back of a truck, and a secure storage metal shed. All very similar to the delivery compounds they'd already visited.

Fifth time lucky, he hoped. If the list proved negative, maybe they'd have to sit up on Harri Subba's care home.

Come on!

The second car pulled into the compound. Rima helped Amin out of the back seat, and rubbed a mark off his face. Finally, she looked around. Her face remained passive.

Rick took photos, and sketched a map. He wanted to pressurise their informant, but stress made people forget.

Rima began to turn around. The roller doors were lipstick-red – but there had been other red doors. The skips, the containers, the hut – but there had been other skips, other containers, other huts. Rima looked carefully; she turned a full circle. Rick turned with her.

She turned around again, slower, Amin pulling at her leg. Another full circle.

Then sank to her knees.

Kasim and Maggie stopped talking. Hunter climbed out of the car and leant against the open door.

Rima shut her eyes and tears streamed down her face. She bowed down to the ground and said a few words in Arabic. Amin started to cry.

Rick walked over.

She opened her eyes and nodded. 'This is place.'

Rick felt hot and cold. If he'd been able to turn an air somersault, he would have done. He grinned at Amin and raised a thumb, the boy smiling uncertainly.

A scooter buzzed along the service road, and a squad of crows took off from the trees.

Rick walked back to the car.

'I'm not sure,' said Hunter.

'I knew you'd say that.'

'Falling to her knees, wailing, all seemed a bit over the top. Like she'd been practising. It makes no difference to her whether we get Khetan or not. It might even be a way of getting her family into the UK.'

'A baby was smothered in that lorry.'

'Only Rima's word on that.'

'For God's sake, Gary, look at the state of her.'

'I didn't say I didn't believe her. I said, I wasn't sure.' Hunter was right, Rick wanted to believe her. His sergeant didn't seem to care either way.

At the gate stood a scooter with two people sat astride. The rider wore a black helmet with a stencil of orange flames. Something familiar about the riders, that helmet. The passenger, wearing a balaclava in place of a helmet, held up a phone toward the compound, toward Rima and the others, and moved it through an arc. Rick didn't like it. Coincidence, sixth sense, it didn't matter. 'Oy.' He walked towards them, but the scooter was already turning.

Rick raced back to the car and jumped in. He fired the engine, yanked the door shut, and drove, pointing through the windscreen at the disappearing scooter. Hunter reached for his phone, Kasim for his radio.

Rick accelerated out of the yard and along the service road. The scooter was already at the roundabout, and whining loudly from the double load. He drove faster, and didn't turn at the roundabout, but careered straight over, the tyres bumping up the low kerb, and the undercarriage grazing the scrub. A bang loud as a gunshot emanated from the front axle. The scooter swerved around the second mini-roundabout. Rick's car plunged forward, but with a rattling offside wheel-arch – as if a spanner had been forgotten at the last service. The scooter reached the main road and slewed to a halt at the central barrier. Cars hooted and swerved. The two riders dismounted and hefted the bike over the barrier. Rick braked hard at the main road. Stopped. Climbed out. Watched the scooter speed away up the side road.

He phoned the control room. They said it was a false plate. They'd send a unit. Rick booted the offside tyre, and climbed back in.

He drove back to the compound, the front of the car sounding like a child playing in a kitchen cupboard. At the gate he wound down the window and shook his head.

Hunter walked over. 'Rima found something. A swastika daubed on the door of the security hut. She'd taken Amin over there for a jimmy when she got off the lorry. Still only her word, though.' Behind him, Maggie waited with Rima and Amin. The boy was playing in a heap of sand between the skips. Rima squatted beside him, letting the sand run through her fingers.

Rick's phone rang. The control room, he thought, but it was Robbo. Maggie had found an old bucket, and was helping Amin fill it with sand.

'Detective Inspector Castle.' Each word ponderous and emphasised.

'The Carmichaels allegation is filed. No further action due to the lack of a victim statement and insufficient other evidence. I've given PC Weatherbeater a formal warning and marked up his personnel record.'

'That's not what I wanted.'

'CPS decision.'

'Law school rejects, the lot of them.' He paused. 'I wasn't in

290

fact calling about that. I had a call from Jim Hazelhurst at the NCA, who said you were asking a lot of questions about trafficking. Have you heard something about Khetan?'

'Rumours, that's all.'

'Really.'

'Really.'

'What about Coniston – have you made any progress on the list of old supermarket sites?'

Rick swore silently. 'Someone was leaking *on him*. 'We're at Chadwick, the fifth one. It's looking promising.'

'You wouldn't tell me if it was any different. Not that it matters now: I'm replacing you. I've spoken to Major Crime, and they've agreed to take the case, and straight away. You're to hand over everything you've got.'

'What if I tell you –'

'You could tell me literally anything.'

'– who's been damaging your Range Rover.'

'La, la, la, la.'

Rick turned the car round. It sounded worse, a toolbox overturning, again and again. It sounded as if it wouldn't make it back to the nick. And if it did make it back, what then?

Amin turned over the bucket. The dry sand cascaded everywhere, and he started crying. Rick messaged Russell to tell him it was sorted, then climbed out of the car and called Maggie over.

'Robbo knows about the list.' He half-suspected Maggie, but he'd already confronted her about going to Bradford.

'Do you lock your office?'

'You know I don't.'

'There you are then.'

Maggie turned and moved back to Rima and Amin.

Hunter ghosted up. 'The security hut would be okay as an observation point. There's chairs, even a girlie mag.'

'Major Crime's taking over. We're done.'

Hunter scowled. Behind him, a murder of crows rose above the trees.

'Rick.'

Someone was shaking him.

He opened his eyes: he'd fallen asleep sitting in his office chair. He felt shivery, as if he was coming down with something.

'You want to wipe your mouth,' said Hunter.

Rick cleaned away the saliva. He felt exhausted and his neck stiff, as if he'd been sleeping on an aeroplane. He up-downed his neck, moved his head from side to side. He walked over to the window. A convoy of three patrol cars slipped out into the gloaming.

'Anything else before I head home?'

Rick shook his head.

A police van stopped at the barrier, its blue lights flickering. The two PCs in the cab stared out like androids.

'Gotta say,' said Hunter. 'I didn't expect the request for cannabis repositioning.'

Rick turned, stifling a smile. He'd not heard it called that before. 'It's legal in Canada, the Netherlands, Uruguay, even in some US states. It's legal here for some medicinal purposes, and fifty-fifty, it'll be decriminalised here within ten years.'

'You're missing my point. I stole it, and you handled it!'

'You know why.'

'But still.' Hunter tutted. 'The white knight Rick Castle, the detective who arrested Hant Khetan. His girlfriend's in a wheelchair, the darling of the top floor.'

'Hardly.'

'The fat man's under pressure from the chief super and the Centre, and had no choice. He still gives you the difficult and dirty jobs because he knows you'll do the right thing, not the easy thing or the quick thing or the procedural thing. But the right thing, the moral thing.'

'Maybe.'

'He also knows you'll never give up.'

The sergeant walked away, his footsteps echoing down the corridor.

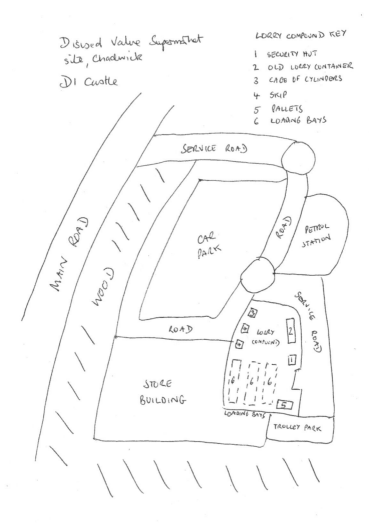

Disused Value Supermarket site, Chadwick

D1 Castle

LORRY COMPOUND KEY

1 SECURITY HUT
2 OLD LORRY CONTAINER
3 CAGE OF CYLINDERS
4 SKIP
5 PALLETS
6 LOADING BAYS

SERVICE ROAD

MAIN ROAD

WOOD

CAR PARK

ROAD

PETROL STATION

SERVICE ROAD

ROAD

LORRY COMPOUND

STORE BUILDING

LOADING BAYS

TROLLEY PARK

46

Calix eased open the back door and crept out. A bat fell away into the darkness. Cars moved in the distance, but the gardens and neighbouring houses were quiet. The air smelt cool and damp. He slipped on his old man's khaki smock, and flipped up the hood. Pulled on his rucksack. A scruffy black cat emerged from under the bench and slunk away. He waited a few seconds for his eyes to adjust, then followed the cat up the garden. According to Darren, a quarter to three was the burglar's sweet spot.

The grass was dewy, and he left a trail. At the wood, he looked back, but there were no lights, and no movement. His socks felt damp and he could hear his breathing. He unbolted the tall gate, walked through, and climbed up to push the bolt home. His heart thumped as if he'd drunk too much coffee.

The undulating sandy paths were easy to follow, and familiar from childhood. The trees stood dark and unmoving, and he caught glimpses of a dull moon through the canopies. A badger trundled toward him. At the last moment, it dived into the undergrowth and disappeared leaving a whiff of granddad breath.

After fifteen minutes he struck off from the path into the

undergrowth, and after another minute reached the holly tree. Its branches trailed the ground like a veil. He pushed his way into the dark interior, and risked a sweep with his torch. The chair was there, rustier but still usable; the porn mags rotted or taken. He slipped off his rucksack and sat down. The hide smelt earthy, and feeling at home, he let himself doze.

He woke feeling chilly. Delved in the rucksack for another top, but instead found Elly's hat which he'd shoved in when she hadn't been looking. He pressed it to his nose, then pushed out the shape. It smelt of her shampoo, and of her glitter. He folded it down, and tucked it carefully away.

Dozed again, dreaming of what couldn't ever be.

Scrabbling at his legs woke him in the pre-dawn. A dog had pushed its way into the holly and nosed around wagging its tail. The dog was a retriever, sleek and dull grey. Calix stroked its head. He fondled its ears, smoothed their glossy interiors. The dog's eyes began to close.

'Rex!' A shout, then a whistle.

Calix had expected it, the dog was in good shape and wore a collar. He pushed the dog to the edge of the hide, slapped its nose and shoved the animal through the prickly branches.

He listened as the dog and its owner moved away. Then sat down again, hands in the pockets of his old man's smock. String and small garden snippers in one pocket. His old man used them to deadhead the roses. A packet of nuts and raisins in the other, army packaging. He tore it open and ate a handful. Maybe he should have done what his old man had wanted, and joined the army. He ate more of the stale nuts. Or what his mum had intoned in her note. His sister Megan might have been more sympathetic, even allied to his cause. He poked at nut shrapnel caught between his teeth. He was doing this for his old man, for his whole family. To make things right.

At midday he pushed out through the trailing branches of the holly. Bright sunlight filtered through the trees and unseen birds called warnings. Wearing only a t-shirt, he walked to the far edge of the common. There was a road, a country pub the Gamekeeper, and a bus stop. He sat against the base of a tree, and waited. His mum being dead rather suited Elly, he thought. He realised he hadn't told Elly about Megan. Elly was like a queen bee: there could only be one.

A bus arrived, a single-decker, almost empty. When it pulled away, one person was left standing on the short stretch of pavement.

Darren Back wore a shiny new tracksuit and immaculate trainers, and held two large milkshakes with straws. Glancing up and down the road, he looked as comfortable as a tourist in a lion-enclosure.

Calix emerged from the trees, and crossed the road. The last time he'd seen Darren was in the visitors' hall at Strangeways. He looked the same but for the rings on his fingers.

'What kind of place, Capeman, doesn't have bus stops on both sides of the road?'

'This kind of place.'

'Q E fucking D.' His former cellmate set down one of the milkshakes, and unfolded a seat. Sat. 'Did the Feds try anything?'

'Castle turned up alone.'

'But?'

'He made a move.'

'You're here.'

'I made a better one.'

'Ha!' Darren grinned. Slurped noisily on his shake.

Calix took the Krugerand out of his pocket, and handed it over. It was wrapped in a pair of his old man's socks.

Darren unravelled the package, and whistled. 'I don't do change.'

A car drew up in front of the pub, and a blonde frizzy-haired woman climbed out. She glanced at the bus stop and went into the pub.

'I need to be going,' said Calix.

'You should take that with you.' Darren nodded at the milkshake on the ground.

Calix picked it up. It felt heavy. He took off the lid. Inside were small wraps of bog paper. He opened one out. It was wheat-coloured with a darker, snub nose. Nine millimetres in diameter. He wrapped it and slotted it back. Replaced the lid. He stood and looked into the windows of the pub. The frizzy-haired woman was on the phone.

'Thanks, Darren.' Calix glanced again into the pub, but the woman had disappeared. 'Walk for ten minutes back along the road 'til you get to a school. There's a bus stop there.' He started to cross the road.

'Capeman.'

'Yeah?' said Calix, looking back.

'Good fucking luck.'

Calix plunged into the scrubby kerbside and into the coolness of the wood. He took a roundabout route, switching paths every couple of minutes. Years of animal tracking had not been wasted. After half an hour, he pushed back into the holly tree hide.

For something to do, he spent the afternoon unwrapping and rewrapping the bullets. There were twenty-six, enough for two magazines, as he'd ordered. He stashed them in his pack and took out his phone. An alert for a missed call flashed up on the screen.

He tapped the screen.

'It's Calix.'

'Dog.' Red's gangster voice, as if he was pretending to be someone he didn't have to pretend to be. 'Your man's living above a car wash. He's running migrants into the UK in secret compartments in lorries, unloads them in northern England.

Usually uses a place once, never more than twice. You might get lucky. Goes without saying, the house is mine whatever.'

Calix could hear drum 'n' bass on the phone.

'Where did he unload them last time?'

'A disused supermarket site in Chadwick.'

'The address for the car wash?'

'You got a pen, dog?'

Somehow, his plan had come together: escape, weapon, bullets, Khetan's whereabouts. His old man might not be proud, but he'd be surprised.

Dusk finally came, but he was determined to wait until the burglar's sweet spot before he returned to the others. He ate the rest of his old man's snack and the sandwiches Elly had made. There were sprigs of parsley from the plant in the Finchams' kitchen.

He heard scuffling close by, and seconds later, Rex wormed his way under the trailing holly branches and bounded over to Calix as if it was his long-lost pal. He patted and stroked the retriever's head, knowing the owner wouldn't be far.

'Re-ex!' A long whistle.

Two options, and he'd already tried one. He started murmuring.

'Rex!' The owner had moved closer.

Still stroking and murmuring, Calix used his knees to clamp the dog's head. He could hear the owner thrashing around in the undergrowth.

Calix snapped his knees tight. Rex released a strange, strangulated bark, and Calix twisted its head, hearing and feeling several clicks. He held the position for a good minute, drool covering his fingers. He released his knees and let the animal sink to the ground, bending down to lower the head until it rested gently on the mulch, and then slowly retracted his hands. Didn't wipe them as a mark of respect.

Preparing for the fallout, he took out his knife and locked it in position.

There was more calling and whistling from the owner. Closer, and further away, and closer. Calix stood, and readied, and readied, and readied, but slowly the man's calling and thrashing faded, and finally stopped.

Darkness fell, and at two forty-five the next morning, he unlocked the Finchams' back door and went inside. The hacksaw and the pieces of Castle's handcuffs still sat on top of the freezer. He locked the door, stood for a moment in the kitchen. Then threw up in the sink.

47

Rick stared out into the backyard. PCs going to the football were loading long shields into the back of a riot van. Hunter was right, he would never give up. But for a moment he was at a loss.

The line of senior officers' cars, Robbo's gleaming 4x4 at one end, was still. Next to the superintendent's car, Maggie's yellow bubble sat in the disabled bay. Which was unusual: normally, she avoided it on principle.

Rick opened the Coniston file and flicked through it. He read some of the statements from the escape at the cemetery. A handful of the house-to-house proformas. Then the statements from Coniston's neighbours in Failston.

He went back to the window. The riot van drove out of the yard, the barrier clunked down, but rose again for a low-loader. The pool car he'd broken the day before stood on the trailer. The garage hand dropped the ramps and reversed the car off the trailer. Still rattling like coins in a washing machine.

Rick turned more pages of the Coniston file. *Antecedents.* Calix's old man a soldier, decorated in the Falklands War. His sister run over in Australia in a cycling accident. The family lived in a big house in Failston. *Had* lived. He knew the Conistons' family history as well as his own. Knew Calix Coniston as well as himself.

He phoned the hospital, and the nurse told him Skye's operation had gone ahead late the previous evening. He asked if he could visit. He couldn't. Could he speak to her. Yes, but later. He asked how it had gone, and the nurse said as well as could be expected.

In the corridor Major Crime pounded up and down, carrying files from the incident room to the photocopying room, and back. He wondered if he'd missed something. Something obvious?

His phone rang.

'Oliver?'

'Is it true about Russell Weatherbeater hitting his girlfriend?' Rick didn't answer. Confirmation or denial would have made little difference. 'And that she's underage?'

'She's not,' said Rick. 'She's eighteen.' Maybe even that was too much.

'Is he going to be charged?'

Like every journalist, Oliver was only as good as his last story. Rick understood – detectives were only as good as their last case. 'Can you let this one go?'

'Not really. The editor's on me. And you already owe me a favour for putting the word out for Coniston and Darren Back.'

'You didn't find them!'

'Weatherbeater?'

'I've got the scoop of the decade for you.'

Huffing and puffing down the phone. 'Well, what is it?'

'Not yet.'

'I need a hint.'

'It's big.'

'Come on!'

'An under-the-radar deal between the US and China. You

could take it to one of the nationals or syndicate it. Might even make your career.'

'Or break it.'

'So?'

'Okay, okay, as it's you. But it had better be as good as you say.'

The line dropped but rang again immediately.

'I'm at work, Mum. Busy.'

'Maggie says you're always busy.' She took a deep breath. 'I went to see Roger yesterday. Seems worse if anything.'

'I'm sorry to hear that.' He mined words used by politicians. 'But it's still too early to tell if it's had an effect.' He walked back to the window. If there wasn't hope, there was nothing.

'Shall I make him another cake?'

'Ideally, one every couple of weeks. I can – I can supply you.' The word hurt to say. Maggie buzzed out of the nick's back door and headed towards her car. 'I've got to go, Mum.'

Maggie opened her car boot and rummaged in the back. She glanced back at the police buildings and moved down the side of her car. Out of sight. Rick kept watching, but she didn't reappear. Keeping his eyes on the yellow bubble car, he edged back around his desk and took out his binoculars. He moved back to the window and raised the glasses. Maggie's head appeared between her car and Robbo's car, then disappeared again.

He kept watching. The bonnet of Robbo's car dropped down to one side. Then dropped to the other side.

Rick descended the stairs two at a time and buzzed out into the yard. As he approached the rear of Robbo's car, he heard the fizz of compressed air, smelt its staleness. Maggie crouched between her car and the superintendent's car, hammer in one hand, nail in the other. She glanced up, spotted him and smiled, laughed quietly. It always made him want to kiss her.

*

'This is how it is,' said Rick.

The two of them sat in his office, the door closed. In the yard, the garage hand, fifty pounds better off, jacked up Robbo's car. The new tyres, he'd told Rick with a smirk, would be two hundred pounds each.

Maggie wore a black and white polka dot blouse, a row of silver bangles. She looked normal, but she was anything but normal. How could one person do that to him?

'He's such a bastard.'

'You've made your point.'

If I follow the rules, you'll be sacked. If I don't follow the rules, and I'm caught out, I'll be disciplined. He wanted to tell her, but he resisted. She knew them. Being her boss confused things.

'Mags, you're a good analyst, one of the best. Soon, you'll be made senior analyst. Heading up the intel unit within a couple of years is a possibility.'

Maggie moved away to the door, her bangles jingling. She opened the door and went out. He wanted to hold her, hug her, reassure her that everything was going to be okay.

He turned pages of the Coniston file. Work, the great distractor. Possibly, the great redeemer.

As a young DC he had never given up. He could still remember the details of his best cases: Will Smith, a fraudster with twenty-seven aliases; a night burglar who targeted shift workers; and the one he'd sung about on his detective sergeant's board, the racist GBH. Following a pub darts match, a group of Asian supporters had been ambushed and attacked with a pair of bolt croppers. The father of three would never walk again. There'd been no direct CCTV, and no forensic evidence. It had been old-fashioned detective work, going shop-to-shop and house-to-house for witnesses. Cross-checking their accounts, convincing a supporter in the opposite camp to talk. Finally, he elicited a name. The suspect had moved address. Rick interrogated every police and open-source database he knew, and discovered the suspect cashed his social security benefits at the same post office every fortnight. It took him nine months, but he got him. He'd never given up, never even thought about giving up.

One lead remained in the Coniston case: the disused supermarket site at Chadwick.

He slipped on his harness, and slotted home the telescopic baton and cuffs. He put on his jacket. He signed out a movement-sensitive camera, and took a car key from the CID office.

And as if the clock had turned back five years, Rick drove out alone on enquiries.

48

Rick returned to Chadwick. The dirty-white clouds were high and passenger planes moved in and out. He was riding solo, a word which reminded him of the flight on a tiny aeroplane from Kathmandu to Lukla listening to Russell Weatherbeater regale mountaineering tales. Solo meant climbing without a partner: you had to get yourself out of trouble.

He drove through the first mini-roundabout. At the second, pieces of metal from his previous pool car littered the road. The garage hand had told him the front coil springs and the inner CV boot needed replacing. Everyone had their world, and lexis.

His world was law enforcement, policing, crime-fighting. DNA, clear-ups, gunshot residue, special warnings.

Manhunts.

Crows rose above the old supermarket. Rick wondered if something had disturbed them. Someone? He drove back onto the main road and parked in a layby. He could phone it in, but he'd seen nothing, heard nothing. A speeding ticker didn't count.

He got out, packed up the camera, and locked the car. He scrambled down the drainage ditch, and headed into the wood.

It was cool and smelt of mushrooms. Scrub pulled at his trousers and scratched his town shoes. He reached the fence and looked through the slats into the car park. It was deserted. He climbed over and walked across the car park, annoyed with the clip of his shoes.

Traffic hummed on the main road, but the delivery compound was quiet. He crossed the service road to the steel palisade fence. It was deserted: no vehicles, no people, the gate open like last time. A rabbit nibbled weeds by a skip.

He should have come at night.

But he might have been too late. He followed the service road to the gate and entered the compound. The rabbit scuttled away. Amin's sandcastles looked battered by decades of war.

He dumped his gear in front of the cylinder cage and set to work. He cut into the cage with pliers, and removed two cylinders. He positioned the movement-sensitive camera and the mini-computer, and switched them on. Checked the app on his phone. He replaced the cylinders and bent back the wire. Checked the view on his phone: slivers of the skips, two of the loading bays, the security hut, and the gate.

In the car he checked the camera via his phone. The compound was empty and still. A patch of nettles near the gate nodded in the breeze.

From Chadwick Rick drove to Coniston's family home in Failston. He parked on the drive, unlocked the padlock on the front door and stepped inside. He eased the door shut.

The hall felt cold.

A mess of post on the floor. Dust on the hall table. A clock ticked in another room, the door open. The distant whir of a fridge.

He searched downstairs, quickly, silently. No dirty plates in the sink, no recent food in the fridge, nothing in the kitchen bin. The washroom odourless, the sink dry and dusty. In the sitting room the TV was switched off at the wall.

He glided up the first set of stairs, pausing to listen halfway, and again on the landing. There was a mark on the carpet. He bent closer. A coin-sized pull of grassy root, not quite dry. From a crime squad boot, or more recent still? He padded up to Calix's loft room. Stuffed birds eyed him. Unimpressed, all of them. He fingered a taxidermy book, a stainless-steel knife on the table. Dusty, everything.

His phone beeped.

He snatched it out of his pocket, pulled up the app for the camera at Chadwick. The lorry compound was deserted – except for a rabbit nibbling at leafy scrub at the back of the security hut.

He went back down the second flight of stairs, to the mark on the carpet. He looked more carefully along the hall between the bedrooms. He found two indentations. Above him was the loft hatch. He found slivers of white paint and a wisp of loft insulation. He clicked down the loft hatch, pulled down the ladder, and climbed up.

The loft insulation was untucked at the ends and the edges, the result of an untidy search.

He phoned DS Davies, the crime squad sergeant. 'Did you search the loft at the Conistons' house?'

'Yes.'

'Under the insulation?'

'No.'

'Did you pull it up?'

'We don't usually, unless we've got specific intel.'

Rick pocketed the phone. Someone had taken up the insulation and recently. It could only be Coniston. Which suggested he was close, maybe even hiding in Failston.

Rick returned to the front door. Listened to the clock and the fridge, sniffed the stale air. He glanced up the stairs and into the front room, letting his eyes roam.

He stepped outside, clipped the padlock and walked along to the next house, the Finchams. They were on holiday, and as he expected, no one answered his knocking. The grass needed cutting. He peered in through a front window, at a pale-yellow sofa and a bookcase covering an entire wall. All appeared in order. He moved on to the next house.

Again, there was no answer. He knocked again, then retraced his steps and tried the neighbour on the other side of the Coniston house.

A tall man wearing a shirt and tie answered.

'DI Rick Castle.' He showed his badge.

'Mike Salisbury, inspector. I chair the neighbourhood watch. No one's been next door, I promise you.' His breath smelt of sardines. 'Except your guys, of course.' He chuckled at his own joke. 'A dog has gone missing, and the broadband's very slow. But that's as exciting as it's been. Have you got time for a brew?'

Rick shook his head. He went to the next house and received the same answer in a quarter of the time. He crossed the road and knocked again. As a trainee detective, he'd always believed if he knocked enough doors, watched enough CCTV, analysed enough phone traffic, he would find something. Detective work was less inspiration, more time-consuming bloody-mindedness. He didn't own hundreds of books or records or follow a team, there was no point.

He knocked a second time. The house was a new build, modern, all glass and steel. Work vans and a cement mixer stood in the drive, and he could hear hammering at the rear. He walked down the side of the house and was met halfway by a man wearing long shorts and a pastel shirt. His eyes were red-rimmed, and a skull cap covered his crown.

Rick showed his badge. He glanced back at the Conistons'

house. 'Have you seen any activity opposite?'

The man slipped off his cap to reveal he was bald. 'Chemo.' He put it back on. 'I don't sleep much. Get up, pad round, already feel like a ghost. I thought I did see a face at the upstairs bay window next door, but my partner says I'm always seeing things.'

Rick frowned. 'At the Salisburys'?'

The man shook his head. 'The Finchams.'

Rick was already backing away. 'When?'

'A day or two ago.'

Rick turned and started running. The Finchams were in Australia visiting one of their children, it was in their statement. A year or two back, their cat had been run over and Calix had preserved it for them. Maybe Coniston had learnt they were on holiday? Maybe they went at the same time every year. He probably knew where the spare key was, maybe even knew an alarm code.

He ran across the road, up the drive and around the back of the Finchams' house, and into a porch choked with old shoes and boots. The back door was locked, but a kitchen window was open. He squeezed his arm inside and flicked the catch. Breathing hard, he climbed in. The kitchen smelt of cigarette smoke and pizza. Dirty plates, dirty mugs, beer cans. One mug used as an ashtray. The sink smelt of vomit and disinfectant. He took out his baton, flicked it out, and listened for voices – there might be two of them, Barney Williams and Coniston.

The house seemed quiet. Another fridge ticked away the seconds. He moved out of the kitchen and into the hall. Peered into the downstairs rooms: they seemed untouched. Upstairs. If he'd been Coniston, upstairs would have seemed sensible.

He crept up the stairs, back against the wall, looking up. The smell of cigarettes strengthened. He pushed open the door of the front bedroom where the bald neighbour had seen a face.

The double bed had been slept in. Next bedroom, two single beds, both unkempt, beer cans on the floor. The rear bedroom was a huge room, and in disarray. As untidy as the parade room. Plates and glasses and mugs and ashtrays. Kitchen chairs, and a table.

He searched every room, and finished by checking the attic. There was no one. He folded down his baton and went downstairs. Found his sawn handcuffs. It had been fun while it lasted: the DI shows them how it's done. No, he doesn't.

On the front lawn a blackbird hauled at a worm. The bald man walked into the drive. Rick opened a window.

'My partner's just popped in. Said he saw a rusty orange car reversing out of the garage this morning. He doesn't live with me, didn't know they're in Australia.'

Rick closed his eyes. Up-downed his head, see-sawed. He saw blackness and flashing stars and guessed it would be something like that at the end.

Rick sat on the bench in the apiary and waited for the place to work its magic. A farmer ploughed a neighbouring field. The next field was brilliant yellow with rape; good for the bees. He closed his eyes, and smelt the sweet, cloying honey. Listened to the buzzing, the air charged with energy akin to electric static. He reopened his eyes. Bees were flitting out from the hive entrances, others returning to the landing boards and crawling in fully laden. Stomachs full of nectar, or legs covered in bright hues of pollen. Others carried water or propolis. Busy as bees. The worker bee, the symbol of Manchester.

Ashen clouds scudded across the sky. He watched a shadow race up to the bench and envelop him, felt its cool embrace. He should get back to the station, work the file, work his staff, work like a bee.

His phone chimed. Chadwick. The bloody rabbit; there was

311

always something. He slipped out the phone, and opened the app.

Between the security hut and the loading bays sat an orange jalopy.

He sprinted to his car like a probationer.

49

The three of them filed into the integral garage and climbed into the car. Calix checked items against a list. They were as professional and calm as if they were dibble. As if he was Castle.

Barney drove. The day was cold and the air smelt of traffic and the city. Elly sat in the back, quietly, like a sullen teenager. She wore her pink hat and a pair of dark glasses, her red jacket beside her. She looked as cool as a catamaran.

The car was tiny, and Calix felt they'd be vulnerable in an accident. His legs were cramped, and Barney's elbows brushed his knees when he turned the wheel. They drove past a layby where a fat woman wearing an apron was selling strawberries. She sat on a garden chair with wooden crates piled behind her. Calix told Barney to go back. His friend did as instructed, and Calix bought a punnet of strawberries. They were decent berries, not over-large or overripe. They smelt of a summer they hadn't had. He gave the woman a ten-pound note and told her to keep the change. He climbed back into the crap orange car and they drove on, drawn like moths to the candle of Khetan.

Calix still felt sick. One big thing to do, but before that a small thing, a minute thing, but it seemed as bad.

A fire engine clanged past. Men in yellow garb stared out of the cab like waxworks, as if they'd always been firefighters, and always would be.

Calix passed the punnet through the gap in the front seats. A hand appeared, and an arm with the palest down. She said they reminded her of parties, and Barney asked if Calix had forgotten him, and the moment was ruined.

Barney took a wrong turning, and they drove down a high street of shops. A post office, a butcher's, and a shop with a pavement display of brooms and doormats. A newsagent's. The wrong turning seemed propitious.

'Stop here, Barney, I need some cigarettes.' Calix's stomach heaved as if he'd eaten a dodgy fry up for breakfast. He'd eaten nothing. He'd drunk a large black coffee and smoked two or three cigarettes.

Barney parked, and Calix leant into the back. 'Elly, could you?' She looked at him as if he was a stranger, and she took her time. She didn't have a choice, but she didn't know that. It would be there, or somewhere near there. Her long black eyelashes signalled assent, but she couldn't get out of the car. The childlocks refused her.

Calix checked up and down for uniforms. He climbed out, opened the rear door. He felt like a chauffeur or a bodyguard. Elly, a celebrity. She stepped out wearing a short skirt and strappy shoes. She stood on the kerb like a lighthouse.

'I'll need some money.' She looked at him as if she knew what was going on, and perhaps she did. She was sharp, and she was surprising, and funny.

'Elly.'

'Yes?'

'How were the strawberries?'

'I think you know.' She took off her sunglasses.

Calix moved closer. He could smell her musky scent, peer into her pale green eyes. Alright, doll. The words were in his head, but didn't make his lips because her lips covered his. Briefly, gently. He gave her the money, she slipped on her glasses and went into the shop. Calix climbed back into the car.

'Drive!'

Calix and Barney drove towards the car wash in silence. Elly would have been useful as a decoy because Khetan knew them both. But Calix had a different plan, and like his old man, a backup too.

They passed a row of delivery scooters outside a takeaway. A helmet perched on one of the seats. Posters and flyers filled the shop window, and it was busy inside.

Calix issued Barney instructions, the car stopped, and he climbed out. He picked up the bike helmet, pulled it on, then entered the ginnel next to the shop. Stinking refuse bins, and a carpet of cigarette butts. Outside the side door sat a stack of pizza boxes. He took the biggest box he could see, didn't look back. The ginnel emerged on the next street. Barney was waiting.

Calix climbed back into the car, took off the helmet and stashed it on the back seat. 'You're becoming a getaway pro.'

Barney pulled away from the kerb smartly. He said nothing, and drove quickly at first, but slowed. He stopped at a zebra crossing for an old man and a dog, braked at amber traffic lights. He drove slower and slower.

Finally, they arrived at the car wash. As directed, Barney parked in the pub car park around the corner.

'You're sure about this?'

'Yes,' said Calix.

He took the wrapped items out of his bag. Unwrapped his old man's Hi-Power from the towel, and released the magazine. He pulled back the slide, checked the chamber was empty and released the slide. He set the gun on the foot mat, and grabbed half a dozen bullets out of the disposable cup. He slotted them into a magazine. Three would take down a bull, six a raging bull. He slotted the magazine onto the pistol.

He grabbed the pizza box, placed the gun inside, and closed the lid. He opened it again, picked up the gun, and pointed.

'*Bang.*'

'You're absolutely sure?'

'I am,' said Calix, replacing the gun in the box and pulling down the lid.

Barney stared out of the window.

'Yes?' said Calix.

His friend looked back. Nodded.

Calix pulled on the bike helmet and knocked it with a fist. 'Wish me luck, then.'

'Do it for Spencer. For my dad.'

'Yeah,' said Calix. For the Williams family, but mainly for his old man.

He climbed out, holding the pizza box and the special delivery. His heart rate was pounding. He was going to do this. Easy as 1, 2, 3.

He walked out of the pub car park, the pizza box horizontal. He was in character. Chuntered to himself. Pizza for you. Got a delivery for you. Your pizza. You ordered a pizza. Special pizza. I didn't order—

Bang!

A kid rode past on a bike. A man talking on the phone. Fifty metres to the car wash. According to TBR, the flat above the car wash was where Khetan was living.

Easy as 1, 2, 3.

The forecourt area of the car wash was deserted. There were no vehicles and no people. The signage was still there, but the doors were closed. There were no lights on. And no lights in the flat above.

Calix walked up the steps with the pizza box. He was no

longer nervous, but angry with himself for assuming Khetan would be in the flat – sitting pretty. For a moment, he wondered if TBR had duped him. But he hadn't transferred the house, so The Big Red had nothing to gain by lying. He kept going.

At the top of the steps, he banged on the door. Peered through the old-fashioned kitchen window.

The room was dark. Cardboard boxes, rubbish, kitchen crockery and utensils.

He knocked again.

There was no response, and no sound from inside.

Calix jogged down the steps, and in the dark space underneath, took the Hi-Power out of the pizza box and shoved it into his waistband. He tossed the box. Took off the helmet, set it on the ground and walked back to the pub.

Inside a tired-looking saloon bar, he asked about the car wash. The landlord, shabby as his bar, told him it had been quiet for two days, and thought they'd gone. Really!

'Any idea where? He owes me.'

'Don't they all.'

Calix returned to the car. He was half-surprised it was still there, and Barney inside. He shook his head.

'Chadwick,' said Calix.

The backup plan.

As they approached Chadwick the sky darkened and lowered. The wind got up. Barney drove around the site while pieces of black plastic whirled around them. In the lorry compound Calix wound down a window. The air smelt of dust, and felt tight as a drum. He directed Barney to the car park, and when his friend slewed to a stop across two spaces, Calix scowled and told him to manoeuvre.

Glancing at the sky, Calix climbed out. There was a rumble of thunder.

They lugged their packs and some blankets over to the compound. The air temperature dropped, and squalls of dark birds arced and curved. Barney tried the huge roller doors but they wouldn't budge. The lock on the metal container was inaccessible which left only the security hut. Calix peered through the grimy window, then sawed off the padlock with the Finchams' hacksaw. Spots of rain marked his t-shirt.

Inside were two plastic chairs and a wooden table. Along the wall nearest the gate were a counter and a bolted hatch. Opposite, the door and a nail with last year's motor-racing calendar. They dragged their kit inside, leaving the door ajar. Barney picked up a battered magazine, turned a few pages of pale flesh and threw it in a corner. Calix wiped the window with a sleeve. It watched the approach, but not the yard. It didn't matter: if Khetan came, they would hear him.

The heavens opened. Rain drilled against the corrugated iron roof, then changed direction and railed against the door.

Calix lit a cigarette and smoked it standing in the doorway. He wondered if Khetan would show. And when. They had blankets, and they had food for two or three days. Then they'd need resupply, or maybe a third plan.

He blew the smoke outside and watched it battle with the rain. He feared the strawberries would spoil, and Elly's hat would lose its shape. He hoped she was okay: he'd given her enough money for a taxi, but he imagined her walking through the pouring rain and singing to herself. Or jumping into a ravine and being washed away.

He stubbed out the cigarette and sat down. Opposite him, Barney rocked back and forth making the plastic squeak.

'Maybe I should start smoking.'

'Maybe you should,' said Calix. He tossed him his pack and the matches. Barney lit a match and blew it out.

Calix took the Hi-Power back out of the towel, released the

magazine. He checked the chamber was empty, raised his arm, closed an eye and aimed at the driver on the calendar. Calix felt the pistol's weight, and its power to threaten, to bully, to cajole. To maim, and to kill. He felt like a gangster, an armed dibbleman, a soldier. He felt like a creator and a destructor. He felt like the lord God almighty. He squeezed the trigger.

Click.

He set the pistol on the table and took out the disposable cup of bullets. He filled the magazine to capacity, and pushed thirteen into a second magazine. There was enough ammunition for a fire-fight. He slotted a magazine onto the pistol, and pulled back the slide. Applied the safety catch. The gun was ready.

And so was he.

He stood by the open door to smoke another cigarette. Pools of water dotted the yard, and the buildings were shiny as if they'd washed for the occasion. He wondered if Elly had only meant she liked the strawberries.

Barney went for a piss in the yard, and Calix joined him.

'Do you think he'll show?' said Barney, looking sideways.

'I do.'

Calix had no idea, but his old man had told him to always stay positive with the troops on the eve of a battle. He sucked his stomach in, and zipped up. Like a dog, he kicked loose earth and stones over his piss.

They went back into the hut. They drank some water and ate some chocolate. Calix cleaned his nails with the knife he'd taken from his house.

'Game?' said Barney. He'd set up the chessboard on the table and held out his fists with concealed pawns.

Calix sat down and lit another cigarette. He might as well kill himself with them as anything else. He tapped Barney's fist. It wasn't a pawn, but a castle. A white castle. He glanced at Barney who was already swivelling the board. The good omen seemed

319

lost on his friend: despite all Castle's resources and experience, they were beating him to the prize.

They exchanged pawns, then knights. Calix picked up a pawn and held it. He looked across at his friend who'd driven the getaway car, and who'd housed him. Calix owed him his liberty, and still owed him, would always owe him for starting it in the first place. For kidnapping him and Spencer in Nepal. Calix knocked the pawn against his teeth.

'Go home, Barney.'

'What do you mean?'

'I mean, go back to college and get your law degree. Become a solicitor. Let me finish this and take the rap. Tell them I forced you, threatened to burn down your mum's house. Mention TBR, they know I've got a connection. Say anything you like, I'll confirm it.'

'I couldn't,' said Barney, and looked down at the board. His eyes were watery. He meant the opposite, and they both knew it.

They played more chess, Calix going through the motions. He lost in half an hour which was a record. He went to the door and lit up. Barney packed away the chess kit, and hefted his bag.

They hugged, Barney's eyes watering again.

Then his friend walked away, to the gate where he glanced back like a child going on holiday, and along the service road to the roundabout, and out of sight.

Calix stood in the doorway, smoking. The yard was quiet, water dripping from the gutters and a flock of noisy rooks hopping around as if it was New Year's Eve. Their greyish-white faces distinguished them from carrion crows. No one knew anything.

He stubbed out the cigarette on the doorframe; he was beginning to sound like his old man.

Barney came back into view. He walked around the

roundabout and along the service road, and into the yard. He walked across to the security hut. Inside, he dumped his bag, and took out the chess set. He set it on the table, and began to marshal the pieces into position.

He looked up, a chess piece in his hand. 'This is my fight, too.'

Tempted to fire a three-volley salute, Calix picked up the Hi-Power. Everyone needed a brother at question time.

He held it up, aimed.

'*Bang,*' he said, softly. '*Bang, bang.*'

50

'Get in,' said Rick.

Hunter climbed into the car, and Rick reversed out of the visitors' parking at the front of the police station. Tyres screeching, the car shot out onto the road causing a council lorry to brake heavily, and the driver to hoot his displeasure. Hunter turned to raise a finger. Turned back, grinning like a loon.

'They'll all come; the whole office. You just say the word.'

Rick accelerated down the centre of the road, hoping the front desk staff weren't phoning senior management.

He drove as if they were in a marked car with a flashing blue light. Hunter made obscene remarks about other drivers while Rick double-declutched and braked hard before corners. His mouth was dry, and his feet sweaty for the first time that summer. He felt like a beat bobby. He felt as if he'd just been given the opportunity to exorcise a growth in his brain.

A stone's throw from Chadwick, Rick pulled into the same layby as before and switched off the engine. The car creaked and groaned as it settled. Steam rose from the bonnet. The windscreen was filthy with dead flies, and he'd not even noticed.

'We'll confirm it's Coniston, then call the office. Even Robbo can't complain if we can actually see him.'

Hunter scratched his shin. 'A woman called for you earlier.'

'Who?' said Rick. His first thought, Maggie, his second, Skye. His sister; Mum? Rima? Someone had died: Skye, or Dad.

'Wouldn't leave a name, said she'd call back. She called from a number registered to Hartford Hall so I sent Kasim round on the QT. The owner had lent the phone to a friend, but wouldn't say who. You thinking what I'm thinking?'

Rick nodded, and they got out. Traffic roared up and down the main road. He slid down into the ditch, Hunter following. Heart thumping, still feeling like he was in uniform. Maybe he would be soon. They stumbled through the mushroom-smelling wood, and emerged at the edge of the supermarket site. The store loomed like an aircraft hangar.

At the fence, they looked through the slats into the car park. The squat orange car was parked near the entrance. It was unoccupied, but too far away to see the licence plate. It had to be Coniston, but Rick had been close before and come away with nothing. The fugitive could be anywhere, or nowhere, but the lorry compound seemed the most likely. If they climbed the fence and walked through the car park they'd be seen.

'We need a drone,' said Rick. He glanced up at the store, three storeys high. The wide pedestrian entrance faced the car park, and alongside the fence, a blank wall.

They tramped up the fenceline to the huge building, pollen and fronds of sticky grass marking their trousers. Above them, Value was written in large blue and red letters across the fluted aluminium siding. They walked further, and came to a small, curved recess in the wall which sheltered a tube ladder. It reached the roof.

Without a word, Rick climbed the fence.

Hunter jumped down beside him, and emptied a shoe of detritus. 'We have jockeys for this.'

The bottom of the ladder was three metres from the ground

and required a second ladder – or combined tactics. Rick smacked his knuckles into his palm in front of him, the sharp crack like a gunshot. Hunter got the idea, and stood under the ladder with his hands cupped against a knee. Rick put his foot in the stirrup, and Hunter heaved up. The sergeant grunted. Rick ran his hands along the smooth surface of the wall and stretched towards the lowest rung.

He couldn't reach.

Hunter let him down. Time was ticking – at any minute Khetan might turn up, or Coniston might leave. Rick wondered about finding a hooked branch in the wood, or attaching his handcuffs to his baton. He climbed the fence and motioned Hunter towards him.

'You're a determined bastard.'

Rick sat, and rested his feet on Hunter's shoulders. He couldn't sleep at night, he couldn't concentrate during the day, he couldn't live. He'd ruined his relationship with Robbo, was losing his sense of fair play, both professionally and outside of work, and was in danger of losing his girlfriend. He stood up using a fence post for support. Hunter gasped, and tottered. The sergeant staggered forward, Rick swaying above him.

He grabbed the lowest rung, Hunter blowing like a kettle below. Rick lifted his feet from Gary's shoulders and straightened out his legs at ninety degrees. He ran his feet up the wall and looped his calves over the bottom of the ladder-like tube. He glanced down, breathing heavily.

'Wait here, I'll see what I can see.'

Hunter nodded, bent-over and gasping like a chain-smoker.

Rick climbed the ladder, and at the top stepped easily onto the roof. There was even a handrail. Glancing back down, he felt a shudder of vertigo. It reminded him of a similar feeling on the suspension bridge near Mosom Kharka. He had overcome it then for the Job, and he'd overcome it now. Maggie was right: cut off his arm, and the Job would be imprinted like a word in a stick of rock. Hunter, now sat with his back against the fence, gave him a thumbs-up. It was a small gesture, impulsive more than considered, but it seemed to matter. Hunter was watching his back.

A keen breeze swept the roof, and the sky was dark. Clouds the colour of gunmetal. The handrail followed the perimeter, but much of the roof was obscured by large vents. Halfway across was a stack of building equipment: scaffolding planks and bars, and a bulky blue tarpaulin flapping at one corner. Two tubs of rusting scaffold joints. Drinks cans, cigarette butts, and a pair of boots lay strewn.

Rick set off, sliding a hand along the handrail. Like he'd done in Nepal. The suspension bridge had been higher, swayed around, and if he'd fallen, he'd have smashed into rocks the size of cars. The supermarket roof in comparison was child's play. He glanced across at the car park, deserted except for the toytown orange car. Beyond it was the wood which acted as a screen to the main road where vehicles sped up and down. The service roads were empty. A gust of wind pushed against him, and he grabbed the rail in both hands and waited. He hoped the bridge and the roof had one thing in common: a Nepalese madman at the end.

As he neared the corner of the store, he ducked down, and then dropped to his hands and knees. He crawled forward to the edge, and looked down into the delivery yard. The vertigo again made him feel queasy.

The yard was empty of vehicles, and devoid of movement. The gate stood open.

Glancing behind him, he surveyed the roof. Further around the perimeter protruded the top of another tube ladder. He looked down again, but nothing had changed. No movement, no detail of note, no one. He let his body go limp and lay down fully. He closed his eyes, felt the gravel imprinting his cheek. He could smell the bitumen on the roof. He could hear the buzz of a bumblebee, even up there. There would be some clover growing in a cleft, or a dandelion in a gutter. He wiggled his toes, curled and uncurled his fingers. If it wasn't Coniston, and Khetan didn't show, then what? Accept his reassignment?

Yeah, right. What did Robbo expect?

He might pretend he had, but he would start by tracing the student – Simons, Simmonds? – who lived in the room next to Williams and who'd phoned the office. Elly, Elly Simmonds. If she yielded nothing, then he would arrest Darren and Anthony Back at the same time and play them off. Apply for bugs on TBR's phone, his car and his h a. It didn't matter how long it took, as long as he was still in the Job, Rick would keep going. In his own time, if necessary.

The deep growling of a lorry cut off his introspection.

He raised his head. A lorry had turned off the main road onto the service road. It was followed by a white van. His phone buzzed with a message.

Is it them?

Rick tapped a button. 'I don't know. Lorry and van so fits the profile. No sign of a reception committee, if it is the Finchams' car. Still can't see a reg.'

'Shall I call the office?'

'Wait, Gary, I want to be a hundred per cent.'

Rick hunkered down again. The lorry reached the first roundabout, and swung laboriously around. It passed the defunct petrol station and turned left onto the service road for the yard. Rick could make out two white men in the cab. He should have brought his binos. The van followed the lorry. Two Asian men in the van. Khetan and a wingman? Ram? Rick thumped the concrete rim. If it was Khetan, it would make sense if the second man was his nephew Ram. *Dharma* and family the two things that fuelled the former FBI's Most Wanted. If he was trafficking, Khetan wouldn't get a second chance.

His phone buzzed with a call.

'Gary?'

'Oliver.'

'Any progress?'

Rick took a gamble. 'I'll send you a post code. Meet my DS Gary Hunter in a layby there. Take a fresh notebook.'

His phone buzzed again. 'Gary?'

'No,' said Emma.

'Not a good time,' said Rick, speaking rapidly. 'Russell's a special constable, and also a professional mountaineer. You've probably heard of him. Last year, he was shot on duty during an operation I was commanding, and he now walks with a limp. The way I see it, he's frustrated and hitting prisoners and Velvet in consequence. He needs a different outlet, boxing or a punchbag. Maybe, they're too literal a solution, you're the expert.'

'It's not Russell's violent predisposition I wanted to talk about.'

'What then?'

'It's yours.'

'Mine?'

'Yes.'

Rick clicked off the phone. The irony had only just struck him. He'd recognised Russell's frustration and consequent substitution of violence for his status quo, but not his own. Thinking about it would have to wait, his phone already buzzing with another call.

'Yes?' he snapped, feeling his neck muscles tighten.

'Is that Inspector Castle?' said a female voice.

'Yes,' said Rick. 'Sorry, did you try to phone me earlier?'

The lorry slowed and drove in a wide arc to enter the delivery yard. Pug-faced white men, the driver wearing a dark blue singlet. It had to be Khetan in the van. And Coniston in the car. Had to be.

'I'm worried about Calix.'

'Are you Elly Simmonds?'

The line went dead. The call made from a withheld number. There were ways, but no time.

The lorry chugged into the yard, and nosed up to a loading bay. It reversed back and forward, straightening each time, and then parked. The van entered the yard. The driver had dark hair. It looked like him. The van turned around and backed up towards the lorry, then pulled forward to leave a gap of ten metres. It stopped. The driver switched off the engine. The lorry's engine chugged on, then powered down.

The yard was quiet, still.

Rick's stomach heaved. He was ninety-five per cent, but not certain. Raindrops hit his neck making him start. A yellow zig-zag split the night-black sky, then a crack of thunder. He counted the seconds only too aware he was on the edge of a roof.

He'd reached seven when his phone beeped with another text from Gary.

So?

The driver's door of the van opened, and the Asian man stepped out. Slim, about five foot six, dark brown tufty hair. He looked like a lot of other Asian men. But even without binoculars, Rick was in no doubt: the driver was Hant Khetan.

Rick shook his head, closed his eyes and reopened them. He was still on the roof, Khetan still in the yard. The Nepalese Most Wanted had had his second chance, and this time incarceration would be for good.

He phoned Hunter. 'Turn the office out, Gary.' His voice a hoarse whisper.

'Aye, aye, boss.'

'Put an armed response team on standby, request an ambulance, and update Robbo. RV with our lot in the layby, and I'll talk you in.'

'AYE, AYE, boss.'

51

God told him to do a recce. He kept listening, but God didn't give any details. The working practice of God was for God.

Hant shut the van door and started the engine. He reversed alongside the cab of the lorry and wound down the window. The driver looked ill. He was white as old marmot bones and blubbery as a government official. A gold-coloured medallion hung down over his stained singlet. He peered down as if Hant worked for him.

'Ten minutes,' said Hant. He raised the window and jerked the van forward. Drove out of the yard, the boy looking back as if he'd missed something.

Rain spattered the windscreen and he switched on the wipers. The weather so random in England. At home it was like clockwork: late afternoon rainfall during the monsoon, otherwise very little. He stopped alongside the boarded-up petrol station. The chains preventing access to the forecourt were still in place. It was deserted and eerie, the only noise raindrops chinking on the plastic roofs. He turned around and drove back, and into the supermarket car park.

A small orange car sat near the entrance. God was right. God was always right. Hant pulled alongside. It would be a reminder for the boy.

He climbed out into the drizzle and stood there waiting, like a Kathmandu housewife. He knocked on the van door. He'd knock on his nephew's head in a short minute. Ram opened the passenger door, and slid down from the seat. He glanced at the gloomy sky and thinking his uncle couldn't see, pulled a face.

Hant clicked his tongue. Ram walked the long way around the van, and took up position behind Hant. Like a dog. *Ramro.* Good.

They walked round like prospective buyers. The car was rusty and old. The tyres worn, the paintwork muted. One wing was caved and there was a dent from a bollard in the rear bumper. Hant felt the bonnet: cool, but not stream-cold. He indicated to the boy to do the same. Hant bent down and looked underneath: the ground was dry. He stood, and looked at the boy. Slowly, Ram squatted down and peered underneath. Hant tried a door. It opened. The door pockets contained de-icer and an A-Z map of Manchester. Tissues and sweet wrappers. Cushions on the back seat. There was no police logbook. He got out. He could hear the dogs barking. They should get back, decant the migrants into the van and get going. It had taken two days to drop them last time; this time, he might not be so discerning.

'Police?'

Ram looked blank.

'*Bandar ko chaak.*' The boy was being intentionally difficult. It was disrespectful both to Hant, and to God. He stepped forward, and cuffed the boy round the head. 'Police?'

The boy turned on his heel and ran off across the car park.

'*Bandar ko.*' Hant climbed back into the van and turned the key. He pressed down hard on the accelerator and the van kangarooed forward. A Coke can fell from the open passenger door. He glanced across, the van slaloming crazily. In front of him, Ram was running like the wind. He was a strong fit boy, brought up in the foothills of Everest. Except for the previous fortnight, his nephew had lived his whole life at altitude. There could be few people who were fitter. He was proud of him, proud of what he represented. God was proud of him.

Hant prodded the brake. The van bowed to a halt and the passenger door slammed shut. He floored the accelerator and the van screeched forward again. Ram was halfway to the perimeter fence, but the van closed the gap quickly. He could knock him down, try to hit him with the driver's door. He could overtake and stop in front of the boy. He could stop and chase the boy on foot. Hant was also fit and strong, had also been brought up in the foothills of Everest. If the boy was scared, then Hant was angry, and it would be a competition of furies. God suggested persuasion. He wound down the window, and decided on Nepali as a gesture of goodwill.

'*Timi kahaan jana lageko?*' Where're you going?

Ram glanced across at him as if he was Ravana. The second time in a week Hant had been so accused. The boy stopped suddenly, let the van drive past, and skipped around the back.

Hant braked and skidded around through the surface water. He drove forward again, the windscreen beginning to mist.

Above them, the dark lid of sky.

Ram ran as if his life depended on it. His life depended on God, and on Hant as God's representative. The boy reached the fence and hauled himself up like a Ghurkha recruit. He raised his legs, and in a smart gymnastic move, swivelled his body over. He dropped down the other side, and out of sight.

Unlike the steel palisade of the delivery yard, the perimeter fence to the car park was made of wooden panels. They were tall but flimsy.

Hant steered so the van was heading at ninety degrees to a section of fence close to where the boy had jumped over. He clipped in his seatbelt and accelerated. God would decide.

There was an intense noise of splintering wood and denting metal.

Wooden panels buckled and broke. Hant felt himself jerk backwards, and forwards again. He felt immediate pain in his neck. The van careered forward and slewed to a halt in the scrub. The engine stalled. He was okay, not too bad considering. He looked up and whispered. '*Dhanyabaad.*' Thank you. He pushed open the door, and climbed out, ready for a fight.

The boy wasn't far, and was standing still. Staring at Hant, at the scratched van, at the smashed fence. His mouth agape.

Hant advanced and grabbed the boy by the arm.

'Small orange car: police?'

'*Chaina.*' No.

'*Ramro.*'

He led the boy back to the van by the ear, and bundled him into the passenger seat. He slammed the door, and wondered how he was going to fix his unruly nephew. With, or without God.

*

Calix craned to see out through a knothole in the security hut; at his shoulder, Barney doing the same. The sky dark as ebony. Dogs barked in the lorry, but the yard was motionless except for the falling rain. The ground was dotted with black-coloured puddles. Khetan and Ram had driven off in the van almost the moment they'd arrived. Either Khetan could see through the hut wall, or he'd forgotten something. Or something else, but Calix couldn't think what.

He grabbed a fluttering Daddy Long-legs and pulled off the legs, squashed the body between his fingers.

Barney sighed and stepped back into the hut. His ear was bleeding from where he'd picked off a scab.

'I want your knife.'

Wiping his fingers, Calix turned.

'You've got the gun.'

Calix took out his knife and threw it over. He understood. Barney the rugby player, the sportsman, plucked it from the air. He opened it and tested the blade on his thumb. Drawing blood, he wiped it down his cheek. He squeezed his thumb and wiped his other cheek. Warpaint, a bleeding ear, and wielding a razor-sharp knife, Barney looked like an Indian brave. The resolve of his friend was more doubtful.

Behind Barney were the blankets, and on top of them lay Elly's red leather jacket. Calix had forgotten to give it to her, and she'd have needed it in the rain. He picked it up. He huffed and polished the metal poppers, and turned away when he realised Barney was watching.

'You look out for a bit.'

Barney shrugged and moved to a spy-hole in the door. Calix sat down with Elly's jacket resting across his lap. He smelt the inside of the collar, and the armpits. Barney made him feel like a pervert. He pushed his hands into the lined pockets and imagined a life earthing up potatoes and tending sheep on a Scottish croft, or on an island in the Outer Hebrides. In the winter, Calix chopping wood, Elly making soup and darning. Or growing bananas and coffee beans in Central America – Honduras or Guatemala, on the coast or alongside a volcanic lake. It wouldn't be such a bad life.

After fifteen minutes they swapped places. Khetan and Ram were taking ages. If Special K had been spooked, it would have all been for nothing.

He spotted a cluster of ladybirds in the hinge of the door. Red and orange with numerous black spots. The white triangle in the middle of their head made them easy to identify as harlequins, the country's newest and most invasive species. They ate native l-birds, including the endangered two-spot, and were already in Scotland. Nothing was perfect. He squashed as many as he could, pasting them against the wood until he had a brownish smear on his fingers.

He heard a vehicle.

Looked out.

The van drove back into the yard.

'Yes,' whispered Calix, raising a clenched fist. At last, his old man's killer was only metres away. He couldn't miss.

Khetan and his nephew climbed out of the van. It was strange to see Ram in England. He'd grown and wore a youth's fluffy moustache. He looked fed up and out of place. So at home in the Everest foothills, boulder-hopping and jumping the silvery streams, but in the delivery yard he looked like a duckling dropped from the sky. Calix felt sorry for him, and responsible. Elly was right, he'd used the boy, and in the end not even needed him.

The men from the lorry appeared, and Khetan held court. The men were heavy and wore tracksuit-type clothing. They looked like cons. In the lorry, the dogs barked like machines. Ram looked all over. While the white men geared up, Khetan and Ram retreated to the back of the van. The boy looked pale and scared. Calix wondered whether it was because the boy knew there were migrants in the lorry. The boy was scared for them, or for the consequences of being caught by the dibble. Maybe there weren't migrants, but if there were, Calix wanted to get it done before they were released. It wasn't their fight. He felt sorry for them, too. Too many people in the world, not enough animals.

'Do you think,' said Barney, 'Khetan will have a gun?'

'Maybe. He had one in Nepal, but in Barnes he used a knife. But if he does, you know what to do.'

Barney nodded. 'You ready?'

Calix picked up his old man's pistol. He'd never been readier.

Togged-up and armed like dog-catchers, the white men opened the back of the lorry. A foxhound leapt out and ran round, splashing through the puddles like a freed con. White base, with black and tan colouring. Foxhounds were an old breed, raised specially for hunting – for killing. Larger than most dogs, with muscular straight-boned legs and boundless energy. Fed on raw meat, like lions. The men ran round and round, and swore and shouted, but eventually noosed the dog, and hauled it toward the cage of cylinders. The animal clawed the ground and fought. They clubbed it down, and tied it up.

'You know I had a thing with her? With Elly.'

Calix looked across at Barney. He felt a great heat flood through him. A thing? He could ask Barney to repeat what he'd said so there was no confusion, or to expand on the detail, but he didn't trust himself to speak.

He slipped off the safety catch on the pistol, and still holding the grip, wrapped a jumper around it. He pushed open the hut door, and stepped out into the sodden day.

52

Rick looked away from the security hut door and back again. Coniston stood on the threshold, his blond hair cut so short his scalp showed through. His right hand was wrapped up in clothing. An injury, but how? The security hut door flipped back, and opened again. Barney Williams emerged. He wore a number eight rugby shirt and boots, and made Coniston look as lean as his old man.

Rick double-tapped his phone. All his Christmases had come at once.

'Gary, they're all here: Coniston and Williams, as well as Khetan.' He tempered his voice. 'How close is everyone?'

'Signal dropped. Just getting back to the layby and the car now, I'm soaked. I'll try again.' He rang off.

In the yard Khetan caught sight of Coniston and Williams. He shouted at the boy in Nepali, and Ram trotted to the back of the van. Khetan then shouted at the men in the lorry, the details lost to the yowling of the dogs. Ram returned with a piece of pipe, Khetan admonishing him as if he'd brought a rolled newspaper.

In the distance, claps of thunder. The rain which had eased increased again. Summer rainfall, heavy and loud, and Rick was also drenched. He hardly noticed.

Coniston's blond hair stood out like a beacon in the yard. Two car-lengths away, Khetan and Ram wielded pieces of pipe.

Rick looked again at Coniston's bandaged right hand. He thought back to the CCTV showing Coniston wearing a sling – on his left arm. Which suggested deception, and Coniston was concealing a weapon.

The white men heaved open the rear shutter on the lorry, and a second cur the size of a small pony leapt out. If anything, the dog was larger than the first. It careered around through the puddles, sniffing at the edges of the skips and pallets. It raced up to the first dog, then shied away, as if taunting it. It stopped and scratched at the ground between the skips. Holding telescopic rods with nooses and short cudgels, the white men advanced in a pincer movement on the dog. Coniston and Williams backed up to the shed, and waited. Khetan tapped the van door with his section of pipe, the sound like a Napoleonic army's drumbeat.

The dogs yowled and howled, the yard noisy as a blacksmith's.

Rick looked around, feeling powerless on the roof. He was too far away. He needed a jet-pack, or a death-slide.

The white men cornered the dog behind a skip. But it jumped up into the skip and scrabbled across the old buckets and packing cases. The animal jumped back down and made off into the yard again. It ran helter-skelter towards the gate, toward Coniston and Williams. It veered towards the two fugitives, increasing to a gallop. Rick expected them to retreat into the hut, but they didn't. They stood their ground. Coniston had a magic touch with dogs according to trekkers on the Mount Mera expedition.

Coniston unwrapped his right hand and wrist. He held a gun.

A wave of nausea went through Rick. The firearm was easy enough to obtain through TBR or even Darren Back, but equally could have been the brigadier's – a memento of the

Falklands. Lots of old soldiers kept a gun in the loft. Rick should have thought, should have realised when he'd been at the Conistons' house and discovered the untidy search. The marks under the loft-hatch? It mattered not. What mattered was the police armed unit only being on standby.

Coniston fired.

The gunshot echoed around the yard. The dog yelped, and staggered. Coniston fired again, the noise ricocheting. The dog fell, and fell silent.

Rick's ears rang. Hypothesis 2a had been correct, Coniston had escaped to do something. To take his revenge on Khetan, and had co-opted Williams to help. With a firearm, the escapee only needed imagination and the motivation, and it seemed he had both. Williams the dupe who would eventually also be sentenced to life imprisonment, but had none of the guile or incitement.

Ram threw down his weapon, covered his ears and disappeared behind the dumped container.

Rick phoned Hunter again. Engaged. He tried Robbo, Maggie, the CID office, the front office, but no one picked up. He switched to text mode.

There was a message from Maggie sent an hour previously. *Need to speak.*

He texted Hunter. *Coniston's got a firearm – a handgun. Has killed a dog. Armed units required on the hurry up.*

The burst of rainfall subsided, but didn't stop. Water dripped from every roof, every ledge, every parapet. Rick's shirt and trousers stuck to his body, and his shoes were full of water. He pushed his hair back from his eyes. He couldn't just wait on the roof and let events unfurl.

He crawled backwards until he was out of view of the yard, and stood up. His trousers sagged. He jogged along the edge of the roof through the puddles, water leaching out of his shoes through the seams. Cows in the nearest field looked tiny. He felt sick, a mixture of vertigo and irritation for not anticipating a firearm.

As he slowed to negotiate a ninety-degree corner, angry voices rose up from below. He jogged to another corner and the top of the second tube ladder, and peered over.

It led down to the far side of the trolley park which had flooded. He turned and looked across the roof. An idea came. He jogged toward the vents and the abandoned building materials. Stopped at the bucket of scaffold joints. He grabbed the handle and pulled. It was heavy, but it moved. He shuffled it towards his original position on the roof edge. Detectives needed special footwear, not slippery-soled town shoes. He swapped hands, tried both together. Red marks appeared on his fingers. He tipped out some of the water, tried again.

He hauled and hauled, and when he was close, he dropped down to his belly and crawled back to the edge.

*

Calix walked forward, as if in a trance. His ears were ringing and his shoulder pulsed with recoil. In front of him lay the great dog, legs folded and still. The second dog howled and tugged at its leash. They were running mates, probably siblings.

He knelt and laid down the pistol. He cradled the dog's head, its hazel eyes vacant. He felt for a pulse under its long muzzle, but there was none. The foxhound had a large black patch over its back, tan rear legs and a tan head. Blood seeped through its fur and dripped to the ground forming a pool. He stroked the hound's back and laid the head gently down. He arranged the limbs so it looked at peace. The paws were rounded, almost cat-like. Dogs so unrefined in life, but majestic in death. Cloaks of fur, like Tudor kings.

The ringing eased, and he could think again. Khetan had disappeared.

A moment of panic.

Calix bent lower and looked underneath the van; the Nepalese man's feet protruded on the far side. He glanced round. Barney stood a few metres behind, and beyond him, the two white men from the lorry scuttled towards the gate. Good luck to them.

'Is it dead?' shouted Barney.

Calix nodded. He stayed on his haunches, staring at the dead foxhound.

'When did you have a thing with Elly?'

Barney frowned, then looked round at the deserted gateway. The lorry drivers had made off.

Calix leant forward and moved his old man's pistol closer to his legs. He picked it up, and scratched his kneecap with the barrel. It was still warm.

'I didn't.'

Calix pointed the gun at Barney, and ushered him forward so he stood between the van and the hound. So Calix could see Barney and maintain tabs on Khetan at the same time.

'I was just saying it to get you mad.'

'What the fuck?'

'Kiwis do the haka before a game. Well, we do something similar in the college team: we get in a group hug and chant, then we pair up and do body charges. You know, like rhinos or bison. I didn't think you were angry enough to do what you had to do so that's why I said that thing about Elly. It wasn't true.'

'I don't believe you.'

Calix absentmindedly stroked the dog's head with the gun barrel. Animals were so superior to humans: no words to hate, cheat, lie, confess. He wiped his watery eyes, then looked up, held the gun steady, and aimed.

He squeezed the trigger.

341

Bang.

Barney screamed and crumpled to the ground. He twitched, his head lolled slowly sideways, and he fell silent and still.

The ringing in Calix's ears returned, and he could smell and feel the heat from the gun. He waited for a few minutes, feeling dizzy, then stood and walked back toward the security hut. Unlike the dog, Barney wore no wound and there was no blood spatter, but Calix hoped it would be enough.

'Calix.' A foreign voice. Khetan's voice.

Calix stopped, and turned.

Khetan stood near Barney's spreadeagled body. He also held a handgun. They'd been right. Khetan wore jeans and a shirt and shiny shoes. He looked like the exec of a start-up.

'Where you go?'

Calix wasn't sure. He wanted to sit down, to lie down. The security hut would do. Home. Not home, he'd gifted it to TBR. The Finchams' house, then, at least until they returned from Australia. Then back to Strangeways, more than likely. He shrugged, and didn't go anywhere. The remaining hound started up again: caterwauling and clawing the ground. Calix understood. He felt like caterwauling.

'You kill you friend. You like you *buwaa*: no *dharma*.'

Like his *buwaa*, his old man. Khetan didn't know it, but it was a compliment. A double compliment: Calix liked being compared to his old man and the subterfuge had worked. He needed a retort, but couldn't think. The dog kept howling. Khetan waggled his pistol. Calix closed an eye. He could shoot but he wasn't confident he would kill the Nepalese man with one shot. He would hit him, but Khetan might also shoot. He wasn't afraid of being injured, but after being so close before, this time he wanted to be certain.

It looked like stalemate.

Barney raised a leg and booted Khetan in the back of a thigh.

Khetan whirled round and Barney kicked out again. His foot connected with Hant's groin and the Nepalese man doubled over. His gun went sprawling.

Calix walked forward, training the pistol on Khetan. He stopped when he was sure he couldn't miss. If he could shoot a dog, an ancient dog, a king of dogs, then he could shoot a man. He pointed at the ground, and Khetan sunk to his knees.

Playacting over, Barney got to his feet.

Slowly, he picked up Khetan's pistol, and also pointed it at the Nepalese man.

Khetan glanced behind him. The hound thrashed back and forth, but was held fast by the chain. There was no sign of Ram which was good. Calix didn't want the boy confusing things. They were all set, as he'd planned during the many months in prison. All he had to do was pull the trigger.

Out of the corner of his eye, Calix saw something falling from the top of the store. There was a loud crash in the yard near the skip. Pieces of metal clanged and flew outwards.

53

Rick didn't wait to see what happened in the yard, but crawled backwards, stood up, and ran along the edge of the roof. A keen wind buffeted. The tiny cows were sheltering under some trees. At the ninety-degree corner, he glanced back and diagonally down into the yard. The lorry obscured his view. He ran on.

At the top of the tubular ladder, he peered down. The foot of the ladder was flooded like the trolley park. On the other side of the fence, wet trolleys glistened.

He looked across the yard, but his view was still obscured by the lorry. Voices punctured the silence. He grabbed the rails. He had to be quick, but not too quick.

His hand slipped.

Stomach heaving, he lurched back from the edge. Climbing down so much harder than climbing up, but he had no choice. Waiting for armed backup always took forever.

He wiped his hands on his trousers and started down the ladder.

Heart banging.

Voices in the yard, becoming more strident.

Rick descended the equivalent of a storey, then stopped to wipe his hands again. If he fell from there, he'd be unlikely to survive. At best, he'd end up in a wheelchair like Mag—

Even as he clung a third of the way down the ladder, he was immediately sorry. Both for his blunder, and to have hurt her. He continued climbing down, wondering about the reason for her urgent text. Tactical advice, a piece of intel, or her decision to leave the Job – and him?

The rungs ran out.

Like the one he'd climbed up, the ladder started several metres above the ground to prevent children – and detectives – from getting into trouble. Going back up or jumping down seemed equally bad.

A screamed shout arrowed out of the yard. He looked across, but still couldn't see anyone. His pulse like a marathon runner's. The huge lorry stood there, water dripping from its bodywork and forming small pools. For a moment, he'd forgotten its significance. So big it was invisible. But inside might be a dozen or more migrants, scared when they started, but here, now, hearing gunshots, they would be petrified.

He worked his hands down so they held the rung above his feet, his body in a squashed C shape. He slipped a foot off the rung, took a deep breath, and unweighted his second foot. He swung forward and back—

But held on.

He waited until his swinging slowed, then one at a time, moved his hands to the bottom rung. He imagined a dozen pairs of eyes on him, willing him on.

He let go.

Bent his legs like he'd been taught at primary school. Mr Holy the physical education teacher had taught them to climb ropes, thick white ropes, and to jump using the springboard, and to fall bending the knees and rolling. Mr Holy, such an odd name he realised now. The memory as vivid as a photo.

Rick rolled through the puddles. Every scrap of his clothing was soaked, but he was okay. He peered through the slatted fence into the trolley park, but couldn't see into the yard. If he couldn't see them, they couldn't see him. He pulled out his phone – the screen was cracked in the corner, the icons fuzzy. He tried phoning Hunter.

'You okay, boss? We got your message.'

Rick half-wondered if he was speaking to the right person. Hunter had never asked how Rick was, never enquired whether he'd had a good weekend, not once. Then again, Rick only knew about Hunter's new grandson Toby because he'd overheard him on the phone.

'I'm on the ground again, behind the trolley park. There's already been a scuffle, and Williams has grabbed Khetan's gun. How long 'til armed support?'

'We've made the request, Robbo did, he's standing with me. But there's only one unit, the rest have been on a pre-planned job in Bury. They want to wait for the others.'

'So stay where you are, DI Castle,' said Robbo. 'No heroics.'

Rick nodded.

'Rick?'

'Okay!'

When the triple line of snaking trolleys ended, he ducked under a barrier, and walked across the service road to the yard fence. A yellow salt bin sat on the corner.

He looked through the fence into the yard, but couldn't see anyone. The lorry stood still and quiet. Too quiet? Migrants had died in containers and made international news: tens of lives lost, and hundreds of family members affected. The incident could worsen yet. Further away stood the white van, and between the two vehicles lay the dead dog. The other dog was out of sight, but still barking like a machine.

Rick followed the fence towards the gate. He hopped onto the verge and pushed his way through the long wet grass. He grabbed at a patch of seedheads and yanking off a couple, tossed them away. He glanced into the yard, but still couldn't see anyone, not even the lorry drivers. If they had any sense, they would have scarpered.

He crept into the yard and backtracked down the fenceline, behind the stack of pallets and, he hoped, out of view of Coniston, Williams, and Khetan.

No one shouted.

He moved up to the cab of the lorry.

Still, no one gave the alarm.

He looked underneath the lorry, but couldn't see anyone hiding or any protruding feet. He drew his baton and flicked it out to the full extension. Twenty-six inches of carbon steel with a puck-shaped end which did the damage. He took out his CS spray and held it in his left hand, thumb at the ready. He felt like David.

The sky was black again, and more rain seemed imminent. Rainfall was the beat officer's friend. It seemed a good sign. He rounded the cab of the lorry and worked his way down the far side. He peered round the end of the trailer and into the centre of the yard. The dead cur lay in a pool of blood.

Coniston wouldn't shoot *him*, would he?

Rick stepped out into the yard. His legs felt like stumps, and he could no longer feel his feet. He walked over to the security hut. Still no voices. He wondered whether all the suspects had scarpered. There'd been no more gunshots so a mess of bodies seemed unlikely.

A raindrop hit the bridge of his nose. He glanced up, and more hit his face. A purple-black sky.

He reached the hut.

Peered through a knothole.

The hut was empty, but he could hear the voices of Coniston and Khetan from behind it. Coniston sounded unsure. A first time for everything.

Rick wished he was wearing his body armour, and he could hear Robbo at a press conference. *Detective Inspector Castle, like every Greater Manchester police officer, has been issued with personal protection equipment and instructed to wear it whenever there is a risk of harm. Not following that advice has unfortunately—*

Rick pressed his cheek up against the damp wood of the hut and peered around the corner.

54

Bounded by the old lorry container and the fence, the corner of the yard was a misshapen and unused area. The tarmac was cracked at the edge and losing to the weeds. A grid had popped and dirty water was gushing out.

Khetan was on his knees, facing the fence. Behind him stood Coniston and Williams, both holding handguns.

Rick pulled back. There was no sign of Ram, and no sound of sirens or a helicopter. Stabs of cold rain began to fall again. He adjusted his grip on the baton and considered his options. He could wait for backup. He could step out from the shed and hope his presence was enough. He could rush them, shouting and spraying CS. Pros and cons to each. Waiting might mean he'd witness an execution, but showing out or rushing them might act as a catalyst to the same outcome.

'Are you sorry?' said Coniston.

Rick edged forward so he could see.

Khetan shook his head slowly. 'You *buwaa* kill my *buwaa*, I make revenge.' Your father killed my father. 'Now you turn. Then Ram take turn.'

Rick thought it as likely as the boy standing for Nepal's federal parliament.

'You're not afraid of dying?' said Coniston.

'You west people, you no understand.' Rick could sense the smugness in the Nepalese man's voice. 'You never understand. For Nepal people death is no the end. *Dharma* is everything. *Dharma* and God.'

Rick rehearsed the four basic tactics of hostage negotiation: to always remain calm; to build relationships with suspects; to prolong the situation; and paramount, to prioritise the safety of all concerned.

Coniston raised his pistol. He swapped hands and wiped a hand on his trousers. He swapped back. Williams glanced across at his fellow fugitive, but Coniston avoided his eyes. He stared at Khetan.

Khetan glanced round. He raised his hands. 'You no do it.'

'Calix,' whispered Williams.

There was no time to build a relationship, and if Rick didn't show out, then he couldn't affect the situation. At least that was clear. As was his aim: prolong the impasse for as long as possible. Rick tightened his grip on the baton, squeezed his thumb down on the CS trigger, and stepped out from the hut.

'Don't do anything stupid, Calix.'

The two white men reeled round and backed up to the end of the old container. Khetan turned around. The four of them in a triangle. Coniston kept his pistol aimed at Khetan, Williams raised his weapon at Rick.

He didn't think Williams would shoot him. Two years ago in Nepal, he'd saved his life, and although Williams blamed him for not preventing the murder of his father, he didn't think the student would kill him for that failure. On top of that he was a police officer. It used to mean something, but maybe it didn't anymore.

Rick was less sure about Coniston. Some days the two of them seemed to have an insight, and an empathy based on mutual respect of the brigadier. Other days, they were Dr Frankenstein and the creature.

The rain strengthened, and water dripped from their faces. Coniston and Williams looked pale, almost ghostly.

Sirens began to wail. Instinctively, Rick relaxed: it was all going to be okay, the armed units were going to arrive and the suspects would put their weapons down.

He took a half-pace forward.

'Khetan's ours now. It's over.'

'You mean he'll go to prison?' said Williams.

Rick was surprised it was the getaway driver who spoke, Coniston always the alpha male in the pair. He nodded. 'Khetan will be an old man when he comes out, if he comes out at all.'

'He won't be spirited away like last time?' said Williams. He was a trainee lawyer and smart, but his was another ruined life.

Rick looked over at Khetan. The Nepalese man moved to sitting cross-legged. He put his hands together in the prayer position and closed his eyes. Rain was striking his face, but he didn't seem to notice.

'Barney's right,' said Coniston.

'Whether he is or isn't doesn't matter,' said Rick. 'If you shoot, it'll be you getting life imprisonment.'

Coniston shook his head. 'Maybe, but for the rest of my life – every single day – I'll know I did it. If I don't, then every day I'll know I didn't.'

Rain pelted the ground between them, bouncing up and giving a silky sheen to the tarmac. The sirens sounded closer. Rick only had to eke things out for another minute or two. 'You *have* done it, Calix. You've led me to him.'

Coniston shivered and lowered his pistol a fraction. He looked cold and uncertain. He'd lost his parents, his sister, and his grandfather in less than five years. It wasn't impossible to feel sorry for him.

'I'm going to put my baton and CS down.' Rick took another step forward, and laid them on the ground. He was close enough to fling himself at Coniston. Better, perhaps, would be to run at Khetan and block the shot that way. 'Now, it's your turn. One at a time, nice and slow. You first, Calix.'

Khetan began to chant. '*Om mani padme hum. Om mani padme hum.*' It was easy to forget he was a kidnapper, a people-smuggler, a killer. He looked peaceful, spiritual, benign. Reminded Rick of Tibetan monks sitting in the road about to set themselves alight.

'Shut up!' shouted Williams. He walked halfway towards Khetan.

'*Om mani padme hum.*'

Tyres screeched as vehicles sped into the delivery yard.

'*Om mani padme hum.*'

'Shut the fuck up!'

'*Om mani padme hum.*'

'This is for Spencer,' shouted Williams.

He fired.

Khetan's voice cut mid-chant and he clutched at his chest. His eyes flickered open, but his look was vacant, as if dealings on Earth were beneath him. He keeled sideways, blood pumping out between his fingers.

Williams fired again, the bullet destroying Khetan's left eye-socket. 'And that's for my dad.'

Khetan convulsed and lay still.

Rick's ears echoed, and his body felt leaden. Across the tarmac trickled crimson-hued rainwater.

55

Calix felt dazed. As if he'd been punched in the face, or Barney
had shot *him*. His friend Barney Williams who'd picked him up
at the top of the graveyard and driven away from the prison
guards like a loon. Who he'd always thought of as physically
strong but mentally weak. He'd been nervy in Nepal when
they'd been escaping and apprehensive throughout the last few
days. But when the final test came, it was Calix who'd been
found wanting, and Barney who'd delivered. His old man would
have been impressed, and disappointed with Calix. He was
disappointed with himself. He realised he was still holding his old
man's Hi-Power. Whorls on the barrel like in a film. He felt like
he was in a film, the rain hammering down around him,
drumming on the roof of the hut and container. The noise so
loud. He couldn't think, couldn't concentrate. Memories
tumbled through his head as if he'd been picked up and shaken.
The suspension bridge in Nepal, Castle negotiating with Khetan,
his old man jumping into the raging river, his old man gone,
only his trekking pole left, floating on the foaming surface. And
why? Because Calix had wanted to be somebody – a player. And
in some ways, he'd succeeded. In Strangeways, the cons had all
known who he was and what he'd done. They were impressed

with his connections to The Big Red and Special K. Impressed he could fix injured birds. But he wasn't going back to prison. He couldn't breathe there, couldn't feed Bird Bird's fledglings, couldn't do what he wanted. Staring at his finger resting on the trigger, an idea came. Still plenty of bullets in the magazine. He'd had some good moments. Convincing Castle, the tireless and thoughtful alpha-detective, to remove him from prison and take him back to Nepal. Escaping in the foothills of Everest before being knocked out and robbed by the Nepalese farmer. He'd lost all his cash and even the last of his mum's flapjacks. No more flapjacks now. She'd gone, his old man had gone, and Megan, too. There was only him left – no one not to do this for. He corrected himself, there was one person: Elly. He'd daydreamed, of course he had. She'd arrived from nowhere, a dreamy introvert who wore a cute pink hat with fishing flies. But Barney had ruined his image of her, and despite retracting his admission, Calix didn't believe Barney's explanation or his retelling. He applied the lightest of pressure to the trigger. His old man had explained how to take up the slack, to squeeze gently – 'gently, Calix!' – as he breathed out. His breathing was heavy and jumpy but it didn't matter. He couldn't miss. A lifetime of remembering that he hadn't done it. Castle was wrong about that – Barney had done it, not Calix. He felt sorry for his friend, and guilty. With Castle as witness, Barney would be convicted in record time and sent to prison for life. So unfair, Khetan the killer, the trafficker. He felt sorry, too, for Ram whom he'd he lured to the UK and would now be deported. More memories surfaced, more recent. Escaping from the guards in the cemetery, being picked up by Barney, hiding in his student room. Climbing out, and meeting Elly. There she was again. Cool as a cat, and possessing an ironic detachment, as if she was half Martian. Rainwater spilled down his face and brought him back to the here and now. In front of him lay

Khetan – Hant Khetan, Special K. Dead as a stone. It should have been him who'd pulled the trigger, not Barney. It was his plan; and it was him who'd sourced the gun and the bullets. Maybe it didn't matter, maybe nothing mattered. He was going to be immortal. The only way to be immortal was to die young. Die young, forever young. Die young, live forever. Look at James Dean, or Diana Spencer, or Kurt Cobain. Dylan Thomas, or Sylvia Plath. Malcolm X, or Martin Luther King. He raised the gun to his ear, and just as his old man had taught him, squeezed the trigger.

56

Rick's ears echoed. The three shots in quick succession had changed everything.

Priorities. As a probationer he'd been taught the acronym COW to deal with traffic accidents: Casualty, Obstruction, Witnesses. The temptation was always to direct vehicles.

Detectives worked a different beat.

The firearms were first. He splashed forward through the puddles and kicked Coniston's weapon under the security hut. Williams set his pistol on the ground and backed away to the fence where he slumped down like a weary animal. Rick toed the second pistol under the hut. Next was Coniston and preservation of life.

The fugitive lay prone, one arm folded across his chest. Blood leaked from a wound next to his ear. His eyes were closed, but he was still muttering.

Kneeling down next to him, Rick jammed the palm of his hand against the flow of blood. Car doors slammed, people shouted. He felt the rain easing.

'Hang on, Calix.' Coniston's eyes were dull, his expression blank. His breathing irregular, and fading. He was dying, they both knew that.

'Why'd you do it?'

Calix's eyes flickered and focused briefly on Rick. He smiled. 'Of all people, I think you know why.' His eyes closed, then opened again. 'Never got to keep any bees.' His head slumped.

Rick increased the pressure on the wound, squeezed Coniston's shoulder. 'Hang on, Calix, damn you.' He looked round.

'Medic!'

He wondered what Coniston had meant. Whether, now his parents had gone, Rick was the person who knew Calix best. He would never forget him, and he doubted whether those who knew of him would either.

'They're over here.' Hunter's voice.

The sergeant arrived with two paramedics. Burly women in green uniforms loaded with equipment. Hunter fussing about evidence like a trainee. The women took over, and Rick stood and backed away.

Hunter surveyed the scene and shook his head. He scratched behind his ear which made Rick want to laugh. The shock, he supposed. Hunter pointed at Williams and Rick raised two fingers. They nodded at each other, and Hunter went back to update the loitering detectives. Every case was the same: it always took a while, but the two of them had gelled. Hunter would get things moving and give Rick two minutes with Williams.

So tired he could hardly stand. Rick walked to the fence, and sat alongside Williams. The student's eyes were closed. Rain dripped off the fence. The sky was brighter, and the black clouds of the summer deluge already in the distance.

'A cold summer,' said Rick.

Williams nodded like a drunk.

'Barney, listen to me.' Rick's third priority after safety and preserving life was the detection and prevention of crime. Justice.

The paramedics worked on Coniston. They wore yellow gloves and military boots. One ripped open dressings and tubes, another tapped a needle. A helicopter landed in the supermarket car park. More vehicles arrived, and a doctor from the air ambulance jogged up. She held a red satchel of equipment.

Rick turned to Williams and grabbed his collar. 'Calix is going to die.' The getaway driver's head flopped all over, as if he was made of beanbags. Rick slapped him. The noise made the paramedics glance across. He shuffled round so he screened their view of Williams.

'I only need you to listen.'

Williams didn't respond. His wet hair hung down, his face shiny with rainwater.

The doctor rocked back on her haunches and stood up. She conferred with the paramedics, then looked over at Rick. She shook her head. A paramedic opened a bottle of water and the three of them drank it in great gulps. They began to clear up the strew of medical waste.

Rick thumped the ground. Suicide was an ignominious end to a resourceful and creative talent. He'd hoped to save Coniston from himself, hoped to do the brigadier a final favour. But he'd failed on both counts.

'Barney.'

The student opened his eyes.

'You shot the dog. Calix shot Khetan, then himself.'

Williams looked at Rick as if he didn't believe what he was hearing.

'Got it?'

Williams nodded. Then sighing heavily, closed his eyes again.

Rick hauled himself up with the fence, and looked out across the glimmering car park. The sun was trying. Behind him, he could hear the excited cries and shouts of migrants from the lorry. Williams didn't deserve life imprisonment for killing a bad man. He'd been blinded by family pain and co-opted by Coniston. He'd never become a lawyer, but he'd still have a life and a chance for a family.

Rick sat on the lip of the car boot. Hunter had chucked all the forensic paraphernalia on the back seat and left him there. He felt like he should be smoking, and if somebody had offered him a cigarette, he might have accepted, just for the hell of it.

A line of ambulances queued outside the yard, marked police cars parked all over. The incident trailer was there, and the mobile canteen. Scene tents, a portaloo, press vans with satellite dishes. Reporters with Dictaphones and notepads and paunches and sly grins. Dozens of uniforms, and detectives from Major Crime. The sun had come out and windscreens reflected the light.

People approached him one by one, as if he'd been widowed. He felt like something bad had happened, and it had. But it could have been worse. Always, things could have been worse.

First was Oliver, the press man nodding like an old school-friend. 'Hunter filled me in, thanks. It'll be a good story, maybe a great one.'

'Don't spare anyone.'

Next was Weatherbeater. Russell wore uniform, and walked with a limp. He always would. 'I've been reinstated, I can't thank you enough.'

A migrant wearing a suit and tie was escorted by a paramedic into the back of the next ambulance. The door closed. The vehicle executed a three-point turn, and drove to the outer cordon. The crowd parted and the constable raised the tape, the ambulance drove forward, and away. The PC lowered the tape and the crowd reformed.

'I've had my first appointment with Emma.'

Rick was still troubled with his word choice, why the word

executed had arisen in his subconscious. Sleep might help, but even then, he might dream. There was no answer: he had to live with himself. He glanced up at the ex-mountaineer, and nodded.

'It wasn't what I'd thought. But I think it helped, and I've booked to go again.' Russell paused and glanced round.

Rick could hear the dog rattling its chain and yowling, but turning around felt like too much effort.

'Velvet's singing at the weekend. Do you want to come – you and Maggie?'

Sabres of light flashed around as the row of ambulances shunted forward. Rick stared at the pulses of intense yellow-white light. His vision furred, and he looked away. He closed his eyes and thought about speaking. He should speak.

'I'll ask her.' His voice sounded normal, but maybe he couldn't tell.

When he opened his eyes, Russell had walked away, and Robbo stood there. He was holding his hat. His stomach strained at his buttoned jacket. A row of blue and green ribbons above his breast pocket which Rick hadn't noticed before. Robbo had done things – brave things, things he probably ought not to have done.

'The damage to my car has stopped.' The superintendent started to rotate his hat as if he was about to throw a frisbee. 'I'm guessing you won't tell me even if I asked, so I won't ask.' He stopped turning his hat and picked a hair from the baize. 'I've been feeding your bees. June gap, they needed it, and I figured you had a bit going on.'

Rick spotted Hunter. The sergeant was talking to a group of detectives from the office. Kasim, Paulson, Woods, and Bennett. Woods was wearing his scruffy anorak. Bennett was fingering his glasses, Paulson eating a Mars bar. Kasim raised a hand at Rick. The young detective said something to the others, and they all looked at Rick. Nodded and waved in their own curious ways. A jolt went through him.

'You should have stayed on the roof, Rick, and directed the armed units in.'

The press officer walked up. She wore a blue and white dress and held a clipboard and a folded umbrella. 'They're ready for you, sir. And, DI Castle, there's a young woman at the gate, asking to see you. Elly Simmonds.'

Robbo put on his hat, and pulled it into place. The press officer backed away a couple of steps. Robbo pulled the front of his jacket down and cleared his throat. 'I've been thinking. We should draw a line.'

Rick nodded. Even that hurt.

The superintendent and the press officer walked away. She said something which made Robbo laugh. They swayed closer, almost touching.

Rick followed them, then peeled off towards the gate. He recognised Elly Simmonds from before. She wore the plain bowl-shaped sunhat of a cricketer or an old person on the beach. But what did he know.

'You wanted to speak to me?' He looked past her, towards the roundabout, but there was no sign of Maggie. He felt tired just standing up.

'Tell Calix, I'll visit. Tell him—' She turned away to hide her emotion. She turned back, her green eyes glassy. 'Tell him, just tell him.'

Rick returned to the car. He couldn't, not there, not then. Didn't trust his own emotion not to spill. He'd ask Beth, the family liaison officer he'd want for his relations, to tell her – and soon.

Hunter walked across. At the car boot he bent down and hauled up a trouserleg to scratch his calf muscle. He straightened up. Behind him, two migrants appeared from the reception tent. They were young, Asian-looking, one carrying a small red suitcase. A gangly ginger-haired paramedic escorted them to the next ambulance.

'Nineteen migrants including five children,' said Hunter. 'All going to be okay.' He watched the two migrants climb into the back of the vehicle. 'The two firearms have been recovered, the two bodies photographed and removed. Williams is being forensicated at the nick. Khetan's nephew has been taken to a place of safety and the two lorry drivers picked up. The detective super from Major Crime wants a first account from you, soon as.' Hunter paused. 'You alright?'

Rick nodded. He tried to find some words, tried to form a sentence. He could hear his own breathing. In front of him, Hunter picked at his knuckles.

'Is she coming?'

Hunter shook his head.

The ambulance turned and drove off. Another took its place. In the neighbouring field the black and white cows stood along the barbed wire fence.

57

The hedgerows bristled with growth. Hazel shoots reached for the sky, and blackberry creepers poked into the road. Bumblebees flitted, and birds flew out ahead of them, calling in alarm. Rick could smell honeysuckle, and the lemony scent of mountain ash. He could hear the trundling of their six wheels, and his rasping breathing.

Despite the exercise, he felt nervous, and a tangled knot sat in his stomach.

They passed the open gate to a field. Inside, two farmhands were tinkering with a hay rake. They were shirtless and their pasty muscled bodies glistened. In the adjacent field a haycutter laboured and the smell of cut grass drifted thickly.

As a boy, Rick had spent a summer holiday staying on a farm. He'd built a camp from hay, and looked for eggs in the barn each morning. Mum had cooked proper breakfasts and packed up lunches. The four of them had tramped miles on country footpaths, and every evening swam in the farm pond. It was cool and dark next to a grove of sycamore trees. They shared it with river boatmen. He'd like to go back there. It was something to talk about with Mum, maybe with Dad.

The memory had helped to pass a half mile, take his mind off both the discomfort and his anxiety.

In front of him waved the triangular red flag on Maggie's rear wheel. Like a dangled carrot, it was always in front, and however close he moved, he never pulled alongside. And he was trying. God, was he trying. Blisters on his hands despite the bespoke gloves, cramp in his quads, a recurring spasm in his back. He'd embarked on numerous pushes for ten, and his lungs were sore. He was desperate for a drink. Desperate to know what she wanted to talk about.

They stopped at a café at the bottom of a hill about ten miles from home. The tables were busy with cyclists, their bicycles leaning against the front wall. Rick eased himself out of the seat and nodding at Maggie, hobbled away to the toilets. There was a queue, and while he waited, he phoned the hospital.

'You can speak to Skye – briefly – but before you do, can you make a payment for her room. Accounts are getting jittery.'

Rick relayed his bank details, and waited while he was transferred. The man in front was stretching against the wall, his cycling shoes making soft clinking noises on the tiled floor.

'Mr Castle.'

Her rough voice always surprised him. Reminded him of a rockstar being interviewed and revealing they ate cornflakes for breakfast. 'How are you feeling?'

'Cold, achey. Like shit.'

'I could take you out for something to eat in a day or two.' The queue shuffled up, Rick was next. 'I'll come by.'

'Okay.' Rick could sense something else was coming, and he waited. 'That place we went last time with the crispy chips.'

He pocketed the phone. In his head, she was always something she wasn't. But she was getting better, that was the main thing. And maybe now, with both Khetan and Coniston gone, his flashbacks and night sweats and outbursts of violence would end, and he could stop seeing Emma.

On his way back, he bought large bottles of water and

bananas, and ordered coffee. Outside, Maggie sat at a table facing the sun. She wore sunglasses, and her garish cycling top and physique made her look like a professional athlete.

'You're looking good for the race, Mags.'

'I'm not doing it.'

'Why?

'That's what I wanted to talk about.'

He pulled out a chair and sat opposite her. They touched bottles and drank deeply, and Rick ate a banana. The smell of coffee drifted. The other cyclists wore bright-coloured Lycra and ate power bars. Talked about football.

A waitress brought their mugs of coffee and slabs of coffee cake. One of the small forks fell on the floor. Rick picked it up, said it was fine. The waitress wore a dirty apron, but smiled at them and walked away. It was a sad, pretty smile. He wondered if she was the victim of domestic violence.

He waited.

'You're a hero,' said Maggie.

Two cyclists pushed off on their bikes; they looked down and clicked their feet into the pedals. They raced away. Thin weathered men with legs like rolling pins.

'And, DCI Castle, you've got your old job back. You must be pleased.'

Rick pushed the handle of his mug back and forth. Despite the two deaths, Robbo was delighted with the result. The chief super looked good, and Robbo could think about promotion again or at least a move away from South Manchester before he retired. Rick's problem was Williams. He'd been charged with assisting Coniston escape from prison, and the CPS were considering a further charge of conspiracy to murder Khetan. Rick still owed Louise a meal at the Taverna for sorting out the Carmichaels file. What she'd demand for a second favour, he didn't want to countenance.

'I've also been offered a new job.' Maggie nodded at him as she forked out a mouthful of coffee cake. 'To set up and run a special investigations unit.'

'Did you take it?'

'I wanted to talk to you first.'

Maggie murmured neutrally as she ate. He tried a mouthful of the cake. Sickly sweet, too sweet. He'd have preferred another banana, and set down the fork. He couldn't wait any longer.

'What's going on, Mags?'

'Do you not want yours?'

Rick shook his head. Like a politician, Maggie had dodged the question by asking another. He pushed his plate across, and Maggie pushed back a banana. He was reminded of Jack Sprat and his wife, and was sure he and Maggie would make a good team.

He glanced over at their racers. Maggie's machine with the red flag sticking up at the back, and Rick's larger and brand-new model from PushPower. He hated riding it. Hated the lack of gears and uncomfortable sitting position.

Maggie followed his glance. 'You bought that for me – for us – didn't you?' She didn't wait for an answer. 'I know how painful it is to start, particularly when you don't have to.' She ate another mouthful of cake. Put down her fork.

He could see and feel it coming, like a tidal wave or a spring tide. He braced himself. He knew it would be bad news; it could only be bad news.

'I'm pregnant.'

'What?'

Pregnant? Had she suspected it and been testing him on the drive back from Bradford? She'd said then she wasn't sure whether it would be with him. He ran a hand along the slats of the table, making a soft clacking noise. It was either the best news of his life, or the worst news, but either way explained why she wasn't competing in her race.

'It's still early days, but I am – definitely.'

'Should you be even doing this?' Rick nodded at their racers.

'I'm not overdoing it.'

Rick nodded. He could hardly breathe. Was he or wasn't he?

'I think we should give it a go. Us, the baby, move in together properly.'

Maggie had tears in her eyes.

Rick took her hands and squeezed them. He was going to be a father. The three of them were going to be a family. He slipped off the plastic chair and dropped to his knees. Shuffled forward and kissed her. She was crying and laughing, and he realised he was, too.

Spontaneous applause erupted from the other cyclists.

The two of them parted slowly, and Rick sat back down. A spotty teenager pumped up his tyres, and stashed the pump in a pocket on the back of his shirt. The youth cycled away, conscious of being watched.

They sat for a while, not saying much, but smiling a lot. Birds called out and rustled in the shrubs and hedges. A robin landed and hopped about for crumbs. Rick thought of his parents, how happy his mum would be, and maybe Dad too, if he ate enough fruitcake. It was a reason to keep bending the rules.

Rick paid their bill. They climbed into the racers and pulled on their gloves. Maggie glanced behind, and smiled, and Rick stuck his thumb up. She pulled out onto the road, and after glancing back at the small stone café and purple flowers in the hanging baskets, he followed. The road rose steeply, flanked by dark overhanging trees.

Lexicon

Nepali	English
baliyo	strong
bandar ko chaak	(inf.) monkey's bottom
Bengal monitor	a large lizard, up to 1.5 metres in length
bhok	hungry
biyara	beer
buwaa	father
chaina	no
chhora	son
chorten	Buddhist temple
dal baht	rice and lentils, Nepalese staple meal
danphe	a type of pheasant; the national bird of Nepal
dekhanunu	show him
dhanyabaad	thank you
dharma	moral code (Hinduism); teachings (Buddhism)
gompa	Buddhist monastery

ho	yes
Kahaan?	Where?
Timi kahaan jana lageko?	Where are you going to?
kayaka	hero
kera	banana
khalti	pocket
Kina?	Why?
kukur	dog
mani	wall or stone carved with prayers
mapha garnuhos	(I'm) sorry
momo	similar to a dumpling, contains meat or vegetables
naan	a flat round or oval bread
namaste	hello / goodbye
naramro	bad
Om mani padme hum.	an ancient Buddhist mantra; literally, praise to the jewel in the lotus
piro	spicy
rakshi	whisky (local)
ramro	good, pretty
Ravana	demonic creature in Hindu mythology
roti	a flat round bread
sahib	sir
Thaahaa chha.	I know.
Thaahaa chhaina.	I don't know.
Thik chha? / Thik chha.	Are you okay? / Yes, I'm okay.

Acknowledgements

I would like to thank my brilliant editors Eve Seymour and Mary Chesshyre. Also, the cover designer Mark Ecob, and Andrew Chapman (Prepare to Publish) for typesetting and all-round publishing knowhow. Thanks again to Lakpa Doma Sherpa for checking the Nepali.

Lastly but firstly, I would like to thank my wife Sarah for her endless support.

If you enjoyed Cold Summer, *please take a few moments to write a review. Thank you!*

You can sign up to James's mailing list at https://jamesellson.com

The Trail

The first book in the DCI Castle series.

**Longlisted for the Boardman Tasker Award
for mountain literature.**

A missing person enquiry leads Manchester DCI Rick Castle to Nepal.

Manchester. DCI Rick Castle is inspecting his bees when his
boss phones. A minor cannabis dealer has been reported
missing. His father's a war hero.
Rick flies to Nepal, and heads up the trail. Through villages of
staring children and fluttering prayer-flags. Brilliant blue skies,
and snow-capped mountains.
He finds a dead body.
Then a second.
Nothing in this world was ever straightforward. Nothing.
Finally, he puts himself in the firing line, and has a decision to
make. Is it the right one? The moral one?

Three missing. Two continents. One detective.

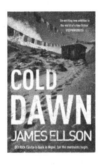

Cold Dawn

The second book in the DCI Castle series.

**Longlisted for the Boardman Tasker Award
for mountain literature.**

Against the rules, Manchester DCI Rick Castle removes a
prisoner from Strangeways and returns to Nepal.
His aim: to bring to justice his nemesis Hant Khetan, rumoured
to be the next Osama Bin Laden.
When the prisoner escapes, Rick and his small team must search
for him along the paths of the Everest foothills.
Trekking in the shadow of snow-capped mountains and
through earthquake-flattened villages,
Rick becomes increasingly desperate.
If they can't find him, Rick can't even begin . . .

DCI Rick Castle is back in Nepal. Let the manhunts begin.